CALABASH

CALABASH
CALABASH
CALABASH
CALABASH
CALABASH
CALABASH

CHRISTOPHER FOWLER

WARNER BOOKS

A *Warner* Book

First published in Great Britain by Warner Books in 2000

Copyright © Christopher Fowler, 2000

The moral right of the author has been asserted.

A CIP catalogue record for this book
is available from the British Library.

ISBN 0 7515 3040 9

Typeset by Solidus (Bristol) Limited
Printed and bound in Great Britain by
Clays Ltd, St Ives plc

Warner Books
A Division of
Little, Brown and Company (UK)
Brettenham House
Lancaster Place
London WC2E 7EN

For Jim

Acknowledgements

I'm indebted to a wide variety of Middle Eastern studies, including R. B. Merriman's *Suleyman The Magnificent*, Raffaella Lewis's *Everyday Life In Ottoman Turkey*, Ilhan Aksit's *Treasures Of Istanbul*, Robert Tewdwr Moss's *Cleopatra's Wedding Present*, Jason Goodwin's *Lords Of The Horizons*, Lynn Thornton's *The Orientalists*, and, of course, *Tales From The One Thousand And One Nights*. I would like to thank my charming and rather glamorous editor, Antonia Hodgson, Nann du Sautoy, my faithful and fearless agent, Serafina Clarke, my international agents, Jennifer Luithlen and Lora Fountain, and designer Martin Butterworth. With love and respect to Jim and Richard for their patience, help and kindness, and, as always, to my family, especially my mother Kath, from whom the idea for this book extends.

Part One

Where lies the land to which the ship would go?
  Far, far ahead is all her seamen know.
And where the land she travels from? Away,
  Far, far behind, is all that they can say.

– Arthur Hugh Clough

CHAPTER ONE

A Visit to the Real World

One minute past midnight. Sixty seconds into the new century. His friends are gathered around his hospital bed, joyously liberating cascades of champagne into plastic cups. He lies beneath their outstretched arms, their tumbling streamers, their cheers and toasts, and though he cannot move, he wishes them all the love in the world.

The century is only new to those who honour the concept of time. The man in the bed draws no pleasure or sorrow from its passing; hours, days, months, years, these arbitrary measurements mean nothing to him. They drift like the snow that passes across the window behind his head. He lies with his arms neatly folded over the counterpane, unmoving but not unmoved, connected to the outside world by a strong and slender thread. He can see and hear, and can sometimes shift his eye line just a little, which is how they know he is still alive. He is a prisoner of his body, but inside his head he is free.

'Here's to you!' says Julia, raising her cup within his field of vision. 'Happy New Year!' And the others chorus her toast.

'Are you sure he can understand us?' asks one.

'Of course he can,' says the nurse, who talks to people as if they are children. 'He can hear everything you say. It's not a vegetative state, it's a coma, they're altogether different. His mind is quite undamaged.' She has seen his test results. Sometimes his EEG line is like a force 8 on a seismograph. On a physical level, though, his neural impulses only allow him to respirate and eliminate. 'He just can't move. He doesn't watch the television, he prefers to be read to; he likes the human contact. We turn him and clean him, and stretch his limbs to prevent muscle wastage, and we feed him from there.' She sounds very matter-of-fact, almost cheerful, as she points to the bag of her patient's drip-feed.

'Poor thing,' says a pretty girl who is new to the group. 'How long has he had this disease?' She mouths the last word softly as though it is obscene.

The nurse thinks for a moment. 'Oh, it must be nearly . . . thirty years?' She looks to her patient's mother for corroboration. 'About that. Of course, he could move about in the early days, but the condition has proved to be degenerative.'

The new girl is somebody's date. Kay has not seen her here before. She is plainly horrified by the casual acceptance of the situation. 'He can't have any quality of life, just lying there. Wouldn't it be better to – well, you know, let him – that is – turn him off?'

There is a moment of appalled silence. The girl is quick to realise her mistake and apologises. 'I'm sorry, I didn't mean – it's just – he looks so sad lying there.'

'I don't think he's sad,' says the patient's mother defensively. 'He doesn't like being pitied.'

'Oh God, I've upset you now.' The girl is a little drunk, and very embarrassed.

'No, love, I think the only person who's upset is you. You mustn't be.' The older woman takes the girl's hand in her own and draws her closer to her son's field of vision. 'It's very difficult for some people. I think of him as being asleep. You know when you're sleeping and somebody talks to you, and you understand what they're saying? It's like that.'

Julia comes forward and touches the girl's shoulder, speaking softly. 'Just look into his eyes, and then wish him a Happy New Year.'

He is so glad that he has come back for this, to hear his mother and see his friends. He will not stay long; the others are waiting for him. He concentrates on the girl for a moment. She is younger than he had first thought. Reluctantly, she bends down and looks into his eyes. Her gaze is tentative at first, then, realising that the others are all watching her, she searches for a sign of life. He tries to send her a message; that everything is all right. A moment later her hand flies to her mouth – 'Oh!' – and she is crying or laughing, maybe both, turning to the others in wonder. Kay has seen this moment of revelation many times before.

'You see?' they tell her delightedly. 'You see now?'

'Oh my God!' she keeps saying, and hugs his mother, and then they are all laughing and crying. His mother turns from the others and her kind face fills his vision. 'Happy New Year, darling,' she says. 'Come back to us again soon.' He sends her love with his eyes. It is time for him to go, to leave the prison of his dormant flesh and be free once more.

As he soars away from the merry little room in the hospital block, gaining height above the town, he leaves behind the sounds of celebration. He looks down at the glowing necklace of the promenade, the fireworks blossoming over the snowswept bones of the pier, and crosses the coastline into phosphorescent darkness, racing low across the midnight sea, as he returns to Calabash.

CHAPTER TWO

Where the Fears Began

'See? There's nothing there.'

I remember my father pulling the curtain aside to let in the light from the streetlamp, spilling sulphurous yellow beams into the bedroom. 'Now will you go to sleep?' I push myself upright and squint into the shadows doubtfully. My father follows my gaze and walks to the wardrobe door. 'And this,' he says, shaking the sleeve of the dressing gown that hangs there, 'is not a witch.'

'Don't close the door all the way!' I call in panic, as he goes.

'How's this?' My father carefully leaves a gap of six inches. It is a nightly ritual. The hall lamps throw a strip of warm light across the racing cars on the eiderdown. 'You know the trouble with you?' He taps the side of his head conspiratorially. 'Imagination. It's a wonderful thing, but it's like a tap you can't turn off. Goodnight now. Go to sleep. Sean will be up soon.'

I feel sure I will lie rigid with terror until my brother comes to bed, but my eyelids grow heavy, and I drift in uneasy torpor. Every night it is the same.

I was four years old when the first of the shadow men appeared. The bedroom was always dark, a suffocating absence of light because my mother had grown used to keeping blackout linings in the curtains. Even though the war had ended thirteen years earlier, she had sewn them in because the new streetlamps the council had installed outside the house were harsh and bright compared to the old gas mantles. It was a warm spring night, and rain was pattering gently against the windows. I lay on my back in itchy blue and white striped pyjamas, facing up into the dark, my thin arms stretched out over the Brooklands racers, when I became aware of a figure standing on the left side of my bed, breathing faintly, watching me. I felt sure that if I turned suddenly I would see the man, a tall thin fellow in an enormous turban, a character from one of my picturebooks.

Scarcely daring to breathe, I slowly drew my arms beneath the sheet and sank down low until only the top of my head poked out from the blankets, but still the shape loomed over me. I was sure I could feel his sour breath on my hair, my cheek. Finally I howled, and my father came running to the room, flooding it with light and life.

My head emerged and I looked around, but the atmosphere of the bedroom had changed. It was smaller and safer with the lamp on and my father there, and I knew that even if I dared to look beneath the bed, I would not be able to find the villain from the shadows. I felt foolish for making such a fuss, but my father did not seem angry. He was an understanding man, scruffy and kind and frustratingly vague. At home he always wore an unravelling cardigan of brown wool, baggy corduroy trousers with ridiculous fluff-filled turn-ups, and moth-eaten carpet slippers. He smelled of hops and tobacco, rolled his own cigarettes, and wandered around humming and jingling the change in his pockets, as if he knew that the world outside was an unfriendly place, and that it was his duty to protect his family and keep us safe indoors. There used to be a television commercial which instructed us to 'get the strength of an insurance policy around you.' It showed a little cartoon man rolling a policy around his family until it became a castle wall, whereupon he would lean over the rampart and knock on the outside to show its strength. I thought of my father as that man. I longed to be as content and sensible as I thought he was, but too many things in the world frightened me. If we walked on the beach, I fretted about the tide racing in and cutting us off. Once I watched my father replacing a fuse-wire, and became worried that when I grew up and left home I would have to sit in darkness, because I had no idea how to mend one.

I felt sure that the man in the huge turban left the bedroom because my father brought too much rationality with him. When you're a child, there are some things you get completely wrong. Throughout my early youth, my mother told me that there was nothing to be afraid of, and I longed to believe her, but fear of whatever might hide in the dark kept me from doing so. Childhood fears are the most memorable, even when they're unfounded, and I was a child capable of unqualified panic.

My mother had told me there was nothing to be afraid of, but she had been wrong. There was the illness, the deep pain in my chest that kept coming back while the doctors whispered behind my bedroom door. There were the strange emissaries who populated the dark corners of the bedroom, the ones who arrived with bears and bats that vanished when the lights were turned on. And, finally, there was my father, who went away one day and did not come back.

My mother's brisk denials were not enough to stop me from being afraid. As the years passed her indulgent smiles faded, and her consolations became warnings. 'It's time to stop daydreaming,' she announced on my twelfth birthday, 'and time to start acting your age.'

Growing up is a slower process for the imaginative child. I was often sick, and during these periods the passing of a single hour seemed to take forever. Years went by and I matured. But the reach of my mind quickly outstripped the strength of my body. And by the time I was a sickly, skinny kid of sixteen, the year was 1970, and it was clear that something had to change.

Perhaps what happened to me could have happened to anyone.

Perhaps it happens to all of us, and some simply forget.

I did not forget.

A Sense of Inundation

That first evening in September, as the sun broke from clouds of dull silver, the struts of the ruined pier revealed themselves like the bones of some great forgotten animal. The wind from the sea ruffled my hair, loosening my attention from the book. I lowered the paperback to my lap and refocused on the fibrous sky as I returned to the real world.

There was a green wooden shelter on the esplanade that could be seen from the pier entrance, and therefore didn't smell of pee. That was where I usually sat reading. It was easy to lose all sense of time and place sitting there. I stared at the glistening beach and listened to the slow drag of pebbles. Then I returned my attention to the book.

Past the pillars of Heracles lay a lush green land cultivated by Atlas's people. This was the kingdom of Atlantis, built around a great white harbour. In the city were palaces and baths with hot and cold taps, race-tracks, garrisons and magnificent temples. Atlas was the son of Poseidon, whose fivefold brace of male twins

swore allegiance atop a pillar in the blood of a sacrificed
bull. But riches turned their heads, and Zeus allowed
the Athenians to defeat them in battle. The gods sent
a mighty deluge that drowned Atlantis in a day and a
night—

A sudden breeze stippled my jacket, covering my arms
with goose-pimples. The light dropped once more, returning
the tideline to a sepia shadow. Slattery and his gang cycled
past, bellowing obscenities, making me lose my place. I tried
to concentrate, moving my finger beneath the words.

Atlantis was long thought to have existed somewhere in
the Atlantic Ocean, but the only inhabited island ever
known to have sunk there is the Dogger Bank, which
was inundated in palaeolithic times. It seems much
more likely that—

'Oi, Goodwin, you're going to get your head kicked in!'
'Hey, Book Boy, get out of town!'
The bicycles made a second pass. The bubble-gum cards
wedged in their spokes made their back wheels ratchet
with ominous slowness. I shut the book and tucked it into
my jacket. They would circle closer and closer like hyenas
scenting blood, and would not leave me alone until I left
the shelter. This was a familiar pattern. I rose and walked off
along the esplanade, keeping my head down, refusing to rise
to their bait. It was best not to show defiance by looking at
them.
I waited until their cries had faded, and lifted my eyes to
the shore. A smear of sickly yellow light led the way across a
grey sea to the dying sun. I wished the tide would rise far
beyond its usual level and fill the town, drowning the

inhabitants. I imagined Cole Bay becoming a new Atlantis, water spilling across the road and pouring into the high street, swilling a scummy detritus of chip papers and half-eaten ice-cream cones, spilling and sucking through the windows of the penny arcades until it was above the rooftops. After the helpless populace had all been drawn out to sea, after the last weak cry had faded to silence, nothing would be heard except the faint ringing of church bells beneath the waves.

I kicked a stray stone on to the beach and glumly made my way back along the esplanade. The lightbulbs edging the Las Vegas penny arcade had not yet come on. The illuminated machines in its cavernous interior blinked and shook in the gloom, like treasures awaiting discovery by some third-rate Aladdin. I stood in the doorway watching a huge old machine light up flushes of outsized playing cards. Each one featured the face of a showbusiness celebrity: Alan Ladd, Alma Cogan, Stanley Baker, Ava Gardner. That summed up our town; out of date and out of step. The year was 1970, but it might as well have been 1958.

As I crossed the road, the sharp scent of brine was replaced with the stench of stale doughnut fat and candyfloss. Even away from the main strip, the sugary smell of warm, freshly-folded rock permeated the pavements. I wondered if rock-making was a purely British coastal occupation. I had never heard of anyone else doing it. Why would they want to? I peered into the window at giant pink false teeth, girls' gartered legs, fake eggs and bacon, babies' dummys, all made of rock. The stuff was inedible, a weird prewar souvenir of a place that you wouldn't admit to visiting, not if you had any sense.

Cole Bay, population 17,650, former fishing village, had been turned into a seaside resort in the 1830s, its bedraggled Victorian atmosphere only surviving above the plastic signs of the chip shops, once regularly visited by daytrippers to the south coast, now largely forgotten but for the occasional mods and rockers riot on bank holidays. The long straight foreshore was bleak and exposed, its delights exaggerated in railway compartment paintings, its shortcomings hidden by artfully arranged clumps of hydrangeas. The promenade was open to the full force of the wind and the tide, and stayed cool even in summer, an agoraphobia-inducing area where you paused to look out to sea and then moved on, despite the green benches dotted hopefully along its length. A series of rectangular lawns were untrodden, and never appeared to grow. The grass looked as if it had been cut with nail clippers. The floral clock was an immaculate disk of tiny yellow and purple flowers, even though its hands had long ago been vandalised into immobility. There was a battered bandstand with an octagonal roof of oxidised green tiles, but no longer any band to play beneath it. Surrounding the kiddies' paddling pool, drained and bare for nine months of the year, were rows of blue and white striped council deckchairs that old couples sat in during the few warm days of summer. Like ripening tomato plants they turned to follow the path of the sun, and folded up at five.

The Pavilion Pier was falling into disrepair. Once a T-shape, now just an L, its wrought-iron pergolas were blighted with rust, its bulb-holders corroded by the salty sea air. Beside the entrance was a theatre called The Crow's Nest that ran decrepit Brian Rix farces and guessable Francis Durbridge mysteries starring character actors who had been around for so long that their faces were more familiar to me than some of my relatives. In an effort to attract audiences to the performances that did not fall on pension day, The Crow's Nest summer season featured pop performers whose most famous songs were often bracketed within their names, like Susan 'Bobby's Girl' Maughan and Frank 'I Remember You' Ifield. This week Scaffold, the ugliest band in the world, were bill-topping with their chart smash 'Lily the Pink'. For Cole Bay, this was a major coup.

But the fun didn't end there. Just along from the theatre, other seaside treats awaited the unwary visitor. There was a Guinness clock that amused the undemanding with an un-reliable robotic parade on the quarter-hour, a telescope that gave you a twenty-second view of the bare horizon for a penny, and a plinth-mounted floating mine that looked like a giant red beachball with teats. Shops stocked practical jokes like 'Fake Soot' and 'Naughty Puppy Turds', and comic post-cards with punchlines like 'Is That Mine Floating Or Is That A Floating Mine?' and 'Come And See My Husband's Little Wotnot Stand'. Beneath the pier were a pair of smelly, haggard donkeys that walked children brief distances for a tanner, although it seemed a crime to put anything heavy on their backs, and a Punch and Judy man whose swozzle-filtered squeals rendered him incomprehensible and frightening.

Across the road were two further dubious attractions. The waxworks (motto – 'Meet The Immortal Stars of Today and Yesteryear!') appeared to feature the dummies Madame Tussaud had rejected. Within its musty basement rooms, long-forgotten celebrities (Jessie Matthews and Robert Donat still featured) leaned from draped pedestals at perilous angles, look-ing extremely mortal, and even ill. None of them seemed to be wearing their own hair; it looked as though someone had swapped all the wigs around. There was no chamber of horrors; presumably the proprietors realised that it wasn't needed.

The Aquarium, on the other hand, appeared to offer nothing at all. This was mainly because most of the fish spent their lives in hiding, and the tanks were hardly ever cleaned out. Many a small boy had been traumatised after spending twenty minutes with his face pressed to the glass trying to spy an octopus in the murk, only to have it suddenly appear in a swirl of suckers an inch from his nose.

Outside, the year-round regulars were taking the ozone; rows of severely handicapped children left gurning at the sea, hunched biddies creeping past on tripod-sticks, ex-military men in blazers and too-tight ties standing stock still at the railings, a smattering of potato-faced nuns. The promenade shelters belonged to blanket-lapped couples who examined paste sandwiches and decanted tea from thermos flasks as if they were still at home.

At the edge of the town was the Cole Bay Kursaal, a funfair more commonly known as The Deathtrap, given its spotted safety record. Several people had flown out of the roller coaster, a child had been interfered with in the Tunnel Of Love and a woman had been slung-shot from one of the chain-chair roundabouts. 'They found her handbag on the other side of the Express Dairy,' warned my mother darkly. Being a sickly child, I was forbidden from going anywhere near the place, so of course I went whenever I got the chance.

The history books have little to say about my home town. All the interesting coastal battles occurred elsewhere; none of the weird historical footnotes you read about in libraries – like St Ethelred having his hair set on fire – happened any-where near Cole Bay; no marauding invaders had attempted to alight on these shores, unless you counted drunken boat-trippers from around the headland. The local museum comprised a single whitewashed room in a fishing hut, filled with musty sailors' knots in cases, driftwood spars, and washed-out photographs of men in waterproof hats and huge wellingtons standing awkwardly beside netting.

Cole Bay had just two claims to fame. The first was a plaque to honour a six-week stay by the young H. G. Wells, who had presumably been obeying doctor's orders and convalescing from an illness that had deprived him of his senses. The second was less salubrious. This year, the resort had snatched the title of 'Seaside Town With The Highest Suicide Rate' from Hastings, and Hastings was glad to get rid of it. Their first famous visiting suicide had been Lizzie Rossetti, the unhappy wife of the artist Dante Gabriel Rossetti, who topped herself with an overdose of laudanum in 1862. Sadly, we could not match this.

Further along the coastline was Eastbourne, a previous holder of the suicide title, where young men killed themselves at more than twice the average national rate thanks to the handy proximity of Beachy Head, a spectacular headland ideally suited for dashing your brains out when you reached your tether's end. Cole Bay's only advantage in the self-extinction stakes was a forehead-clutching air of melancholia, largely induced by the overpowering odour of fish that scoured its way across town from the gutting sheds.

The weekend trippers stopped coming before the start of the Second World War. Although the town was just seventy-eight miles from London, there were only two ways of getting here, via an unreliable Southern Region railway network that required two changes and operated virtually no service on Sundays, or by car on the nightmarish A21, and then on to a variety of convoluted traffic-choked B roads. In every sense, Cole Bay was the end of the line.

I turned into my street, a lopsided run of terraced houses with pebbledashed bay windows (pebbles being an extremely available commodity), and stopped before the only property with scallop shells still jauntily set in its front garden wall. As I approached the glass front door indented with frosted yachts, I heard my family before I saw them. As usual, there was an argument in progress. I quietly pushed open the door and waited in the hall. My mother was telling Sean not to use the house as a hotel. I could see my brother standing before her in his courier leathers and motorcycle helmet, waiting for her to finish. Bob was slumped deep in his armchair trying to watch the television through my mother's body. He possessed the ability to screen out family complaints and only hear electronically transmitted signals, no matter how faint. Bob preferred the television to his wife. It had an off switch.

I closed the front door as gently as I could and headed for my room, but was spotted at once and forced to divert to the lounge.

'You, don't you try and slip away. Do you still own a watch? Do you realise what the bloody time is?' Pauline, my mother, switched the focus of her wrath. Sean used the momentary distraction to slip out into the kitchen.

'You were supposed to be here a bloody hour ago, Kay. Your dinner is dried out. And where's your scarf? You were wearing it when you went out.' I felt inside my jacket collar. My mother never missed a trick. I realised I might have dropped it while leaning over the end of the pier trying to see if any more of the stanchions were rusted through.

'You've lost it, haven't you? I give up. Sometimes I don't think you're on this bloody planet. Well, you'll have to eat your dinner as it is. Then Bob wants a serious talk with you.' Bob's eyes flitted in our direction at the mention of his name, like a dog hearing the rattle of a lead.

I knew what the talk would be about. This was the moment I had been dreading; Bob had received the letter from the school. To my horror, he reached forward and turned off the sound of *Up Pompeii* just as Frankie Howerd was about to remark on a slavegirl's cleavage. Apart from *Doomwatch* it was the only programme he never missed. This was serious. He studied me for a moment, long enough to allow my mother to leave the room. I was suddenly alone with my step-father. I braced myself for the onslaught. Instead, Bob pinched the bridge of his nose and said wearily, 'Get your dinner, lad. Then I think we should take Gyp for a little walk, don't you?'

It was too late to pray for an oceanic inundation now.

Letting the Side Down

Gyp was a short-haired brindle cross-breed that Bob had found abandoned in a cardboard box outside the Scheherazade Hotel. What exactly Gyp had been crossed with was a mystery, but it presumably hadn't been another dog. He had tall ears, a long, lean body, short legs, a docked tail and a tongue that was too big to fit properly in his mouth. He looked like the unhappy result of intercourse between a draught-excluder and a fruitbat.

Sean was still in the kitchen, foraging, and caught my eye. He drew a thick finger across his throat and grinned. I cheerfully mouthed 'fuck off' back. As sibling rivalry went it was like Castor and Polydeuces, only with more jokes and swearing.

It was almost dark now, and the streets belonged to elderly ladies in tea-cosy hats who cast their eyes to the sky while their dogs trembled on their haunches and attempted to protrude hard white stools into gutters on command. Bob and I stayed away from the promenade, which by this time belonged to the Chavs, grim little knots of chainsmoking kids who spent their evenings standing around in bus shelters looking hard. We headed towards the park instead. Gyp was trying to strangle himself on his lead, and made gasping, retching noises as he clawed away at the pavement.

Here, the local council had filled the branches of the plane trees with diseased-looking illuminated gnomes in an attempt to create an enchanted grotto effect. Disfigured plastic faces leered through the leaves beside us, buzzing with errant electricity. Snow White and her four-and-a-half dwarves hung out in a fag-end-filled clearing with Little One-Legged Riding Hood. A deformed Miss Muffet had collapsed in agony over a plaster tuffet, while Little Blind Peep, squinting forlornly towards the bingo hut, appeared to have lost her mind as well as her sheep. A bridge troll bore an eerie resemblance to the man who sold racing forms on the front, and there was something poking out of an elderberry bush that was presumably the only remaining billy goat gruff. As a small child, these fairytale gargoyles had terrified me. The councillors voted to reinstall them every season, like Christmas tree lights brought down from the attic and draped around a coffin. It seemed appropriate that they should surround me now, in my darkest hour.

'Your mother's very upset,' said Bob finally. 'Very upset indeed. She doesn't know what to do with you, Kay. She doesn't understand you. And frankly, neither do I. You're a clever boy. You're always bloody reading, some of it must have gone in. But you're not making the grade, lad. You're letting the side down. I know you've been sick a lot, but at this rate you won't be able to stay on at school. They've written and said as much. The headmaster is very dis-appointed by your grades. Miss Hill reckons you're her best pupil, but she's the only one with anything decent to say. The others are ready to write you off.'

'Don't want to stay on anyway,' I mumbled, feeling the

heat growing behind my National Health spectacles. Bob halted before a crackling tableau and released a thin, high fart that he thought wouldn't be noticed. One of Sleeping Beauty's eyes had dropped out. She had a dent in her head, and the kids had drawn crimson felt-tip nipples on her breasts.

'Don't talk stupid. What would you do with yourself if you had to leave school, hang around here like the ones on the front? Christ, it's bad enough that your brother's let your mother down, bloody motorcycle courier. Do you know what he wanted to be when he was a kid?'

'Doctor.'

'A doctor. He had big plans. Look at him now. "Take a padded envelope to a firm in Margate". Not exactly the big time, is it?'

'He likes bikes.'

'He could still like bikes if he had a proper career. And now you're going to follow him. You were doing so well, catching up on all the time you lost in hospital, taking your O Levels a term early. Now it turns out it was a waste of sodding time. You won't get another chance to make something of yourself. What are you going to do? I've no spare cash, and neither's your mother. How are you going to live?'

'Get a job.'

'Around here? Do you know what the unemployment rate is in this town?'

'Thirty-six per cent.'

'Don't be smart. What would you do? Be like the bloke who mends the slot machines? The man who gets put in a sack and escapes from handcuffs at the end of the pier? They used to set fire to him until the council put a stop to it. He nearly dies at every performance, and still has to go around with a cap.'

We stopped beside an arrangement of cankerous shoe-maker's elves. Gyp scrambled over the low wall and attempted to wee on an elf until he was yanked back.

'You've got to pull your socks up, and fast. You're behind in everything except English, and that's no bleeding use to anyone. From now on you're indoors, not down at the library.' Bob puffed out his cheeks, thinking. 'Regular meals at the table. Homework. A set bedtime. And you can try watching some telly for a change, like normal people. I'm putting my foot down. This is your last chance to make something of yourself.' He examined the sky for a moment, trying to remember whether there was anything he'd missed. 'Well, I've said my piece. Now it's up to you.' He pulled a bottle of stout from his jacket pocket and snapped off the cap with the little opener on his key fob. Obviously it was a bottle Pauline had somehow missed. Usually she conducted a furtive search before he was allowed out of the house.

This was probably the longest speech Bob had made since he had married my mother. It was almost impassioned, almost as if he cared. I considered this radical idea as we walked back, then dismissed it as far-fetched. I knew that Bob was just following orders from Pauline in order to have a quiet life, just as I knew that he would chew a stick of peppermint gum after he'd finished his beer to stop her from smelling it on his breath. Bob was not my biological father; that honour fell to the cheerful man who had come upstairs to quell my night-time fears, someone who now existed in little more than a few faded photographs taken on outings. Pauline had divorced Phillip in 1960 and remarried two years later when I was eight. Apart from my night-time memories, attempts to recall the image of my real father yielded less each day. Faint recollections of summer afternoons, resting against a garden wall, a pleasant feeling of warmth and safety, music playing on a portable wireless; impressions as light as those on recently flattened grass, blurring even as you watched them.

I felt that some justification was in order, an explanation as to why I had failed so badly in my examination results, but instead I allowed the silence to stretch between us on the walk home. I knew that any excuse I gave would be a lie, because he would not believe the truth.

I was aware of what I was doing. 'Letting the side down,' Pauline called it, as though we were all rooting for the same thing. My stepfather was not a bad man, he wasn't unkind or bitter. He was what would later become known as a 'functioning alcoholic', a banqueting manager at the Scheherazade Hotel on the esplanade, and he worked long hours so that he could provide us with the few simple luxuries that he thought we needed to hold together as a family. He came from a time, not very long ago, when that was all it took, and he couldn't see that everything was changing, that what he wanted wasn't what I wanted because there was nothing I wanted in the life I saw around me, nothing at all. And it frightened me so deeply, this emptiness at the heart of things, that I could barely speak without insanity pouring out instead of the chatter they all expected. And so I bit my cheek and hid my thoughts and burrowed down into my books, because only there, inside those warm white walls of words, did I have the strength to survive this hell.

My dreams of Atlantis were pointless. The sea had already risen and drowned my world. Though I was only sixteen, all I could see before me was a grey waterscape of drifting corpses, and I could not believe that passing a few exams would save me from becoming a part of it.

Anticipation of Arrival

Doctor Trebunculus fluttered his hands impatiently at the palace guards who stood beneath the great bronze dragon lanterns on either side of the East Gate. The guards were bald mutes, and barely twitched their pupils as they swung aside to let him pass before returning to their official positions, with their legs astride and their fat blue-black arms folded over the enamelled handles of their scimitars. The lobes of their ears were pierced with heavy sapphires that stretched their flesh and required constant protection from the knives of brigands, so the guards were eternally vigilant. These stones were worn from birth by the palace staff as a sign of loyalty. It was said, although unverified even by the doctor, that the Sultan's eunuchs wore similar gems inset in their groins. The palace was rife with such stories, of course, and though unfounded, they often became truthful in the retelling.

The doctor straddled the limestone stairs, taking them in pairs until he had almost reached the top. His legs were as thin as stalks. His long chin was thrust purposefully forward, and his coat-tails flew out behind him. He moved like a heron striding across mudflats.

'Doctor!' A young girl's voice was calling from one of the modesty windows. Rosamunde pushed back the latticed rosewood shutters and stepped from the calm of her private quarters on to the balcony. Her braided chestnut hair fell across the nipples of her bare brown breasts. Her arms were wrapped in spirals of gold wire. Leaning forward beneath the edge of the beaten copper baldachin that covered the balcony, she hissed down at him, 'Where on earth have you been? He's absolutely furious! He's cutting the heads from the canaries! It'll be Egyptians next! You know how he hates to be kept waiting. And why are you alone? Where is the *ajnabee*? Has something gone wrong?'

'What could I do?' gasped Trebunculus, pressing his knuckles against his heaving chest. 'I could hardly drag him here against his will, could I?'

'I don't see why not. Time is not on our side.'

'*The caged animal has just cause for grievance*,' muttered the doctor. He gave another impatient wave of his fingers. 'Go, run ahead and tell your father that I am arrived. I cannot enter his presence unannounced.'

Rallying himself, Trebunculus stepped through a tall carved arch of interlocking brass stars and jade hexagons, past blue glass jars filled with fragrant jacaranda, around the piddling sapphire fountain scented with cedar oil, and into the courtyard of the great palace. Here the world descended into a delicate fretwork of shadows, as cool and still as a painting, but fraught with a tension that saturated the air like ozone.

The doctor was the only man in the city who was allowed to enter royal quarters in civilian clothes, because of the haste in which he was usually summoned. All others were expected to wear silken sashes of honour in order that their rank could be instantly divined, but dressed in his purple velvet suit and stovepipe hat Trebunculus stood out in any crowd. As the only man of science in the kingdom, he occupied a unique position at court. Unfortunately, the Sultan tended to impatience and inattention, causing him to misunderstand almost everything he was told. This was very frustrating for the doctor, whose own mind tended towards the intellectual and abstract. The more the doctor spoke of paradigms, paradoxes and panaceas, the more the Sultan thought of his stomach and his concubine. Happily, the Princess Rosamunde was as worldly as she was intelligent, and acted as a bridge between them.

From within the courtyard came the suspirial drone of an *arghul*, and in counterpoint the plaintive twangling of the *rababa*, a two-string bowed instrument that was an Eastern ancestor of the violin. The Sultan only allowed such peasant music to be played when he was feeling very depressed. Pausing to draw fresh breath and kick off his leather pattens, the doctor entered the ornate arena.

'Do you realise what the time is?' bellowed an uncontradictable voice. 'In a land which finds no use for the measurement of the hours, did we not determine to present you with a pearl and bloodstone timepiece when our daughter was delivered? Trebunculus, I'm talking to you. Take your hat off, man. Demons of Trezibond, where the hell do you think you are?'

The doctor hastily doffed his headgear and slipped it behind his back. He took stock of the situation. The Sultan was enthroned – never merely seated – upon a veined marble dais swagged in saffron cloth and dusted in marigold petals. Every time he moved, showers of flowers sifted to the ground around him. His fat right fist held a silver blade. In his left, a minuscule canary was incarcerated, yet sang on. The heads and bodies of a dozen yellow birds lay scattered at his sandalled feet.

Whenever the Sultan grew especially petulant, he killed all the songbirds in the courtyard. It was a small cruelty that upset everyone within the palace grounds – the birds were a symbol of freedom and happiness – yet most of all the gesture hurt the Sultan, who loved the sound of birdsong. In terms of the customs of his land the Sultan was not a particularly malicious ruler, but his position was one of absolute power, and he occasionally felt the need to remind his subjects of the fact. He was flanked to the rear by the Dowager Sultan, or Queen Mother, a bulky, impractical woman swathed in grey silk, most notable for the alarming mass of copper hair that perched on her head like a sea-sponge, the Sultan's lovely daughter Rosamunde, the melancholy royal consort, who was not allowed to have opinions and whose name no-one could quite remember, the lugubrious Lord Chancellor, whose eyes glistened like black beetles, the ancient, one-eared, smelly Semanticor, a pair of sullen eunuchs and a couple of palace dwarves, who had been invited simply to prevent the retinue from forming a hard line (the Sultan had a horror of right angles – they bore the stamp of death). Before him stood the doctor. Everyone except the Sultan looked uncomfortable. Nobody moved a muscle; the Sultan detested unnecessary movement.

'I am alone,' Trebunculus stated.

'Yes, I can see that. O celestial heavens, stop that infernal warbling.' He made a threatening gesture at the court musicians, who fell silent and shuffled back into the shadows. 'Where is the *ajnabee*?'

'I endeavoured to locate him, your grace, but the celestial portents ... my calculations were somewhat inaccurate. There were complications.'

'I think what the doctor means,' began Rosamunde, 'is that the process is not as simple as you think.'

'The doctor is quite capable of speaking for himself,' warned the Sultan, raising his hand. 'Go on, Doctor.'

'The transition site has a habit of shifting about. It's something to do with their weather. So much rain. My efforts were only partially successful.'

'What do you mean, *partially* successful? Were you successful or not? That's like saying you fell *partially* pregnant. You dropped *partially* dead. You were *partially* roped across the ignited mouth of the Imperial Battlement Cannon and blown to shreds. You were *partially* entombed alive in the floor of the Royal Ossuary. As there is nobody with you I can only assume that you failed to bring him here, and that registers as a total and utter lack of success in my book.'

He reached back and snapped his fingers impatiently. The Dowager Sultan gave the Semanticor a painful nudge, waking the old teacher with a start. He hastily produced a small gold-trimmed pocket dictionary of English from his embroidered robes and passed it, open at the appropriate page.

'Here we are,' observed the Sultan. 'Failure. A negative result. A bungle. A botch. Incapacity. Insufficiency. Inability to fulfil a promise. It's probably a beheadable offence.'

'That may well be so, Your Grace, as indeed most things are, and I'll admit that the person whom we seek is not corporeally present as such, but I have managed to establish that he is—' Trebunculus corrected himself, '—was – in the exact spot where our calculations predicted that he would be found.'

'Oh really? And where was that?' The Sultan's knife slipped across the canary's throat and silenced its singing. Its tiny head fell to the floor like a bottle-cap being popped, landing in the centre of the congealing crimson pool where all the other heads were mired.

'In the percheron field beyond the vale of cyprus trees. Sort of over . . .' He endeavoured to point through the wall of the palace.

'I'm not calling you a liar, Trebunculus, but why by all the *bektashi* bodies of firmament and fundament should I believe you? Do you have any proof at all that he was ever there? Are we getting anywhere?'

'Well yes, Your Grace. If you will permit—' Flustered, he dropped his hat and rooted about in the battered black leather medical bag that hung from his trousers. Finally, he produced a muddied brown woollen object with a flourish. The Dowager Sultan wrinkled her nose.

'What – what – what – is *that* disgusting thing supposed to be?'

'His scarf,' said the doctor, much taken with his small triumph. 'I found the boy's scarf.'

CHAPTER SIX

Lack of Calibration

I spread the photographs carefully across my threadbare racing-car eiderdown. It was normal, I knew, for teenagers to become excited by magazines in the privacy of their bedrooms, but I was probably the only teenager in Cole Bay ogling blurred photographic studies of the suggested sites of ancient Babylon. My brother's favourite personal reading matter was a specialist monthly entitled *Birds 'N' Bikes*, which featured heavy-set girls in white PVC thigh-high boots bending awkwardly over Triumphs and Nortons. I, who could not tell a carburettor from a castanet and wasn't much more accurate with the opposite sex, owned a single battered copy of the weird naturist magazine *Health & Efficiency*, which I kept on top of the wardrobe, but all the interesting bits of the nude women had been airbrushed out, so that they looked like eerie lifesized dolls. They also seemed unnaturally cheerful about playing volleyball and tennis in wintry woodland with no clothes on. The resulting effect was the opposite of sex, on a par with thumbing through Bob's medical dictionary.

Downstairs I could hear my mother arguing with Sean.

These days her voice never fell below a certain hectoring volume, maintaining the uncomfortable see-sawing timbre of a distant factory alarm, something to be endured until the battery had worn down. I wormed my fingers into my ears and read on.

The capital of Southern Mesopotamia, Babylon was at the height of its splendour during the 7th and 6th centuries BC. Nebuchadrezzar's city was the largest in the world. Through it flowed the golden Euphrates, and within its eight fortified gates, decorated with enamelled lions, bulls and dragons, stood the 300 foot high Tower Of Babel, with a splendid temple in blue glaze at its summit. Greek tradition refers to its extraordinary Hanging Gardens as one of the seven wonders of the world—

'Kay! Beans on toast, it's on the table and getting cold.' Her voice penetrated my defences, and besides, I was hungry. Deciding to chance the atmosphere downstairs, I folded away my maps, charts and photographs, and stowed my Plasticine scale model of Babylon in the wardrobe (Gyp had tried to eat it on several occasions but had only managed to masticate part of the Shamash Temple). Sean was supposed to be taking his girlfriend back to her flat for the evening, but wasn't allowed to leave the house without having a hot meal. His girlfriend's name was Janine, commonly considered by my mother as She Who Can Do No Wrong. Janine worked in a bakery, which explained the doughy texture of her skin and the fact that she continually wiped her hands on her slacks, as though trying to remove icing sugar from the whorls of her fingertips. The gesture was fast developing into a nervous tic that I morbidly imagined would grow and stay with her until the day she died. She already had a permanent ridge in her hair from having to wear a paper hat. Her bum was restrained by slacks that prevented her from sitting upright without first sticking a finger down her belt.

Janine was so sweet that she was only bearable in small doses, and usually arrived carrying paper bags filled with sickly pastel slices of Battenburg cake or pastry horns filled with artificial cream. I found her habits very annoying. When watching the evening news her reactions chimed with my mother's. If it was announced that an entertainer had died, Janine would remind us that 'he was no stranger to personal tragedy,' or that 'he brought so many people pleasure in his lifetime.' When a news presenter described the capture of a murderer, she tutted and said, 'hanging's too good for him.'

I could not stop myself from responding. 'What *would* be good enough for him then, Janine?'

'What?' She looked across from her armchair, genuinely puzzled.

'If hanging's too good for him, what would be good enough?'

'Pack it in, Kay,' admonished my mother.

'It's just an expression,' said Janine, returning her gaze to the screen. But for a moment I knew I had got to her. Her eyes unblanked and I could see her thinking. Then clouds passed across her brain once more, and I let the subject drop because I didn't want to annoy Sean. My brother was loyal and decent and true. I didn't think he loved Janine in the way that I had read about people grandly loving one another, but then Janine was more robust than women of the past. She didn't moon about. She was sturdy and got on with things, and had this way of making Sean go quiet around her, the way Bob did with Pauline. I didn't think it was love so much as fear of upsetting her.

Sean had never allowed his girlfriends to be made fools of, and I thought this was a good thing. Physically, my brother was everything I was not: broad-chested and beefy-fleshed, blond and thick-necked. But not thick-skinned. He always stuck up for me, even when he thought I was talking rubbish. It was important to keep Sean on my side. In the war of attrition that was my life, I needed every ally I could get.

'There's a new restaurant opening in London that has topless waitresses,' said Pauline, reading from her newspaper. Her lips thinned out in disapproval. 'It's unhygienic, while you're trying to eat.'

'Could pep up the catering industry,' murmured Bob. He knew my mother thought it was disgusting because she thought that anything new or different was somehow wrong. When pressed for a more detailed explanation, her reasoning fragmented and she became angry. She once explained to us that she'd had enough of change during the war.

The easiest way to get her started was to mention Princess Margaret's divorce, which she saw as some kind of defining cataclysm which would lead to the fall of the monarchy, the collapse of law and order and, ultimately, to the end of the world. She was an avid follower of royal appointments, and liked nothing more than to hear titled folk giving us proles the benefit of their opinions. As most of the royals only gained popular support by keeping their mouths shut, why the condescending remarks of these people interested her was hard to say. I wasn't a big fan of royalty. Princess Margaret had once been scheduled to visit the Cole Bay Children's Infirmary to open a diphtheria inoculation station, but had cancelled due to fog. They closed the hospital for two days in the middle of an epidemic to dismantle the viewing platform.

'They've managed to get sixteen people in a Mini,' complained my mother.

'Who are "they"?' I asked.

'What?'

'You said "they". Who, car manufacturers? Scientists? The government? Is this being hailed as a breakthrough in miniaturisation?'

'Don't be clever, you.' Pauline slapped the paper shut and poured more tea. My mother studied the local papers for reports of poor self-control, and viewed every small change in postwar behaviour as a fresh social transgression that would eventually drag us into a moral stone age. It didn't pay to get her started on haircuts.

I ladled another forkful of beans drenched in brown sauce into my mouth and chewed, watching as she reached for her needlework scissors to clip out the offending article. Somebody somewhere was going to be slapped with a grim little note of complaint. She mailed a dozen such missives each week, usually to the *Cole Bay Mercury*, expressing her disgust with everything from the condition of public toilets to the unruliness of bus queues, and persisted until she received acknowledgement. Oddly, it didn't take much to assuage her, just a form letter thanking her for drawing attention to the matter. There was such an air of inevitability about my mum's disapproval that I would find myself reading out newspaper items just to inspire her to whip out a Biro and some Basildon Bond.

According to Janine's latest issue of *Reveille*, London remained the centre of the universe, and was still filled with a hedonistic generation of groovy swingers even though Paul was leaving The Beatles and the Fab Four had all been turned strange by psychedelic music, Eastern philosophy and drugs. But nobody knew whether the capital's cool would last far into the new decade. The portents were poor. The Conservatives were back in power, Jimi Hendrix had died of an overdose the month before, and pop music was relapsing into kiddie tunes; you couldn't turn on a radio without hearing Mungo Jerry singing 'In The Summertime'. Everything was still very English then. The only American pop culture I recall from that time is 'Peanuts' starting on the back page of the *Daily Mail*, *Mad* magazine and *Butch Cassidy And The Sundance Kid*, held over for a fourth week at Cole Bay's only cinema.

As far as I was concerned, London was seventy-eight trillion miles away, and all the tales of swinging hip affairs that Pauline and Janine read out to each other in tones of hushed horror might as well have been happening on the far side of the sun. I had no part in the world that my mother grimaced over in her magazines. I had no role in the modern world at all. Everyone at my school seemed obsessed with the new sciences. They were all looking forward to some kind of magical electronic future in outer space, but no-one was bothered about what they would have to surrender to get there. And no-one was interested in finding out why they had ended up here instead.

Looking around Cole Bay, I could see why. Everything summoned up the past in its worst possible sense: gloomy bed and breakfast lodgings, damp arcades, cheap postwar office blocks, grumbly old folk, desperate-looking foreign students, corrupt town councillors, noticeboards banning anything that people might really want to do, dead-as-a-grave Sundays, esplanade buildings that were losing their crepuscular battle with the corrosive sea air, and one road out that led to London, a city I had only ever visited with my parents to see the Christmas lights in Regent Street, although I had also managed to drag Bob and Pauline around the British Museum. They'd lasted almost twenty minutes before heading for the cafeteria.

There was never a moment when I felt attached to the rest of the world. I remember watching live footage of the Apollo moon landing on the tiny television set in the school recreation room. The broadcast, which ran throughout the whole day, was very slow and deathly boring. Admittedly, picture reception was poor because the third-formers had a habit of flying kites above the ariel on the roof, and the pieces of silver cigarette-pack paper they attached as weights interfered with the signal. Even so, I kept having to remind myself that this was a milestone in the history of human development, especially when I read that Neil Armstrong had got his words wrong, having been supposed to say that this was 'one small step for a man, one giant leap for mankind,' instead of which he said that it was 'one small step for man,' which meant the same thing as 'mankind'. It felt strangely appropriate that the first sentence spoken by a human being on another planet should turn out to be wrong.

The spacemen looked as if they were at a loss for something to do on the surface of the moon. They took several more giant leaps for mankind across the planet's surface, acting as if their parents had left them behind on a bouncy castle. They planted a flag and saluted. They took pictures of each other. The moon's landscape appeared as inviting as Cole Bay's beach at low tide. Finally they got tired of bounding wide-legged past each other, returned to a spaceship that looked like a Chinese takeaway on stilts, and came home. I imagined them sleeping on the way back, then rubbing their eyes as the hatchway was opened and asking each other if they were home.

What was the point of going to another world if you didn't do something interesting there? And why spoil the event by not allowing the spacecraft to look like a proper rocket with fins? Nobody asked themselves that. My teachers were only concerned with the technical statistics of the event. They could tell you how many gallons of fuel were required to achieve lift-off, but not what the point of it was. The people of Cole Bay were not interested in the universe, or wars in other nations, or even problems affecting other parts of the country. One hundred and ten years earlier they had anxiously read of the battles that were raging in the Crimea. Fifty years after that they followed the drama of the Boer War in their daily papers. In 1970 they discussed which footballer was dating which pop singer, and none of that was even true, just nonsense thought up by promoters to sell things. If I could figure this out at the age of sixteen, why couldn't my parents, who were old enough to know better?

I retreated to my bedroom after wolfing down my beans, and returned to Mesopotamia. It was a world I could control. History books provided the bare bones, but the rest was up to me; if I decided that the palace guards wore rings through their noses, then it was true.

I was hard at work colouring in defence sections of the city when the doorknob started to turn. I started shoving the maps, diagrams, battle plans, timelines, weather charts, population tables, war documents, trade agreements, flora, fauna, armour and weaponry sketches back into their folders. They weren't secret, I just didn't want anyone in the family to think I was obsessive. Very little of my documentation was based on fact, anyway. Whenever I lacked details I extemporised.

'Can I come in?' Sean opened the door and leaned cautiously inside.

'What are they watching?'

'Some kind of game show.'

'I thought there was a lot of screaming.'

'A woman just won a kitchen.'

'Perhaps she's never seen one before.'

'You'd think so. She's wetting herself.' Sean cleared aside some of my fantasy-Mesopotamian temple layouts and sat on the end of my bed. 'How's your chest?'

'All right.'

'Breathe for me.'

I drew deeply a few times. 'All right?'

'Still a bit wheezy.'

'That's my jumper creaking.'

'Make sure you use your inhaler.'

'You don't have to keep checking up on me.'

'After three bouts of pneumonia—'

'I know, my lungs are like a pair of old dishcloths.' I had seen the inside of my first oxygen tent at the age of two. There had been a serious recurrence at nine, and another more prolonged life-threatening experience the previous year that had landed me in hospital for nearly two months. Pauline was fond of telling people that it was a miracle I had survived.

'You were wet when you came in tonight. You're not supposed to do that any more.'

'The rules are unreasonable, like don't run upstairs and don't lose your temper. I mean, how can you not? I thought you were going to take Janine home, anyway.'

'She wants to walk back.'

'Only there was a rough lot hanging around the esplanade earlier.'

'Janine can take care of herself. She's got her boots on.'

'Yeah,' I grinned, 'she's not exactly the Elizabeth Barrett-Browning of the confectionery world, is she?'

Sean spread a big tanned hand across one of the maps, ironing out the creases. 'So, smartarse, how are you going to catch up on your homework?'

'I've been reading a lot.'

'You've been reading a lot since you were six.' He gave a rueful smile, looked at the drawings on the walls. 'It's not really the right field of study, is it? Not exactly on the curriculum.'

'More interesting than school.' I spread out one of my half-finished maps and started to draw a neat pencil line along the edges of a desert.

'You're supposed to get yourself interested in something useful. You've got to be able to use your knowledge, Kay. Can't do that unless you get good exam results. Have you thought any more about what you want to do?'

'I thought I might join the Imperial Indian police, like George Orwell. His lungs were buggered, just like mine. Has Mum been having a go at you?' Sean usually left the vocational guidance counselling to others. He wasn't much of a role model for the ambitious Cole Bay school leaver, but he seemed happy enough. He didn't talk to me about his own life. Analysis was less important to him than just getting on with things.

'No,' he replied, 'not really,' which meant yes. 'You're worrying them. They think you lack confidence.'

'And you don't.'

'I think you've got a bit too much. You're an annoying little sod, and you reckon you're too smart for this town. But I suppose you may be right there.'

'I'm not allowed in the water, I'm stuck here breathing the rotten sea air, and I can't go to London, how crap is that?' My last bout of pneumonia had damaged my respiratory system enough to make the doctor ban me from the sea and the city.

'I think you're looking at this the wrong way. It wouldn't be so bad if you made some friends.'

'I've got friends.'

'I'm talking about people of your own age.'

'People of my age are only interested in pop music and finding someone to snog.'

'And of course you're above all that.'

'I'm being realistic, that's all. I can't stand Simon and bloody Garfunkel. I wear the same duffle coat John Noakes wears when he climbs up things on *Blue Peter*. And the only two girls I know are Julia, who's given up on men, and Janine, who's going out with you.'

'You don't exactly put yourself out. You're not a bad-looking kid, you could make an effort. Grow your hair a bit and cover those ears, buy some jeans and a leather jacket instead of wearing your school raincoat everywhere. I reckon girls would go for you, if you could find something to talk about other than dead civilisations.'

'That should be a subject of interest to everyone living here.'

'Put down the pencil for a minute.' I looked up and saw that Sean was wearing his stern older-brother face. 'I know what this is about, Kay. You can be honest with me.'

'I am honest with you.'

'I heard what you said to Dr Forrest.'

'I didn't do anything.'

'You asked him about your long-term prospects.'

'He wouldn't give me an answer. I know what that means. Doctors don't lie, they just miss things out. What's a check-up for if he can't tell me everything?'

'Listen, you've got to have a more positive attitude. All this stuff about dying, it's bollocks.'

'You don't know that.'

Sean's angry glare could have taken the distemper off the ceiling. 'None of us knows anything! They might find out tomorrow that beans on toast gives you cancer. The point is, you're not going anywhere, so you just have to get on with life and start measuring up.'

'I can't calibrate myself against anything out there.'

'You need to find a way of making things work.'

'Otherwise what?'

'Otherwise – I dunno. You go barmy. Wander off into your own world.'

'It's got to be more fun than this one. Isn't that why you and your mates smoke dope all the time?' I knew that Sean deserved better than this, but could not help myself.

'They're making allowances for you because you've been ill, but you can't ride on it forever.'

'So what are you saying?'

'I'm saying don't piss away your chances, that's all.'

'It could be worse,' I told Sean's retreating back. 'I could be hanging around on street corners selling drugs.'

'Don't worry, Kay.' Sean turned in the doorway. 'There's still time.'

'Yeah, I thought I'd keep that particular career opportunity up my sleeve for next year, if I make it that far.'

Sean slammed the door shut behind him, and I returned to shading the map, scribbling at the paper until I tore through it. My heart wasn't in Mesopotamia any more that night. I knew I had overstepped the line with Sean, and was disgusted with myself.

Persistence of Memory

'You teenagers are always getting het up over little things. You're hyperactive. It's to do with glands. Or is it hormones?' Dudley Salterton selected another chip from his paper cone and ate it carefully. He had a dental plate. 'How's Mesopotamia?'

'Unsatisfactory.' I looked over at his cone. 'Have you got an onion?'

'Give over. I'm on in an hour. Breath. My pensioners don't like it.'

I looked out at the horizon. The grey-green edge of the sea was darkly softening with rain. 'It's going to piss down.'

'That'll drive them in. Eight people there were last matinée, not a cloud in the sky. More backstage than in the audience.' Dudley performed in the theatre next to the pier. He did a Mr Memory act, and a bit of ventriloquism with a lascivious sailor-suited dummy called Barnacle Bill. He also led singalongs and managed a few basic magic tricks, tearing ladders from newspapers, producing bouquets of coloured-feather flowers from unusual places, that sort of thing. He was ageless in a way that wasn't good, somewhere between postmenopause and postmortem. He dyed his hair and eyebrows a really weird shade of gingery-brown, and thought nobody noticed. His false teeth looked too big for his mouth. He never shaved properly, leaving a patina of stubble around his chin, and always wore a grey pin-striped suit with a greasy collar. When he had his stage makeup on, he looked like he'd been badly embalmed. We sometimes sat on the pier and had chips together before his Wednesday matinée.

'Can you not find anything in the library?'

'About Mesopotamia? You're joking. Their historical shelf doesn't go back further than the First World War. It's all romances and thrillers. One of my teachers is trying the London bookshops for me.'

'Dolores always used to say that the past is another country.'

'How do you mean?'

'Very different. Hard to understand.'

'Oh.' I thought for a bit. 'I like that.'

'I don't think she made it up. Someone else said it first. Still.'

I never had a conversation with Dudley where he didn't mention Dolores, his deceased wife. She used to help him with the act when they were resident in Blackpool. She'd been dead for years, but he still missed her.

'When the person you love dies, you never get over losing them,' he told me once, 'you just get used to living with the memory.' It seemed grimly appropriate that he was often billed as Mr Memory. Dudley was quite depressing to be with, but I liked him. He never bothered trying to impress me. Then again, it would have been pretty hard to do; I'd seen his act.

'Dolores used to do this turn where she put a sparkly tube around her neck, and I'd thread a balloon through it.'

'What for?'

'What do you mean, what for? It was an optical illusion. It never really worked. We tried it with a sword but I kept nicking her, so we went back to the doves, until someone called the health inspector in.'

'Why, what did they want?'

'Well, there's this trick where you show your top hat to the audience and tap the bottom, and the dove's in a triangular black box that clips to the brim at the back of the hat. As you turn the hat over on the table to bang the top with your wand, you drop in a little explosive pellet, nice bang and a flash, see, then you release the catch on the box and the dove drops into the hat. But the box we had wasn't big enough. I found out later it was meant for canaries. We got through a fair few doves before I twigged.' He looked at my watch. 'And those that made it didn't last too many performances because the explosives made them very loose down below. I'd best be off. Do you want a comp?'

'What are you doing?'

'Barnacle Bill's Saucy Sea Shanties, "If You Were The Only Girl In The World", magic mirrors and either "Love Makes The World Go Round" or "You Need Hands", depending on which music Eileen's brought with her.'

'Ah – no, not today.' I balled my cone and potted it into the nearest bin. 'I've got a lot of homework. Maybe Saturday. Who's top?' The programme changed on Fridays.

'Brian Poole and the Tremeloes. They had something in the charts once, I thought you'd know. Scruffy looking shower. Makes you wonder where he finds them.' 'He' was Mr Cottesloe, the crimson-faced booking agent who spent most of his life topping up a huge scotch in the snug bar of The Jolly Anglers at the end of the pier.

'Dudley, can I ask you something personal?'

'I suppose so.'

'Is that your real name?'

He looked at me. 'For a smart lad you can be right soft sometimes.'

'Why do you stay here?'

'Well.' He stuck out his stubbly chin, thinking. 'It's regular work. You can get a good crowd in. And the sea air settles me stomach.'

But as soon as I asked him, I knew the real reason. He didn't really notice being here, because 'here' was inside his head, with Dolores. She made it home for him, wherever he was. Funny that. I'd always thought of him as a poor old sod. His act was really terrible, feeble tricks and ditties no-one remembered, sung in a thin, cracked voice. That Wednesday afternoon I watched him plodding back down the pier just as the first drops of rain spattered the boards, and I wondered how he could keep going without much of his dignity left, without his beloved wife. Back then, I didn't understand what kept him alive. I do now, but a lot has happened to me since those stormy grey afternoons on the pier.

CHAPTER EIGHT

The Searching Scimitar

The dying sun caught the sweat-sheened forelocks of four-and-twenty Arab stallions belonging to the *sipahi*, the imperial horsemen, as they trotted forward in a gentle arc. They stepped with such precision that the tiny glass bells on their martingales jingled in a clear glissando, the sound of angels heralding the night. They were ridden by the city's emirs, men of the greatest gravity, resplendent in their emerald turbans and sashes, their hooked brown noses turning neither right nor left, their amber eyes never dropping from the horizon.

Dr Trebunculus rode with Rosamunde in a tumbril at the far end of the line. The Sultan's daughter had been leaning from the carriage window, watching the tails of the horses switching from side to side as they raised and dropped their hooves. She flounced back on to her seat, raising a cloud of fine dust from the embroidered upholstery. 'Perhaps you made another mistake in your calculations.'

'That unfortunate slip occurred in Menavino's transcription, when he misinterpreted a fracturing beam of sunlight,' the doctor bristled. 'The calibrations of the astrolabe are measured by the turning of the stars themselves. There can be no margin for error. And their world is so very wet, the condensation plays havoc with our instruments. Menavino triple-checked the paperwork with me and agrees with my findings. If there is a fallacy, it begins in the heavens themselves.'

'Be careful, Doctor,' warned Rosamunde, 'that sounds remarkably like blasphemy. We'll have to turn back soon. You know the rules.' The sun would soon be setting, and the Sultan's horsemen were not allowed to ride after nightfall because the unlit ground was treacherous, and there were *akinci* – mounted raiders – operating in the area.

Trebunculus was mindful of his delicate position. He was allowed great liberty within the house of the royal family, and had always been careful not to abuse the trust he had earned. But the longer the promise he had so rashly made to Rosamunde's father remained unfulfilled, the worse it grew for him. He had told the Sultan that he would find a replacement, and time was fast running out. His hard-won reputation was at stake, and Rosamunde's mother was no longer alive to protect him from the Sultan's wrath.

The doctor thrust his head from the window, allowing the cool evening breeze to fan his face, and looked to the emerging stars for help. He glanced back at the Princess as her pearl-sheened eyelids closed to the rhythmic dancing of the carriage, and ran his hand through his dusty beard. He remembered the day he had delivered her into the world, and how he had fought to save the life of poor Eliya, her mother. The infant had been born so silent and still that for a moment the doctor felt sure he had lost her too. But Rosamunde, at least, came back. And here in the desert oasis she had blossomed – there was simply no other word for it. Her fearlessness, her compassion, her intellect set her aside from the other ladies of the palace; she was in every way her mother's daughter. The Sultan saw it, and his joy was tempered with sorrow for his loss.

But even Rosamunde did not know the truth of her birthing day. Only Trebunculus had seen the goblet of blue crystal from which the Sultan's wife had drunk. He alone had found the tiny black granules of poison in the bottom of the glass. How he had agonised over his discovery! Suicide was unthinkable, for the Sultan's marriage was the happiest in the kingdom, but the spectre of murder was just as difficult to confront, in a land where peace had reigned unbroken for so many years . . .

He had kept the goblet's residue, carefully drying and sealing it within a jar in his laboratory. And there it had remained while Rosamunde grew. He had hoped one day to solve the riddle of Eliya's death, but now more pressing concerns had overtaken.

He thought of young Menavino lying on the floor of the laboratory, surrounded by astrological charts and calculations. The boy was barely out of his teens, but instinctively understood the principles governing the mystic foundations of the world. He would make a fine successor, and might yet save the day. As the doctor's abilities faded with his eyesight, the talents of his apprentice blossomed.

'We'll ride a little further,' he decided, 'to the *meydan* by the river basin. You must understand that there is more than mere geography involved in this convergence; the will must be on his side. But the Westerner's appearance is inevitable, you need have no fear of that. I shall find him for you.'

'It's not for my father's sake that I pray you succeed,' the Princess murmured sleepily, her brocade fan wilting in her fingers, 'but for all of us.'

The curving line of stallions rode on, the tan carriage positioned at the base of the arc like the handle of a great scimitar, sweeping into the sunset.

Paying Respect

'I'm thinking of having my name changed by deed poll,' said Julia, 'except my mother would kill me if she ever found out. How much money have you got on you?'

'Twelve and six. It's all right if you shorten it to Stakis.' Julia's surname was Stakisvakapolos. Julia wasn't her real name either, but she was never prepared to discuss the subject. I knew she was embarrassed by her family background, which was Greek Cypriot Catholic. Her mother spoke very little English. I wanted to talk about how this made her feel, belonging to one of the few foreign families in the area, but sensed that the issue was taboo. I was sure that if I ever mentioned it she would act surprised and pretend that the thought had never occurred to her, when it was probably an obsession. In 1970, on the south coast of England, if you were anything other than Church of England people talked around you as if you weren't there.

'I meant "Julia", change it legally to "Julia". Doesn't matter, I was thinking aloud.'

I seized the chance. 'Come on, then, what is it really?'

'Forget it, it's my bloody mother's fault for being so religious. I'm not telling you. I had enough trouble in the Junior Mixed Infants. We'll have to go halves today, Kay, if we want to buy popcorn and Kia-Oras.'

'We normally go halves anyway. Why don't you call yourself something she likes?'

'She likes the name Crystal. Thinks it sounds sophisticated. Chandeliers and sparkling lights and that. Makes me think of those birds at the fairground who give you a chalk poodle if you get three darts in a card.' Julia looked down at her stomach and ran her hands across her fawn duffel coat, smoothing the rain from it. 'I never seem to be able to change anything. It's like I know I'm always going to be fat. It's in my mother's genes, and the bad genes always win out, so if your dad went bald you'll go bald.'

'My dad's not bald,' I said defensively. Julia had no idea that Bob was not my real father. 'Your mother's built like a hippopotamus. She's never going to let you change your name legally, so you might as well learn to accept it.'

'I can't, it's really awful.'

'Tell me. I promise I won't tell anyone.'

She searched my eyes. This was a big deal for her. 'You swear?'

'On my grandad's grave.'

'It's Mary And Joseph.'

I stifled a laugh. 'What, both names, hyphenated?'

'It used to be popular in parts of Greece. Please, Kay, don't ever tell.'

'Yeah, all right. It's a good job your surname's not Carpenter.'

'It's easy for you to talk. Kay's not your real name, is it? Your real name's Kevin but you hated it so much when you were a little boy you told everyone to call you Kay, even though Kay is a girl's name. Your mum told my mum.'

'It's not 'cause I don't like Kevin, it's 'cause I like Kafka. Actually.'

'Here, are you two in the queue or what?' asked an elderly man behind us.

'Yes we are, thank you,' said Julia loudly, turning to me. 'Why do they always let the coffin-dodgers in half price on matinées?'

I moved up to the window and laid out our money. 'Two at the front, please.'

Taste the Blood of Dracula was an X-certificate, but the cashier of the Cole Bay Roxy used to go out with Julia's older sister, and he let us see anything we wanted so long as the manager wasn't about. The only problem was that they had to sell adult tickets for Xs, so we were forced to pay the full amount. We liked the balcony seats, but prices had recently risen to 7s/6d, so we made do with a couple of eye-strainers in the stalls.

'I don't think I like the look of this,' Julia complained, studying the lurid foyer poster which bore the legend DRINK A PINT OF BLOOD A DAY. The feature was double-billed with a psychological thriller called *Crescendo*. 'It's not going to be scary, is it? Not like that thing we saw in the tube station, where the plates flew up in the air and there were grasshoppers from Mars.'

'I take it you are referring to *Quatermass and the Pit*,' I said witheringly. 'I know you don't like films with an element of the *fantastique*. You've told me often enough. I'd have gone with someone else if I could have found anyone.'

'You might hang around outside and offer to pay a stranger.'

'I've bought the tickets now. Come on, fatty. You know you've got nothing better to do this afternoon.'

'I really hate you sometimes. I can't help being like this. I'm retaining water.'

'You're retaining chips. And quite a lot of grease.'

Julia was fifteen and glistened with sweat on the coldest days of winter. Her eyebrows joined together at the top of her nose. She lived on chips and crisps, and spent the whole time complaining about her skin, but as soon as we were past the ticket booth she was drawn hypnotically towards the popcorn counter. And yet, sometimes it was like there was another person inside her, behind the eating and the sarcastic banter, someone very wise and beautiful that I could only ever glimpse.

'You're never going to grow up,' she said nastily. 'First chance they get, the kids in your class will all leave and you'll be left behind with your boring old history books. In London everyone's wearing bandsmen's tunics and lime-green plastic frocks with holes in them and opening boutiques and being trendy. My dad sent me a picture of himself in an orange lace polo-neck shirt that fastens with Velcro. He's met Twiggy and Justin de Villeneuve. He's very with-it. He's thirty-five and still looks cool in sideburns and hipster flares. Nobody thinks he's my dad at all.'

I could have said something cruel, but let the moment pass.

'I've seen what happens to people who get left behind. Don't think I'm going to be stuck here with you.' She ordered the largest carton of popcorn they sold. 'As soon as he comes home we're moving back to London.' Julia always said this. I knew who she was trying to convince, and it wasn't me. Her parents had separated two years earlier, and her father clearly had no intention of ever returning to Cole Bay. He handled public relations for a travel firm and sent her postcards from Mediterranean resorts, and rang her up when he was drunk, and she interpreted these teary swaggerings as an imminent return.

'Tell me if this stuff tastes off.' Julia waved her popcorn bucket in my direction. 'How's Mesopotamia?'

'Bleeding awful,' I replied, wriggling a straw into the top of my Kia-Ora. 'Old Dunmow didn't get up to London. He's on a crutch. He was crossing the miniature railway and they changed the points. I think he was pissed.'

'He goes drinking with your dad.'

I ignored her implication. On the rare occasions that he was sober, Mr Dunmow taught us history, and to say that he failed to bring it to life was a severe underestimation of his inability. We called him the Dunmow Flitch because he had a face like a side of bacon.

'The trouble with Mesopotamia is you get three or four recognised authorities and they all cross-reference each other, so you keep coming across the same information, over and over. I don't know how to get the kind of access I need. There are reference systems you can phone, but they never give you the right material. To be honest, now that the Flitch has let me down I'm not sure what to do. There must be another way to find out about the past.'

'Why don't you just pick something else?'

'Egypt's been done to death.' I peered through the porthole in the auditorium door, but the last film hadn't finished. Christopher Lee was screaming and slashing himself to bits on a huge stained-glass crucifix. It was probably not the ideal film to take a Catholic girl to, but I thought Julia could handle it.

'You could do Constantinople.'

'It's Istanbul, not Constantinople,' I told her. 'And there's no point. It's the same problem with the Ottoman Empire. I've had a volume of *Suleyman The Magnificent* on order for six months. The librarian thinks it's been stolen but he's not sure. He says there's not much call for it these days.'

'Then do something else for a while, give your brains a rest. Look at you. You could join the rowing club, build yourself up a bit. Your arms are like pieces of wet string.'

She was right. Recurring illness had robbed me of muscle growth when I most needed it. I was as thin as she was fat, and Julia was exceedingly fat. She had beautiful eyes, but her kinky black hair was held down with huge tortoiseshell slides, and she wore paint-stained dungarees to annoy her mother. Still, she was the only girl I knew who would spend time with me, just as Danny and I were the only blokes in Cole Bay who would bother with her. Of course, Danny didn't count in the traditional way of male–female relationships because he was as gay as a French trombone.

Julia ate all through the first film, stopping only to smear pale blue mascara on my shoulder during the scary parts. Usually she bought a Jubbly, a deep-frozen drink in a triangular carton. The trouble with these was that once you had sucked the flavour from the top corners, the whole ice-block had to be carefully lifted out and turned over, and she inevitably shot hers on to the floor. Her incessant snacking annoyed me because I knew she wasn't following the plot properly, and I expected my cinema companions to appreciate the films we saw, even if they were bad. Julia's attention kept wandering off, to her clothes, the ceiling, the people in the row behind. In key scenes she would get up and go to the kiosk, and on her return she never once asked what she had missed. To someone who was interested only in the world on the screen, this kind of behaviour was incredibly infuriating. During the main feature she vanished for ten minutes to talk to a girl on the smoking side of the stalls. I was determined not to let this annoy me, and concentrated hard on the film.

After Dracula had been noisily dispatched once more we left the cinema, and I was ready to discuss the historical context of vampirism.

'The Dracula legend is loosely based on the real-life atrocities of Vlad the Impaler,' I explained enthusiastically.

'My mother's expecting me, Kay. We're going shopping.'

'Christopher Lee was good, though, wasn't he?' I never gave up without a fight.

'I suppose so.'

'You *suppose* so?'

'Which one was he?'

'What do you mean, which one?' I exploded. 'He's Dracula! Fangs, cape, red eyes, always turns to dust at the end, you've seen him loads of times!'

'I'll be late if I don't go, Kay. I'm meeting her outside McFisheries.'

'I don't know why I bother with you,' I sulked.

'I'm not one of your mates, Kay, I'm a girl. How about giving me a little respect?'

I couldn't make her out at all. I trudged back towards number 14 Balaclava Terrace feeling unfulfilled. Half the fun of going to the pictures was arguing about the film afterwards. Julia took that pleasure away and replaced it with something else. It was something I couldn't quite get a handle on, but I had a sneaking suspicion that it was to do with sex. There was nothing to rush home for now, so I wandered around the backstreet bookshops for a while, in the forlorn hope of finding reference material. I didn't find any – I hardly ever did – and within minutes of re-entering our house, managed to get myself into trouble again.

My mother had problems with her back, flares of pain that acted as some kind of early-warning system for osteoporosis. When she passed through these phases, she grew very angry.

She hadn't expected to feel old so soon. Resentment flew about her like a fireball, exploding on random targets: the dirt behind the cooker, the common woman next door who allowed her children to eat baked beans from the tin, the halfway-house for young offenders in the next street, the councillors who allowed the construction of the Las Vegas arcade on the front.

She asked me about school, and I told her about old Beardwood the headmaster giving us a start-of-term lecture. 'Life is a race,' he'd said, beadily scanning the assembly room, 'and you are all in competition. We are here to push you hard and to build winners. Nobody likes a good all-rounder. Neil Armstrong didn't get to the moon by being a good all-rounder. We only want champions.' He made the place sound like Crufts.

'So why did you get sent out?' she asked me.

I hesitated for a moment, then described how I explained my problem with Neil Armstrong to the headmaster, pointing out that astronauts should be made to pass grammar as well as physics. I said I thought the system was wrong, and that French students were probably right to confront their educators. Now, the news items that had most annoyed my mother in the last eighteen months were the ones about the Paris riots. So we embarked on a huge argument that ended with me going to my room and ripping up my old plans of Babylon. This had been the project before Mesopotamia, and was actually quite hard to destroy because I had laminated several of the maps, and was forced to work on them with a hacksaw blade, my mum's best breadknife and a pair of secateurs before they'd fit in the bin.

On the way to school the next morning I saw another of the acquaintances my family considered unsuitable for me. She was heading for the bus-stop, half-obscured beneath a gigantic yellow golf umbrella. Ruth Hill was my English teacher, but everyone called her Miss Ruth. She was rumoured to be several years older than the pier. Someone said she remembered it being built, but this had to be a lie because according to the guide book – a slim volume available from the English Heritage bookstall, extortionately priced at 19s/6d – the pier was constructed in 1865. Miss Ruth had a face the colour of the old dried newspapers you find under floorboards, and periodically felt it necessary to justify her state of spinsterhood by telling me, 'there was only one man I ever wanted, but it didn't work out so I never married.' She used to say this with such an air of distant melancholy that I usually felt obliged to flee, but on this day she suited my mood, so I walked with her for a while.

She took very deliberate steps in great square-heeled boots of shiny leather that defied all the traditional old lady pavement traps and would probably have seen her to the shops in a blizzard, like some kind of orthopaedic snow tractor. From the side she looked like a question mark. She smelled of lavender, not the crushed-bud-between-your-fingers kind, or even granny bottles, but more overpowering, like a toilet block. I was sixteen years old, a physically underdeveloped, mentally overactive boy verging, as they say, on manhood. It was not natural for me to enjoy the companionship of a woman as old as a tree, I knew that.

My grandparents on my mother's side were both dead, and Pauline hadn't kept in contact with those on Bob's side because they didn't approve of second marriages and had stayed away from the wedding. Miss Ruth was a logical extension of the women within my circle. First there was Julia, adolescent, fat and invisible to boys; then came Janine, anxious to please and preparing for marriage; then Pauline, disillusioned and disappointed by men; and finally Miss Ruth, an eternal virgin who had dedicated herself to being alone. It didn't conjure much as a composite of womankind. I got the idea that the lifespan of the opposite sex consisted of roughly four stages: mooning around over boys, becoming hysterical about settling down, spending the married years wiping floors, and finally not looking or sounding like a woman at all. All I can say in my defence is that my experience was limited, I was a late starter and it was 1970.

The problem was simple; I put the women I didn't know on pedestals and treated the ones I did know like men. If I'd have been an Incan priest it would never have occurred to me to shout up at the sun god, 'Listen, Ra, instead of me chucking you a virgin, how would you like a woman who's been around a bit, someone who's a bit of a laugh?' I think I needed to look up to women because I knew in my heart that respect was due, but did not really know why.

Miss Ruth had been considered quite a scholar at one time, but people had forgotten her prodigious intelligence because it was of no use in the present school curriculum. She used to lecture on classical mythology at the old college, but the council closed the place down and the new building was too far for her to travel to – she didn't drive – so all the knowledge that she had accumulated had nowhere to go, and stayed wasting within her unless I lingered after school to discuss the Greek myths. She also used to teach singing, and showed me how to respirate my way through a nervous attack. Bob always gave me an odd look when I told him I'd stayed late to talk to her, as if it was the weirdest thing in the world to show an interest in something other than football, cars or girls. But she taught me how to breathe, which was more than he ever did.

But now she, too, was displeased with me. 'I think it's a

shame, you giving up on your schooling. You enjoy learning, I don't understand it. All you have to do is work hard for a couple of years, resit your exams and get some decent passes, then you can choose what you want to do.'

We reached the bus-stop and stood beside each other, peering ahead at the empty yellow ribbon of road. Because I was wearing plimsolls and she had on her I-Survived-Black-Ice boots, she was slightly taller than me.

'It's true,' I said, 'an entire world of opportunity could open up for me in Cole Bay. If I play my cards right I could become a mobile rep for a string of exhaust replacement centres and have customers as far as the greater Bexhill-stroke-St Leonard's area.'

'Sarcasm is not a substitute for wit, Kay. If you choose to be somebody small, that's entirely up to you.'

'I'm not afraid of hard work,' I told her. 'But they say I'll peg out if I go and live in a city. I'm too young to be thinking about dying.'

'Teenagers are always thinking about death; you stop as you get older. Perhaps you haven't found the right city yet. Don't be in such a rush. Finish your learning, then worry about where to go. Does that look like a bus to you?'

'You want your glasses on, Miss Ruth. That's a boat.'

She leaned perilously forward, then back. 'Oh yes.' She sometimes carried a stick with her, but I got the impression that this was for waving about rather than leanage. If determination played a part in staying active, she had enough for both of us. To be honest, there were days when she appeared to have more energy than me. We had this weird unspoken rule, that if anyone from my class came to the bus-stop we would cease speaking to each other. This was initiated on her part, not mine. She was more worried about my reputation than I was.

I sometimes thought of Miss Ruth as a weird counterpart to Dudley Salterton, a grim example of what happened to older people who stuck around in Cole Bay. Lost in dreams and memories, defiantly alone, marching on to nowhere. Was this all that a life of hard work amounted to? It seemed a pretty poor reward for living so long. Unlike the other kids in my school, being around old people didn't annoy or bore me, because they had always been so kind when I was ill, and yet the mere fact that I got on with them made me some kind of an outcast.

I wasn't very good at remembering who I was supposed to hate. But later that day I was given a reminder of who to fear.

Getting Together,
Coming Apart

At school that morning, an awful spirit-crushing sense of disaster hung over the morning maths test, mainly because I hadn't studied for it. The questions involved stupid things like working out the lengths of trains that passed through stations at different speeds. What was the point? If somebody knew how fast a train was going, he would surely have a rough idea how many carriages it was pulling, because he'd be a controller. And there was this problem with a farmer and his boat that could only ford a river holding himself and either a duck or a cabbage, and how many trips would it take to get all three across. I mean, what difference in weight would a cabbage make? And anyway, why not tie the duck to the boat and let it swim behind? The maths teacher told me my thinking was too lateral, which I would have thought was a good thing, and gave me no marks.

After lunch the same feeling of impending doom invaded the weekly physics test, which was something to do with fulcrums that, needless to say, I hadn't a clue about, having spent too much time on Mesopotamia. *Fulcrums,* I thought.

Come on, you can do it, concentrate. I thought hard, but could only conjure an image of circus performers jumping on to each other's shoulders from seesaws.

I was standing in the cloakroom absorbed in the task of turning my overcoat the right way out (my classmates thought this trick was sufficiently amusing to pull every day), when Malcolm Slattery dropped one-handed on to the bench opposite like an orang-utan descending from its climbing bars, and began to hoot with laughter. This, I have to say, was not a pleasant sound because he had serious sinus problems, and produced mucus with every breath he drew. When he exhaled he sounded like the wind blowing through a damaged harmonica. You would have thought we had enough in common to be friends.

Slattery was intelligent to the point of lunacy, and apparently had a great future ahead of him in applied mathematics. He reckoned that computers were going to be the next big thing, and saw himself making a lot of money. He was the sort of person who would, too, because he had a crafty charisma that attracted the weak. His parents were pushing him to succeed, and in my opinion they were pushing a bit too hard, because he was completely nuts. He had a particular fondness for breaking things; damaging furniture, scarring cars, ripping kids' jackets, smashing shop windows – a psychiatrist would have had a field day with his childhood fantasies. I discovered what Slattery was snorting about when I put my hand into my overcoat pocket.

'What's the matter, Goodwin, 'snot what you expected?'

'It's what I'd expect you to expectorate.' I withdrew my gummy fingers, wiped the contents of his nose on to the paisley handkerchief I kept tucked inside my left shirtsleeve and attempted to ignore this latest assault on my dignity, but the problem lay with my mouth. I had a shoddy sense of control over the technical brain device that edited my thoughts for aural consumption, and found myself suggesting aloud that Slattery's mother was, how can I put this, no stranger to the embraces of barnyard animals, the upshot of which was that, unsurprisingly, I got seven thicknesses of shit kicked out of me. The cloakroom stayed mysteriously empty until he had finished.

'And the next time I see you outside school,' he warned in a drawl copied from Clint Eastwood's spaghetti westerns, 'you're dead.' There were rumours that Slattery owned a gun. I wondered if he was planning to shoot me. The bare hatred that showed in his eyes branded me a natural enemy. As I forced my aching body from the floor, I made a decision to be more wary of him in the future.

The school nurse made me go and sit in the A&E department of Cole Bay General until I could get my head X-rayed. It turned out that I had a couple of hairline fractures in my nose, and some bruises that made me look like a maltreated panda. It wasn't enough to keep me out of school, but I liked to think that Slattery had ruptured his fist on my face. I'd have made a good flyweight boxer, one of those wiry little things that keep bouncing back on their feet despite the giant blows raining down upon them.

Afterwards I hobbled off to the Pavilion Pier and watched my homework pages gently unfurl like parachutes into the sea. Then I sat staring between the rusting white pillars at the secret love of my life.

The first time I saw her head poking up between two nodding skulls, I fell so deeply in lust that I got a stiffy every time I saw the skeleton that hung beside the blackboard in Biology class. I knew that her name was Katherine, spelt with a K, which was a good omen, that she was seventeen and didn't have a boyfriend. She worked on the ghost train taking the tickets. The front of the ride was a lifesized green railway carriage with nodding skeleton passengers in its windows, and as she faced towards them collecting money it always looked as if they were agreeing with her. That first time I had just been reading about Hylas and the Sea-Sirens, and it was quite weird because as I walked past her the ghost train siren went off, which I took to be a sort of sign. She also worked on the candyfloss counter, wrapping pink sugar clouds around sticks. Sometimes she had tea with the flat-chested girl on the helter skelter, and they stood beside each other breathing lightly on to their polystyrene cups.

I spied on Katherine from a dozen carefully chosen vantage points (back of the dodgems, behind the gents' toilets, side of the shooting range). She favoured breast-moulding ribbed sweaters and jeans, and looked a bit like the actress Julie Christie. I saw her on the beach once, stretched out across the pebbles on an August Sunday when the air was hot and still and the sea was bottle-green glass. She had long bare legs, shiny brown hair that brushed her shoulders, and a smooth white midriff that became exposed as she reached back on the stones. She shifted her legs slightly, stretching her miniskirt so that the hem between her thighs lifted until it was taut. You always remember things like that.

I allowed Katherine to enter my dreams under cover of darkness. I had been reading a book I'd bought at the Cole Bay Quality Used Paperback Centre about erotic psychic attachment. It said that once you found your psychic sexual soulmate, no physical distance could part you. It didn't tell you how to actually talk to her, though.

I bought a bag of chips (without an onion, in case this was the day that we would finally meet) and hung about in the arcade talking to Danny, but he didn't know anything about Katherine beyond the fact that she shared a flat on the other side of town with a girl who worked in Boots, and had once told him that she couldn't stand marzipan. Danny was more interested in a boy that worked on the dodgems at weekends, but was frightened to go near him in case he got his head kicked in. Katherine finished work at ten and I followed her off the pier, the lightbulbs flicking out behind me as I walked, as though my secret ardour was draining off their electricity.

I had been planning to ask her out for some time, but the moment had to be absolutely right. I knew that I would have to wait for my facial bruising to subside, and anyway I couldn't decide on an opening line. I figured I'd say something like, 'You don't look like someone who works in a funfair.' And she'd say, 'Oh, how do they usually look?' And I'd say, 'Sort of hard and trashy,' and that would be that. I longed to be casual, but everything I came up with in my head just sounded smartarsed and creepy. All around me kids like Malcolm Slattery were treating girls like rubbish and, incredibly, getting off with them. I just couldn't do it. I couldn't treat females as if they were a race apart, lying to them as a matter of course, simply because that was what you were supposed to do. I was rude to Julia all the time but only because she was rude to me, and that made us equal.

Apart from its suicide record, Cole Bay provided some kind of benchmark in the number of teenage mothers who spent their days wandering around its high street with prams. If you hadn't fathered a few illegitimate offspring by the time you were sixteen, you were considered a poof. We had the birth-rate and the death-rate sewn up; we just didn't know much about the part in between.

October 1970. Swinging London was starting to slow down, Cole Bay was turning like a corpse in the breeze, and I was coming apart at the seams. Something had to change before it was too late. I needed to discover a different destination, and quite accidentally, I did. But it was the last place that I expected, and in the last place that I expected it to be.

CHAPTER ELEVEN

A Shift in the Cosmos

It was an unseasonably warm, wet afternoon at the end of the month. The esplanade shone and smelled of seaweed. Malcolm Slattery had been following me for over half a mile, and I knew he was going to beat me up again, and I knew that this time he would hurt me very badly. With him was a weaselly-looking boy called Laurence who functioned as some kind of protean henchman. The words that best described Laurence were ones of finality and termination: bottom of the class, end of the line, last one out of the gene pool, back of the queue for brains, lowest point of the food chain. He had long ginger hair, wonky pale eyes, and a weird high laugh that sounded like a seagull with a bone stuck in its throat.

There was nowhere to hide on the esplanade, and I could tell they were gaining on me. They wore Blakeys on their boots, clattering closer like nefarious tap-dancers until they were just a few yards away. It was starting to rain again, and my chosen-for-cheapness sneakers had hardly any grip left on their soles. I heard Malcolm snort back mucus, then the high 'heeehn-heeehn' of Laurence's laugh, and thought, *this time they're going to cut me up*. It was common knowledge that Malcolm carried a switchblade knife. He hated me because I was top in English, because I had a smart mouth, because I was exempted from football and chose to take fencing lessons instead, because I'd been seen talking to Danny, whom everyone feared and detested, and because I was the kind of sickly speccy twit who deserved to be crushed. But this particular day he had another reason for hating me.

I've always had a high regard for the value of books. I could never bear to see harm come to them, so when I saw Malcolm tearing the first page from a hardback Burton edition of *The Arabian Nights* I knew he was doing it to remove the evidence – the first page always carried the school stamp – and I blurted out to Mr Davis the librarian that he was stealing them and selling them to secondhand shops. This was common knowledge among the other kids, but suddenly I was a snitch and a grass and breaking into a loping run along the esplanade as Malcolm and Laurence ticker-tacked closer behind me, and I felt a searing stitch in the pit of my stomach as I wheeled sharply to my right and vaulted over the turnpike on to the Pavilion Pier without paying the gaffer his shilling. (Actually, the gaffer, Mr Aylmer, was hardly ever there because he spent most of his time under the pier in the girls' lavatories with a hand-drill, and was subsequently exposed after making improper suggestions to a Brownie.) I galloped into the Paradise Penny Arcade, housed in the great dome that ran down its centre, hoping to lose myself between so many flashing lights, but the place was almost deserted. I ran on past the Skee-Ball slides, the Jolly Jack Tar, the Driving Test, the Flick-A-Ball slot machines, the Laughing Policeman, the Penny Rapids, the pinball tables called 'T-Bird' and 'Ace In The Hole', the faded automata in glass cases that bore titles like 'The Drunkard's Dream' and 'The Condemned

Man', and emerged from the top of the arcade, taking a quick look back to see the pair of them dividing on either side of a boxer's punchball, shouting to each other.

My chest was bursting. There was nowhere to go. The pier didn't lead anywhere. Of all the stupid moves I had ever made, this was the worst. I must have been mad running into a blind alley. As soon as I heard them behind me again, I knew I was done for. I wheezed past Katherine's closed candyfloss kiosk, the shooting gallery and the booth where they made glass animals. The helter skelter was shutting up, but the ghost train was still running. I glimpsed the back of Katherine's red plastic rain mac – she was loading a fresh roll of pink paper tickets – hopped over the railway tracks before she saw me and slammed in through the doors of the ghost train ride.

The interior of the structure reeked of oil, electricity and damp painted sailcloth. After a few moments I could make out faint grey lines where the walls didn't fit together properly. I moved to a chink of soft light and looked down at the sea drifting between my feet. It felt as though I was suspended in space. Gradually I was able to make out more detail. Wooden beams hung at crazy angles all around me, painted black. At the height of my head dangled pieces of knotted string. You were supposed to think they were spiderwebs. Somewhere in the darkness ahead there was a mechanical shriek, like a ghost calling through a hooter. The wailing sound rose and fell. It was meant to be spooky, but was also a sign to anyone working inside that there was a car on the track. I ran ahead, beyond the first set of hairpin turns, to where the luminous skeleton came out of its day-glow mausoleum.

I had only ever been inside the ghost train in a carriage, but had ridden it so many times that I knew every square inch of its route. There was an acrid tang of zinc as the entrance doors banged apart and the little steel car rattled past, sparking and shaking. Malcolm and Laurence were squashed into a single carriage beside each other. They looked ridiculous. The car began twisting back and forth on its miniature track with a crackle of voltage, and I readied myself behind the skeleton's plywood tomb lid. Just as they reached the ghost, I pushed hard. The 'tomb' divorced itself from its moorings with a creak and fell on top of them, jamming itself across the track and stopping the car, and both Laurence and Malcolm screamed like terrified toddlers. Shocked at the effect of my own actions, I stood upright and cracked my head sharply on an angled steel beam.

It was all I could do to stop myself from exploding into peals of hysteria as I flew from the back door of the haunted house into the pelting rain. I galloped around the black-painted hardboard sheets at the rear of the attraction, skidded across the steel-plate floor of the dodgems and made my way towards the fisherman's platform at the undamaged L-end of the pier. Below this reserved section was another platform, similar in construction but half the size, a rusted metal matrix built close to sea level that I had never descended to because there was a padlock and chain across the top of the steps, and a sign that read 'DANGER KEEP OUT This Area Declared Unsafe By Cole Bay Council', but now I dropped beneath the chain and ran down until I was just above the height of the waves, praying that my pursuers would not be able to free themselves in time to see where I had gone.

I was surprised to find that the area was protected from the wind and rain by the overhang of the pier. It was suddenly calm and quiet, and I was alone with the water heaving and falling like a great green meadow, inches below the grill upon which I stood. Here the stench of brine and old seaweed was overpowering. I looked over the edge of the rotting iron lattice into the ocean, hypnotised by its closeness as the clouded olive crests rocked back and forth, almost touching my feet. Something opaque passed below the surface, a large domed jellyfish trailing tendrils, transparent and opalescent. I felt the chill of the wind on my neck as it changed direction with the shift of the tide. I briefly closed my eyes and sensed the sway of the sea, lapping coronas of phosphorescent life and refracting light. My stomach rolled over. For a moment I thought I was going to be sick.

And something happened . . .

Because when I opened my eyes I was looking at the jetty, but now it was made of pale scoured wood and its smooth posts were bound with reeds; the sky was the brightest blue I had ever seen, and I stepped forward from the rocking boat as if finally reaching home after a long ocean voyage.

And there, lining the top of the harbour, were dozens of smiling people, whose faces broke into grins as they watched. Some actually began laughing and applauding, as if I had achieved some momentous feat. They beckoned, and raised their caps in greeting, and I started forward for the stairs, their arms reaching out as if they wanted to pull me up and help me to the top. Then they were touching me, and I was surrounded by raucous delighted people who patted me on the back and pressed my arms encouragingly, and one of them stepped forward to lead the way, as if he had anticipated my puzzlement. His barrel-shaped body swayed on stick-thin legs as he strode forward. He wore a stovepipe hat, wire-rimmed spectacles and a purple velvet suit, and was nearly in tears as he cried out, 'My dear boy! We've been expecting you! The stars themselves are blessed! I'm so pleased, so very pleased!' and the others laughed and congratulated him, too, as if he had somehow been responsible for bringing about my long-awaited arrival.

I looked around and saw that the men were wearing white linen shirts open to their navels, with bands of red satin around their waists, and baggy muslin trousers tied with ropes and knots of shiny red cotton. The women had similar bands loosely woven through their hair, but more intricately arranged and richly patterned. And all around I saw white teeth, black hair, olive skin, silken tulips, sapphire sky, darting yellow birds like scraps of windblown gauze, topaz sea behind me, emerald hills in front, and clothes like collisions of rainbows, people moving through prisms of brilliance, the very air shimmering with diamond light, and the warm, dry smells of fruits and flowers and spices, the scent of a safe haven.

Sensing my confusion, the man in the stovepipe hat threw out his right hand and gripped my fingers, shouting above the tumult, 'I am Doctor Trebunculus.'

'Where am I?' I called back, barely able to hear my own voice above the cheering crowd.

The question caught him by surprise. He looked around, and suddenly a gust of exhilaration rippled over his features. 'Why, you're in Calabash, of course!' he laughed, and the merriment ignited, tumbling through the crowd, catching from one face to the next until we were all roaring up at the cloudless, endless, impossibly indigo sky.

CHAPTER TWELVE

A Cause for Jubilation

I had arrived at the harbour that stood at the entrance to the city of Calabash. On either side of the quay, great sandstone athletes knelt facing the sea. Though proudly decorative, they also acted as lightermen, for their shields were beaten into concave discs of bronze and copper and angled to reflect the sun along the exact path of the harbour's deep water channel as a guide to shipping. Trebunculus later informed me that the shields could also be tipped to blind enemies and burn their boats, but they had never been required to do so.

I could see the city from where I stood, a kingdom of ivory-tipped minarets, domes and spiral towers. Rising within its crenellated walls were slender silver spires inlaid with mother-of-pearl, and at their heart, a great marble-tiled palace surrounded by gold-mosaic courtyards and glittering sapphire fountains. Beyond the city walls were twisting fresh-water streams and banks of ancient cyprus trees. My sense of disorientation lasted only a short time, for I had arrived in a paradise on earth, and it felt for all the world like coming home to a place that had long existed in my dreams. There was no sense of danger, only the warmth of belonging, and an eagerness to explore. The everyday fears I felt in Cole Bay had no hold on me here, and yet I was surrounded by strangers who, for all I knew, meant me some hidden harm.

As our donkeys picked their way along the chosen route, farmers waved to me from their fields in welcome, and Trebunculus waved back, pointing gleefully at his guest. In just a few minutes we arrived at a wide limestone stairway that heralded the formal entrance to Calabash.

I tried to understand what had happened, but my mind came up with nothing that made any sense. The breeze that ruffled my hair felt subtropical, and the air resonated to the ticking beat of distant samba music. I could smell nutmeg in the air. The city that rose before me appeared to be an amalgam of everything I remembered about the Ottoman Empire; a living painting of the Arabian nights. But there were so many anomalies - the doctor's purple velvet suit, the samba, the modern language. Then there were the bare-breasted women who brazenly rose in the fields as we passed, shading their eyes to watch us. I knew from my studies that in a Muslim society their bronzed bodies would have been covered and locked away from male eyes, protected in paleness and privacy.

Within the walls of Calabash, the colours and textures grew more prolific and intense. Instead of the dim narrow alleyways and souks I had expected to see were sun-glazed squares and fountains where fruit sellers sat with wicker baskets filled with oranges and pomegranates. Toothless brown women laughed together, rolling mounds of green figs from sacks. A pair of greyhounds lay beside one another in the shade, as motionless as clay statues. An old man poured fragrant tea into small metal cups at a wood-faced salon in a bazaar, the craquelure of his walnut face attesting to his years spent serving in sunlight. A lithe young woman passed by in drifting white cotton and slim gold sandals. On her head was a gold turban with a flamboyantly enamelled aigrette. '*Cattir helu*,' Trebunculus muttered, smiling at me with a helpless shrug. 'Very beautiful, no?'

As a small child I had owned a book filled with reproductions of oriental paintings by French travellers. What it was doing in my family and where it had gone remained a mystery - but what I saw all around me now was what I had seen in those pages. A mosque with orange-and-white striped arches, its penumbral calm undisturbed by worshippers, a sun-mottled courtyard where scholars and students lounged, conversing and drawing on copper narghiles, a merchant selling tiger pelts, another offering kaftans sewn with crimson sequins and silver tissue, a dervish angrily peppering himself with dirt, a dromedary with its legs folded beneath its body, its tail rhythmically switching at flies, a cross-legged musician playing a gourd-like instrument with a long handle, producing long high notes that blended perfectly with the sound of the soft, hip-swaying samba that seemed to permeate the air.

'This must all be rather new to you,' Trebunculus called from his donkey. His English diction was formal and immaculate, without carrying the nasality of an upper caste. 'Not, I suppose, what you are used to.'

'Not at all,' I replied. 'Where are we going?'

'We have an audience with the Sultan and his daughter. They are most anxious to meet you.'

I leaned back as a pair of bright blue parrots fluttered between us, aware that my thin limbs were as pale as the sand. 'How did I get here?'

'Ah, that is a matter of some ... here we are.' The mute palace guards swung to attention as a tiny brown girl appeared and began to tether our donkeys. I climbed down, and she indicated that I should bow my head. I looked to Trebunculus.

'Just a formality.'

She removed my blue nylon windcheater and cardigan, then slipped a tangerine-coloured satin sash over the narrow shoulders of my school shirt. Gathering my fingertips together, she guided them into a copper bowl filled with lavender-scented water. Finally, I was bidden to remove my shoes and don padded slippers of bright green cloth. Embarrassed, I tried to hide the hole in my sock.

Trebunculus squinted approvingly. 'Oh, you'll do.' He picked up my sweater and gingerly examined the lettering on the collar. 'Marks and Spencer,' he intoned solemnly, before dropping it back on the ground.

'Am I to bow?' I asked as we passed through a series of courtyards, each exquisitely decorated in iridescent tiles of turquoise, amber and jade. Intricate patterns covered every surface. There were no dead spaces. The corners of the court-yards were cut off, as if to exclude the possibility of shadows.

'No salaams today,' laughed the doctor. 'The Sultan will want to show off his English manners.'

Some courtyards contained bronze gazebos and shallow pools where mutes and buffoons played. Others had tall fountains glazed with the painted shells of ostrich eggs. In the most interior and spectacular of these rooms (although there were silks hung between the topmost corners of the walls, they were still open to the sky) was an area in the shape of an elongated oval, richly decorated with friezes encircled by a wide braid of hatayi blossoms. Here sat the Sultan, extravagantly enthroned on his marble divan, surrounded by pashas. These military commanders, I later learned, were dis-tinguished in rank by the number of horsetails they displayed in times of war, and included the admiral, the vice-admiral and the rear-admiral of his fleet. The division generals of the Sultan's army had not been invited to attend the welcoming ceremony in a deliberate snub that stemmed from the Sultan's ongoing feud with the commanding officer of his land troops, General Bassa.

The Sultan eyed me from beneath drooping lids and smiled, revealing a row of golden pegs. His face was virtually a caricature of an Eastern potentate, with its broad hooked nose and pendulous cheeks. His headdress of amber silk was so heavy and laden with bejewelled royal crests that it rested on his eyebrows. Into the pointed tip of his white goatee was woven a little ebony bar bearing a carved script. Rosamunde later informed me that it was there to remind her father of an ancient saying; that every man's fate was written on his face.

The Sultan's smile turned to a grimace of pleasure. 'We have no need of a *dragoman*, for today I speak the English,' he shouted. 'You are an English, yes?'

'Yes,' I managed nervously. The sharpened scimitars of the guards had not escaped my notice.

'We teach it in our schools,' he bellowed back. 'You're very white.' He turned to the others. 'He's very white.'

'There's no need to shout,' said the Sultan's mother, fanning his voice away.

'Come forward, don't be afraid. We're not going to eat you.' The Sultan released a burst of laughter and looked about appreciatively. 'We're not going to eat him, are we?' His mouth gleamed gleefully. 'May the Prophet of the Seven Burning Stars look down upon this most auspicious occasion. May the Goddesses of the Mystic Silver Moon-Chalice bless this meeting.' He took a weary breath. 'And so on and so forth. Now we shake the hands.'

The Sultan made a sudden lurch forward. Everyone fell

back in alarm. His right fist vigorously pumped mine until I felt my arm loosening in its socket.

'I am the Grand Sultan Mehmet Selim Bousaada Charenton Mustapha al-Hakim Raduan Sur-Guillaumet. I don't expect you to remember all that. The Queen Mother, the Valide Sultan, our gracious Fathmir of Cordoba, my beloved daughter the Princess Rosamunde, and the Royal Concubine Carmelia, a gift from the Saracens for something-or-other.'

'The relief of Scutari,' prompted a short, elderly man with a bulbous nose and a gigantic blue turban pinned with a topaz.

'The Semanticor,' Trebunculus explained, close to my ear. 'Former head scholar of the court of Shey Terrazin, now seconded to the Sultan to teach his children about the world. He is a man of many strange beliefs, one of which is that it is spiritually hazardous to wash the body. Best to stay upwind of him.'

'Ahem.' A cadaverous bald man in robes of black moiré silk cupped a cartoonish cough into his fist.

The Sultan dropped his plump ringed hands to his knee-caps. 'Ah yes, and my Lord Chancellor, Septimus Peason.'

The Chancellor snaked a slim bony hand into the light and clutched at my fingers. 'My father was once the British Ambassador to Calabash,' he explained, 'but he left his family here when he returned to London.' One eye fluttered in a grotesque half-wink. 'Certain delicate affairs of state diplomacy, you understand.' I did not understand. Nobody else had tried to explain anything to me since I arrived, and I was just getting used to the idea. Peason withdrew his cold hand and slid back into the shade. For a moment the space he had occupied remained chilly. He reminded me of the man who had invaded my childhood dreams. Everything about him was so thin and distorted that even the bones beneath his robes appeared to be twisted. At well over six feet in his black satin slippers, he was the tallest man I had yet encountered in the kingdom.

'Well, Trebunculus, I take back everything I said,' the Sultan decided. 'You did it. Septimus, you may reinstate the songbirds. Now perhaps we'll have some peace and I can get on with the running of the state. Let us have sherbet.' He waved his arm in the direction of a row of tall china vases, cut to expose their contents of rhubarb, tamarind, ambergris, rose and lemon. 'So, what happens next?'

'Next, Your Magnificence?' asked the doctor, as if the thought had not occurred to him. 'I hadn't made any plans for our young guest.'

'Whose name we still do not know,' pointed out Rosamunde, whose scarlet robes only reached the winking ruby in her navel. Her bare breasts were capped with tiny cones of gold filigree. She watched me with steady frankness. I tried not to stare back.

'Um, Kay Goodwin,' I announced, adding preposterously, 'of Balaclava Terrace, Cole Bay, southern England.'

'England, Septimus, you're hearing this? "Dreaming spires". "Green and Pleasant Land". Samuel Taylor Coleridge. Yes?'

'Quite so, Your Highness.'

'You are hungry, Kay, yes? We use the first name, yes? Of course you are hungry. We don't know much about English food except the sheep, and we have sheep, too, so today a Calabash feast, yes?' He clapped his hands and a glass gong boomed in the building behind us.

The dining area was another oval courtyard similar to the one in which I had been welcomed, but this was enclosed and carved with panels of multifaceted rock crystal. The arched ceiling was faïenced with black and gold mosaics, and perched upon a dozen octagonal-sided cobalt pillars – a man-made celestial dome. Tall moulded windows released spider-webs of light through gesso mosaics. I glimpsed mysterious doorways leading to other quarters, closed with fine gold chains and framed with incense burners.

The members of the welcoming party seated themselves on embroidered bolsters while bare-chested young men in trousers of silver brocade poured mint tea from twin-spouted mataras. The Sultan's mother sat behind him to one side, and the Royal Concubine was relegated to a place further behind her, clearly an establishment of the household's pecking order. Rosamunde seated herself beside me.

I had never appreciated the aptness of the term 'almond eyes' until I saw hers. They were large and luminous, like flames seen through a honey jar, and were drawn to such fine points that when I first looked at her I saw nothing else. There was no guile in her face, but a frank and unconscious beauty that I had never before imagined could exist in a girl. I fell instantly in love with her because she was impossible to attain, in the way that one can look upon a perfect memory and never fully capture it again. Rosamunde held the spirit of Calabash in her eyes. Even though the years would finally succeed in dimming my memories, I knew I would always see her almond eyes.

The Sultan clapped his hands.

Apart from the dozing dromedary in the market place, I had yet to spot a camel in the kingdom. The one placed before me now was hairless and steamed. Six men set it down on cedar poles, so that its head was facing the Sultan. Grapefruits filled its eye sockets. A muscular man dressed in a brass-studded loincloth and sweating heavily appeared beside it, and with a bloodcurdling scream brought a scimitar down hard across the creature's hump. The tender flesh sprang apart to reveal, once the clouds of steam had lifted, a whole goat, horned, pale and drenched in spice-oils. The scimitar flashed once more. Inside the split goat was a peacock dressed in metallic green feathers. Another scream, another shear of the blade. Inside the peacock was a chicken, and inside this a sand-grouse, then a quail, then a guinea pig, then a sparrow, and finally a canary. The man in the loincloth pushed a long-handled spoon into the canary's opened chest and dug out half an ounce of brown granules, which he brought to a silver plate and laid before me with the greatest delicacy. Everyone looked at me expectantly.

'See!' said the Sultan, pointing proudly to the side of the plate. 'Knife and fork!'

They were all waiting.

'Don't let it get cold,' said Rosamunde drily.

I raised my fork and lifted the savoury brown blob to my lips. It smelled of citrus, but had a subtle nutty taste.

'Speciality of Calabash,' said the Sultan proudly. '*Molida.*'

'*Molida?*' I chewed carefully. 'It's very nice.'

'*Molida!*' Everyone smiled and began to eat.

'Roasted mashed cockroach in fruitbat oil, seasoned with lemons,' explained Rosamunde. I managed to mask my surprise as I swallowed, and tried not to cough. As we ate, I noticed that Rosamunde was still watching my every move. My white skin seemed to fascinate her. Once she reached out and touched my wrist, only to recoil as if electrified. The Sultan eyed her and issued a displeased 'Harrumph'. Nobody spoke, but concentrated on the serious business of enjoying the extraordinary repast.

'Well, I expect your journey has wearied you,' the Sultan decided after the last of several courses had been cleared away. He pushed aside a tray of torn-open lemons and released a series of baritone belches that were roundly applauded. 'When you are fully rested, Mister Kaygoodwin, we expect to hear all about your land, its people and customs, its arts and sciences, yes? Especially its sciences.' He winked knowingly at the Lord Chancellor. 'We must be friends. There are so few young people in the palace these days. I wanted you to meet Scammer, but apparently he's stuck in a chimney.' He leaned back to his mother and said loudly, 'Is he still in the chimney?' She nodded, her chins rippling. 'Well, next time, perhaps. Now that you are here you must treat my humble palace as your home. You can sleep in the Kiosk of the Circumcisions. Or, if you prefer, the doctor will take you to his village, yes?'

The palace was a spectacularly beautiful edifice, but only hospitable to those who were its subjects, and given the choice I knew I would be more likely to relax in an atmosphere of less formality beyond the guarded walls. Making my decision known to Trebunculus, the doctor gave a shy smile. 'A wise choice,' he whispered. 'I have just the very place for you.'

So, amid much complimenting of the sun and moon and stars, and much low bowing and scraping and walking backwards, our visiting party took its leave of the Sultan and his retinue, crossed back through the cooling courtyards and remounted the donkeys at the base of the palace steps, to ride gently with full stomachs towards the setting sun.

CHAPTER THIRTEEN

The Criteria for Happiness

I began to feel cold. The shoulders of my windcheater were soaked, and my teeth were chattering. Someone was shouting at me. 'Oi, in bloody dreamland you are. I'm trying to close up here.' Mr Church pulled a sodden green tarpaulin across the coconut mats at the bottom of the helter skelter. He was responsible for opening and closing the pier, and took his job too seriously. On wet evenings when there were few visitors he shut the place early, and conducted convoluted arguments with anyone who dared to point out that they were entitled to finish their stroll. I snapped from my reverie as if someone had thrown a bucket of cold water over me, and looked back at the pier end, trying to make sense of what had happened. I checked my watch. Only half an hour had passed since I had fled from the ghost train. I wanted to return to the lower deck, but Church was busily ushering me out. How did I get back up the steps to here?

I walked home in a daze, my head still filled with sunlight. Had I imagined everything? I gingerly explored the back of my skull with my fingertips. A tender welt from the ghost train's steel beam, no broken skin. Could it just have been an extremely vivid hallucination?

A van almost ran me over as I crossed the promenade. I remained lost in dreams until I reached my front door. The house smelled of boiling cabbage. Janine and Sean were over for dinner, and were arguing about buying a motorbike. Janine didn't want to ride in a sidecar because she used to ride in her father's and the smell of the acetate windows on a hot day made her sick. She had entered the *Daily Mail*'s competition to win a Mini Minor with a Union Jack painted on its roof. Pauline complained about a butcher who had been caught using contaminated bonemeal in dog food, reminded us all that since the Fray Bentos scandal she still didn't trust corned beef, and rose from the table in the middle of her meal in order to clip out an article from the paper about council cleaners refusing to clear up dog's muck left on the esplanade. Bob stared at the television even though the sound was turned off. I had no stomach for two grey lamb chops coated in elastic gravy, and toyed with the dry meat before excusing myself from the table at the first available opportunity.

Up in my room, I set aside my precious maps of Mesopotamia and all of my notes on ancient Babylonian burial sites, sealing them in labelled plastic bags and placing them on top of the wardrobe. I cleared a space on the floor, pulled a fresh pad of A2 cartridge paper from under my bed, and began to sketch out a city unlike any other I had attempted. The sights, smells and sounds of Calabash lived on inside me. Everything had been so intense and alive that I could not believe all this had simply sprung from a crack on the head. I wanted to get back to the pier as quickly as possible. I needed to understand what had happened; whether the area below the fishing deck was somehow responsible for fostering this fever-dream, or if something truly mystical had occurred, and I had actually crossed a point in time and space to arrive at a different part of our planet. The harder I thought, the less it made sense. For Calabash to have once occupied the same spot where the pier now stood, surely the world needed to have stopped spinning.

One thing was certain; I had to return there, if only to talk to Trebunculus. The doctor appeared to have fulfilled some kind of promise to the Sultan, who had congratulated him on his success. Trebunculus held the key to my appearance. To occupy my mind I scoured my atlases in search of any city remotely resembling the one I was sure I had visited in person, but nothing like it existed in the Near, Middle or Far East. I dragged books from cupboards and examined historical timelines going back through thirty centuries; nothing. I checked the names of British Ambassadors to the East, but there was no mention of anybody called Septimus Peason. I recalled what Sean had said about drifting off into one's own world; I had not expected the sensation to feel so real. Could I have spontaneously imagined something as fully formed, as detailed and colourful as Calabash?

'I have to get out of this bleeding town, it's getting on my nerves. I tried to buy a kipper tie in the high street and the woman laughed at me. She said, "You want to try the fish shop, love." Obviously not a dedicated follower of fashion.'

Danny considered the residents of Cole Bay to be common and out of touch with rest of the country, but he'd been born here just like me. He wouldn't eat at any of the Wimpy Bars or cafés on the front, so he treated me to a set lunch in the Buckingham. This was Cole Bay's smartest hotel. Once it had been a popular retreat for wealthy landowners, but during the war it was occupied by the military, who billeted troops there because of its commanding position on top of the cliffs, and the building had never quite recovered from the shock. The restaurant was a slim glass box swagged with dusty festoon curtains. It ran along the cliff edge to take advantage of the view, which meant that the wind moaned forlornly around it even on a still summer's day, and every third winter half of its salt-caked windows blew in. The waitresses were morose teenagers in ill-fitting black dresses and white caps serving grapefruit cocktails and dry pork chops with plates of watery mixed vegetables, but there was a wine list presented in a red mock-leather folder, and an elderly quartet played Bach in an alcove. To Danny it represented a step up from the seafront restaurants where the smell of batter permeated the curtains and all meals came with slices of white processed bread and a cup of milky tea.

The other reason we ate up there was so that no-one would see us and start making trouble. Danny was fond of describing himself as the Queen of Cole Bay, by which he meant that while he was not the only gay man in the area, he was the only one who went out of his way to look it. He wore fitted-waist stripy suits with flared trousers, orange lace roll-neck shirts that fastened with Velcro, and wide white patent-leather belts. His blond hair was cut in a fringe so that he looked like Justin Hayward from The Moody Blues, but the effect was spoiled because he also had a thin, long neck (which my stepfather once referred to as 'breakable') and a prominent Adam's apple.

He carefully unfolded his napkin across his knees and leaned closer. 'Look at her over there.' I looked for a woman, but only saw a man eating alone. 'That's a wig. I think it's a trannie.'

I thought a 'trannie' was short for 'transistor radio'. 'What do you mean?'

'You know, Venus with a Penis. Honestly, what's she like?' Danny called men 'she' sometimes, especially after he'd been listening to *Round The Horne* on a Sunday lunchtime. Frankly, I felt that Danny had been standing a bit too close when the gay bomb exploded. He adopted the elbows-in-wrists-up mannerism that I associated with effeminate posture, but only when others were looking. I had long suspected that he was only pretending to be camp in order to be noticed. What gave him away most of all, though, was his determination to dress as if he was going to a fashionable party in London, when in reality he was stranded here on the south coast along with the rest of us. He usually tried a few screamy shock effects when we met up, then went back to behaving normally when he realised that I was indifferent to his routine.

Danny was a display manager – 'not a window dresser,' he was quick to point out – at Ramsey & Danforth, the old-fashioned department store in the high street, and we had become friends because he was often on the pier visiting an older man who owned the postcard shop, who I now think might have been gay as well, although he was married with a daughter. I suppose I had no problem with Danny being that way because I had always understood it from an historical perspective. I knew about the Romans, the Greeks and the 'army of lovers', holding hands as they faced death in battle. I knew about the homosexual kings of England and Leonardo Da Vinci and Nero and Michaelangelo and Oscar Wilde. I knew that Sir Richard Burton, the translator of *The Arabian Nights*, had openly supported gay rights, as had Tolstoy and H. G. Wells. In fact, I knew a lot more about the subject than he did. But Danny wasn't interested in the academic aspects of being homosexual; he just wanted to meet someone nice and fall in love. He had no political motivation at all. When activists in London rallied to fight for equal rights, he went off to Amsterdam with a Spanish waiter from the Cole Bay Trocadero.

The fact that I was the only heterosexual male he knew who would talk to him as if he was an ordinary human being made him my lifelong friend, although of course he would never admit that this was the reason. He seemed incapable of standing up for himself. Wearing outrageous clothes and being sarcastic was the best protest against conformity that he could muster. 'What can I do, darling?' he said helplessly. 'The butch look just isn't me.'

I somehow expected all outsiders to be angry with their status and prepared to do something about it, so it always came as a shock to me to find that people were fully prepared to remain marginalised for the whole of their lives.

Although Cole Bay had missed out on the Summer of Love, it was experiencing its first public flirtation with drugs. Marijuana was easy to obtain, as were amphetamines, and on a Saturday night the front was full of kids off their faces, but Danny liked to make friends with a bottle of gin. Alcohol was his big weakness. He drank too much and became a little too vocal in his condemnation of the town. I was worried that one day someone was going to bash his head in. He handled his problems in what I considered to be a typically English manner. Instead of acting upon the calling of his heart and moving to London where he would be free to grow, he remained in Cole Bay and moaned about his life. And so we amused ourselves by pretending to be posh at the Buckingham, and by making fun of others we felt better about ourselves. We laughed all the time when we were together, and if Danny drank too much and became maudlin I would try to cheer him up before steering him back in the direction of his flat, and we would promise to meet again some other time. It was a comfortable friendship, undemanding and easy. I could ask him the sort of questions anyone else would have thought soft, and I knew that he wouldn't laugh at me.

'Danny.' I waited until the waitress had plonked a custard jug between us. 'Do you think there's a place where you could be completely happy?'

'Depends on your criteria for happiness,' he replied.

'Somewhere nice and warm. Where people treat you properly. Sort of like . . . in an old painting.'

Danny tipped the jug over his apple pie, but the skin seemed determined to hold the custard in. He prodded it with a fork. 'Oh well, it would be nice to think that charm and style and grace still counted for something, somewhere in the world. I don't know though. Some of those old paintings have all sorts of trouble going on. Hidden serpents lurking in unlit corners. Besides, a perfect world is your actual contradiction in itself.'

'But imagine being able to do whatever you want.'

'They've promised me a promotion in the new year. If I can get some money together I can move to London, apply at one of the big stores.' He peered into the jug. 'There's something wrong with this custard. It's supposed to fall out. Sod it, let's have another bottle of wine. By the way, how's Addis Ababa?'

'Mesopotamia. Stalled, I'm afraid. I'm working on something else for a while.'

'Forgive me, but I don't entirely see what you're trying to do, recreating all these dead kingdoms. What do you hope to achieve? Nowhere's perfect. People don't exist in a vacuum.'

'What do you mean?'

'Forget it, it doesn't matter.'

Later we stood on the edge of the cliff, looking down at the sea as it smashed over the shale. A gale was roaring so loudly in our frozen ears that we had to turn sideways to hear each other. I was worried that the windshear might react with Danny's fashions and whip him over the edge.

'Sometimes you can see the coast of France when it's clear,' said Danny. 'It's different over there. The cafés are all open-air, the bars never close, everyone's drinking, laughing. At it like rabbits. People are up to all sorts of things. Not over here. Everything's shut. Everyone's hiding indoors.'

'Why don't we go there, then? Calais, Boulogne, Dieppe. Ferries go back and forth all the time. All you need is a passport and a few quid.'

Danny drew a great breath and exhaled slowly.

'It's a long way though, isn't it? They don't speak the same language as us. Probably wouldn't want us coming over.'

I decided there and then to tell no-one about my discovery of Calabash. Not Danny or Sean or Julia or Dudley Salterton. I wanted to get back to the platform, to see if I could make it happen again, but today was Saturday and the weather was fine, and I knew that the pier would be full of people. I resolved to get up early and go there the next morning, when it was supposed to rain once more. My instinct told me that there could be no-one else around to witness my escape.

I had to go somewhere, do something. Even if it was only in my head.

CHAPTER FOURTEEN

A Crystal Constellation

The sky was the colour of greaseproof paper. Rain scythed in grey sheets across the sea until I could no longer see the horizon. Even the ghost train was shut. I stood at the end of the pier facing the DANGER KEEP OUT sign with my left hand steadying myself against the railing, and pressed my right palm over my beating heart. I felt as though I was about to do something highly illegal. Below my feet, waves churned around the pillars of the pier, the downward suction of the eddies revealing struts covered with dripping black molluscs, thousands of shiny razor-sharp shells. I leaned forward and looked down. Every third wave swamped one end of the lower platform.

Fearful that I would change my mind if I waited any longer, I ducked beneath the chain and made my way down the spray-drenched steps. The metal floor of the platform creaked and groaned like an old ship, but felt sturdy enough to hold my weight. It was slippery though, and the only railing consisted of metal chains slung between posts. Directly in front of me a ten-foot section was missing. I tried to remember where I had been standing, and realised with a sinking heart that it had been right at the back, in the darkest corner, where the ocean seemed to be rising to its highest level.

With the wind tearing at my navy blue gabardine school raincoat, I edged my way around the platform until I could no longer see any light between the pier's struts. I wondered how long it would take them to find my body if the sea rose to a full swell right now. I was a poor swimmer because I had trouble catching my breath when immersed in water. I had crept out of the house before anyone else was awake. Nobody knew I was here.

I twisted around, hanging on to the corner post, trying to see if the world was changing, but there was only the shifting storm-mottled sky and the tilting, angry sea. It felt different this time; none of it was right. My mood and the landscape had changed. I was too desperate to make it happen. The idea that I had opened a doorway between the planet's temporal and spatial dimensions was the stuff of science fiction. How could I fashion a workable explanation for what had happened to me? In Calabash all of my senses had functioned to produce a complete experience, and now the only way I could think of getting there was to duplicate what I had done before.

I needed to open up my mind and cast the world I knew away from me like a bad dream. But as I looked about, trying to recall my exact movements on the platform, everything felt too calculated. All I could feel was the sharp brine on my face and the gloomy, oppressive mass of the pier. Releasing my grip on the handrail, I tacked to the rear edge of the platform and groped my way into the darkest corner, where the roar and suction of the tide boomed against the underside of the pier. I turned and raised my eyes to the horizon.

And for a brief few seconds the cloudbase broke, and I saw

paths of light dancing out across the green water, and knew that they were made by the reflecting shields of the harbour warriors, converging beams of brilliance that would guide me back into the port of Calabash. I stared at the point where the lines crossed. There was a sharp stab of sunlight in my head, and a concoction of strong odours: old leather, metal, earth, sea. I gripped the iron post at my back. My stomach twisted and I felt consciousness slipping . . .

. . . And I was on the butte above the harbour with the azure sea spread below me, the hills at my back, and the tang of fish burning in my nostrils. My hair rose about my ears in the warming summer breeze, and it felt as though I had come home again. No longer afraid, I slowly turned and, sure of my way, began to walk.

My senses opened to my surroundings. The low sweep of a seagull, lifting to hover in the air above my head. Ridged brown fields beyond, newly planted with maize. An ass tethered to a pump. Hares outrunning the breezes that feathered the meadows. A road that became a street built in ochre stone, with a faintly unkempt air. Rocket and dandelions sprouting between paving slabs.

Dogs and chickens raised the alarm in courtyards as I passed. Girls with summer flowers braided in their hair turned slowly, so slowly, as I walked by, and smiled secretly at me. I had arrived in a village, oval in layout, within sight of the city of Calabash, with a well at its centre and arable fields to the west, gardens and the sparkling sea to the south. I had headed here instinctively, and now that I looked about myself, I knew exactly who I would see.

Dr Trebunculus and his apprentice hailed me as though they were bumping into a neighbour on their way to the shops. 'Ah, there you are,' cried the doctor, striding up the path waving a walking stick. 'We wondered where you'd gone. For a horrible moment I thought we'd frightened you off. This is Menavino.'

I found myself facing a young man of similar build and height, but the top of Menavino's head was as shaven and smooth as an olive. He had a little pigtail at the back and wore several engraved golden rings in each ear, but was more simply apparelled than his mentor, in a long white kilt with a sky-blue waistcoat. He was about to bow, but remembering English courtesy, tentatively shook my hand.

'I thought that before you settled yourself too comfortably you'd like to see my laboratory,' said Trebunculus. 'It's not far from here.' He made no further mention of my reappearance, and it seemed that any explanation of where I had been since the Sultan's welcoming feast was unnecessary, so I followed the pair, happily taking each moment as it came. Being in Calabash seemed to encourage such an attitude.

The laboratory was situated at the junction of two winding paths near the road into the village, which was differentiated from other roads by the large ditch running across it. This was supposed to be kept filled with water in order that anyone entering the village under the cloak of darkness would be heard by the splashing of their horse's hooves, but as there was no threat of marauders from without, the practice had fallen into disuse.

There were two entrances to the doctor's house, on different levels. The rear of the building was built into the hill that rose steeply behind it. The lower door was unlatched, as were the doors to all the houses in Calabash. The room we entered was filled with long wooden benches, the surfaces of which were cluttered with mechanical arms, cogs, ratchets, springs, toggles, sprockets, and the tools required to fix them in place. None of these items, individually or in combination, gave any clue as to what was being constructed. The floor was so entirely covered with charts and calculations that I found myself unavoidably walking on them. The doctor did not seem to mind. A piebald piglet and a half-bald cat lazed in a corner, following us with their eyes.

The far wall, which backed into the hill, was lined with shelves containing dozens of turquoise glass jars, their contents obscured in murky fluids, their purpose forgotten even to the doctor. Beneath these were remnants of other failed investigations: the lenses from the experiment to gauge the power of the sun that had set fire to the rotunda of the royal conservatory; the honey-smeared arrows from the attempt to follow the paths of bees that had resulted in Menavino almost being stung to death; some perished elastic bonds from the test of gravity that had broken both of the cook's legs; the pitcher of hyena's urine intended as an aphrodisiac for the Royal Concubine, which had proven more useful in ridding the palace of an infestation of weasels; the jars of fine sand designed to measure time – well, it transpired that they had proven more successful than most of the doctor's other plans.

Beneath the central skylight stood a tall iron contraption which appeared in imminent danger of collapse. Its myriad arms sprouted concave mirrors set at angles to catch the light and redirect it about the room. In one corner stood an orrery made entirely of glass and calibrated to the brass workings of a clock. As the mechanism ticked, its crystal planets lurched past each other in their orbits, catching reflected beams of light and refracting them into prisms, fiery colours splitting and spitting into the corners of the room, splinters of crimson and indigo dancing across the walls. Medicine was not the only science that interested the doctor.

The warm, heavy air made me pull off my coat. 'What are you making?' I asked.

'Calculations, dear fellow, always calculations,' the doctor answered, waving his hands about in a distracted manner. 'How else would we have known that you were coming? Menavino, prepare some refreshment, will you?' The boy hurried off into a curtained area as Trebunculus hung up his jacket. 'Much of our work is hypothetical, of course, but the Sultan is only interested in results.'

'You knew I was coming?'

'We knew *someone* was coming. That was the whole point of keeping the doorway open.'

'I don't understand.'

'We're not barbarians,' exclaimed the doctor indignantly. 'We live simply but we have enquiring minds. We know there are other times and places, it's just a question of access.'

It seemed inconceivable to me that anyone would want to open a doorway to my world. Calabash to Cole Bay felt like an unfair transaction. My mother had told me that in the 1950s many West Indians had travelled to London to become bus conductors. I thought they must be mad, giving up the beauty and abundance of the Caribbean for a dingy bus depot in Clapham.

'You can teach us about your world.'

'Why?'

'Why do we look up into the nightly starfield and wonder what we might find if we could go there?' Trebunculus seated himself on a stool. 'To satisfy our curiosity. Expand our knowledge. Enrich our existence.'

'What if you went there and found out that it was really horrible? If you came to where I live you'd hate it. It's damp and boring and everyone's miserable.'

'Perhaps it only seems that way to you. Here.' The doctor rolled open a hand-inked map, weighting down its edges with small clay pots. 'This is what we know of the world.' In the centre of the map was a neat pink circle labelled 'Calabash' in elaborate calligraphy. Several of the surrounding cities were familar to me: Benghazi, Alexandria, Sofia, Baghdad – but the rest of the map was wrong. The countries were skewed in shape, as though viewed through a distorting lens. And as the chart progressed outwards it became more nebulous, until there were great bare patches of nothing at all. Its borders were cluttered with silly-looking sea serpents and fat cherubs blowing gales.

Menavino arrived with the tea, which smelled of buttered flowers in hot brandy, scalded my lips and made me light-headed.

'Your homeland is over there somewhere.' Trebunculus gestured vaguely at the edge of the map. 'But of course I have no proof. Your world is as invisible as the past, but I choose to believe in it. Life's possibilities must be drawn out of us by others, Kay. Look.' He rose and beckoned me to the ticking orrery. As we watched the circling crystal spheres, I realised that the glass of each globe was tinted a different shade, so that as they passed, they altered the light they threw upon each other; now mauve, now amber, now emerald. 'Everything affects everything else,' intoned Trebunculus. 'When we stop learning, we start to die.'

I studied the doctor through the shifting glass. 'Did you bring me here?'

'You brought yourself here.'

'Why?'

'I would have thought the answer obvious.' He smiled gently, old and wise. 'To save a desperate situation.'

'But how did you reach me? How did you know that I was—'

'Your questions will be answered all in good time. Let me give you a piece of advice. You must think of Calabash as your means of escape. Come here whenever you are tired, whenever you are frightened, whenever you feel alone, and all will be well again.'

I felt a hotness behind my eyes. For a moment I could not find the power to speak. 'I don't know how to show my gratitude,' I said finally. 'I always thought there might be somewhere – people who would—'

'Oh, don't think it's all one way. We'll do what we can for you, but I can assure you that you're doing something just as vital for us.' A chart on the floor caught his eye, and he bent down to study it.

'I'll help you in any way that I can,' I offered. 'Just tell me what interests you.'

'Well, *everything* interests me, of course, but it is more for the sake of the Lord Chancellor. We could start by seeing him, if you like.'

As we made our way back to the royal palace, Dr Trebunculus attempted to answer my questions. 'The Sultan believes that wars destroy empires which are in mature stages of development, such as ours. Our kingdom is very old, and its ways are hard to change. That makes it vulnerable. The Lord Chancellor feels that a better understanding of the world's scientific advancements would place us in a safer position.'

'I'm not sure I can provide him with much technical detail,' I warned. 'But I'm sure I can find out some things if he makes specific requests.'

The Lord Chancellor's apartment was situated in a rect-angular high-domed kiosk-pavilion to the rear of the royal harem, which at its height had housed four thousand sterile concubines for the sole pleasure of the Sultan's great-great-grandfather.

'He must have been quite a man.'

'Oh he was, but those were dangerous times. Fratricidal

law meant that he had no cousins, brothers, nephews or uncles to challenge his authority, and the chances of surviving for long in high office were slim. Anyone suspected of acting as a threat to the throne was placed in a *kafe*, a suspended cage, and kept there.'

'For how long?'

'Until they went mad. But now, mercifully, we are more civilised.'

'You've done away with the cages?'

'No, but prisoners are allowed to survive until the end of their natural days, mad or not. Ah, here is Septimus.'

The Lord Chancellor drifted out of the gloom in a rustle of black silk. He held aloft a pale hand and shook mine with exaggerated solemnity. 'How kind, how thoughtful, for you to come and visit my humble abode, *Aslanim*.'

I shot Trebunculus a quizzical look. 'It means "Little Lion", a great compliment,' he whispered. There was certainly nothing humble about Septimus Peason's apartment, I thought, marvelling at the gilded baldachins and the pink porphyry walls revetted with blue faïences, each bearing inlaid mother-of-pearl inscriptions of indecipherable complexity. This was the only room in the palace that ever became cold, and where I was to find dark shadowed corners.

'The boy is most eager to provide you with information,' said Trebunculus, gesturing me to be seated. 'For his knowledge may help you to ensure the safety of our kingdom.'

Two small girls entered bearing trays of mint tea and tall clay pots in which burned sandalwood incense. We waited until they had completed their tasks and departed, then Peason bade me speak.

'Our land is very different to yours,' I explained. 'Our main concerns appear to be more scientific, and perhaps less human.'

'Ah ha.' The Lord Chancellor gave Trebunculus a knowing look.

'We have, for example, put a man on the moon.' This was, in hindsight, probably the wrong place to start, and the *we* part was a bit of an overstatement.

'On the moon.' Septimus Peason raised a bony forefinger to the heavens. 'The yellow moon above us.'

'That's right. They went up in a rocket.'

'Ah. Raised by gunpowder?'

'Not exactly, no.' I struggled with the concept of jet propulsion for a while, but finally had to abandon the topic. 'I can find out more from a book,' I finished lamely.

The Lord Chancellor cricked his knees as he leaned forward, steepling his fingers over one kneecap. 'If I can explain the problem of life in Calabash,' he confided, 'it is one of overconfidence. Nothing has changed here in generations. The Sultan – may the heavens themselves be praised for bestowing him upon our unworthy people – believes that no harm can ever befall us. Since the loss of his wife he has grown – how can one best put this – complacent. Once his eagle eyes would spot the faintest stirring on our most distant borders. Now those eyes have turned inward. Celestial warriors, smite me from this miserable life if I should suggest a particle of disrespect, but our people have been made too comfortable. Our soldiers have grown plump and lazy. Our outposts are gradually being withdrawn. Where once our ships plied trade routes across the seven seas, we now have little contact with the outside world. Our lives have become settled. We are ripe for attack. Only General Bassa knows this. He and his son regularly patrol our northerly quadrants, and they have seen the unrest for themselves. Dangers await at the edges of our land.'

'Then why don't you persuade the Sultan to allow his army

a show of strength?' I asked. 'A series of border parades. Drills of the utmost military precision. Perfect lines of uniforms. Feats of great daring. Canter your horses fearlessly through cannon fire.' I had read about such performances in my books on Mesopotamia. 'Act as though you believe no-one is watching, but of course you will be observed with the greatest interest. This is something to make all invaders think twice before crossing your borders.'

'Truly the boy has the wisdom of gods,' cried Peason, raising his hands up to his face. 'You speak sagely, but there is a difficulty, my dear *Aslanim*. Man for man, we are quite outnumbered. A parade would reveal our weaknesses as much as our strengths. Our supremacy can only be conveyed through displays of superior scientific advancement. If we were able to show our might in a manner that has never been witnessed by infidels before, some invention of war from your world perhaps . . .'

I thought for a moment, but the weapons that sprang to mind were far too terrible to contemplate: land-mines, hand-grenades, mustard gas, fragmentation bombs. There had to be something the Lord Chancellor and his General could display that would not undermine the stability of their own kingdom. After some further discussion, I agreed to give the matter more thought and return with my findings at a future date.

'Dearest Doctor, you have done well to find someone of such obvious intelligence as this charming young man,' fawned Peason as we took our leave. 'I can hardly bear to wait until our next encounter.'

'Come,' gestured Trebunculus, 'I will ride with you as far as my laboratory.'

'Well, what do you make of our Lord Chancellor?' he asked as soon as we had remounted our donkeys.

'I don't trust him,' I replied. 'He's far too polite.'

The doctor cackled happily. 'I know what you mean. His deferential manner grates, but he is a diplomat, and he must place the welfare of the state above all other considerations. The Lord Chancellor's loyalty to the kingdom is utterly beyond question. The Sultan has no male issue at present, and unless he remarries, which is unlikely, the safety of the kingdom will be compromised. It is true that he has never been the same since the death of Eliya. He is merely the faintest whisper of his former self. I wonder . . .' He reigned his donkey back until he had drawn close to my side. 'In your land, have you perfected the grinding of crystal lenses?'

'You mean like my glasses?'

'No, we also have those. I was thinking of a more precise tool.'

'Certainly. We have microscopes that can examine worlds inside a single grain of sand.'

'And could you get me information on the precise construction of such an instrument?' he asked eagerly.

'I can do that easily.'

'I would be so very grateful if you could.'

I thanked the doctor, who bade me farewell in a vague, distracted manner, suggesting that we would see each other again very soon. As Trebunculus retreated once more into his room of travelling colours, I followed Menavino to a house in the village that had been prepared for my return. Everything came so naturally here that I felt no need to ask what was expected of me.

The sun had disappeared behind the hills, and a soft ruby glow filled the sky. The villa was a low ochre building lit with oil lamps that suffused the dim air with hazy halos. There was fruit and warm bread on the table, and a thick down-filled mattress had been laid out on the floor. I felt weary with the passing of the sun. My limbs grew heavy as I moved into the warm shadows of the villa. Menavino touched my arm and smiled mysteriously, watching me, awaiting my approval. I returned his smile and the boy backed quietly from the room, closing the door behind him as I sank gratefully into the bed.

As I slept, I dreamed of the crystal constellation and its gently changing colours, and the worlds that brushed against each other without quite touching.

When I awoke, I found myself back in my narrow bed, tucked beneath the faded candlewick counterpane in my chilly bedroom in Cole Bay.

CHAPTER FIFTEEN

A Stab at Existentialism

'You keep your bedroom like a rubbish tip,' said my mother, using her chin to hold the case while she slipped the pillow in. 'It's a wonder we haven't got rats.' She dropped the pillow on my bed. 'It's like a dirty old museum in here. Can't you put up some posters, brighten it a bit?' She had a long wait if she was expecting me to cover the walls with pictures of busty birds, footballers and E-type Jags. There was a Victorian etching from the Lang edition of *The Arabian Nights* entitled 'Zobeida Prepares To Whip The Dog' that I quite fancied pinning over my bed, but it wasn't exactly hot stuff.

Pauline ventured to the fireplace and gave the mantelpiece a cursory dab with a damp cloth, then began thrusting at it in earnest. 'Look at this dust. With your lungs. I don't know.' She worked on, leaving the air filled with unspoken griev-ances. I tried to ignore her but she moved to the wardrobe, and at that moment I realised it had been a bad idea to let her in, because she opened the door and began folding clothes – an occupation she was capable of stretching infinitely – and I knew that she was waiting for a reassurance, just as I knew that I had to tell her of my decision.

'Mum, I have to talk to you—'

'How do you get your things in such a state?' she asked, holding up a shirt with orange stains on the shoulders. 'And where's the nice cardigan Janine bought you?'

'Mum, I'm leaving school.'

'Your clothes don't seem to last five minutes. What do you mean, leaving?'

'I'm not going to stay on to do A Levels.'

Pauline turned from the wardrobe, her features setting in stone. 'Oh yes you are, Kevin. Don't think you're not.'

Uh-oh, I thought, full name warning. 'I'm sixteen,' I warned. 'I'm old enough to decide for myself.'

'Then you can decide to get some common sense into your head. I've never heard of such an idea. Your first set of O Level results were poor because you'd been ill, that's all. You missed most of the revision tests. Your teacher agrees. You'd be throwing away your chances.'

'That's not why I do badly in tests.'

'I don't see what other reason there could be.' She shifted about the room, looking for a chore with which to busy herself. 'You're a bright boy, Kevin, brighter than your brother ever was.'

'I don't see the point of passing exams,' I tried to explain. 'I'm not going to work in an office I hate for years, until I finally retire with just an engraved carriage clock to show for my life, like Grandad.'

'Your grandad fought in the Great War,' she snapped defensively. 'He couldn't do much after that because of his nerves.'

'I've made up my mind. There are other ways to live your life, you know. I'm going to be an existentialist, like Jean-Paul Sartre.'

Although Pauline was unfamiliar with the concept, she had a gamely stab at discerning its meaning. 'Oh yes? How could you without proper training? You have to work your way up to become anything. It all takes planning, even exist— whatsit. There are children in Africa with no books to study from. One of them could have taken your place if we'd known you weren't going to bother.'

She left the room and the house fell ominously silent for a few minutes. Then Bob's weary feet trod the stairs. I could hear him hovering undecided on the landing before he came in.

'Your mother says you want to leave school and become an expressionist.'

'Existentialist.'

'Listen, you can work in the Express Dairy as far as I'm concerned, so long as you put a brave face on it, but your mother is expecting you to stay on and make something of yourself. She's had enough of all this dreaming and moping about.'

I needed Bob to sign the papers, without which the school would refuse to release me. My only hope was to appeal to his sense of logic. 'My best subjects are English and History, right? The only way I'd be able to improve my knowledge is through higher education at university, and all that can train me for is lecturing, or being some kind of historian.'

'I thought you were interested in becoming a journalist.'

'Not any more. I thought about it and decided I didn't want to be stuck covering flower shows for the *Cole Bay Mercury*.'

'I think you should stay on. It's for your own good.' Bob seated himself on the end of the bed. 'You'll see the sense in the long term. There's good money to be made by those in the know. A lot of people are out there getting their noses in the trough.'

'What if I don't see the sense?' I asked. 'What if I don't want a place at the trough?'

'Well, I suppose the main thing is to make sure that you're happy. You're old enough to choose for yourself.' The moment the words fell out of his mouth Bob realised he'd made a mistake. Sensing defeat, he considered retreating downstairs and sinking the best part of a Watney's Party Seven, but decided to stay and argue it out. His heart wasn't in it, though. This was a man who spent his days ordering portions of boil-in-the-bag coq au vin and arranging paper napkin deliveries for the Churchill Suite of the Scheherazade. The high point of his week was getting pissed with Roy 'Boy-O-Boy' Maloy And His Big Band Combo after the Friends of Rommel dinner and dance on a Saturday night, while his wife sat at home watching *Armchair Theatre* with her arms tightly folded across her cardigan and her lips and eyes bitterly narrowed to slits.

I wondered if Pauline knew that Bob was having an affair. It was, perhaps, a little too exotic to describe it as an affair. He had an occasional fumble about with a woman called Doreen who was one of the hotel's senior housekeepers. I found out because two years earlier he had been seen at the Roxy with her. Bob never went to the pictures, and would certainly never have gone to see *Funny Girl*. Then, in the wastepaper basket of the bathroom, I started finding wrappers from those skinny little packets of pink soap you get in hotel rooms. He was coming in and washing upstairs before having his dinner, so that Pauline wouldn't smell perfume. Once Bob had triggered my strange-behaviour sensors, I turned the searchlight of my attention fully on him, and there was no escape. I noted the discrepancies in his timetable, watched the hotel through binoculars and stalked him to tawdry backstreet trysts. Bob didn't actually seem that keen, and I got the feeling that he only went along with it because Doreen made all the arrangements and kept him topped up with miniatures from her minibars. I knew there would be hell to pay for all of us if my mother ever found out, so it was in my best interests to make sure that she didn't.

I wondered how my parents would reply if anyone asked them whether they were happy. Phrases like 'mustn't grumble' and 'can't complain' came naturally to their lips. Number 14 Balaclava Terrace was a happy home, according to 1970 levels of happiness. There was no domestic violence. There was no thieving, no starvation-level existence. Only small cruelties occurred, each day as inconsequential as the one before, and the sheer accretion of routine crusted our little house into a prison. How much easier Calabash would have been to explain if I had suffered neglect or abuse. As it turned out, the situation didn't prove to be quite that simple.

I figured there were four things I needed to escape from Cole Bay: money, guts, health and imagination, and I had one and a half of them. Unfortunately, the one and a half I had weren't the one and a half I most needed, and staying on at school could offer little assistance.

Even though my mind was made up, I decided to hold a democratic vote. Pauline was Against. I put Bob down as a Don't Know. Sean couldn't vote on my future because he'd left school at sixteen. Janine, another early school leaver, now enjoying a successful career in Bap Management, was another Don't Know. Julia, largely because she was planning to take a degree in Biology and felt that it was wrong to waste the opportunity to continue studying, was Against. Miss Ruth, obviously and violently Against. Dudley Salterton was For, on account of the fact that he had left school at twelve(!) and had never looked back. Danny was Against because he argued with pristine logic that a university course would get me somewhere other than here, be financed by the state, provide me with a sex life, independence, good times, wider horizons and possible long-term happiness. But Danny had failed to escape himself and was a fine one to talk. And not one person who thought I should continue at school and stay in the system could come up with an answer to my basic problem, which was: what if you didn't believe in the system? All across Europe and America, students were questioning the world their elders had created, and were dropping out rather than become a part of something they could not believe in. They had no illusions. They could see that the old ways were no longer working, and so could I, although in Cole Bay this made me some kind of visionary. And what did it matter if reality was lousy when I had somewhere fantastic that I could visit whenever I liked?

I suppose I began to detail my life in Calabash because I had to prove to myself that in some sense it was real. That morning I went down to the stationers and bought half a dozen hardcover notebooks. Then I began at the first page of the first volume and started recording my visits. I placed my chronicle of this other reality in a shoebox and kept the box taped shut, hiding it beneath the wardrobe. I came up with a variety of methods to booby-trap the hiding place, pasting hairs across gaps and tying fine threads to floorboards. I had never bothered to hide my Mesopotamia maps, but now Mesopotamia felt as though it had been a dry run for Calabash, and what was this city if not all the ancient cities of the world rolled into one? Byzantium had become Constantinople, and Constantinople had become Istanbul. The epicentre of one of the greatest civilisations on earth, yet historians knew next to nothing about it. My visits to Calabash reminded me of the lurid fever-dreams I had experienced in times of illness, with one vital difference. In

Calabash, unlike anywhere else I had ever been, everything made sense.

And I had already solved one mystery. The scarf and cardigan I had lost. I had been reunited with both items in that impossible land. And the shirt my mother had complained about; it had been stained orange by the dyed satin sash I had worn to the Sultan's banquet. To me – perhaps only to me – the city of Calabash was real.

CHAPTER SIXTEEN

No Life Before Now

It was on my third visit to the city that Trebunculus attempted to provide a new reason for me to pass more time in Calabash. The doctor had encouraged the Sultan's theatrical troupe to stage a performance of *The Pirates of Penzance* in their guest's honour. Ricketty benches had been constructed on the packed white sand of the palace parade ground, with awnings of saffron muslin hung from the branches of the almond trees to keep the afternoon sun from the faces of the audience. The main entertainment was preceded by a number of baffling marionette shows. The familiar overture, now rescored to Eastern taste and played on *rababa, tabla, kawal* and *sagat*, bore only a tangential resemblance to the original, and for the first time its Cornish setting incorporated the braying of camels. It seemed ludicrous to witness these proud, extraordinary people squeezed into Victorian corsets and bustles, but I understood that they were doing it to please me.

Rosamunde, the Sultan's daughter, had been cast as an absurdly sultry Mabel. The pirates looked like bedouins. The cast had learned their parts by rote, and very little of the recitative, tackled as it was at great speed, with the endings of sentences clipped off, made any sense at all.

Throughout her bizarre ululating rendition of 'Poor Wandering One', Rosamunde rolled her eyes at me and all but sat in my lap. Halfway through her chorus in 'When The Foeman Bares His Steel', she found the tight high-necked blouse too constraining, tore it free and threw it on the floor, finishing the song with bare breasts. The ladies of the court fell about laughing. The palace guards nudged each other with knowing leers. Only the eunuchs remained unmoved. At the end of the performance, the Sultan noisily showed his appreciation. He summoned me to his side.

'The English sing-song is popular in your land, yes? Taradiddle, tarantara, yes?'

'It used to be, Your Majesty,' I replied, not wishing to offend him. 'Music changes just as people change.'

The Sultan was affronted. 'People do not change here. Change brings trouble. We try to change as little as possible.'

'But how can you grow?'

'Plants grow. Kingdoms must endure. Every empire runs its course. You are English, surely this you understand.'

'Certainly. We are no longer an empire, but we endure. There was a time . . .'

'Time, bah! Time is an enemy that enslaves the weak. We have no use for clocks here. We do not wish to harbour the seeds of our own destruction.'

'But time itself can't destroy you,' I explained, 'only the mismanagement of it.' I could sense Trebunculus tensing up as I disagreed with the Sultan.

'You are young and foreign, so I forgive your impertinence. I dismiss it.' He waved a hand across his turban. 'I overlook it, yes? Here there is only the rising of the sun and its sister, the moon.'

'You must understand,' explained Trebunculus, 'that while the concept of time *per se* exists in Calabash, its calibration can only lead to the demands for increased economic efficiency. If the passing of time can be measured in detail, the weaknesses of the nation's workforce can be discerned so that—'

Now Rosamunde arrived by her father's side to act as an ambassador. She was still draped in the torn white costume that had so constricted her lustrous breasts. 'Father once gave the doctor a unique timepiece, a great clock specially constructed by the palace jewellers from an old drawing. It was a gift for saving my newborn life. But he did not allow the jewellers to make hands or an interior mechanism for the clock, for fear of spreading the infection of time throughout the kingdom. He believes that time is a thief that can only work best in the hands of our enemies.'

'But I thought you had no enemies.'

'*Exactly*,' said the Sultan. 'Here sensuality rules over science. How else can you have a notion of your life?' He rose with a grunt and moved off to the cool interior of the palace, trailed by the Queen Mother, the Lord Chancellor, the Royal Concubine, the Semanticor and a number of irritating dwarves who were part of an acrobatic troupe that performed tumblings during scene changes. Rosamunde lingered at the rear of the entourage, watching me and smiling, until summoned from my sight by her father.

'Ah, I thought as much,' said Trebunculus as the rest of the audience filed away. I noticed that he had been observing me closely during the performance. He saw how I had reacted to the leading lady's romantic overtures. 'Of course you are enchanted by her, as who would not be?' he sighed, but shook his head and said: 'The Princess Rosamunde is not for you. She cannot marry an *ajnabee*. Her future husband must be of royal extraction, and has already been selected.'

'But the way she looks at me . . .'

'She is probably just trying to annoy her father.'

'Why would she want to do that?'

'Because he has plans of his own for her, involving the son of the Lord Chancellor. You must put the Princess from your mind. It is simply that she enjoys seeing the confused effect of her flirtations. How do you think Menavino lost his tongue?' Trebunculus spoke as if the answer was obvious. 'Besides, I know of a girl who will please you just as much. It's time for you to meet someone more . . . appropriate. Menavino will take you to the house of Parizade. I thought you should have a companion of your own age, someone in whom you can confide. Although Menavino is young and clever, alas, his dumbness is a hindrance to true companionship. Of course, he is also a boy, and while mutuality of gender is not always a hindrance to intimacy, I think perhaps Parizade will be more to your personal liking.'

Menavino led the way across the little village of pavilions and villas. Even here, curving marble embankments formed canals which led to pools and artfully constructed cascades, designed for no other purpose than to bring pleasure to those who passed. When the boy stopped before a small square house of coral stone, his face broke into a broad grin. Gesturing that I should follow, he made his way to a tiled courtyard at the side, and entered through a curved arch. A fountain pattered in the late afternoon sunlight. A black and white cat slept in an unshaded part of the garden, while a pair of cranes made careful progress along the edge of the roof. Menavino crossed to a low door and lightly rapped his knuckles on the wood. Then he made a sharp little bow and was gone.

The door slowly opened, and before me stood a girl of sixteen with thick, dark hair knotted loosely away from her face. It could not be said that Parizade was beautiful – her nose was a little too long, her figure a little too full, her face still a little too undefined – but she exuded a soft sensuality that took my breath away. She was an opening bloom, and everything of her suggested freshness and beginnings, a world of endless possibilities. 'I am Parizade,' she said, smiling, 'and this is to be your house.' And with a shy gesture of welcome, she invited me inside.

The villa into which I stepped was furnished with simple gifts from Parizade's family: copper pots and great clay bowls, bright loose-woven rugs and a few items of polished wood. The rooms were plumbed and heated beneath their floors, although the nights rarely grew cold enough to require additional warmth. Bougainvillea smothered the ochre walls of the garden, forming a carpet of petals on the terracotta tiles, and an arched tunnel, open at one end, looked out across the sea.

Parizade lived with her mother in the next village, and told me that if I chose to spend the night with her, her family would be greatly honoured. She had been invited to the villa for the express purpose of delighting me. When I asked her if she minded, she looked upon me as if I was mad.

Beyond the arched tunnel, on a marble bench whose cushions were fastened with nails of emerald, we sat after supper, Parizade and I, watching the sun sink into the sea. It seemed that our names were intended to be linked, like a pair of lovers who had never been apart. When the light had gone we lit the oil-lamp in the courtyard and drank mint tea, and retired to the divan of soft green damask that Parizade's mother had sewn for her, and there we made motions of love until the oil burned low in the glass.

I awoke just before dawn and lay with my arm beneath Parizade's cool neck, looking up at the ceiling. I turned to study her face, the faint gloss of sweat on her brow, the sheen of pearldust on her closed eyelids. It seemed almost impossible to imagine a life before this. I felt great peace and contentment.

But I felt no love for Parizade. She had been provided for my pleasure, and knew nothing but her duty. It was almost as though she was being used as a lure to keep me here. Besides, Rosamunde had stolen into my soul so deeply that thoughts of her strong body, her soft eyes, her open-mouthed smile became as familiar as breathing. It was more than simply wanting something I couldn't have. She stood at the heart of the kingdom. I felt a compulsion to pursue her. It was as though, through her, I would discover my real purpose here.

The time I passed in Calabash was as idyllic as ever. It was easy to allow the questions that formed in my head to fade into half-memories, and to remain unanswered until answers became unwanted. But a sense of restlessness was at work within me.

I knew that I would risk everything to make Rosamunde mine.

CHAPTER SEVENTEEN

A Quest for Air

Pauline spent the morning seated on a stool in the kitchen with her hand absently at her lip, staring at the floor. Bob's reaction was more straightforward. He simply refused to sign the forms. Sean grew frustrated and came fairly close to hitting me. Nothing affected my decision. One evening, Miss Ruth made me stay behind after class and told me that I was behaving like an idiot.

'It may surprise you to know, Kay, that I believe you have a talent worth nurturing. Staying on at school may seem like a waste of time now, but you must set that thought against this; I have watched pupils with great potential pass through my classrooms, and the ones who choose to leave usually remain here in Cole Bay. You boys tease me about my eyesight, but I can spot the failures a mile away. Nothing can hide their anger, their bitterness.'

She was trying to use shock tactics on me, and very nearly succeeded. But sticking around in Cole Bay didn't seem so bad, now that I could retreat to Calabash whenever I wanted. I stayed away from school so often over the next two months that eventually a curt letter arrived from the headmaster, summoning my parents. They disappeared for the evening and returned with faces like thunder. Further lectures followed, usually along the lines of 'You're letting no-one down but yourself,' but I felt a new freedom. I had been formally requested to leave. Miss Ruth was so upset that she refused to speak to me.

'You're a funny lad,' said Janine one afternoon, as she removed a stash of purloined Eccles cakes from her macramé shoulderbag and dumped them on our kitchen table. 'You're just like your brother.'

'How do you mean, Janine?' I had lately taken to speaking in rhyme with her, just to see if she'd notice.

'You won't listen to what's good for you. You're stubborn.' She guiltily eyed the cakes, then broke off a small chunk and popped it into her mouth.

'You'll never be lean, Janine,' I warned.

'Are you being rude?' she asked, dabbing the crumbs from her lip gloss.

'I'm far from obscene, Janine.'

'I give up with both of you,' she snarfled through her cake, suddenly close to tears. 'I try to be nice. I'm always pleasant. Why can't you just be a little more – normal?'

'I don't know where you've been, Janine.'

'Oh, for God's sake!' She whooshed out of the room in search of a Kleenex. It was like shooting fish in a barrel.

There was nothing now to distract me from my new life in Calabash, and yet I found myself unable to make more than a few visits there. The weather was too fine, the sea was too still, or there were fishermen casting off from the upper platform of the pier. On those days I returned home in a foul mood and spoke to no-one. All I could think about was spending a night with the Princess. When I sent Parizade back to her village, Dr Trebunculus visited to ask me if she had displeased me in any way. No, I had truthfully replied, it had simply felt wrong. And my thoughts returned to Rosamunde, and how we would one day swim naked in the secluded bay near the harbour, while silver fish darted about our legs—

'What's the matter, lad? You look like you've lost half a crown and found sixpence.' Dudley Salterton fell into step beside me. He had redyed his hair the colour of those orange trolls you used to stick on top of pencils, and it appeared to glow against the slate sky. The bright dry tufts that stuck out from the side of his head reminded me of his ventriloquist's dummy. The two of them were starting to look like each other.

'You young people don't know when you're well off. You should have my problems. I had an OAP up on stage on Thursday, popped him in my knife cabinet and as the first blade went through he weed in the box. They don't half take fright easy, those old 'uns. Then the head came off Barnacle Bill during "You Need Hands". His lips have been going home for years – he's knocking on – he was old hat in the Great War, Dolores used to say – well, the joins are painted leather and it cracks in the damp. The act's not what it was. These new comics are coming along and it's all just smut, but Mr Cottesloe thinks they're funny so they're topping the bill. It's not right but what is? What's the matter with you? You've a face like a wet weekend.'

I couldn't tell Dudley that a few minutes earlier I had tried to get to Calabash and failed. Although for most of the day a storm had hung threateningly on the horizon, it had bypassed Cole Bay to attack a town further along the coast. The sea had condensed to green glass, and the air had settled into gelid stillness. Worse, some painters had moved their scaffolding equipment in front of the gate to the lower fishing platform, and I had not been able to climb down.

'I hear you've left school.'

'How did you know that?'

'Your brother told me. He's a big lad. Gave me a hand loading me props on to the van. Cottesloe's trying to do away with shifters. A cost-cutting exercise he calls it. I know what I call it. He was looking for you, was your brother.'

'When was this?'

'Not an hour ago. You'd best go and find him.'

'I will in a minute. Dudley, have you ever been abroad?'

'Aye lad, I was posted in the Middle East, and later in Malaya with ENSA.'

'What was it like, the Middle East?'

Dudley thought for a moment. 'Hot and flat. Full of flies. And there was a lot of rubbish everywhere. You could see for miles, though. My pal Dickie Parker – we used to call him "Nosy" – dehydrated on desert patrol after a night on the town, then drank too much cold water and died of it. Hardly any electricity about. You could get some right saucy post-cards. The food wasn't up to much but there was always eggs.'

I thanked him, none the wiser. 'I think I'd better go.'

'Don't get me wrong,' he called, 'it were a dry heat, good for a boy like you. And they're bound to have better plumbing by now.'

My departure from school had proven anti-climactic. I left with few goodbyes, earning disappointed scowls from the teachers, and instead of a sense of freedom found myself embarrassed to be one of the early leavers. Miss Ruth was off sick; I was glad that I did not have to confront her. Malcolm Slattery saw me go, and I felt sure that he knew I was not coming back. As I walked across the quadrangle towards the main gates, I could hear a class distantly reciting a physics theorem. Their voices were flat and disinterested, as if they had no sense at all of what they were saying.

I took to wandering the streets of Cole Bay in an aimless fashion, feeling unconnected to the people around me. They seemed less real somehow, drab grey counterparts to the residents of my dream city. They had once seemed funny, but now I just felt sorry for them. On rainy afternoons on the esplanade I witnessed random acts of stupidity, of sadness, of hatred and harm; a young man shaking a girl by her thin shoulders, shouting in her face until her cheeks were flecked with his spittle. Two boys stamping on cans of orange drink to make them explode. Another disconsolately cracking pieces of glass from the window of a telephone box with the end of a spoon. A gang of girls on the wet brown beach throwing stones at one of their number, who was screaming and stumbling away from them. A middle-aged woman in a plastic rainhood angrily crying in the green shelter by the sea, who told me to piss off when I touched her sleeve.

So many people looked alone: old men smoking thin rollups, sitting motionless in bright cafés, smoke eddying above their heads. Silent couples seated in cars along the seafront, staring out through their windscreens, slowly chewing sandwiches. A spindly boy in short trousers sulkily kicking out the toe of his sandal on a paving slab while his parents argued. A couple patiently watching an old man trying to park a three-wheeled invalid carriage, not offering to help as he repeatedly hit the vehicle behind. If there was some way that they could make their lives better, wouldn't they have taken it? Was it this paralysis that made them so angry, so petty?

If the streets were grim that winter afternoon, the atmosphere at home was worse. Pauline was sitting at the kitchen table with Janine. It looked as though they had been on a major tea binge. Janine had eyes like red golf balls. Bob was in the lounge, seated in his usual armchair being furiously ineffectual, and Sean was slamming around upstairs. I stood in the kitchen dripping rainwater on to the lino. 'What's going on?' I asked.

'It's nothing to do with me,' said Pauline darkly. 'Ask your brother.'

Sean was standing on a chair in his old room trying to get an ancient brown suitcase off the top of the wardrobe. 'I came looking for you,' he grunted, freeing the case in a cloud of dust. 'I wanted to tell you first.'

'What? Has Uncle Harry died?' It was the only thing I could think of. 'What's going on?'

'I'm off.' He thumped the case on to the bed and tried to pry its lock open. 'Where are the keys for this?'

'What do you mean?' I asked stupidly. 'Where are you going?'

'Singapore.'

'Singapore? But you don't know anybody in Singapore.'

'I know Mickey O'Donnelly.' Mickey had been in Sean's senior year. All of the remaining O'Donnellys – and there were a lot of them – still went to my old school.

'He's in the army, Sean. He's off his head. He tried to kill someone.'

'He's in the right job, then.'

'You can't go, not to Singapore. It's miles away.'

'Mickey reckons he can get me a job doing the same thing I do now.' He dug a penknife out of his pocket and began hammering at the lock. 'Trust them to lose the bloody keys.'

'What about Janine? Is she going with you?'

'No, she's bloody not.'

'I thought you two were getting married.'

'Yeah, that's what she thought and all. I never said I wanted to. I've lost count of the number of hints she's dropped, leaving magazines open at bridesmaids' dresses, suggesting churches, picking out three-tiered cakes, do we want marzipan? Bloody marzipan!' He turned and threw the penknife aside. 'We haven't even talked about whether we want to spend our lives together, what we want to do, what we expect from each other. She's already picking out bungalows.'

'They're for old people who can't get upstairs any more.'

'Well, that's how I feel.' He softened. 'I'm just not comfortable around her any more. I can't relax. I've started going the long way round on my deliveries, just so I can drive my bike fast. I know how you feel when you need your inhaler. Look, I'm sorry and that, but I've got to get out. It's driving me mad.'

'You never said before.' I studied the carpet. Brown with stale yellow swirls. 'Take me with you.'

'I can't, Kay, you know that. You'll change your mind about school. You'll miss your mates.'

'I'm not going back there, Sean.'

'I can't look after you. You're big and ugly enough to do the job yourself. I'm sorry, Kay. Sod it.' He sat on the bed and shoved the case on to the floor. 'It won't be forever. Just until I've made myself some money and she's got over the shock.'

'That could be years.'

'You're right there.'

'To be honest, I always thought she was wrong for you.'

He gave me what my mother used to call an old-fashioned look. 'Did you now? You might have said earlier.'

'I thought you could tell. She likes *Coronation Street* and you like motorbikes. The only thing you both like is chocolate. You can't build a relationship around a mutual respect for confectionery. She's going to eat herself sick if you go, and get a really big arse.'

Sean laughed. 'You're a cheeky bugger. You've got to be nice to her, all right? It's not her fault we're different. Bloody hell, Kay, I wish I could take you with me but I'll barely have enough cash and energy to sort myself out.'

'I could find work.'

'And what if something happened to you? How do you think that would make me feel? No, Kay. This is one I've got to figure out for myself. I've already bought my boat ticket.'

'You can't get anywhere on a boat. It takes ages. You'll get scurvy. You have to fly there these days.'

'You don't if you're broke. I'm going overland. On a bus.'

'Let's see the ticket.'

'There.' He pulled a folded carbon copy from his back pocket and smoothed it out on his knee. 'Eight-twenty Friday morning from Dover.'

'That's the day after tomorrow!'

'I'll write to you every week.'

'You say you will, people always say they will, but they never get around to it. It's like thank-you letters.' We stared at each other for a minute. 'You're serious, aren't you?'

'I'm afraid so.'

'Hang on then.' I went to my room, dug about in the drawer beside my bed and came back. 'Hold out your hand.' I held my fist over his palm and opened it.

Later, I wished I had never given him that damned key.

CHAPTER EIGHTEEN

The Importance of Balance

'He will want to know more about us soon,' wheezed the Semanticor, slapping chalk-dust from his ermine robes with a liver-spotted hand as he seated himself. The old teacher wore his ratty fur cloak even in the fiercest of heatwaves, and although he never seemed to sweat, exuded a most extraordinary odour, something between unharvested cauliflowers and monkeys on heat. He was very old and greatly venerated, if generally avoided. Even camels stayed away. 'The boy has an enquiring mind. It will not be enough to simply provide him with a safe harbour. What will you tell him when he asks more awkward questions, eh? How will you explain the absence of the muezzin call, the empty mosques? He is Church of England, yes? He will ask if we are Muslims. He will want to understand us.'

'I don't foresee a problem in the granting of such a desire,' replied Dr Trebunculus. 'There are ways of answering the most difficult questions.'

'There is the truth and there are lies, if that's what you mean.'

They were taking mint tea together on a sleepy afternoon in the Garden of the Osman Janissaries. The square was silent but for the insistent piddle of a star-shaped fountain and the occasional snores emanating from a trio of stupefied weavers and their slumbering dromedary. 'He is a good boy, and quite in thrall to us, surely you must see that.'

'I cannot imagine why,' moaned the Semanticor, looking around at the somnolent inhabitants of the garden. 'His own home must be exceeding dire, worse than that of the boy before. I don't understand how you may be so sure that he will return.'

'Then you have forgotten much about the curiosity of the young. You've been teaching too long in the palace. A spell back in the village classroom might do you some good.'

'This is easy for you to say. You received all the accolades for bringing him here, but what if you're wrong, eh? What if he does not return? They're getting harder to find with each passing term, you must be able to see that. Soon there may be none left at all. Do you need reminding of the fate that befell the Valide Sultan Kosem?'

'*There is no past, there is no hereafter, all is in a process of becoming*,' replied Trebunculus, looking into the middle distance and blowing on his tea. It was a quote from the poet Bedreddin, but its point was not lost on the Semanticor.

'I just think we should be on our guard. The boy sent Parizade away. Sent her back to her village. Said it wasn't right that she should be provided solely for his pleasure. The poor girl was devastated; she has lost standing with her family. He has a mind of his own, this one. The Lord Chancellor is anxious that we should keep him away from the Princess Rosamunde. He has seen the way they look at each other. There must be no disruption, only continuity.'

'I take your point. I shall assuage his inquisitiveness.

Upon his next arrival, we must take the boy on a tour of the kingdom. There shall be no question we refuse to answer bravely and honestly.'

'No question?' The Semanticor raised his thick grey eyebrows.

'No question.'

'And suppose he then chooses not to tarry here? What will become of us?'

'You might well ask what will become of them,' replied Trebunculus philosophically. 'What would they do without us? You can't have one without the other. *Balance, harmony and light*. Thus is it written.'

The Semanticor pulled a grim and disbelieving face. 'Or eternal darkness for all,' he warned.

CHAPTER NINETEEN

The Benefits of Progress

'**Because in** Calabash,' explained Trebunculus with a certain amount of exasperation, 'some things are taken for granted. For example, everyone knows that singing is compulsory on Feasting Day, visible sorrow has been forbidden without a signed warrant from the Sultan, there must be no sharpness of sound or movement in any areas trodden by the Royal foot, and the discussion of court affairs must cease when Scammer is in the chimney.'

'Why?' I asked. 'The last part, I mean.'

'Because Scammer is a spy in the pay of the Lord Chancellor. Just as the royal monkey can be relied upon to bite the Lord Chancellor whenever he stamps on its tail, so Scammer reports back each dusk with his latest discoveries.'

'Why does he stamp on its tail?'

'Oh, he says it has the *jettatura*, the evil eye. Our Lord Chancellor finds the evil eye almost everywhere he looks. It is said that he carries his last will and testament in his robe, next to his heart, for fear that his life will be taken at any moment.'

'So the state of Calabash does have enemies, then?'

'Evil can breed in any dark corner, even in Paradise,' replied Trebunculus evasively.

I sat back and allowed the sun to warm my face while I considered the point. The queasiness of my crossing had already faded. Although it had been raining when I left, I had chosen my clothes more carefully for this, my latest trip. On the pier's lower platform I had tied my plastic Pakamac to one of the iron posts and waited patiently in the sheeting drizzle, confident of my ability to cross over. Underneath the mac I wore the shirt I had borrowed from Sean. It was a little long in the sleeve, but was made of cheesecloth and had a wide orange collar with looped buttonholes. I untucked it as soon as the transition had been made, allowing the sumptuous warm air that enveloped me to dry it out.

As always, the doctor had been there to greet me. This time he was accompanied by the Princess Rosamunde, who had apparently insisted on coming. She was wearing a tunic of lemon cotton and had strings of tiny yellow flowers in her hair, and she greeted me with a hug after Menavino had touched my arm in friendship. Behind them, fringed with vivid green date palms, stood Calabash. It was the shape and tone of an apricot stone, a city of calm arcs and flourishes, glittering in sunlight, the lives within it unfolding in graceful curves, like the bolts of cloth in the merchants' displays, like the wings of cranes in lazy, looping flight. Existence in Calabash was a series of rich ellipses, each one gliding into the next. In a sapphire sky unseamed by cloud, a pale crescent moon receded. In the air hung the sharp tang of orange blossom. My shirt steamed on my back. I could hear crickets rasping in the grass, the distant incessant ticking of a samba beat, and felt drunk with pleasure.

We had begun to walk around the city. Rosamunde looked

over at Trebunculus, then raised her finger slyly to her lips as she slipped her hand in mine. The doctor had not noticed. He was too busy pointing out various locations as the sites of scandals and legends, reciting parts of tales within tales that had no end.

'And here,' he explained, pointing to a large rusty nail embedded in the ground, 'is the spot where the Akond of Manchia met his gruesome fate. On a visit to our Sultan's great ancestor, Ahmet The Obscure, it is told that the Akond brought with him the rare gift of a golden salamander for our court alchemist, my distant predecessor, in exchange for a barge of onyx so intricately carved that it was said to float upon the waves by trapping air bubbles in its fretwork frame. The salamander is, of course, a symbol of cleansing fire. It lived inside flames and looked like a gigantic worm, and made a skin around itself that could be spun and woven into a cloth so pure that any garment fashioned from it would emerge from the fire forever clean, and would protect its wearer even within the hottest inferno. Ahmet's most favoured concubine wove him a shirt from the salamander's skin, but she failed to notice that her thread had become entangled with the thread of an ordinary silkworm, and the shirt was impure, so that when Ahmet wore the shirt and stepped into a cauldron of fire to impress his adversaries, he was greatly burned.

'Furious that his enemies had been able to witness his suffering, Ahmet ordered that the Akond be taken to the town's old marketplace, which was here, and had this nail driven through the left foot of the well-meaning visitor, pinning him to the ground. He then ordered coals to be banked around the Akond in a circle. The coals were set ablaze, and the Akond was forced to turn himself around the nail, constantly facing his least-burned side to the searing heat. In this way he was scorched with such evenness that he was perfectly cooked, and upon his collapse was fed to the palace dogs. The salamander was returned in the onyx barge, which had its air bubbles punctured with a thousand gold pins, causing it to sink, thus drowning the salamander and extinguishing its flame forever.' Trebunculus looked with satisfaction at the blood-rusted nail. 'I think there was a war,' he concluded with a resigned heave of breath, 'but it was all a long time ago.'

Rosamunde rolled her eyes at me, bored by the doctor's tale, and allowed her smooth brown fingers to roam over my arm. The doctor moved hastily on from this location to the next. Every site revealed its own fable, but gradually his stories grew shorter and shorter. 'I must get you back to your father, Princess,' he told her.

'Although of course I respect and honour my father,' said Rosamunde hotly, 'he is not my keeper, and I am free to roam wherever – and with whomever – I see fit. I may return to him when I choose, until the time comes for me to marry. It is the lot of women to be obedient to their husbands, but until then I shall decide the course of my own actions.'

'I meant no disrespect,' the doctor apologised, removing his velvet hat and mopping his brow.

'Then let us rest for a while. Poor Kay's head must be spinning from your stories.'

Finally, not a little footsore, we came to a halt in the shade of a twisted old fig tree, where a small, clear stream ran across pale stones.

'Everything is so still.'

'Calabasians are not much given to movement,' said Trebunculus with some pride. 'It expends too much energy.' He reached down and cupped his hand in the stream to sip some water.

'We wish to enjoy our days,' said Rosamunde. 'Why hurry through your life?'

'What do your people do with their time?' I asked.

'They celebrate the beauty of their world, in verse, in work, in duty, in repose, in being,' Trebunculus replied. 'Although there are lunar clocks and sundials in the royal palace, their purpose is purely decorative. As I explained, our people do not mark the passing time with hours or minutes. They have no use for measuring instruments. It is enough for them to know that they are born and will die. The rest is simply being alive. This is not to say that I entirely agree with their philosophy. Menavino and I have devised our own systems for the calibration of time and distance. We are progressives.'

Rosamunde dipped her hands in the stream and raised her cupped palms to her lips, gesturing for me to do the same. The water tasted cold and sweet.

'The Sultan encourages your investigations?' I asked, wiping droplets from my chin.

'Indeed not. But we are all curious about our enemies, no? And the Sultan cannot feast upon a honeycomb without demanding to understand the flight of bees.'

'And political intrigue? Does he demand to know the strengths and weaknesses of his rivals?'

'The Royal Sultanate has no rivals. Our old enemies are ravaged, shattered and dispersed. This era has known only peace. Most of our political concerns now stem from the deployment of our army, and these matters are under the control of the Lord Chancellor.'

'Septimus Peason. Hm.' There was something bothersome about him that I had yet to determine.

'Enough. Come, let us return to the city.' The doctor rose on creaking knees, brandished his malacca cane at the distant walls and set off at a brisk pace.

'I still don't understand where I am,' I said, as we passed beneath the curving archway of the Eastern gate. 'Where exactly is Calabash?'

Rosamunde looked at Menavino and tittered silently, as if I had asked the most foolish question imaginable.

'It is,' Trebunculus paused to frame his answer, 'on the other side of the world.'

'But not in my time.'

'Always you must know about time,' said Rosamunde with a sigh. She paused before another fountain in the shadow of a vine-skeined wall, and raised one small foot, tipping a stone from her slipper.

'I just want to learn.'

'Hah! I knew you were also a progressive,' laughed Trebunculus. 'It is a rare thing to find such a person. Look up there.' I raised my head, shielding my eyes with my fingers. Ahead of us a small dark stain darted across the gleaming blue tiles of a roof, vanishing behind a golden dome. 'Scammer is going about his work.'

'I don't understand. Why does Septimus Peason need a spy?'

'It is the duty of a Lord Chancellor to search for enemies, even if they are imagined.'

'And what happens if he should catch one?'

'Why, they are taken to the detention house, where he extracts confessions and then puts them to death. A traditional method. Slow compression of the testicles.'

'It sounds unnecessarily cruel.'

'Cruelty is only unnecessary when it achieves no purpose. Calabash is as old as it is new, and has its own unique way of going about its affairs.'

'I see,' I said doubtfully.

'No, I don't think you do.' Trebunculus looked upon me

with kind, knowing eyes. 'You think we are not democratic, that we are some kind of benign plutocracy, and perhaps there is some truth in that. But there is a balance here.'

'And harmony.' The Princess made this last word almost musical.

'Then how should I think of you?'

'Why, as your inspiration.'

'Look there now, Kay.' I followed Rosamunde's pointing finger to a tall turret shingled in shining gold. 'Every evening our Queen Mother, my grandmother, the Gracious Fathmir Of Cordoba, sits in that tower with her maids of honour, and weaves a tapestry that chronicles the lives of the people all around her. It is said that just as the sun slips below the horizon, it touches her stitches with tongues of fire, and for a brief moment it brings to life all of the characters she has created, and in this moment she can see the fate of everyone within the tapestry. And if she should see something that saddens her, she unpicks the stitches and remakes their destinies.'

I was going to ask Rosamunde something about kismet, but did not wish to appear foolish. I couldn't help associating the idea with terrible old Hollywood films. Legends and fables were all very well, but they failed to explain the life of the city.

'Do you have electricity?' I asked the doctor instead.

'Of course!'

'You do?'

'Most certainly. It accumulates in the sky when storms bring the rain, and is discharged into the earth. You must have it too, it is a part of nature.'

Whenever we embarked upon a question-and-answer session, it never seemed to get us anywhere. 'Then do you have television?'

Trebunculus gave the word some consideration. 'I think I understand what you mean,' he replied uncertainly.

'Little moving pictures you can watch, in a box.' I attempted to demonstrate with the use of my hands.

'Ah. No. We are clearly not talking about the same thing. I thought you had truncated the words. Telescope-Vision. Television. Seeing distances. Now you're saying some kind of puppet-theatre.'

Rosamunde dropped down on to the mossy edge of the fountain beside Menavino, giggling again. 'Kay is making fun with you, doctor.'

'I'm not,' I replied in some earnest. 'We have an invention, a box like a little theatre, it runs on electricity. You plug it into the wall.'

'You have electricity in the wall?'

'Yes.' I could see that we were about to be sidetracked again.

'You catch it from the air?'

'No, we make it ourselves.'

They all had a good laugh at that one.

'But seriously,' said Trebunculus when they had settled once more. 'It is in the walls of your houses?'

'Yes.'

'How?'

'It is carried by wires from the places which make it, great big turbines that build up huge amounts of electricity, very powerful, millions of volts, and then it comes into our houses and we turn on the little box and it gives us the news.'

'A messenger.'

'Sort of. And adverts. Selling things.'

'A merchant.'

'And it tells us what the weather will be.'

'An oracle.'

'And it acts out stories. It shows you what life is like.'

'A prophet.'

'Sort of.'

'But what can it do that a man cannot?'

'Well, nothing really.'

'And for this you have to make your own storms?' They shrugged at me. 'Seems a lot of effort.'

I tried to think. Every time I asked questions about Calabash, I ended up having to justify something about my own world. 'All right,' I said, finally thinking of something useful, 'we can light a room with electricity.'

'So can we, with candles.'

'But not very well.'

'How much light do you need?' Trebunculus gave Rosamunde one of his looks.

'Ah, but a candle burns you if you stick your finger in the flame.'

They laughed again. 'Of course, if you stick your finger in the flame, but why would you be so stupid?' asked Rosamunde.

'So electricity does not hurt if you stick your finger in it?' asked the doctor.

'Well, yes, it hurts very badly. It can kill you.'

'There you are. Better to stick with candles.' We were back to where we had started. The doctor's bones cracked as he folded his long legs and joined us in the shadow of the vines.

'Why do you distrust electricity so?' I asked.

'Because it belongs in the natural place of things, in the angry summer air, not in boxes. If it can be put in a box and used to drive mechanical devices, and set to a multitude of uses, cannot its masters then be tempted to wage war against those who do not possess such science?'

'Well, yes,' I conceded.

'So be it. What else have you got?'

'Cars.'

'Short for . . .' Trebunculus searched. 'Caravans, yes?'

'No. Not short for anything, really. You drive them about.' I performed a hopeless mime. 'Open the door, get inside, start the engine, off you go.'

'Ah! An engine!' He leaned forward to nod knowingly at Menavino.

I ignored the diversion I was being offered. 'Then you drive away. You can travel at great speed, get where you're going a lot faster.'

'Faster than a horse?'

'Faster than many horses.'

'This thing, what is it made of?'

'Metal alloy. Steel. On wheels, like a cart, but you get right inside it, and it's much, much faster than any old horse or camel.'

'Why?'

'What do you mean, why?'

'Why go so fast?'

'So you can get there quicker.'

'Why?'

'To . . . arrive there . . . earlier.'

I could see that this wasn't going to lead anywhere useful either. The doctor raised a bony tanned forefinger. 'And.'

'What?'

'If it is made of metal and going very fast, why does it not hit things?'

'It does if it's not driven properly. You have to have lessons.'

'People go to school for this?' asked Rosamunde. 'To not hit things?' Behind them, Menavino snorted with laughter.

'I'll tell you what. Forget about the cars.'

'No. Now I am interested. They run on electricity?'

'No, on oil.'

Incredulous faces. 'Like the *lamps*?'

I had a brief vision of streets in Cole Bay choked with traffic. 'Look, let's change the subject. We'll talk about something you have here.'

'Good.' Rosamunde cocked her head to one side. 'Listen. You hear those sounds in the distance? Do you like the songs of the samba?'

'Very much,' I replied, baffled and cheered. 'The beat. It's sort of like dance music.'

'Oh yes, it makes you want to do like so—' She rose and shook her hips seductively.

'Come. Let's go and dance. Menavino will stay here with the doctor.'

'Oh, I don't, um . . .' I made a face. 'I've got two left feet.' They all looked down at my feet. 'Uh, it's just a saying.'

'Oh come, we dance. I will teach.' Rosamunde grabbed my hand and gently reeled me up to her. She had a tiny silver ring in her navel, on which an ice-blue diamond turned.

'I'm sure Kay would rather learn about our kingdom,' huffed the doctor. 'I've much to show him. We've barely begun the tour.'

'There are other times for your lectures, I think,' warned Rosamunde. She pulled me closer. Beneath a tang of oranges I could smell the scent of her warm flesh.

'Well, Menavino and I have been neglecting our studies of late,' Trebunculus decided. The apprentice showed the whites of his eyes and shook his head vigorously.

'Really,' sighed the doctor as Rosamunde pulled at me and we ran off down the hill towards the beat of the drums. '*O! Call back yesterday, bid time return.*' He watched us for a moment, then, followed by his loyal apprentice, strode off in the direction of his laboratory, shaking his head at the transient follies of youth.

In The Tower of Trezibaba

We danced like dervishes for an hour in the crowded market square where the band played its strange, skirling sambas. The music sounded as though its origins lay in Spain, ancient Arabia and the Upper Nile, but there were also modern Latin elements, and something else hiding within the rhythms, something very English that I could not identify. Everybody danced: shopkeepers, weavers, fishermen and camel-drivers, mothers, children and grandfathers; all were swayed by the hypnotic power of the band's strange melodies. Dancing had been forbidden within the imperial palace since the death of Rosamunde's mother, but it survived in these streets, where the Princess always came to enjoy the companionship of her people. Nobody seemed awed or uncomfortable in her presence. She was barely noticed as she passed through the cavorting crowd.

Afterwards Rosamunde presented the musicians with a handful of ducats, and they encouraged us to slake our thirst on a sharp fermented nectarine drink that was poured on to our parched tongues from tall clay bottles.

'I hope you still have some energy left for climbing,' said Rosamunde, wiping her mouth and pulling me away. 'Come, I want to show you something.'

We left the market square and re-entered the city through the great South Gate, making our way to a slender, pale obelisk that bulged from the outer wall.

'This is the Tower of Trezibaba,' Rosamunde explained, pushing open the door in its base. 'Seven storeys high, built of a rare white brick made from china clay and ground ivory. Trezibaba was a brave warrior who was felled by his enemies when he was ordered to march into battle after dusk. In those times, nobody waged war beyond the setting of the sun, and the fate of Trezibaba and his loyal men was sealed upon the loss of his honour. The tower was built as a rebuke, against the orders of the Emperor Sun-Mo-Tsung (for during this period the kingdom was ruled by a Chinese warlord). It was constructed by the sons of the troops Trezibaba commanded, the children whose fathers died for him. It was made seven storeys high so that its shadow would sweep like a pendulum across the palace, touching the Emperor's quarters with its shadow each day to remind the royal dynasty that the misuse of time can destroy an army, and, by inference, a kingdom. We must go all the way to the roof.'

She ran ahead of me, vanishing and reappearing in the fierce shards of light that were cast by the narrow embrasures. Twice I was forced to stop and draw fresh breath before I reached the top. A narrow balcony circled the turret, which was lined with tiles of beaten gold. I looked down at the tower's shadow, which cut across the city like the minute-hand of a clock, the only measurement of time in the land. Rosamunde stood with her hands spread wide on the railing, her head lifted to the sun.

'Feel the air,' she said. 'How fresh it is up here. Cooler, yes?'

'Yes.' I stood beside her and looked down at the kingdom spread beneath us. 'What is that?' I asked. To the south-west of the city walls a grey building, squat and sinister, stood surrounded by sentry boxes.

'It is the military compound containing the drill grounds, General Bassa's quarters and the interrogation chambers.'

This bird's eye view of the kingdom brought my Mesopotamian maps to mind. 'Why doesn't the army protect the city from within?'

'From the time of Trezibaba onward, the militia remained separate from the royal state. It receives its orders from the Lord Chancellor, not the Sultan. The army has no divine right, but draws its strength from political will. We attempt no crusades here.'

'And that, what is that?' Below the compound a dark wood grew, its wild, dense trees hiding the ground completely. Lined by tall hedgerows on every side, it appeared from above to form an impenetrable green fortress.

'It is the oldest part of our land, a territory forbidden to outsiders.'

'Why?'

'*Ajnabee*, always you ask questions. It would be best for you to stay away from there. Remember my words and heed them well.'

'Is there something I'm not supposed to see?'

'It is sacred ground. Old gods, you understand? Nobody goes there. Enough.' She turned to face me, brushing her hair from her face, and readied herself for my embrace.

'From the moment I saw you . . .' I began.

'It is best not to say.'

I had no way of stopping myself. 'You know I'm in love with you.'

'I know.'

I seized her hands, but it was she who succeeded in drawing me to her. To try to explain or describe that first kiss is pointless. Even now, though, I remember the silkiness of her skin and the touch of her lips, and will remember them at the moment of my death. I have no idea how long I held her atop the white tower, but by the time we came to leave, the sun was setting and the tower's shadow lay beyond the city walls.

'I want to be with you,' I said foolishly, not caring because I felt sure that none of this could be real.

'And so you may,' she replied, 'but it must be our secret. I am sure the doctor has told you that I am soon to be married. My husband-to-be is Major Maximus, the son of the Lord Chancellor.'

'Do you love him?'

'I have never been alone in his company.'

'Then you have no way of knowing if you do.'

'It is not a matter of love, but of honour and duty. I will learn to love him. This marriage is for the good of the state. To reunite my father with his people.'

'I don't understand.'

'My father and General Bassa. Well, let us say there are misunderstandings. These problems go back many years, perhaps as far as Trezibaba himself. My marriage is – what is the word – a stratagem.'

'But will you be happy?'

'If I succeed in performing my duty. And if you love me as you say you do, you will be happy for me.' She nodded to herself. 'We must understand this, you and I. Abide by my terms and we shall know happiness.'

'But for how long?'

'All happiness is fleeting. Your kings take mistresses, no? I will never betray my husband with a lover. But I will be with you until Maximus comes for me. I know it will be difficult for you, but you are the outsider and I am the Princess, and my sacrifice is greater than yours, yes?'

'Yes,' I agreed, reluctantly.

'So – you must leave the tower first. Make sure no-one sees you go. Accept my situation and I will be yours. It is an agreement?'

'You make it sound so formal.'

'I have to. I am the Princess. There is no other way to proceed.'

There was a nobility about her when she spoke of her duty. I wanted to argue, to say that she could run away with me, but knew that doing so would doom any chance I had of seeing her again. At the foot of the stairs we kissed in the dark, and then I was back in the bright afternoon, darting through the streets and checking to make sure that my departure was unwitnessed.

For me, the world of Calabash had taken a further step into the light. Everything was becoming clearer, sharper. It was a world whose people followed rules I understood, who behaved and who thought as I did.

It was my world.

CHAPTER TWENTY-ONE

The Necessity of Belonging

Menavino's calculations had begun to show results. One sultry afternoon – was there ever any other kind? – stood out in my memory.

'Ready when you are,' called Trebunculus. He was leaning at an angle of forty-five degrees in order to keep the fat elastic cables taut. The heels of his pattens dug into grass. Rosamunde stood by with her hands at her mouth. Menavino settled himself in the narrow hide seat and adjusted the strap of his goggles over his new-grown tonsure, a symbol of his completed apprenticeship. He licked a finger and raised it in the air, then gave the thumbs up, a gesture I had taught him. There was a collective holding of breath. Rosamunde raised a scarf of amber silk to check the wind speed, as she had been shown.

'Now!' The doctor swung down his arm and released the elastic. The pale balsa contraption lurched forward and toppled over the ramparts of the Jasmine Terrace, which was built at the second-highest point of the kingdom. For a moment none of us could bear to look.

The sound we had dreaded hearing, the splinter of wood, the tearing of limbs, did not come.

'Look! Look!' The doctor was jumping about like a child and pointing down. Far below us Menavino swung gracefully over the fields, then up across the face of the sun. He was silently laughing into the sky. His feet worked the pedals that controlled the silk wings of the little craft. Catching an up-draft he tilted alarmingly, then levelled out. Farmgirls stepped back from their barley baskets and shielded their eyes, turn-ing to watch as he passed over their heads. Children chased the shadow of the craft across the meadows. From a distant silk-draped window in a palace turret, the Sultan's entourage applauded politely.

The doctor was ecstatic. 'Proof that man can be made lighter than air! This is just the beginning!' His enthusiasm was not dampened even when Menavino crashed into the top of a fig tree and had to be cut down from his harness. We galloped across the fields to right the shaken but elated boy, and dragged the broken-spined craft down through the branches. Then we seated ourselves beside a stream to discuss the next step.

'I suppose the skies of your home are filled with flight devices of every conceivable nature,' suggested Trebunculus, sucking on one of the fallen figs that surrounded us.

I found myself reluctant to discuss scientific progress in my own world. I had a horrible feeling that somehow we would end up discussing Neil Armstrong's walk on the moon. Every time the doctor enquired about a particular invention it seemed to me that a coolness crept into the air, a chill that warned against advancing too quickly and upsetting the precious balance of life here. The Sultan had no agenda for the modernisation of Calabash, and seemed far too preoccupied with his various internecine military disputes to consider how the kingdom might be ameliorated. His methods for dealing with the simplest problems seemed circuitous to say the least. For instance, after being informed by the Lord Chancellor that the palace staff were failing to complete their housekeeping duties before noon, the Sultan sanctioned the construction of a gigantic golden statue that portrayed him as a benevolent half-human, half-cockerel, to 'improve the vital humours' of his staff and remind them of the benefits of an early start. His thinking was impossible to guess. Still, the people and their land existed in such easy, ancient symbiosis that to alter any part of it would risk damaging the whole. And I did enjoy our conversations of comparison.

'Our aircraft are forged from steel,' I explained, 'into great carriages that can hold over a hundred passengers at once.'

'But how can something so heavy rise into the heavens?' asked Rosamunde, slipping her hand in mine, much to the doctor's disapproval.

'I'm not really sure. It has something to do with sucking in air.'

'Have you ever been up in one of these carriages?'

'No.'

'Ha!' Rosamunde slapped the ground, happy to have caught me out.

Trebunculus frowned. 'Kay, perhaps you can tell me something I don't understand. Today we have seen Menavino ride on the natural currents of the air. But to put a hundred people in the sky is so obviously against nature that it must invite disaster. Why would you wish to tempt fate?'

'Progress, I suppose,' I replied dejectedly. 'My science teacher used to say that if you weren't going forwards, you were going backwards.'

'What did he mean?'

'I don't really know.'

We looked down at the city basking in the afternoon sunlight, the stillness of the sleeping streets. Menavino rubbed his bloodied knees with a soothing leaf.

'I think you are not happy when you go home,' the doctor decided. 'Perhaps you should spend more time here.'

I thought of my family, and a more troublesome problem clouded my mind. 'That's just it,' I admitted uneasily. 'As happy as I am here, this place can't be real. It's born from my imagination. It's what I wish the world was like.'

Rosamunde leaned forward and pressed her warm lips against my bare arm. She took my hand and placed it on her smooth stomach. 'Then I am not real?' she asked. 'Can you not feel my body?'

'Princess, I would ask you to remember your station,' admonished the doctor. 'But Kay, how can you be so sure of what is real? You tell us your brother has travelled to a faraway land, but how do you know that it exists? Why must reality contain bad things in order to prove itself to you?'

'I guess that's what makes it real,' I replied. 'It doesn't always go the way you want it to. Reality is unexpected. This is all so – perfect.'

'Then we must make ourselves less predictable?'

'No, you don't have to do anything like that – I don't know how it works.'

'Too much head. Not enough heart. Trust more to instinct, I think.'

'You're probably right, Doctor. I suppose it will sort itself out. Now I must go home.' As much as I hated the thought of returning to Cole Bay, it felt necessary to keep one frozen foot there. I gently disentangled Rosamunde's hand and rose. 'I'll be back in a day or so, I promise.'

As I walked down through the swaying fields towards the

harbour, I looked back and saw the little group unmoved beside the stream, Rosamunde in her silken saffron shift and bracelets, her brown face tilted to the sun, Trebunculus sporting his velvet top hat, Menavino peeling figs, surrounded by his great feathered wings, and for the first time I began to fear their loss.

CHAPTER TWENTY-TWO

The Conundrum of
Eliya's Chamber

'I have something for you,' I told the doctor on my next visit. 'Go on, unwrap it.' Trebunculus lifted the paper package from my hands with the tips of his bony fingers and carefully peeled it open. He slid the glass lozenges into the palm of his hand and examined them. 'Dear boy!' he grinned, 'you found lenses for me. Oh, well done!'

'Machine-ground, as you asked.' I had removed them from Sean's old school microscope. It had been broken from its mount during one of our more boisterous fights, and was now beyond repair. My latest crossing to Calabash had been the easiest yet, and I was pleased to be doing a service for my new friend.

'Machine-ground, my! You have no idea how exciting the prospect of a degree of accuracy is to me. There is so much guesswork here. Menavino, look!' He held the lenses up for the boy so that they caught the light. I looked down for the piebald piglet that usually wandered between my feet.

'Where's that little—?'

'Oh, I kept tripping over Cerastro, so we stuffed her with

figs and ate her. Seat yourself on that stool over there.' I watched Trebunculus busying himself in the laboratory. 'There are many formal experiments I wish to conduct, but first I must use these to answer a question that has dwelt in me for many years. Perhaps you should not bear witness, Kay, for my intention is a seditious one,' he whispered.

'I'm an outsider,' I reminded him.

'Very well, then.' He crossed to the shelves that lined the rear of the room and stretched until his hands seized upon a small iron box. Setting the box upon his workbench, he produced a key from the chain around his neck and inserted it into the lock. Inside were two glass vials containing what appeared to be identical red crystals, the colour of ground rubies. He spent the next hour hunched over the bench. First he suspended the crystals in two separate solutions, then boiled them down in iron pots. During this process, he fitted the lenses I had brought him into a sliding set of rods, by which he could adjust their distance from each other. Then he dried and scraped the residues out of the pots and set them beneath the lenses.

Menavino darted about preparing each stage of the test for his master, leaving the doctor free to concentrate on the technical specifications of his experiment. When Trebunculus finally rose from the bench, his face had lost its colour. 'It is as I have always suspected,' he said. 'Poor Eliya.' He tipped one of the vials out on to his bench and separated the crystal residue with a pair of wooden tweezers. 'Both samples are the same. The poison is fast-acting and causes total muscular paralysis. It comes from a scarlet octopus found in the deep sea beyond the harbour. The fishermen know about it and are careful to avoid its breeding grounds, yet the roasted flesh of the creature may be eaten because the poison is only found in the tips of its tentacles, and in low concentration. To prepare a toxic dose you simply need to milk the octopus and boil its poison to a crystallised sediment. This is the sediment I found in the glass that was set on the table beside the Sultan's wife as she gave birth to her daughter.'

'Do you know who put the glass there?'

'Well, of course.' The doctor's face fell further. 'I put it there. It was a difficult birth; I had prepared a sedative potion for her.'

'Somebody wanted you to be blamed for her death.'

'But why? I am the court physician, I bear no political interests.'

'The Sultan trusts you. He almost treats you like one of his family. Whoever divides his trust weakens the power of the hand that rules.'

'You think so?'

I had read too many books on dynastic collapse to believe anything else. Fallen civilisations were my specialist topic. 'Tell me, Doctor, what else do you remember of that day? Why did suspicion not fall on you? Why were you not arrested?'

'Because as his wife died, the Sultan let out a terrible scream and collapsed. The court was in turmoil. For three days he lay unconscious, until my potions and the crying of his newborn daughter roused him back to life.'

'And by then the crime scene had been cleared.'

'That's right. Eliya's effects had been removed to her burial vault, but I found the shards of the glass I had prepared for her awaiting disposal beside the headquarters of the royal nursemaid. When I examined the shards I saw that a solution coated one side.'

'What aroused your suspicions?'

'Eliya was a strong woman, in good health. The delivery should not have killed her.'

I asked him who else had attended Rosamunde's birth. Trebunculus stroked his long chin for a minute. 'I see things in my mind's eye. And yet it was all so long ago.'

'You must try to picture the scene,' I told him.

'Very well. I remember the gathering in the jade chamber, the flickering of the balsam lamps. The room had no windows, and only one door. I prepared the sedative outside and took the glass in to Eliya myself. After helping her to take a few sips, I set it on the octagonal table near her head.'

'What else was on the table?'

'Nothing. By rights the table should not have been there at all. It was tall, carved in onyx, and set with five carnelians. Onyx is regarded as an evil stone, you understand. The carnelians temper its harmful nature. It was considered bad luck to even have it in the room, but the piece was a favourite of Eliya's and so it stayed. She looked so small in that great bed. The swan-bed, carved from rosewood, as smooth as her own fair skin.

'The Sultan was not in attendance for the delivery. He was only summoned to the bedside after his wife began her death throes. The Valide Sultan – the Queen Mother – was in attendance, of course. Eliya's own mother had died several years earlier, and Fathmir had adopted Eliya as her own blood family. They were very close. The two handmaidens of the inner court were also present. Eunuchs guarded the doors. Oh, and the Lord Chancellor was present when Eliya's contractions began to quicken, but was ushered from the room for the sake of propriety.'

'So he had access to the sedative glass,' I replied. 'Of all people, surely suspicion must fall most heavily on him?'

Trebunculus sucked thoughtfully at his teeth. From the opposite side of the bench, a great convex mirror exaggerated his gnu-like features. 'I understand your reasoning, but you must realise that the Chancellor had everything to gain by the birth of a royal daughter. His own son was four years old and destined for leadership training under General Bassa. It meant that, for the first time in decades, there was the opportunity to heal the division between the sovereign state and the militia by means of a marriage. The glory from such a strategy belonged – and still belongs – to Septimus alone.' The doctor's tone grew confidential. 'The Sultan is not the man he was. He can no longer afford to risk internecine war with his own military powers. The unity of the kingdom is essential, and it is the Lord Chancellor who has engineered this miracle where so many others have failed.'

I tried another tack. 'Did anyone approach Eliya apart from yourself?'

'The handmaidens bathed her forehead with strips of wet cloth.'

'And the glass remained on the table?'

'It stood at the head of the bed, so I suppose both Septimus and Fathmir were within reach of it. My concern was for Eliya, you understand. She began to convulse moments after I had cleared the baby's lungs.'

'Whoever added the poison to the glass must have done so between your setting it down upon the table and Eliya's first sip.'

'But there was only the briefest of moments between the two events, I am certain. Poisoning is not uncommon in our kingdom's history, but it remains a delicate art. To introduce granules to the glass is not a momentary action.' Trebunculus slumped forward at the bench, distraught.

'I don't understand. Why not?'

'For the simple reason that too much poison would have taken action immediately, risking the life of the unborn child, a child everyone in that room needed. Too little poison and there would have been time for me to administer an antidote. You see our dilemma, Kay. The poison from the scarlet octopus is so powerful in concentration that a single grain would make a difference in its effect. The exact amount of toxin had to have been measured out at the bedside. But I ask you, how would that have been possible?'

'I agree, it is a puzzle,' I admitted. 'But perhaps not beyond solution. Would it be possible to visit the jade chamber?'

'Why, the room was dismantled after Eliya's death upon the order of the Sultan, and everything in it destroyed, except for a few items which were buried in the royal vault along with Eliya.'

'Then we must visit the vault and examine the body.'

'Impossible!' cried Trebunculus. 'Such an act would constitute the purest form of sacrilege. If caught we would be tortured for weeks, slow compression—'

'—of the testicles, yes, I remember.'

'And then, if we were very lucky, we would be beheaded.'

'*Very* lucky?'

'Oh, beheading is an honourable form of execution.'

But even as he spoke, I could tell that he was already thinking of a way to achieve our goal.

CHAPTER TWENTY-THREE

Farewells

There had been a storm in the night; huge puddles covered the car park. The air was damp and everything smelled of seaweed. Not that there was anything new about that.

'What's all this stuff?' Sean asked, peering down into the plastic shopping bag.

'Supplies for the journey. Fry's Mint Chocolate. Teabags. Seasick stuff. Your old bobble hat. Uncle Harry's number in Beirut. It wasn't my idea, Mum wanted me to give it to you.' Uncle Harry was the nearest relative we had to Singapore. Pauline's thinking here was that if Sean had some kind of emergency he would automatically ring us in Cole Bay, and if we were out he would phone the next nearest living relative, not counting my step-Grandad, who answered his phone but could never understand the person on the other end. Beirut was still a beautiful city then. Uncle Harry was five years away from suffering a fatal heart attack after his apartment was shelled.

Sean stuffed the bag into his holdall. He wiped his blue nose on the back of his hand and looked towards the ferry, the great blue and white wall rising motionless beside the dock with its deck lamps glowing coldly in the grey dawn light. It didn't look like a boat at all, more like a factory on night shift. 'Well, I'd better get on or it'll go without me,' he said. 'Everyone else is already on.'

Bob and Pauline were sitting in the car, looking uncomfortable. Pauline said the waiting around was too damp for her back. Janine had, unsurprisingly, opted not to see my brother off.

'And what's this?' Sean took the slim plastic case from me and turned it in his hands.

'Open it and see.'

He unclasped the lid and removed the fountain pen from its holder. He gave a low whistle. 'This must have cost you a bomb, Kay.'

'There's six ink cartridges too. Just remember your promise.'

'You daft bugger. Come here.' He made a lunge for my head and squeezed it so hard against his chest that his coat buttons made marks on my face. 'I'm not going for ever, you know. I just need to sort things out in my mind. Like you do with your maps. But you have to stay here and do it. And look after them two. Everything will be all right. Here.' He pulled a hand free and took a tiny paper Union Jack pin from his lapel, some kind of flag-day offering. He shook the fountain pen. 'Is there ink in this thing?'

'Of course, I filled it up last night. Had to make sure it worked.'

Uncapping the pen, he wrote his name on the back of the flag, twirled it dry and handed it to me. 'Put me on one of your maps. I'll write and tell you exactly where I am, and you can keep track of me, is that a deal?'

I smiled. 'A deal.' I carefully pinned the flag on to the lapel of my overcoat. When I looked up, Sean was walking away towards the silent ship with his suitcase and his shopping bag, his big boots making no noise on the concrete plain. The weight and sway of his confident walk stayed in my mind long after his form had blurred into the thickening sea mist. I looked back at the car, at Bob and Pauline staring out through the condensation on the windscreen, and felt lost, stranded between ever-widening points.

The best way to forget about losing my brother was to get as far away as possible from Cole Bay. While I waited for Trebunculus to plan our excursion into the royal burial vault, I passed my time with Rosamunde. The Princess brought a seductive, elicit rhythm to my days and nights in Calabash. I could not stop thinking about her, especially when I was stuck at home with Bob and Pauline. Her luminous beauty, her swaying body, the guileless advances she made in my presence, combined to enslave me. Lying on a wind-freshened hillock, I waited for her to pass on Ebu, her favourite mare, a prancing, angular creature with powdered withers and kohl-lined eyes. As the sun set I watched her undressing in a conical room lined with wicker, silk and tortoiseshell, where the concubines were arranged for royal presentation. And one day, hiding no more from public view, not caring if the Sultan himself saw us, I approached her in the courtyard below her apartment, and embraced her in the shadows of the great columnade.

I knew I was behaving like a lovesick idiot, and that Rosamunde was soon determined to leave me for the Chancellor's son. The last thing I wished was to upset the balance of this finely-run kingdom, but I also knew how little the laws of logic counted in matters of the heart. Night after night, the Princess drew me to her chamber and kissed my bared chest as I slid her warm brown thighs around my waist. Unmindful of the dangers of discovery, we lay within the rumpled bedding until dawn restored the voices of the palace canaries.

I knew it was too good to last, of course.

'You have to leave,' urged Rosamunde one morning, kissing me anxiously. 'My maids will arrive at any moment.'

'I just want to be with you,' I begged pathetically, half-pushed towards the door in my unbuttoned shirt. 'There must be a way.'

She held an unsealed note before me. 'I have received word that Maximus Peason has been awarded the highest honour of his rank in General Bassa's annual review of troops. He is arriving today to claim his bride. There are military documents to be signed by all parties, then the ceremony of our betrothal will be set to take place at the quarter moon.'

'But this is terrible! Is there no way you can stop him?'

'I warned you of this moment, *ajnabee*. There has been further strain between the monarchy and its military force of late. I must make this marriage work for the sake of my father, so that his weakening power may be restored.'

'Marriage for love is the only kind of union that can ever last,' said I, who knew absolutely nothing about the subject.

'Poor Kay. It is not quite over yet for us. I will see you until the eve of my wedding, and then no more.'

Sulkily I took my leave, clambering through the tangle of briar below Rosamunde's bedroom window just as the servants arrived for her morning toilette. The Sultan's daughter was a prize worth fighting for. I imagined witnessing the arrival of her future husband's military courtege, a confrontation with Major Peason at the altar, a duel during which my fencing skills would finally come into play, a blade at his throat, acquiescence, the carrying off of my treasure.

I also remembered that I was an incredibly hopeless coward with a thing about pain, that I had left school before the conclusion of my fencing lessons, and that I was a low-born commoner with no hope in hell of marrying a member of a royal family that didn't even exist outside of my fevered imagination.

But hey – it didn't hurt to dream.

'You're lying to me,' said Julia, shouting above the clatter of the winch. 'If you really did have a girlfriend I'd know about it. Someone would have seen you out together and told me. What's her name, then?'

I looked over the side of the car at the passing white-painted struts. It didn't look very safe. The roller coaster was the most forbidden ride in the entire off-limits amusement park. It had been closed down for yet another safety check last month after some kid fell out at the top and broke his back. 'I'm not telling you. You don't know her, she's not from around here. You wouldn't recognise her if you saw her.'

'Then how did you meet her? You never go outside of Cole Bay,' she bellowed back. We were nearly at the peak now. 'What happened, did she get washed up on the beach one afternoon while you were down there chucking stones in the water? Did you give her artificial respiration and bring her back to life? Is she a mermaid or something? You're making it up, you lying little sod.'

'I'm not.'

'You are. You know how your imagination always gets the better of you.'

The clattering stopped as we came off the chain. The little car levelled out and curved around on its track. For a moment, the only sound was the wind in our ears.

'There's no point in telling me this sort of thing, anyway,' shouted Julia. 'If you were really in love you'd be shouting about it from the rooftops.'

The car tipped down and gathered speed as we began to scream our heads off.

If my trips to Calabash were a secret that I could not share, then falling in love with a girl who in all probability did not exist was even worse. I had been stung by Julia's sarcasm into hinting about the situation, but could not face any further risks from disclosure until I had made a few decisions about my other life.

I began to lose count of the number of times I returned to Calabash. Nothing disturbed the safe calm haven of the days I passed there, the warm expectant eroticism of the nights. Every minute spent apart from Rosamunde seemed to me like time irretrievably lost. She was a wilful, thrilling lover, who used the lonely hours of darkness before her impending wedding in lustful escapades with her traveller from across the sea. What passed between us on those hot nights was almost childlike, free from guilt and responsibility, free, I suppose, from reality. Whenever I came back to Cole Bay, I found myself cold and dog-tired, physically and mentally bereft. A familiar depression settled over me, and always lasted until the moment I decided to return.

Our last night together was – at least on my part – beset with melancholy. I sat on the edge of the royal counterpane and stared glumly out at the indigo hills, and generally moped about like a dog whose owner had been shot. Rosamunde was calmly accepting of her fate. We did not make love; I had no wish to renew the pain I felt, and she was preoccupied with the practical arrangements for her wedding day. When my hand brushed her arm she moved away from me, and I knew that our time together was over. As lovers part, their final words are supposedly imbued with import. 'Well, I'd better be off then,' probably won't go down in history as one of the great romantic farewells.

'Kay – wait,' she called back, unclasping something from the chain at her neck. 'I want you to take – this – with you.' Her hand revealed a smooth oval gemstone, the colour of flames through honey, the colour of her eyes. 'It belonged to my mother. Now it belongs to you, as I cannot.'

She turned her back and brushed her fingers across her face. I would like to think she shed a tear, but I knew that she was already lost to me, growing distant, thinking of her future husband. She was fully prepared to follow the path of her duty, and setting aside her childhood in order to grow up was part of the process. She made me feel immature.

I dropped the polished jewel into my pocket and left.

So my Rosamunde was married at the quarter moon, in a ceremony of such might, splendour and opulence that its sights and sounds could be sensed throughout the kingdom. Unable to keep myself away, I attended the procession from a distance. Maximus Peason was pretty much as I expected him to be, tall and tanned and shaven-headed, with a shovel-shaped beard and a merciless gaze. He was bedecked in silver braid, and his high-collared sapphire tunic acted like a neck brace. He was a commander of men, whose military training dictated his movements and revealed itself in every measured step he took. Rosamunde made a proud and dutiful bride, bound tightly in yellow lace and purple violets, unfaltering in her instruction. She stared ahead from the palace steps and smiled as if periodically remembering to do so. The Sultan was absurd with pride. His Nubians showered the couple in jacaranda petals, and fired a couple of gold-painted dwarves from cannons. Hurrying beneath an arch of shining unsheathed scimitars raised by the Sultan's *sipahis*, his personal cavalrymen, the Princess was spirited away by her new husband, but not before she had been taken to the heart of the cheering populace.

Although I tried to engage her attention, nothing I could do would encourage Rosamunde to catch my eye. But just before the Major raised her up to his carriage door, she cast back a fleeting look of such sadness that it was all I could do to keep from pushing my way to her side.

That evening, I trudged back to my village feeling unworthy and miserable. There, in the shifting shadows of the bougainvillea, Parizade was waiting to draw the sting from my pain with the sweet balm of her body. It crossed my mind that she had been sent for. Whether she had or not, I was glad of her company. She stayed until it was time for me to step back into chill reality.

Back to the coast of England.

Back to Cole Bay.

Whenever I returned to that rainblasted pier, I wondered what it was that kept me coming home at all. Right through that appalling winter, when the seashore silted up with dirty snow and pensioners froze to death in their flats, when angry scraps of cloud glanced across the clifftops, and seafront shops boarded their windows against the hammering of the wind and the ice-green sea, I remained in my bedroom, marking my brother's position. The flag he had given me was now flanked with rows of colour-coded pushpins chronicling his travels. He was working as a courier and making frequent business trips to Thailand, a country I still preferred to think of as Siam. A letter arrived from him every Friday morning. He wrote of glittering temples and floating markets, saffrongarbed monks, elephants and water buffaloes, women frying trays of squid by the side of the road, noise, squalor, life. I left the pages open on the dining room table for Pauline to read. She treated them as if they were infected, leaning forward to verify Sean's handwriting and turning them over with the tips of her fingers. She never commented on his adventures.

The Christmas decorations came down from a biscuit tin stored in the attic, the tree was tied with musty garlands, the minty ends of paper chains were licked, the tissue bells, so knackered that their metal fastening clips had snapped off, were hung within scorching distance of the front-room fireplace, then everything went back upstairs. Janine came around to finish off the dates, nuts and candied orange slices. She only stopped eating after a chocolate tree ornament left over from the previous Christmas made her sick.

The new year set out in subzero temperatures that slowed life down. Daylight barely entered the house. Pauline hoovered round Bob's legs and Bob took the dog on a lot of unnecessary walks that detoured past Shepherd Neame pubs. Janine sat in our kitchen and sniffled. She had formed an alliance with my mother that involved cataloguing complaints about men, individually and as a breed. The only sound of happiness in our house came from the tinny audience laughter of television shows, not a human sound at all, more like the drag of pebbles in the tide.

As usual, the pupils from my school passed their winter break standing around in bus shelters looking hard. And I returned to the end of the pier, to tumble back into a world of my own making, safe in the knowledge that no-one from Cole Bay could touch me there. I knew it was a life I could have no other way. In Calabash my stifled imagination ran riot, and all the things that were denied to me in the real world were available. I could breathe. I could laugh. My company was sought. My ideas were considered. My opinions were appreciated. In the royal court and the village streets I was treated with honour and honesty. Yet still the question lingered – was it entirely imagined or somehow real? And if it was imagined, why couldn't I access it from anywhere else? I always arrived back in Cole Bay feeling drained of life and energy. Nothing in the real world held any importance for me. I had no money, no job, and no ambitions save to return as soon as possible to the world where my fantasies were made flesh.

Gradually I learned that there were visiting rules. I could only be guaranteed of reaching Calabash at certain times – just before sunset was easily the best – and it did not seem possible to cross on dry, sunny days when the sea was flat, or when there were too many other people about. Also, it was easier to make the transition if I was in a state of agitation, although the process usually left me with a churning stomach. After my earliest arrivals at the harbour, my reappearances caused no further disruption to the city's well-ordered life, and the locals welcomed me with the same casual accord with which they greeted the gull-blown fishing boats returning from deep water with full holds.

My life was not schizophrenic, because the real world ceased to matter much at all. My mind became criss-crossed with chunks of half-remembered myth and fairytale, from a timeless land that, in my darkest days, I supposed I had cobbled together out of storybooks, to make up for the fact that I would never have any genuine adventures.

I wonder now how on earth I could have failed to see so much.

CHAPTER TWENTY-FOUR

Midnight in the Burial Vault

1971. The year London stopped swinging and John Lennon told us that the dream was over. The utopian reveries of hippies drifted off in an aromatic haze. The first British soldier was killed in Ulster, gunned down in a Belfast street. The underground revolution withered away from lack of interest, and Pauline discovered fresh cause for complaint in the national changeover to decimal currency. Looking back, it seems that the commercialisation of the planet began there. As the tunnel of time opened out into a broader vision, the lunatic optimism of the Sixties simply became a nose thumbed to postwar poverty, not a beginning at all but a final desperate fling.

If things were bad before that date, they really went downhill fast in its wake.

In February I began to look for work, but the only jobs available were the kind that could be taught to moderately bright chimpanzees. I managed a month sweeping up in a butcher's shop until I could no longer stand the smell of offal. My job hosing fish guts from the floors of MacFisheries' sheds lasted until I caught a chest cold and the doctor forbade me from working in a place which required me to spend half the day soaked in cold water. I recovered to pass the next six weeks stacking shelves in Cole Bay's first supermarket, but quit after my former classmates began coming in for the specific purpose of shoplifting in front of me, and while there was a certain level of satisfaction to be gained from building towers out of boxes of Daz, it wasn't a cornerstone on which to construct a career.

Back on the esplanade, Malcolm Slattery swapped his chopper for a motorbike with a tiny tank and extended front forks, like the one in *Easy Rider*. He still cruised patiently by, watching and waiting for my reappearance, the weaselly Laurence hiding around corners, acting as his spy. I cut new paths through the back alleys of the town, where my detractors would not find me. I began to believe that I had no friends, only friendly enemies.

But in Calabash . . .

'I think I've found a way,' the doctor informed me at last. 'These plans; there are tunnels.' He unrolled a vast crack-backed map across his work table while Menavino secured the top with pins. 'A bit of a problem, though. I have no idea which way up this is. There are no compass points . . .'

'Here, let me.' I pulled a stool up to the table and examined the chaotic mass of broken lines. 'I'm good at this sort of thing.'

The burial chambers were easy to locate, but the cartographer's use of scale was haphazard, and it was hard to tell if any of the passages to the sarcophagus rooms were intended for human use, or whether they were merely sluice channels. 'Why would there be tunnels?'

'The chambers are not permanently sealed because decorative work continues on them long after the body arrives, and our artisans need access gates. Death can be sudden, but such chambers as these are the labour of lifetimes.'

'And the workers continue to complete the burial vaults after they are filled?'

'Sometimes for years.'

'How do they get back inside?'

'With a set of special keys. Like so.'

Menavino stepped forward and gave a broad grin. Digging into his tunic, he produced several twisted snakes of gold with a magician's flourish.

'We have from midnight until two hours beyond it. Only at this time are the gates accessible. Some kind of safety mechanism is built into the locks. We must return before the keys are missed,' explained the doctor, tugging on his jacket. 'Any later, and Menavino's head will roll. You say you understand the map?'

'I think so.'

'Then let's go.'

The entrance to the chambers was a diagonal door embedded in the hard-packed sand. Menavino set his oil-lamp on the ground and worked the first lock. The door – the first of three – pushed inward to a set of dry stone steps. We resealed it behind us as we moved forward in the gloom. The air was dusty and oppressive, but cleared and cooled with the passing of the third door, whereupon we found ourselves in the first of a series of small stone vaults. Our inexperience with the intricacies of the door locks meant that they took a considerable amount of time to open, and it felt as though over an hour had passed before we managed to reach the first chamber.

I directed Menavino's lamp over the map and pointed. 'We are here now. Which chamber belongs to Eliya?'

'There are many rooms divided off from the central passageway,' said the doctor. 'I have never been down here. The only ones who are allowed to visit the chambers of the dead apart from the artisans are blood relatives. I do believe, however, that the males and the females of the royal line are kept on separate sides of the compound.'

I studied the map again, trying to remember what I had read about such burial chambers. 'In that case the women are most likely to be buried to the left, in correspondence with the moon. The men will be on the right. They'll be arranged by generations, but more importantly by social standing. As the Sultan's wife, Eliya was of high rank, and should be one of the first we encounter.'

Eliya's final resting place proved to be the chamber immediately connected to the one in which we were standing. Our lamp revealed walls of intricately patterned gold-leaf, and pictorial mosaics that chronicled the lives of those who had passed over. There were very few artifacts to be seen scattered around. In the centre of the chamber was an oblong box with thick clay sides and an open top.

'Lower the light.'

Menavino refused to come closer to the coffin, so I took the lamp from his trembling hands and set it on the edge of the wall. The flickering light illuminated the box, revealing a small dried body clad in bright woven robes, brown skin stretched tightly across a skull that still displayed a luxuriant head of brown hair. Her eyelids were sewn shut with gold thread, and her lips had shrunk back to reveal rows of perfect tiny teeth set in leathery gums. Her head was resting on a deep pillow of saffron velvet. It was, in its way, a beautiful corpse, its lack of ostentation imbuing it with an air of peaceful dignity.

'My lady,' said Trebunculus softly, bowing his head. 'Oh,

my poor lady.' He raised his sad eyes to mine. 'I think I cannot bring myself to touch her.'

'Perhaps we won't have to.' I picked up the lamp and lowered it over the side of the coffin, carefully studying everything I saw. A few personal items had been included beside Eliya's body: some tortoiseshell combs, a tapestry footstool, the octagonal onyx table topped with carnelians. These gemstones were identical in size and colour to the jewel that Rosamunde had pressed into my hand. Laid at the corpse's tiny feet were some gold-embroidered slippers, an oval mirror, and some kind of stringed musical instrument. I thought about Eliya's death, her poisoned agonies mistaken for birth pains, and my mind began to form an idea.

'Doctor.' I raised the lamp out of the sarcophagus and looked for a place to set it safely. 'Who chose the items that would be buried alongside Eliya? Doctor?' But the doctor was not by my side. Hearing a sudden scuff of boots, I looked about and saw Menavino being dragged off by a pair of shadowy figures. In my surprise, I dropped the lamp on the ground, extinguishing its flame. Before I could speak, a broad hand clamped itself over my mouth and an arm locked itself around my waist, hauling me backwards out of the chamber.

We were taken back through the gates and released into a tall grey room, cool and windowless, illuminated by high balsam-burners, where we were lightly chained. This was General Bassa's interrogation quarters, and the General himself was waiting for us there. His corpulent form was constricted within the crimson work tunic of his regiment. He was leaning over a disgruntled leopard in a cage and dangling pieces of goatsmeat through the bars.

'I don't know what to do with you, Trebunculus,' he said. 'You're always creeping about, poking your nose in where it doesn't belong. This time you've gone too far.' The doctor, Menavino and I were arranged against the far wall of the room. The doors were guarded by palace Nubians, presumably the same ones who had removed us from the burial vault.

The General was, it was said, prone to fits of melancholy. You never knew when one would come. He left the leopard cage in the corner and paced across the floor, then stopped suddenly and leaned forward until his forehead touched the wall, looking for all the world as though someone had left a cello lying out of its case.

'What to do, what to do.' He pushed himself upright and swivelled his beady eyes in the doctor's direction. 'You have commited a treasonous offence. I've a mind to have you and your meddlesome friend garrotted, and have your heads mounted on sticks above the garrison where your eyes can be pecked out by the royal lyre-birds.'

'I do not think such an action would be appreciated by the Sultan, General.' The Lord Chancellor was standing in the doorway. Bassa gave an angry shrug of the shoulders and strutted back to his feeding plate. He tore off a piece of meat and gave it a desultory flick into the cage.

'I am sorry, Doctor,' Peason apologised, stepping forward. 'The military mind. Our General sees no subtleties in the lexicon of courtly intrigue.' He turned to the leader of the Sultan's army. 'I understand that nothing was touched. There was no desecration, merely trespass.' Behind him scuttled a small hunched figure, running through the shadows as quickly as a crab. I knew then that Scammer, the Lord Chancellor's spy, had informed his master of our night escapade. But how had General Bassa's men known about us?

'Bah! I recognise the laws of the land, Peason, and I see when they are being trampled by those who do not accord us with honour.' The leopard pressed its muzzle against the cage and licked its lips, waiting for another tidbit. The General tore off a strip of dripping meat and dangled it through the bars. 'Entering the burial crypt is a sacrilegious act.'

The Lord Chancellor swept past us with a crack of his cloak. 'Think, General. The kingdom is so close to unity once more. The Princess Rosamunde is now my daughter-in-law. Maximus has been welcomed into the royal family with open arms. Your army is to be reunited with our state. No harm has been done, and no-one needs to know. We cannot allow a small – infringement – such as this to endanger all we have worked for.'

'Not to punish these three would make a mockery of our laws. I must demand some kind of reparation. What were they doing in there?'

'How did you know we were in the chamber?' I countered. The doctor cast a fearful look at me for speaking out.

'Keep your silence, *ajnabee*, unless I address you directly,' barked the General. 'If you want to keep your head.'

'Let him speak, General.' The Lord Chancellor smiled wanly at me in what I took to be encouragement.

'We meant no disrespect, General. The Sultan himself asked the doctor to teach me the ways of your kingdom, and I explained that I could not possibly learn more without seeing the honour you accorded your dead. The highest civilisations are marked by the manner in which they respect their ancestors.'

General Bassa looked at his pacing leopard, then back at me. 'Hmm. Is this true, Doctor?'

'Most certainly,' said Trebunculus, following my lead. 'It was necessary for us to visit the burial vaults in order to fully explain our history to the boy. If you want him to bring us scientific advancement, he must be entirely cognizant of our ways. Science, dear General, nothing further can be achieved without it. The boy will yet prove himself useful.'

'And just what can we expect him to do?'

'He will do anything we want, won't you, Kay? He doesn't want to cause any trouble.' The doctor smiled nervously at me.

'I will certainly do whatever is within my power,' I said.

'Then you must fulfil the promise you made to the Lord Chancellor.' The General's smile revealed a mosaic of pointed yellow teeth. 'Bring us something from your world. Something that will grant our army scientific superiority.'

'And you will release us without a word to the Sultan?' asked Trebunculus.

General Bassa returned to his leopard cage and watched the animal sniffing the air, then tipped the last of the meat in, flecking the walls with blood. 'I will release you, but the Sultan must be informed of your actions.'

'He trusts me,' said the doctor. 'I have cared for his family since I was little more than an apprentice. I live for the honour of his patronage. It is my whole world. If he should choose to banish me . . .'

'Then you must accept your punishment. It is the law of the land.'

The Lord Chancellor shook his head sadly. 'General Bassa is right. The Sultan must be told. He alone can decide your fate, Doctor. In this matter even my hands are stayed.'

'But you can speak to him. Explain that I only act for the kingdom's good, explain that I mean no harm.'

'Indeed I shall, Doctor, you may take no fear in that. But remember that many a kingdom's downfall has been caused by a subject who meant no harm. Have your men release these chains, General.' Septimus Peason approached, studying my face with his strange yellow eyes. 'And as for the *ajnabee*.' His nostrils flared with faint distaste. Gone was the respect he had accorded me at our earlier meeting. 'As the General said, there must be something given in return. I think now the *ajnabee* will bring us the science he promised.'

CHAPTER TWENTY-FIVE

Winter's Angel

Three things preoccupied my mind: how I could trick General Bassa, what I had seen in the burial vault, and how I would ever be with Rosamunde again. But once I had returned to Cole Bay, life there found new ways of turning aside my intentions.

Cole Bay General Hospital never tried to hide the fact that it dealt with pain and loss on a daily basis, and brooked no nonsense from its mostly elderly patients, who were angered or at least bewildered by their sudden change in fortune. The watchwords of its operational procedure were hygiene and efficiency. The matrons had no time for mollycoddling. The doctors were blunt and precise. They told our next-door neighbour Mr Harrington that he was going to die, and if he hadn't lost the will to live before he'd attended the appointment, he certainly had by the time he caught the bus home. Any man who laid his best suit and tie on his bed before dying had to be fairly sure of his expiry timetable.

I was more familiar with the chest X-ray department than most of the doctors. I'd passed many dismal hours slumped in the waiting room, which comprised a curtained section of corridor, three green metal cubicles and a folded stack of floral open-backed shifts, their cotton thin with overwashing. Melancholy old ladies in NHS wheelchairs sat with their hands pressed against grey foreheads. Others misunderstood instructions, anxiously asking passing strangers about travel arrangements, or forgot their dates of birth when questioned by orderlies, or simply wandered off after being told to stay put, like disobedient children, then reappeared to find that they had missed their turn. I was always the youngest person there, cajoled by nurses who were more used to loudly lip-synching their requests to the terminally confused than dealing with teenagers.

After posing for my X-ray ('Shoulders against the machine, chin touching the top, don't breathe in until I give the word'), I took some grapes to Miss Ruth in the Sir Humphry Davy Women's Ward, and found her in a bed with no visitors at the far end of a green and white room that smelled of disinfectant. She had lost weight, and her wispy hair stuck out from her skull in an anaemic auriole. A saline drip hung from her skinny left arm. I had expected to find her surrounded by stacks of books, but there was only a dog-eared *Woman's Realm* on her bedside table. She had, rather pathetically, pinned a cameo brooch to her bedjacket.

'I told myself I wouldn't scold you.' Even her voice had shrunk. 'But I do wish you hadn't left school, Kay.'

'Haven't you had any visitors?' I asked, noticing the lack of 'Get Well' cards.

'Some dreadful woman from the social services dropped by, full of the joys of spring. She offered me a visit from the Unitarians. I feigned sleep. Virtually had to pass into a coma before she left. But you – look at you.' She raised a feeble hand and prodded me. 'Wasting your talents, it's shameful. Working in a supermarket.'

'How did you hear about that?'

'Oh, the old lady network.' She smiled up from her pillow. 'Better than Russian spies. Tell me something, Kay, have you really so little faith in the world?'

I could not bring myself to answer.

She watched me. 'You feel – disconnected – from other people, don't you.'

'Nobody else sees how horrible everything is here. They don't seem to mind.'

'Oh, you'd be surprised. Perhaps you need to change your point of view.'

'School didn't let me do anything.'

'Nor does shelf-stacking.'

'It was just a job,' I said defensively. 'I don't want to end up like my mum and dad. They act like their lives are over. They just watch from the edges and complain all the time. Once they must have been free to do whatever they liked, but they didn't do it. Now they can't, or won't. Our biology teacher said animals only grow old in captivity.'

'Don't be so hard on them. They love you.'

'I'm already starting to think like them. My brother left while he still could.'

'Oh, Kay. It's not as simple as going or staying.' She turned her head aside to the window. 'My Lord, it looks so cold out there. Once when I was a child, I remember the sea froze solid. Frosty white peaks, like the icing on a cake, lapped by a cold green sea. I wanted to walk on it, but wasn't allowed. Little girls weren't allowed to do anything in those days. "Children should be seen and not heard", my mother's favourite motto. Sundays were the worst.'

'Didn't you ever want to leave?'

Calabash

'It wasn't so easy in those days. It was hard for a girl to travel alone. One needed independent means, and a certain confidence that came from having money. My father died, my mother became bedridden. She needed to be cared for. I wanted to run round the house making such a noise, just to make up for all those years passed in silence, but I didn't. I had to rely on my books to take me away. By the time she died, I no longer wanted to make a noise.'

'Can I get you anything?'

'Mm. A new heart. The one I have is worn out, apparently. What are we going to do about you? Help me up.' I propped pillows behind her narrow back. 'You have to be practical about this, Kay. People who don't grow up get left behind. You don't stand still in the world, you know, you go very gently backwards. Sometimes so gently that you don't notice it happening until it's too late. You must do something, use what you have. Imagination is both a gift and a curse. You say your head is filled with fantasies. Why not try to write a book about them? Publishers long to discover talent at an early age. How I'd love to take credit for discovering you.'

I felt then that if I had let anyone down it was her, a sick old woman I barely knew. I wanted to tell her about the notebooks I filled, my one precious link between Cole Bay and Calabash. But I didn't. Instead I allowed silence to grow between us. Embarrassed by my failure of nerve, I tore a grape from its stem and ate it. It had no taste at all. 'Have they said when you can go home?'

If she heard my question, she chose to ignore it. 'I miss my books. They're the only things that really mean anything to me. Belongings become so necessary when you live alone. I have some volumes I know you'd especially appreciate, Kay. By an old pupil of mine.' She gave a sharp little nod. 'They shall be yours. They just sit on my shelves unread. Books should never go unread. I never shared my knowledge enough.'

'Are you sure there isn't anything I can get for you?'

'You could be an angel. Go to my flat and bring me my big bag. There's something in it I'll be needing now. I don't want the social services poking about. The front door key is in there somewhere.' She pointed to her locker.

Miss Ruth lived on the first floor of a purpose-built Edwardian block, at what was considered to be the genteel end of Cole Bay. The streets here had less litter and were more residential. There were fewer doorbells, chip shops and poster sites. Her apartment was dark and very still. All the rooms were lined with books, even the toilet. The lounge smelled of lavender polish, and felt as if nothing had been disturbed in years. Its broad bay window overlooked the esplanade and the beach. I looked through the salt-rimed glass and wondered how she could live so close to the edge of the land. It was a constant reminder that across the sea were places she had never visited. The water heaved slowly against the distant pier, dense with cold. In the kitchen, I noticed that the immersion heater was turned off at the timer. Odd, I thought. I went to the fridge and saw that it had been emptied and scrubbed clean. Only tinned food remained in the cupboards. The pedal-bin beneath her sink had been drained and disinfected. I checked the other rooms. The bed was stripped of its linen, the blankets folded into neat stacks on the mattress. I realised then that Miss Ruth did not expect to come back.

I found her bag waiting beside the front door, ready to be collected, and took it to her. She died four days later, of 'complications', a useful medical catch-all that meant nothing. I didn't find out until I called by to see her the following

Saturday, and discovered the bed occupied by someone else. The doctor said she had asked for me, but nobody knew where I lived.

I was wondering what would happen to her beloved books when a terrible thought struck me, and I wished that I had checked the bag I took to her.

'There's something in it I'll be needing now,' she had said. 'Be an angel.' I didn't like the sound of that.

There are things in life you never find out.

I became a Friend of Cole Bay General shortly afterwards, visiting patients without families once a week to read to them. I'd like to think it was purely an act of altruism on my part, but of course it was mainly born of guilt. I wanted to do something more for Miss Ruth. 'Write about your fantasies,' she had suggested. And that was what I decided to do.

CHAPTER TWENTY - SIX

A Means of Communication

'Absolutely not,' bellowed the Sultan. So loud was his cry that the doves that his Master Of Eunuchs had troubled to have painted in every imaginable hue burst into startled flight from their positions along the roof, like a rupturing rainbow. 'It is out of the question. Can you imagine what would happen? We do not want people prying into our lives. There is a very good reason why we have no royal scribes at court.'

'You had them all beheaded,' said his mother, looking up from her tapestry.

'Apart from that. We do not want information falling into the hands of our enemies.'

'But I would be writing about your kingdom from an outsider's point of view,' I pleaded. 'I could create a work that describes all the good things about your reign.'

'For the benefit of whom? For the English, yes? No, I forbid the production of such a volume.' He wagged a thick brown finger at me. 'Do not attempt to appeal to my vanity. Oh, you English. You chronicle, you calibrate, why must you do this? Your measurements steal away the power of dreams.

Such awareness is unnecessary. My mind is set. We shall not speak again of the matter.' He raised his palm in a gesture of cessation. 'Why, even the idea is treasonous.'

It seemed that my own imagination was rebelling against me. In order to write a book, I required access to the imperial palace, and as I considered Calabash a land of my own imagining, I assumed that such access would be automatically granted. But it appeared that this was not the case. The court had forbidden me to use the one tool that might eventually free me from Cole Bay. I was angry, but apparently powerless to argue against the royal decree.

'I have overlooked your act of trespass in the tomb of my lamented wife. I have even granted a pardon to Dr Trebunculus for his part in the desecration of sacred ground.' Although the Sultan could never afford to be seen as a weak leader, he had a soft spot for the doctor, and the news of what had transpired in his burial vaults had not been made public, so he felt able to act with leniency. He was anxious to be seen as an educated man by outsiders, and the Semanticor had explained to him that moderation was considered a sign of cultivated behaviour.

'For this kindly act – this *civilised* act – you should be grovelling at the worms beneath my feet.' The Sultan caught his mother's disapproving eye, and softened. He beckoned to me and placed an avuncular arm around my shoulders. 'But I remember you are young, Kay, and the young are the same in every land. The General is a rigid man, as befits his station. He believes that superfluity breeds slavery. In time you will come to understand the principles of our state.' He gestured to his concubine. 'Carmelia, take our young friend to the ostrich races. See that he enjoys himself and forgets his foolish ideas.'

I realised I had not chosen my time well, making my

request so soon after our pardoning. I could tell that the Sultan was missing his beloved daughter. He wasn't the only one. Rosamunde had been taken away by Maximus, her new husband, and was not expected to return until General Bassa released his officers from their duties at the northern border. In addition, the Sultan's council was sitting today, nervously awaiting the arrival of Bayezit The Grim, an elderly uncle of the Valide Sultan Fathmir of Cordoba, who, it was said, only communicated in Ixarette, the forgotten sign language of the seraglio. A political matter, the doctor had explained vaguely, something to do with the building of a bridge. He had tapped the side of his nose and added mysteriously, '*the dog barks, the caravan moves on.*' None the wiser, I was dismissed with an impatient rattle of bracelets. Despite my privileged status I was still an *ajnabee*, and it was clear that my presence was not desired at court today.

Usually they all seemed so anxious for me to remain in Calabash. More than once, the doctor had suggested that I should give up all ideas of going home, and live here forever. 'What has your world to offer you that we cannot provide?' he asked petulantly, and although I could not furnish him with a satisfactory answer, I was reluctant to close the door to my other life completely.

Carmelia appeared at my side. 'Come to the races, Kay, there are not only ostriches but ichneumons and sables, and a dancing bear.' She slipped her hand in mine, but I pulled free.

'I'm going to take a walk,' I told her.

'But you will miss the start of the gala.'

'Oh, I'm sure there'll be others. There always are.'

I stalked away rudely and left them staring after me. Soon the palace was far behind. Ahead, my village lay entranced in brilliant sunlight. To the left was the harbour, where the red and blue sails of the fishing boats clicked back and forth at the dock. On my right were the fields and the hillside, goats bleating over clanking bells, the village where Dr Trebunculus lived.

As I watched, a cloud lifted free of the sun and light raced across the woodland beyond, illuminating something angular and grey that squatted brokenly between the pines and cypresses. It looked like the remains of a temple. Yet why had I never seen it before? I realised that although I had looked down on it from the Tower of Trezibaba, it had remained hidden beneath the cover of the foliage. Intrigued, I set off in the direction of the wood. There, beyond the cultivated trees of cherry, walnut, olive, lemon and apricot, the wild black-pines grew within a misty bed of succulent ferns.

As I reached the shaded edge of the wood, I spotted the fallen shaft of a corinthian column protruding from the undergrowth. I stepped from the sunlight of the meadow into the cool, loamy air, and found myself standing between the ruined peristyles of a temple. A chunk of its dentil, seven or eight feet in length, lay half-buried at my feet, carved stone acanthus leaves blending with the pinnate blades of the ground foliage.

I saw now that I was within the ruins of not one temple but a dozen or more. Their fractured columns had fallen like shafts of solid sunlight between the verticals of trees. An air of great melancholy saturated the place, as if something terrible had happened there, and even nature was determined to cover it.

I walked through the weed-cracked naos of a temple floor, studying the mosaics beneath my feet. The style of architecture was distinctly different to that of Calabash; the remnants of the buildings were undoubtedly Greek. What, I asked myself, were they doing here? The slow curling cry of a peewit caused me to look up. I glimpsed the sky in the tops of the trees. The sole of my sandal came down on a smooth surface. I stepped back and searched the floor, and a shiny blue object caught my eye. I bent down to dig around its edges, wiping aside the dirt and dead leaves, and found myself looking at some scraps of paper from an old school exercise book. Only the inner parts were intact. The edges furthest from the staples had been burned away. I tipped the shadows from it and read from one piece.

Lee Hill Grammar School For Boys South Do

On the back, on what would have been the inside cover, was half of a carefully pencilled oblong.

This homework book is the property of Simon Jonathan Saun

An English name. It made no sense. How could an English boy have been here before me? How could I have shared my dream kingdom with someone else? I pushed the leaves aside with my shoe, and found one other trace of the schoolboy's presence, a chewed stub of pencil.

The ferns nearby exploded in an animal scuffle. Unnerved, I jumped back, my heart pounding. I threw down the remaining pieces of the book, but stuffed the part I had read into my pocket with the pencil, then ran hopping over the ferns and nettles, out of the wood, back into sunlight.

I walked on until I reached the harbour. My discovery had unsettled me. This land was mine. To share it with a stranger from my own world would be to spoil it. I wondered what the doctor would make of my find, but decided not to risk telling anyone else, for fear of sparking something harmful, something unstoppable. But even now the gentle torpor of Calabash worked its wonders once more, and calmness returned as I reached a halt beside the jetty.

A fisherman with a face like a bag of nuts cheerfully broke from net-mending to offer me a bottle of wine. Here, among the lopsided baskets of fish, I seated myself on a ledge of warm stone and dangled my feet over the water. I pulled the stopper from the bottle and drank, gazing out into the sparkling azure ocean. I would find a way to solve the mystery later.

When the wine bottle was empty, I took the pieces of exercise book that concerned its owner's identity from my pocket and turned them over, scribbling my own name and address on the back with the stub of pencil. I twined the paper into a tube and poked it into the bottle, which I resealed with the stopper. Rising unsteadily to my feet, I threw the bottle as far as I could. If another schoolboy had managed to find his way here from England, what were the chances that a message in a bottle could make it home across the sea?

CHAPTER TWENTY-SEVEN

The Desire to Believe

But of course there was no sign of it in the churning grey seas at the base of the pier. This time, I told myself, I would be rational about Calabash. I was back on the fishing platform, standing precariously near the edge, when I realised that the proof was in my pocket. I felt inside my jacket and my fingers closed around the remaining scrap of the exercise book. My excitement was short-lived, however, when I turned it between my fingers and saw that it provided no proof. It looked like a piece of litter torn from an item you could find in any stationers. What else could I bring back from Calabash to prove its existence? A piece of fruit, a rock, the jewel that Rosamunde had given me? There would always be reasons for not believing. The gemstone was safer in my villa. I had not brought it back for fear that it might turn into a pebble.

I knew then that I could not go on without some kind of an answer. I could not return to Calabash until I was prepared to take some action on the part of its inhabitants, and I was heading for a similar situation in Cole Bay. Somehow, I was screwing up in two different worlds at once. It was time to do something, to take a bigger step. I would have to involve someone else. Tell someone the truth, perhaps try to take them there from here. But who? Sean was still away. Danny was visiting friends in London. Dudley Salterton was a walking safety hazard and would never make it. Who else was there?

I decided that it would have to be Julia. This, I saw, had an advantage. She was so pragmatic, so grounded, I felt that if I could just get her to believe in me, it must be true. Perhaps we would be able to travel to Calabash together. I hadn't seen enough of Julia lately. She had recently embarked upon a punitive diet that was making her tense and bad-tempered, and had cancelled our last planned trip to the cinema. I called her as soon as I left the pier.

At first she refused to meet me. Finally we agreed to take a trip to the Roxy, on the condition that I paid for both of us. The film was *Countess Dracula*, which starred Ingrid Pitt as the savage siren Countess Bathory, and was only very loosely based on historical facts, being aimed at pubescent males who saw their teachers as fanciable older women. I noticed with some satisfaction that several of my old classmates were seated near the front. I drew an odd comfort from the fact that, though they had stayed on at school to better themselves, they still enjoyed trashy movies. Personally, I was always disappointed by the lack of historical documentation in such films, and it was a mark of my immaturity that I never got used to the feeling.

Julia had lost loads of weight but was still wearing her old clothes, so she looked like someone who had been attacked with a shrinking ray. Deprived of any calorific pastime she was patently bored, and talked all the way through the film, about her biology exam, about a classmate who was pregnant, anything but the Countess Bathory. This time, though, I was determined not to get annoyed. After the film I suggested a walk on the pier. 'But it's bucketing down,' she complained. 'And I told Mum I'd be back for dinner.' As we had arrived late at the cinema, I had not yet found an opportunity to raise the subject closest to my heart. I decided that it was now or never.

'This won't take long, I promise. There's something I want you to see.'

'I know what's down there, Kay. A crappy ghost train, a pub, some dodgems and a helter skelter with mats that shed on you.'

'This is something new. Suppose I told you that I'd made a discovery. Something right at the end of the pier that nobody else knows is there.'

'Give over, there's nothing to see. I've been there a million times.' But still she followed me through the turnstile, her high heels skidding on the wet planks. It was raining hard by the time we reached the ghost train. 'Everything's closed,' she said anxiously. 'It'll be dark soon.'

'Listen to me, Julia, you know we talked about where we would go if we could leave here? If I told you I'd found a place, would you believe me?'

'Where?'

'Somewhere you can only reach – from there.' I pointed down at the chained-off fishing platform. The clouded sea was swelling up through the lower grille, lifting the strands of mildew-coloured seaweed that clung to the pylons.

'I'm not going down there. It's dangerous, look at the signs. You must be out of your mind.'

'You have to trust me. No harm will come to you, Julia, I promise. I'll look after you. Have a little faith.' I held out my hand.

'Really, Kay.' She was serious now. 'This is crazy. There's nothing down there.'

'You're wrong. You can reach a place. It's safe, I've done it loads of times, come on.'

Before she had time to consider the matter further I seized her hand and pulled her down behind me. 'It's fine if you keep hold of the rail.'

We had nearly reached the bottom when she hesitated. 'I can't, Kay. My heels—' She looked down at the half-submerged grating.

'Give me your shoes. Just do this one thing for me, Julia, and I'll never ask you to do anything like this again.' She looked at me, then reluctantly removed her shoes and clasped them in one hand. The rain-laden wind had moulded her shirt to her breasts. Suddenly self-conscious of her body, she pulled her coat across her chest with her free hand.

'It's okay, I've got you.' I locked her fingers with mine. 'Now, you have to look over there, right in the corner.'

'I can't see anything,' she wailed, peering nervously forward. 'I don't know what you want me to see.' I realised with a shock that she was scared of me, and that I was forcing her forward to the edge of the platform as the sea rolled around us.

'Let me go, Kay, there's nothing there!' She was close to tears.

'But you must be able to see it!' I shouted above the rising wind. Conditions were perfect. I could always get to Calabash on days like this. I stared into the deep green gloom but saw nothing. The struts of the pier reminded me of the old pine forest where I had found the ruined temples. I became aware of Julia's body, so close to mine that we were almost touching. Her hip brushed against the top of my leg. I gazed down into the turbulent darkness as it lifted and dropped around us, and willed our passing over into light. We would tumble through the maelstrom together, and emerge in a dazzling new world. I tried to feel the familiar ripples of nausea I experienced when the journey began. I squeezed my eyes shut and visualised the sparkling sea, the warm stone harbour.

But nothing was happening.

A heavy swell rose up over our feet, rocking the platform. Julia screamed. I saw now that I was holding her on the very edge, gripping her hand so tightly that it was white to her wrist, and that the next wave would tip us both into the icy water.

'Let me go, Kay!'

Coming to my senses, I allowed her to drag us back. She was sobbing and stumbling towards the staircase, trying to wriggle free of my hand.

'I'm sorry, Julia, I didn't mean to—'

'Get away from me!'

She broke free and fell hard against the steps, cutting her hand. She scrambled about on all fours, tearing the knees of her tights, dropping a shoe. It bounced on a lower step and fell into the water.

'Please, just let me explain.' I followed her.

'Keep away!' she screamed, ducking under the chain. I tried to grab her but she was too quick for me.

'I just wanted you to see what I've seen,' I shouted. 'I wanted you to come with me!'

I watched her sobbing and hobbling off across the rain-lashed walkway between the rides, and suddenly I knew I had destroyed my truest friendship, and had perhaps lost something else, something far more precious than a friend.

CHAPTER TWENTY-EIGHT

The Fear of Inheritance

I was sure that Calabash existed, so why had it not appeared? Because I had tried to bring somebody across with me? Paradoxically, I also knew that it could not exist because life there was exactly what I wished for.

So many doubts surfaced. I had frightened Julia into thinking that I was trying to kill her. From that time on she refused to take my calls; her mother always answered the telephone. Eventually she told me not to ring anymore. And the Sultan had refused my request – how could that be if he was a figment of my imagination? Could my mind no longer be obeying me? I could not now return to Calabash as a neutral bystander, but was expected to aid General Bassa in his search for 'scientific superiority'. Our discovery in the burial vaults had forced me to become a partisan. The good faith that had existed between myself and the Sultan had been compromised. If it had not been for the diplomacy of the Lord Chancellor, we could have ended with our heads on poles. Perhaps it was lucky that Scammer acted as his secret eyes and ears . . .

And there, right there, I knew that something was wrong,

that a flaw existed in what I knew, some anomaly which would allow me to gain a foothold in solving the mystery of my imagination.

Dudley Salterton always told me that adolescence was a time of confusion. He got that part right. Still, I had continued to chronicle my alternative life in the notebooks I kept behind the wardrobe, including my discovery that a stranger had set foot in the kingdom, my tentative explanation of the circumstances of Eliya's death, and my abortive attempt to take someone else across the divide. Events in Calabash were forcing me to take action. Each night I tried to work things out in the pages of my notes, and felt that I was growing closer to an answer. But before I had time to make any sense of these developments, real life intervened once more.

As another month passed without work, I was forced to join Cole Bay's expanding dole queue. Although it had reached the top of my priority list, moving out of my parents' house was not an available option, because even in a half-derelict coastal town, property rent was too high for my meagre pocket. March was the coldest month I could ever remember, but the atmosphere in our house was chillier than any sleet-swept seafront. My mother had taken to addressing me through a medium, either Bob or Janine, and only spoke when circumstances demanded a practical reply. Requests for dirty laundry were placed with mealtime orders, and all casual banter was bypassed. Bob mooched about with his hands thrust deep in his pockets, staring from unfrosted patches of the lounge windows, whistling tunelessly and jingling the change in his pockets before offering to walk the dog. He missed talking to Sean about arterial roads. He was a mine of information about the fastest way to drive from Caterham, where his sister lived, to Orpington, where her daughter-in-law had moved to, and assumed that because Sean was a courier he shared an enthusiasm for the navigational possibilities of 'B' roads. I could not drive and was therefore impossible to engage in such conversations. Fresh wrappers from pink hotel soap piled up in the bathroom wastepaper bin as Bob spent more time with Doreen and her minibars.

On the last Saturday of the month I spent the afternoon at the Roxy, sitting through an excruciatingly unfunny Carry On film. As I twisted my key in the lock of number 14 an uneasy feeling filled the pit of my stomach. Like a dog, I could always sense when a storm was brewing. Or perhaps I could simply smell something burning.

She had been in my bedroom. The wardrobe was moved from its usual position, and my Calabash notebooks and all my Mesopotamia plans were gone. I found Pauline in the garden with her cardigan pulled about her narrow shoulders, standing over a metal wastepaper basket, watching the low blue flames.

'What are you doing?' I asked, trying to sound reasonable, already aware of the answer.

'This is the problem, this,' she said, stabbing into the flames with a poker. 'All this nonsense. Stuffing your head with rubbish, fairytales and what have you. Dancing girls and flying machines. It's my own fault. I let you read too many books when you were young. Now all of – this – won't go away.'

'What did you want to do that for?' I shouted.

'This is why you couldn't study, spoiling your brain with this tripe. Bloody fantasyland, all of it.'

'You've no right to touch my stuff.'

'It's for your own good.'

'They're just stories! They can't hurt you.'

'Can't they?' she shouted back, her sallow face contorting above the flames. 'Ask your father. Ask him!'

'Bob doesn't mind me—'

'Not *him*,' she spat, ramming the last of my notebooks into the thin fire.

'I don't care. It's all in my head, I can write it out again.'

'Not under this roof you bloody won't,' she said, and that was the end of it.

I waited until she had gone in, then ran back to the make-shift brazier and tried to salvage some pages from the ashes, but she had been thorough. My hard work was gone, all of it. Defeated, I went back into the house and pretended to watch television with Bob, who was slumped in front of a pro-gramme about baboons, wisely keeping his head down. *Not him*, she'd said. Not him. My real father.

'I was wondering when that would come up,' said Bob in answer to my question. He thought for a slow minute, then sighed. 'I can show you, perhaps that's the easiest way.'

We went out to the car and drove in silence for five miles or so, beyond the edge of town. Bob turned into a sidestreet away from the shore and pulled the Hillman up in front of an ugly Edwardian house with tall narrow windows.

'Your dad was originally from London, but his family moved up north somewhere when the war broke out, and he came down to live with his aunt. Phillip was a clever man by all accounts, too clever for around here. But after they were married your mother didn't want to move, so they stayed on in Cole Bay.' This much I knew already, but there was some-thing bad coming, because Bob wouldn't look at me. 'He wasn't a very practical man, your dad, couldn't change a fuse, she said.' That's funny, I thought, changing a fuse was the one practical thing I remember him doing. I had always thought he was so sensible. Things can get turned upside down when you're very young.

'Your mother had to sort out everything. He had his head

in the clouds. They had some very hard times. Sean was little and you were coming along. She was always finding him positions – a desk job on the council, administration – but he had, well, a breakdown.' Bob looked up as if expecting to see his predecessor at one of the darkened windows. 'Do you understand? He lost his grip. He couldn't stay at home. They put him in there.'

I stared up at the grim slate roof, the tiny attic windows. 'It's horrible. You'd never get better in a place like that.'

'He was none the wiser. Couldn't remember the names of his visitors. They used to give patients a test: name who's on the throne, who's prime minister, what day of the week it is. Ten questions. He couldn't manage them. In a world of his own. It killed her to see that he didn't know who she was. She's frightened, that's all. Scared you'll take after him if you don't do some growing up. You're the dead spit of your father. She sees him in you. You have to understand your mother, she's not – well, she's not a happy woman, the way things have turned out for her. Sean's gone off to God knows where, hardly a card from one week to the next, he won't be told what to do, you're all she has left.'

I had never thought of Pauline like that. I had never imagined that we were the cause of her anger. I thought of something Julia had once said, about bad genes predominating. I pressed up against the railings and tried to see into the shadowed rooms, but all I could see was a reflection of myself staring in, scraps of bright cloud at my back like drifting ghosts. I forced myself to look away. The lawn needed cutting. The building looked abandoned. 'How could she let him stay here?'

'I don't think she had a lot of choice in the matter. He'd become very unstable, a danger to himself. The doctors had him on tablets for years, all sorts of experimental trials, but they didn't really do much for him.'

I suddenly had a terrible thought. 'He's not still here, is he?'

'God, no. When he died, your mother felt you were still too young to properly understand. She meant to tell you, of course. It was never the right time. And you with such a mouth on you.' He exhaled wearily. 'They were going to turn the place into flats but, I don't know, fire regulations.'

'All this time. I wish she had told me.' But she couldn't have, of course. She still felt bad about having him put away. Perhaps she had just married Bob so that we would have a father again.

'Pauline said it was the worst day of her life when she had to sign the papers.' Bob turned back to the car. 'Come on, son, it's getting cold.' He caught my eye across the roof. 'Probably best not to say anything about this.' That was how it always was in our family. We would hold in-depth conversations about proposed motorway routes before we touched on anything remotely personal.

I felt as though I understood my mother a little more, and felt sorry for her. But it hadn't set things right between us.

CHAPTER TWENTY-NINE

Sealing the Door

That process didn't start until a few days later.

I was walking along the esplanade one Sunday evening. The pavements were slick with rain again, and the streetlights had just come on. The Roxy had these special Sunday double-bill matinées when they paired up old films, and they had posters showing for *The King and I* and *South Pacific*. I was just about to pass the entrance when something made me stop, and it was a good job I did because there was my mother coming down the steps, looking up at the sky and tying a plastic rainhood around her hair. I saw at once that her face was streaked with tears. She blew her nose briskly into a Kleenex and stepped out into the rain. I was surprised to think that Pauline's heart was touched by the thought of romances in faraway places, but suddenly I knew that she had sat alone in the dark mouthing the words to all of the songs. I had seen the dusty soundtrack LPs lying under the radiogram, but had never considered that they might belong to her. This kind of behaviour didn't fit the picture she had given me at all. Now the picture began to change, and it altered a little more on the day I finally left home.

I was surprised to find that all my worldly belongings fitted into three cardboard cartons. Surely I had managed to accumulate more than this during my sixteen years on earth? But the books were mostly from the library, and finally had to be returned, the records were borrowed from Sean, and the few remaining maps that hadn't been destroyed fitted into an A2 folder. Also into the boxes went Sean's flagged itinerary, which had not been updated for three weeks. In went the strange tapes of classical music Danny had given me for Christmas to 'broaden my horizons'. In went the cuddlesome gifts Julia had bombarded me with at yuletides and birthdays.

It was Dudley Salterton's booking agent, Mr Cottesloe, who started the ball rolling, just before my seventeenth birthday. A few days after my row with Julia I returned to the end of the pier, planning to cross over into Calabash once more, but something stopped me. It was now April, and the winds of change were in the air. Seagulls rode high above the helter skelter, looking towards the horizon as if waiting for summer to arrive. I secretly watched the shapely Katherine rolling candyfloss around her tub like pink spiderweb, flirting with the boys who hung around the stall. She was more beautiful than ever, but now she seemed aware of it. Her movements were choreographed for her admirers, her disdain for them exaggerated. Cottesloe saw me hanging around from the window of the saloon bar, and knocked on the glass with his signet ring.

'You're Kay, aren't you? Old Dudley's pal? Have you thought about getting yourself a job?' Cottesloe's spectacular stomach stretched his shirt over the top of his trousers like a water-filled balloon, and forced him to perch on his stool with his legs apart. He ordered me a bitter without asking me what I wanted.

'Here, is he old enough?' asked the barmaid.

'Of course he is, Doris, give over, he's left school. You have, haven't you?'

'Yes. I've only been able to find short-term work, though.'

'That's the bloody trouble with seaside towns, everything's built around the season. Have you seen Dudley today?'

'He's gone up to London to buy a new lip for Barnacle Bill.'

'Not before time. You can't understand a bloody word that dummy says. I'll get to the point. It pains me to see a lad hanging around in all sorts, doing nothing. You know I own the Las Vegas arcade on the front?'

To be honest, it had never crossed my mind that such places were privately owned. I had assumed they all belonged to Cole Bay council, which was legendarily corrupt.

'No,' I replied.

'You probably think I'm loaded. Well, I'm not. The rates are an arm and a bloody leg, the place is empty for half the year and my last manager buggered off with a month's takings in his suitcase. They'd like to close me down, the council, they say it lowers the tone of the esplanade, but it could make money, Kay, given a bit of effort from someone with half a brain. I'm too busy, fingers in too many pies. Do you think you have half a brain?'

'I'm not very good at maths,' I admitted, trying to be honest.

'I'm not looking for a mathematician. The bank tots up the pounds, shillings and pence – or should I say the new pee. It's more a matter of making sure the machines work and getting the punters in. It's not rocket science, lad, just common sense. If I can get this one turning a decent profit, I'll open another. It's worth doing just to watch our lady mayoress's face drop a foot. She wants to tear down the Kursaal and put in a bowling green, so she can have coachloads of sour-faced old biddies filling their thermos flasks at her brother-in-law's tearooms. Now, I suppose you want to know about money. The wages aren't fantastic, but they're commensurate.' He liked the sound of the word, even if he wasn't entirely sure what it meant. 'Yes, commensurate.'

Commensurate with watching bored teenagers trying to tilt the Penny Falls machine so that it paid up, I thought. And before I knew it, I'd somehow agreed to take the job, and Cottesloe was ordering two more pints from Doris.

The previous manager of the Las Vegas had rented rooms above the arcade. The windows were grey from the salt sea air, their frames rotting with damp, but the place was still available and very cheap. This, I later discovered, was because the landlady's husband had died in the lounge two years earlier, and she was uncomfortable with the idea of turning a profit on rooms that had hosted a wake for a loved one.

'I suppose you'll be bringing me your washing,' was all Pauline said when I left, but her tone implied that she wanted me to. Bob guiltily stuffed some notes into my top pocket, 'in case of emergency' as he put it. I would have thought that in an emergency he'd have wanted me to come back. The dog saw me with my coat on and thought it was about to be taken for a walk. It was the only thing in the house that showed any uninhibited emotion.

Pauline hovered awkwardly while I packed my stuff. She was only ever comfortable when she was busy. She looked like she wanted to be somewhere else, scrubbing something clean. We were never a very demonstrative family, and I left without making any physical contact in order to spare their embarrassment.

I stepped out on to the street with my boxes and filled my lungs with cold sea air. As the front door shut behind me, part of my life was left back inside. Closing the gate, I looked over my shoulder. Pauline was standing as still as a statue in the bay window of the front room, the room we weren't allowed to use in case we had visitors. She looked as if she might break into pieces if she moved. I suddenly felt very sad for her. When I was small, she saved up for a dining set of bone china and carefully installed it in the glass-panelled sideboard in the front room, ready for smart guests to come and eat sherry trifle with forks. But the years passed and the guests never arrived, and the bone china sat in the sideboard unused. Instead she got Sean pulling his motorbike apart in the hall, me boiling flour-and-water paste in the kitchen to glue together cardboard cities that no-one was allowed to touch, and Bob sitting in the kitchen taking the clock to bits. She had every right to be disappointed.

Two days before my birthday, I pushed open the brown painted door to the side of the Las Vegas arcade and lugged my cartons to the top of the stairs. The place smelled as if someone had been boiling cabbage on the landing for about forty years. I tried to open the lounge windows, but they were stuck fast with layers of paint, and besides, the wind from the sea would probably have blown everything out of the room. The carpets were the kind you found in bad Indian restaurants. There was a dead mouse in the kitchen. An ancient immersion heater made gastric noises that rumbled through pipes above my head, and when that stopped I could hear the endless bonk-squeak-bonk-squeak of the electric slot machines on the floor below. It certainly wasn't much, but at least it was mine.

A pair of threadbare wingbacked old-lady armchairs stood in the lounge. It looked as though the landlady's husband had died in one of them. Something had certainly wet itself on the cushion. I pulled the other one over to the window and sat looking out, thinking, this is where I start to gain control over my life. This is where the real Kevin Goodwin begins. But I wasn't sure I believed it. My disinterest in reality was damaging me, and my fantasies had to be sealed beyond reach before I could live normally. I thought of my ruined father, lost within the recesses of his imagination, and became frightened by the idea that the same thing might happen to me. I would take my leave of Calabash, and never look back. Start behaving like an adult. Pay bills. Get married. Have children. Buy a house, learn to drive, put up shelves and mend a fuse. I had already taken the first step. It was time for the next.

I resolved to pay one final visit to my kingdom. Obviously, I couldn't just leave them all without taking care of unfinished business.

The Time for Confrontation

I went back as soon as I had the whole thing worked out. How to trick the General, how to help the doctor solve his mystery, how to take my leave of Calabash with honour, dignity and respect.

I was waiting on the tide-rocked platform making final adjustments to The Plan when a horrible doubt assailed me – but by then it was too late to stop the process and I was on my way, spiralling out of sordid reality and off into the horizons of my mind.

The sun was high in the cyanic sky, gulls and cormorants plunging into the water, a mist of yellow butterflies drifting over the dock, the boats rocking, the city still and heat-becalmed in the distance. I moored my little fishing boat to the dock capstan and set off for my villa, sweat already dripping between my shoulderblades.

Well, of course, I knew that no-one in Calabash would want me to leave. Parizade proved to be inconsolable. She sat on the verandah and wept when I told her, mopping her tears with the end of a cream silk shawl. It was a glorious day to be alive, a terrible day to say goodbye. Sharp noon sunlight dappled the garden, piercing the trees with spears of fire.

'How could you even think of going?' she asked. 'You know how I have grown to love you. Have I done something wrong? Have I offended you in some way? I only intended to please you.'

'It's nothing you've done,' I mumbled guiltily. How could I explain that the entire kingdom was a figment of my mind, that she did not even exist? To say such a thing would be unnecessarily cruel, not to mention bizarre.

'I don't understand. You have everything you could wish for here. Why would you want to leave it all behind?' Her amber eyes welled once more as I slipped my arms around her waist. 'What is there in your land that you cannot be without?'

I sighed. Coming back had made my choice even more painful, but I was determined not to waver. 'I have to go,' I said, rising. 'The blame is entirely mine. I don't mean to hurt you, but I must stand by my decision.'

Parizade pulled away from me and turned to the sea. I rose and quietly left the garden, ashamed. I could still hear her crying when I reached the street. I thought of the glorious Rosamunde, encamped in a tent in some great desert with her husband's troops. I wondered if she would sense my leaving, and if she, too, would mourn.

Next I went to see Trebunculus. I found him in his laboratory, mixing noxious yellow gases in a pipette.

'Ah, good, there you are,' he said absently. 'We're experimenting with the melting point of ambergris, and hoped to enlist your help. It's not going well. We've already scalded the cat to death and given the parrot mange. Its feathers have fallen out and it's not at all happy.'

'Doctor, there are some things we need to talk about,' I

began firmly. 'You must request an audience for me with General Bassa.'

'Oh, he's been asking for you, by the way. His men came here yesterday. I told them I didn't know where you were.'

'Can you arrange a meeting between us?'

'That's easy enough. All I have to do is flash a mirror from the roof and he will send a man to fetch you.' The doctor's sharp grey eyes appeared over the top of his spectacles. He had replaced the thick, uneven lenses with new smooth-ground glass, based on his examination of the microscope pieces I had brought him. 'So, what have you got for the General? Nothing too dangerous, I hope. He has no patience for learning. He nearly blew his army to bits experimenting with cannon-powders. His "self-reflexive musket" blinded a *kadi* from Constantinople, took the ears off his horse and caused a diplomatic incident.'

I could appreciate that the doctor and the Lord Chancellor were both keen to advance the kingdom scientifically for its own good, but I could see only further harm coming from providing the General with the practical means to vanquish his enemies.

'That's the thing,' I explained. 'I knew if I failed to bring something truly scientific, he would see through my ruse. Instead, I've decided to give him something so technically advanced that he cannot hope to duplicate it.'

Trebunculus released a high bird-like laugh and gleefully laced his bony fingers together. 'Too much science – oh, very good!'

A horseman in a regimental turban arrived at the gate within minutes of the doctor's signal. At the garrison, the General was waiting in the weapon-house in his corset-tunic, paired with his valet, a white eunuch armed with an arquebus and a small hatchet, who squatted on the floor at his feet and never moved a muscle. Bassa could barely conceal his excitement.

'What do you have for me?' he asked, rubbing the heels of his palms together.

'Something very special, General. A military advancement so great that even the warlords of my nation are still learning to employ its might.' I pulled the light plastic object from my pocket and carefully removed the handkerchief in which I had wrapped it. I set the grey plastic Airfix model down on the bench in front of me.

The General moved forward and bent down, puzzled. 'What is it?'

'It's called a jet engine,' I told him. I opened the accompanying assembly diagram and pointed out the various parts. 'This is the turbine compressor shaft, here, and these are the turbine blades. The fuel spray manifold is above the annular combustion chamber, here, these are the centre bearings, there and there, the axial-flow compressor houses the rotor blades, the inlet guide vanes are here beside the nose cone and at the back you have the exhaust nozzle and pipe. Simple, really.'

'Hmm, I see,' he said, clearly not seeing at all. 'But what does it do?'

'You fix it to the wing of an aircraft and it flies. Just think, the power of flight will be yours. A flying army, General, imagine the look of terror on the faces of your enemies when you rain bombs on them from above.'

The General paced around the little kit, keeping his head directly above it. 'It's very small.'

'This is only a fraction of its real size, a scale model. Obviously I am not able to bring a full-sized jet engine back with me, so I brought you a model and instructions for its assembly, so that you could copy it.'

'A flying army, you say.' I could tell the idea appealed to him. 'A ghet.'

'That's right.'

'What powers it?'

'Oil.'

'Ah – like the lamps.'

'Exactly.'

'The flying craft goes underneath?'

'No, General, between. You must make two engines.'

'For balance. I see.'

He rose and puffed out his cheeks, thinking. Finally he clapped his hands to his sides, raising puffs of dust from his tunic. 'Well, this is brilliant. Just what we needed.' He waved towards the assembly instructions. 'And this tells us all we need to know about construction, yes?'

'Yes,' I lied.

'I will set my finest men on to it at once. Well, I think you have repaid your debt to the Sultan.' He clicked his heels together in acknowledgement of my gift. 'This calls for a celebration. You must be bathed.'

'I'm sorry?'

'It is customary at such times, when a promise has been fulfilled.' He clapped his hands together and a pair of slim brown handmaidens entered the room. 'They will take you,' he said with a wink. 'Just leave your body in their dextrous hands. I promise you will feel most refreshed.'

I had just been led to the door when he called out.

'One other thing, Kay.'

I turned, half expecting to be felled in my tracks. 'Sir?'

'Until this "ghet" is built, don't wander too far. We may need your advice.'

'Of course, General. I understand.'

The handmaidens took me to a grotto shaded by willows behind the garrison, where they stripped me and lowered me into a warm, clear pool of running water. Discreetly disrobing and slipping into the water by my side, they poured fragrant oils across my stomach and chest, and massaged me into a perfumed, languorous stupor.

An hour later I rose and dressed, buoyed by my triumph with the General, and moved on to the second part of my plan. Returning to Dr Trebunculus, I found him beneath the overhanging cliff at the rear of his laboratory, where he stood with a cloth across his face, igniting phials of a disgusting sulphurous substance.

'My scarf!' I cried in surprise. 'You have it wrapped about you.'

'I only meant to borrow it,' said Trebunculus in some embarrassment, 'to prove to the Sultan that we were fetching you. You smell nice.'

'So you did fetch me.'

'Not exactly,' he flustered, setting the choking experiment aside. 'We merely ensured that the conditions were – conducive – to your crossing. But tell me what the General thought of your scientific invention.'

I grinned. 'He admired it, but it'll do him no good. He hasn't the means to manufacture such a device, or power it. The metal must be tempered in a manner beyond his disposal, and the oil must be refined and purified. It's impossible to make it fly with the instructions I've given him. I have no doubt that he'll spend a good deal of time trying, though.'

The doctor clapped me on the back and released a squeal of laughter.

'But now I must speak of something graver,' I said. 'The death of the Sultan's wife.'

'Dear fellow. I'll have Menavino draw some tamarind tea.'

We sat in the garden and drank as the afternoon shadows lengthened, and as the evening flowers opened their scented petals, I carefully laid out my proposal.

'I first had my suspicions when you told me that it had been impossible to introduce the poison into Eliya's sedative glass in the brief time that your back was turned, because of the exact measurement that was required. The door to the jade chamber was closed, and there were no windows. I first thought of Scammer, who seems to be able to secrete himself in the smallest corners, then dismissed the notion. No-one could have dashed in and up to the glass, measured the poison to the grain then rushed back out without others seeing, no matter how small or agile they could make themselves.'

The doctor inched forward, his hands planted on his thin, cracked knees. 'Go on.'

'I looked at those present at the death: the Valide Sultan, representing the royal family, yourself, acting as court physician, Septimus Peason, representing the interests of the state, two handmaidens, and a eunuch at the door. None of these six had a known grievance with the victim, I'm sure of that, but one person knew that her death could further his own purposes – the Lord Chancellor.'

'How do you reason so?'

The air around us had grown cooler, and the bench on which we sat was now steeped in shadow. 'If the mother is dead and her only child is a girl, there is no heir to the throne. The Sultan is the last of his bloodline.'

'But that is against everyone's interests. I have no great love for the Lord Chancellor, Kay, but I can assure you that he has the kingdom's welfare at heart. Look at the marriage he arranged between his own son and Rosamunde.'

'That's just it. With the Princess's marriage, the power balance has now been shifted to the militia. Rosamunde is headstrong, but she'll have no say in her husband's affairs. Major Maximus reports to his General . . .'

'Do you really think it could have been the Lord

Chancellor? But how? I can assure you he knows very little about the administration of poisons.'

'Well, that's where this comes in.' I dug my hand into my pocket and removed the red jewel that Rosamunde had given me. 'It only began to make sense when I saw the onyx table that was buried with Eliya. You told me that onyx created bad luck, and had to be tempered with carnelians. This gem, presented to me by the Princess, belonged to her mother and is identical in every facet to the ones set in the tabletop. But if it was taken from the table, there should only have been four stones remaining in the onyx, and you specifically told me that there were five. Let us suppose, then, that one of them was false. An answer to the puzzle presented itself when you told me of the scarlet octopus. The poison and the gem are the same colour. Couldn't the poison be most precisely measured by grinding it up, setting it into a lozenge, and putting it on the table in the space the missing stone once occupied? All the poisoner would have had to do then was scoop it up and drop it into the drink in a single motion. The lozenge dissolved, leaving the residue you found.'

'Celestial heavens, I believe you may have solved the conundrum. If this is true, then the Lord Chancellor must have chosen to side with the General long ago, and his plans have been slow to reach fruition. There has been so little intrigue in the court these past few years, we have quite grown out of the habit. And now that Rosamunde has performed her duty, Peason's power has been gathered, ready to harvest. But answer me something. Why did the Princess give you her mother's gem?'

I must have reddened.

'You didn't,' whispered the doctor.

I reddened further.

'Oh, you *didn't*.'

'We were secret lovers before she took her marriage vows, and I wish we could be again.'

'But this is terrible – don't you see what you've done? If you have lain with the Princess, then Septimus knows of the affair. Scammer watches the royal apartments night and day.'

'I don't see your point,' I said dimly.

'He has been toying with you, foolish boy! He knows you have committed high treason, and he can have you both beheaded.'

'Then why hasn't he come after me?'

'I imagine you still serve some useful purpose to him.'

'But I've presented his General with the scientific advancement he requested.'

'*Just* presented him . . .'

'Oh no.'

'If all that you've said is true, Bassa's men will be coming for you right now – and that will be just the start of our troubles.'

I rose in a panic. 'But why did he have me bathed instead of killed?'

'He had you bathed?' The doctor's eyes widened. 'You were bathed?'

'Just before I came here.'

'He cannot kill you while you still bear the sweat of your motherland. You have to be cleansed in the waters of Calabash before execution.'

'Why?'

'It is a tradition that goes back to the *sekban*, the military auxiliaries who once occupied the land of Nicodemus Tapica. Tapica was a notoriously smelly ruler who once decreed that—'

'I don't think there's time for your histories now, Doctor.' I looked back at the city. I was sure I could see dust rising from horses' hooves. 'I must go.' I ran to the gate. 'This is all turning out wrong. Forgive me.' And, like a rat deserting a ship of state, I fled, not trusting myself to look back.

Even so, Trebunculus and Menavino managed to catch up with me as I reached the foot of the great statues at the dock. 'What are you doing?' asked the doctor breathlessly, 'you can't just leave us like this.'

'I'm sorry, Doctor, I'm leaving for good this time, I'm afraid.'

Trebunculus was dumbfounded. He brushed the dust from his velvet hat and shook his head in wonderment. 'But what will become of us? Don't you care? I thought we were your friends. Menavino, don't just stand there gawping, run and tell the royal emissaries. We must talk some sense into this poor deluded boy before it's too late. We must find a way to fight back, if fight we must.'

Menavino's eyes widened as if he had been slapped, and he set off at a great pace.

'I've made up my mind,' I explained. 'I just came back to sort a few things out.'

'Heaven inside the Earth, you're serious.'

'I need to be in my own world, Doctor. I fear for my sanity.'

Trebunculus looked about himself wildly. He hopped back and forth as if trying to impart a secret. 'And suppose I told you that we need you too? What do you say to that? Suppose I told you that our very lives depend upon your staying?'

'But they don't. You were happy before I arrived. And I will die if I stay.'

'There is no before, just as there won't be any after.'

My God, I thought, *he knows that I've imagined all of this. He's the only one who sees the truth*. The thought of never seeing Rosamunde again was heartbreaking, but leaving someone who knew that he would shortly cease to exist was even worse. Drawn by the panic in the doctor's voice, a crowd was starting to gather around us. Menavino was spreading the word, although quite how the dumb boy was managing it was a mystery. I had to leave before the Lord Chancellor's men arrived.

'What am I going to tell the Sultan? Who knows how he'll react? Someone will pay, someone will be chastised.'

'Not slow compression—'

'—of the testicles, no, much worse: the punishment of the hooks.'

I knew about the punishment of the hooks. The great French artist Alexandre-Gabriel Descamps, who specialised in Eastern scenes, had painted bodies being thrown over a wall from which protruded hundreds of steel hooks.

'Isn't there anything at all we can do to make you stay and help us fight back?'

'I wish there was, believe me, but I have to go. I will miss you all so much. I can't do anything to help you. This is your land, not mine. I'm sure everything will sort itself out the moment I've gone.'

'And suppose it doesn't? Suppose General Bassa and the Lord Chancellor stage a military coup and have us all beheaded?'

'The invention I gave them is unworkable. You'll be protected from its use. I'm sorry, Doctor.' I turned and looked down at the little boat. I knew that the moment I stepped into it, I would be returned to the fishing platform below the Cole Bay pier for the very last time.

I looked up at the sad, expectant faces around me. A hush had fallen on the assembly and a sense of puzzlement charged the air. I knew I was letting everyone down, yet it was the doctor who looked most as if he had failed.

'It's best for all of us if I do this quickly. You've been so kind, and I've failed to repay you. If you hear from the Sultan's daughter, please tell her—' I hastily checked the thought. 'Send Rosamunde my fondest regards, and extend the poor unworthy thoughts of this lowly commoner' (for I had learned the language of paying respect) 'to all the royal family. Tell Parizade that she will always hold a special place in my heart. It's best for all of us this way.' What I meant was that it was best for me.

In the distance, I could indeed see the gleaming pikes of several horsemen galloping towards the harbour. I took one final long look at the shimmering spires of the distant city, the verdant fields, the muted villagers, the sad face of the doctor, who stood clutching the brim of his velvet hat.

Ashamed, I turned away from them all and began my descent to the boat.

Part Two

Now I have nothing. Even the joy of loss—
Even the dreams I had I now am losing.
Only this thing I know; that you are using
My heart as a stone to bear your foot across . . .
I am glad – I am glad – the stone is of your choosing.

Stella Benson

Real Time

And so my real life began.

I put Calabash out of my mind. All childhood fantasies were stored away. No more jollies and follies, no amber-eyed girls and trotting horses, no valleys of smoky ambergris, no cobalt skies, no golden kingdoms. It was eyes down, nose to the grindstone, all aboard the workers' bus for the dungeons. And the perfect time to do so.

1972 was the year in which the country grew angry. Protestors burned the American flag in Grosvenor Square. In the North, traditional industries began shutting up shop at an accelerated pace. In the South, rapacious property developers began to rip the capital apart. Inflation and the new decimal currency doubled prices. British Rail shut down its services, the miners went on strike, and power cuts caused the Heath government to declare a state of emergency.

For the first time since rationing, national crises managed to affect us in Cole Bay. Most noticeable was the change of mood, a new pessimism on the streets. Militancy reached its highest peak since 1926. *A Clockwork Orange* opened at the

Roxy, and nobody was really that shocked. The first computers began to appear in the offices of the Scheherazade Hotel. Britain began to package its history in preparation for the coming of mass tourism. In America, the Watergate break-in started a chain of events that would lead to a worldwide loss of faith in leadership. A crafty kind of dumbing down began. It was no longer a time to be innocent.

On the day of my birthday I opened a bottle of sparkling wine and drank it alone, watching from the smeary window of my flat as the pier lights flicked on with the settling of night. I had furnished my lounge with a ricketty table and chairs that the Ocean Breeze restaurant three doors down had thrown out during their refurbishment. I had scrubbed and varnished them, but the odour of stale batter lingered. In the weeks that followed, I slouched into my new life. It was easier than I'd expected; all I had to do was stop thinking.

I grew my hair long. I reached an uneasy truce with Bob and Pauline, visiting them on Saturday mornings, usually with my laundry. Sean stopped writing once he discovered I'd moved out, and his only contact with the family was the odd reverse-charge phonecall to my stepfather asking him for money. Even the dog got stomach cancer and had to be put down, which left Bob without a legitimate excuse for escaping the house.

Everything seemed to be going wrong. In addition to setting my fantasy life aside, I should have stayed on at school and studied hard, but decisions never work out that neatly. One morning while I was seated on my stool at the back of the arcade reading the paper, Danny came in looking for me. He had cropped his hair short, and was dressed in the kind of clothes he never normally wore: a black roll-neck sweater, boots and tattered old blue jeans. He looked casual, natural, even unfashionable. The lapels of his scruffy afghan coat were covered with Gay Liberation Front buttons. Instinctively I knew that he was leaving town and had come to say goodbye.

'Doesn't the noise in here get on your nerves?' he asked, glaring at some children who were rowdily playing the nearest pinball machine. 'Couldn't you just strangle these kids?'

'You get used to it.'

'Look, I wanted you to be the first to know, I'm going off to work in London.' He grinned. 'How about that, then? But not as a window dresser. Press officer for a monthly magazine, very radical and new. The pay's not much, but it's for a good cause.'

'I thought you wanted to work in a big department store.'

'I did too, but the major shops are having a lean time of it. Quite a few are closing down. Well, what happened was—'

He had fallen in love with somebody called Dennis who lived in a squat in Notting Hill and was involved with gay liberation. Dennis had persuaded him to come and lend a hand to the movement. It sounded to me as though Dennis was dodgy.

'I know what you're thinking, right, he's using his sexual charisma to enlist cheap labour. Well maybe he is, and maybe I'm using him to get out of Cole Bay. Is that so wrong?'

'You're always going on about sex these days,' I complained.

'I'm just getting the amount of sex that straight men would get if women would let them,' he replied tartly. 'Anyway, you never think about sex at all. You're a late developer, you.'

I decided not to answer. I had too many other things to worry about.

'Dennis has found me a flatshare. I can't move in with him because he's still with his old boyfriend. They're sorting things out. We'll see what happens. It's all terribly adult.' He sighed. 'And to think I used to imagine that lunch at the Buckingham was the height of sophistication. They had tomato juice down on their menu as a starter, for God's sake. Anyway, what I wanted to know was, do you want my facial solarium? I'm not taking anything with me. It needs a three pin plug.'

'That's kind of you, but no, I'm fine.'

'You don't look it,' he sniffed. 'Very pale and thin, but you always were thin. Is Janine not feeding you cream buns anymore?'

'She's stopped going round to my mother's. I think she's finally realised Sean isn't coming back.'

'I thought so. I saw her on the front last week with some lad who works at Pickfords. They were snogging so hard I thought their teeth were stuck together. She's the size of a bungalow. He'd have to be as fit as a butcher's dog to climb up on her. Listen, when I get settled I'll send you my address, how would that be?'

'Yeah, sure.'

'Maybe you'll come up to town. I know you've got your lungs and everything, but maybe for a short visit.'

I smiled. 'Maybe.'

'Don't close the door on any friendship, Kay. Who knows when you may need someone?'

'Haven't you got a bus to catch?' I said, only half joking.

'Yeah, well.' He turned to go, then stopped. 'I don't get you sometimes. You've got so much going in your favour, and you're pissing it all away in this dump. It's like you're doing it deliberately, just to spite yourself. There are kids sleeping rough on the streets of London, and it'll happen down here eventually, you wait. Things were going forward for a while but now they're sliding back again. We're going to have to fight for what we want. The sexual revolution is just the tip of the iceberg. It's a bad time to be without a purpose.'

I knew that this was not Danny talking. He'd been fed some

rhetoric by his new man. The idea of discovering a cause through a lover was new to me. Up until that moment I assumed most people got their opinions from reading or watching television.

'It's easy for you,' I replied hotly, 'swanning off without any worries. I can't do that.'

'You think it was easy for me? I told my dad at the dinner table I didn't fancy girls, and he stuck a fork in my arm. I had to have stitches. The only person in my family who'll still talk to me is my mother, and she's just been diagnosed with cancer. She hates my old man. I'm all she lives for. I feel like I'm running out on her, but what will happen if I don't take my chance? I might never get another one. It tears me up to think of letting her down.' He stared at me oddly. 'I don't know why I'm wasting my breath. I thought you'd be pleased for me.'

'I am, Danny.' I didn't sound as if I meant it.

'You say that but look at you, the light's gone from your eyes. I've seen that look all over this bloody town.' He stared around at the beeping machines. 'This bloody town.' And he was back on the street, walking briskly away before I could find the right response. The kids came over to complain about losing their money in one of the pinball tables. I shouted at them for tilting it.

Losing Danny wasn't the worst thing that happened that month. There was no telephone in the flat, and the only way of contacting me quickly was to ring through to the cashier in the arcade, so I was surprised to be called to the phone a little after eight o'clock one morning.

'I've had a letter from your brother,' said Bob, sounding strange. 'I think you'd better come over.'

The typed sheet lay unfolded in the middle of the kitchen table. Bob was pacing about, unsure of what to do. Pauline was nowhere in sight. I carefully picked up the letter. 'He's in a hospital in Bangkok,' said Bob, pre-empting the contents. 'Some kind of overdose. He very nearly died. The police are involved. They're talking about pressing charges.'

I was so used to taking vast amounts of tablets for my condition, my first thought was that Sean had accidentally swallowed some kind of medication. 'What do you mean, press charges?' I asked.

'They haven't decided what to do with him yet. That's his bloody so-called pal for you, O'Donnelly, getting him into bad ways. Employing him as a courier. Courier! Bloody drug courier.'

The letter was from the British Consulate. Sean had been caught smuggling cocaine out of the country and had tried to swallow the evidence. He had passed out in a public toilet. He was expected to pull through but there was a possibility of lasting damage. If he survived, he faced a minimum jail-sentence of ten years, and there was even talk of a death sentence. There was a telephone number for Bob to ring, but it was clear that he had no idea how to go about making an international call. Eventually we worked out the time difference and arranged for the operator to complete the connection. A series of tinny British voices peeped from the phone as the call was shifted around various extensions. Finally, they found someone who seemed to know about Sean. I edged as close as I could to the earpiece.

'I've been to see him, he was in relatively good spirits, and I think it's safe to say that he is going to be all right . . .' a posh voice at the British consulate explained.

'Well, that's something.'

'. . . but he has had to lose his left arm below the elbow.'

'What? They've not – chopped it off?' asked Bob incredulously.

'No, no, when he became unconscious in the toilet he cut off the blood supply to his arm. It's quite a common occurence in these cases, apparently. You understand that your son will need legal representation. There's no question of his pleading not guilty, and drug smuggling carries a mandatory sentence in these circumstances. Only the severity of the punishment is open to negotiation.'

'Oh my Lord.' Bob settled on his chair like a deflating balloon. He listened to the consul for a few more minutes, then replaced the receiver as though he was afraid of breaking it. 'I might have to go over there,' he said, clearly horrified by the prospect. 'I shall have to get a passport.'

And so it was that the good name of our family was dragged into disrepute when the local press mysteriously got hold of the story and milked it for human interest. 'Local Couple Tell of Son's Drug Tragedy,' read the headline on page seven. Photo caption: Robert Goodwin, seen here receiving top catering management award. 'I can't believe my son was mixed up in drug trafficking.' Distraught mother unavailable for comment. Younger son not asked to provide one, unfortunately. 'My faith in him is gravely diminished,' brother of tarnished hero figure would have admitted.

Endings, that year, nothing but endings. One more that month, God going for a fully representative set of tragedies. Dudley Salterton was found dead in his flat. He'd been there for three days before a neighbour noticed that the milk wasn't being taken in. You'd have thought Barnacle Bill would have called someone. He'd just been given a new lip. There was gratitude for you. Two weeks after Dudley's funeral, his posters still adorned the advertising sites on the railings of the promenade. I freed one from its case, took it home and pinned it up in my kitchenette. The little monochrome photograph showed Dudley in his striped summer jacket, mugging for the camera as he adjusted the straw hat on Barnacle Bill's head, the fading image of a performer in a happier but already forgotten time. At least you've gone to join your beloved Dolores, I thought. She's waiting for you on some celestial stage in her spangly leotard, posturing beside your cabinet of swords. I wondered if Parizade still waited for me, seated in the garden beneath peach blossom and bougainvillea, looking up from her book and listening for the distant sound of an approaching fishing boat.

CHAPTER THIRTY-TWO

Staying Behind

Summer came, and with it the arrival of those few visitors to Cole Bay who had not opted for the new Spanish holiday packages. In the face of unsettled weather they meandered along the esplanade looking for something to do, dissatisfied with the dated amusements on offer and ill at ease with each other, until the first warning prickles of rain drove them into my arcade. The summer of 1974 would go down as the hottest in living memory; it was the summer that changed Cole Bay forever. But that was still two years away, and if the past was another country, then so was the future.

During the out of season period my job had reached zen-like levels of boredom. Despite the electronic racket ricocheting around me, I found myself drifting into a trance state that only the electrocution of a screaming child on the Bally Ski-Rally could awaken me from. I tried not to think about Sean, now recovered but missing part of an arm and languishing in a Thai custody centre, still awaiting his court appeal. Bob had been out to see him – a disastrous trip by all accounts, due to misinformation from the British Embassy and delayed flights that resulted in Bob missing his meeting with the consul in charge of Sean's case. My brother's chances of a reduced sentence were either fair or nonexistent, depending on who we listened to, and the degree of variation was less to do with the circumstances surrounding the arrest than our government's unwillingness to upset Thailand while its building programme relied on British imports. Bob and Pauline were told that they had to view the case as part of a bigger picture, which must have been a comfort to them.

Sean wrote to me a few times, meandering apologetic notes that embarrassed both of us. He had always been honest with me, but was uncomfortable with any discussion of the events leading to his arrest, so his letters became like my conversations with Bob and Pauline, where nobody ever said what they meant, or what they really wanted to say.

The Scheherazade Hotel announced that it was going broke, and would be laying off many of its staff in order to downgrade from three stars to two. It cut everyone's pay and asked Bob to work overtime without remuneration. One evening when he had to work late, I decided to go around and see him. The Scheherazade employed a doorman who wore an outfit that was meant to look exotic and Middle-Eastern. It was made of shiny orange nylon, and came with a sequin-trimmed cape, curly-toed shoes and a purple fez with a feather. The trousers didn't fit properly, and hung below his crotch. The ensemble made him look like a children's entertainer of below normal intelligence. He wouldn't have lasted a minute in Calabash.

'Oi, you can't come in here dressed like that,' he told me, holding up his hand.

'Why not?' I asked.

'Plimsolls.' He pointed at my feet. 'This is a smart establishment.'

'You must be joking. Take a look at yourself. I wasn't aware that there were any man-made fabrics in the Ottoman Empire. Anyway, I'm on business.'

'Oh yeah? How d'you work that out?'

'I've come to see my dad,' I explained. 'He works here.' I thought the doorman might be reasonable and let me in. We looked about the same age. 'He's the manager of catering services.'

'I don't care if he's the genie of the lamp, you're not coming in with those things on.' I peered over the doorman's shoulder. In the foyer two very old ladies were slumped in armchairs, fast asleep or possibly dead. There was no-one at the reception desk.

'Oh, come on,' I said, 'there's nobody about.'

'Go on, you, piss off back to your arcade,' he said nastily, shooing me off the step, and I realised with a shock that he must have noticed me sitting there on my stool. Seeing my job through his eyes suddenly made me feel ashamed. He clearly considered it on a lower social scale than his own. Depressed, I went around to Balaclava Terrace and sat with my mother. The anger, or at least the tetchiness – for there were no large emotions on display in our family – seemed to have departed her, leaving only a weary acceptance that manifested itself in an inability to decide anything: what to cook, what television programme to watch, what to do next. After a few hours of this agonised pottering, I found myself longing for the days when she and Janine sat together in the kitchen moaning about topless models.

The rain refused to let up. It was as though there was some kind of dial controlling the weather, and it had become jammed. Some days the temperature rose enough to make the pavements steam, but nothing dried out. I shifted my stool to the front of the arcade and stared up at the incontinent sky like some malevolent pixie, aware that I was slowly becoming a Cole Bay character, like the escapologist who used to dive into the sea in a straitjacket from the side of the pier, or the scary old man with the boil on the end of his nose who had dispensed 99s from Guiseppi's ice-cream counter for about thirty-five years before being put away for tampering with his electricity supply. Meanwhile, a wave of vandalism swept Cole Bay with the force of an exciting new trend. Sixth-formers smashed several of the pinball tables while I was out getting a sandwich, and although I was sure that Malcolm Slattery was the most likely ringleader, I had no proof to offer Mr Cottesloe. Incredibly, Slattery had opted to stay on at school, thus defeating the time-honoured tradition of bullies leaving early to drift into lives of petty crime. It didn't seem right that he was to be the recipient of higher education while my own communication skills were reduced to shouting, 'Oi, mate, don't leave your cola bottle on the mechanical grab.'

It was difficult to read in the arcade because the lights were dimmed to prevent reflections in the glass cases of the games. Also, several of the machines 'talked', and though some could be turned down, none could be silenced. Especially grating was a Texan voice that counted down from ten to 'three . . . two . . . one . . . BLASTOFF!' every minute or so.

To say that I missed visiting Calabash was like saying the Germans were disappointed about Dresden. Not a day passed when I didn't long to be back in the palace bedchamber with Rosamunde, holding her gently in my arms upon sheets of quilted crimson silk. I even thought of Parizade on her crescent bench of white marble, high above the sea, an open book unread in her lap, her eyes focused on the dimming horizon. It felt as though I had lost the only piece of my life worth living for. Part of my mind was always thinking about going back. The only way I could return to the problems of the real world was by reminding myself that Calabash only existed as a fanciful form of escape, that what I had actually been doing on all those occasions was standing on the lower fishing platform for hours in a state of mental aphasia, risking my life and half freezing to death until the cold and the wind finally snapped me out of it. I told myself that I could have killed Julia, that we could have fallen into the sea and drowned, and if that didn't work I reminded myself that I had started to behave like my real father, running away from reality to live in some childish world of make-believe. Thank God, I said, that I saw sense in time and stopped being foolish.

It didn't stop me from missing Calabash.

Hell, everyone retreated from trouble, they just had different ways of doing it; my mother with her letter writing, Bob with his solitary drinking, Sean with his dreams of escape, Janine with her illusions of a storybook marriage. Had Calabash been such a harmful alternative? Here I was, trapped like a rat in a maze, working six days a week in the arcade, making barely enough money to live on, unable to save, unable to move, and for what? At the end of June, during the first really dry week of the year, my chest infection returned and put me back in the hospital for a fortnight. Cottesloe grudgingly kept my job open, but only after remarking that it would have been easy for him to find someone younger – and, he implied, cheaper – for the position.

Around this time, Bob lost faith in British justice when it became clear that my brother was going to lose his appeal. The death penalty was ruled out, as it was proven that Sean had been deceived by his employer. The Thai justice system sounded a lot more organised than the British Consulate. Although there were all kinds of clauses and riders attached to the ruling, the basic sentence amounted to six years in jail, and the consul ominously warned my parents that as life there was tougher than in British jails, we should expect a big change in his appearance when we next saw him.

Soon after my lungs had sufficiently recovered, I returned to the end of the pier and stood watching Katherine, who was still rolling clouds of candyfloss around her drum and selling tickets to the ghost train. Now she had heavy black stripes of kohl around her eyes and dyed red hair. She had taken to wearing a studded leather jacket, tight torn jeans and motorcycle boots. It was an image I'd seen on a lot of recent rock albums. I decided that the time had come to meet her. I did this over a number of days by buying a lot of candyfloss and throwing it away once I had walked around the corner.

'Can I ask you something?' she said during my sixth consecutive visit.

'What?' I tried to look surprised as I accepted another great pink sugar-swirl on a stick.

'Why do you buy this muck?'

'I like the taste.'

'No you don't.'

'I do.'

'You chuck it away.'

'What do you mean?'

'You get round the corner and chuck it away.'

'No I don't.'

'It floats. She sees you chuck it over the side.' She pointed at her friend on the darts stall. 'It floats right past her. Even the seagulls won't touch it.'

'I like the look of it, I just don't like the taste.'

'That's what Larry told me the other night,' called her friend, and she laughed coarsely. This wasn't going at all how I'd imagined.

'Then why don't you just watch me make it instead of buying it?' I knew she was teasing me, but there seemed to be no way out of this conversational trap.

'I don't mind buying it.'

'You're not doing me a favour, you know, I'm not on a percentage.'

'All right,' I said, exhausted. 'Next time I'll just watch.'

'It'd be quicker if he just asked you out,' said the friend, who talked to Katherine as if I wasn't there. I decided to call her bluff.

'All right, do you want to go out?'

'Depends. Where?'

I hadn't prepared answers for anything this far down the line. 'Er, do you like the pictures?'

'No, it's boring. What about a drink?'

'Yeah, all right.'

'You know the King Edward?'

'The pub?'

'Well, I'm not talking about the potato.'

'Yeah.'

'You could meet me in there after I finish, about eight-thirty.'

'Yeah, all right.'

'When, then?'

'Um, tonight if you like.'

'Yeah, all right.'

I was glad I hadn't opted for a display of Shavian wit. Katherine was clearly more straightforward than I had imagined. As I walked away, I heard the two girls laughing together.

The King Edward was frequented by bikers from London. I had to walk past it from the pier to the arcade. It didn't seem like a good place to get to know someone, but maybe that was the idea.

I don't suppose I need to point out that the evening was a hopeless disaster, but to give you some idea of just how horrible it was you have to picture me squeezed on to a red plastic couch next to Katherine's friend and her neanderthal biker boyfriend, opposite Katherine and her boyfriend, who turned out to be the psychopath of Cole Bay Grammar, my former nemesis, Malcolm Slattery. Thundering heavy metal music shook the glasses on the lager-swamped table as the tittering weaselly Laurence did tricks with a beermat, and Slattery ominously reminisced about the fun we hadn't had together at school. The knowledge that Katherine had invited me to the pub was presumably his only reason for not duffing me up.

'Remember the old bitch who took us for English?' he asked. 'She died of cancer.'

'I know. I visited her in hospital.' Slattery gave me an odd look, and seemed on the verge of an insult, then snapped his mouth shut and grabbed his beer to take another noisy draught. Every two minutes he abruptly stopped chewing his gum, turned and clamped his mouth over Katherine's, as if franking the postage on to a parcel. Her pleasure at my squirming discomfort seemed only slightly higher than the enjoyment she clearly gained from receiving Slattery's fat tongue in her throat. Each time he attacked her face, she raised her legs from the floor with pleasure and seemed about to jack-knife into the couch.

After half an hour of this torture, during which time I was expected to keep them all supplied with beer, I went outside to get some fresh air and didn't go back. I avoided the pier after that. Knowing that she and her friend were still there helped me to avoid the temptation of being drawn back to Calabash. Katherine had come down from her pedestal with a vengeance.

The dead days were only enlivened once more that summer, by an unannounced visit from Danny, who had changed his appearance yet again. This time he had grown his hair into a glittery mullet and was wearing eye shadow. (This was about the time Mary Quant started selling black and silver 'Glam Rock' makeup kits for men.) He told me he had taken a few acting classes and was understudying a part in *The Rocky Horror Picture Show*, which was then playing in a derelict cinema in the King's Road, Chelsea. He wasn't sure how long the job would last, but he was enjoying it. I asked him about Dennis and his work with the GLF.

'Who?' he asked, puzzled, then remembered. 'Oh, him. That was absolutely *yonks* ago. We didn't see eye to eye. He wanted me to go on protest marches all the time, but the people were so awful, shouting about politics and badgering people in the street. The flat was always full of students having stupid arguments about Marxism. They'd sit on the floor burning holes in the carpet with their joints, hang around until they'd emptied the fridge and drunk all our booze, then go home and wait for me to restock. I couldn't see what wanting to shag men had to do with striking miners, so I moved out. I see you're still here, then.' He scratched his nose with a varnished fingernail. 'How's it going?'

'How does it look?'

'Like you died and went to hell.'

'How astute of you to notice.'

'I guess there's still no work down here.'

'Not unless you want to be a deckchair attendant. Of course there are plenty of other skills to be had. Why, only yesterday the man on the soft ice-cream counter was telling me how you can cheat customers by keeping the edge of the cone close to the nozzle as you fill it, thus creating a central hole in the ice cream that doesn't collapse until after you've sold it. And I can thrill you with tales of wafer technology, but I'm sure you haven't the time.'

'At least you don't have to make your own amusement.' He waved a hand around the beeping, blinking room. 'Sorry, I suppose that's not very funny.'

'Not very, no.'

'Look, I really do have to go. My mother's back in the hospital, and it doesn't look like she's going to come out this time. I can't visit her at the same time as my dad because they won't let him smoke and he won't sit in the waiting room with me. You should come up and catch the show before it ends its run. You look like you could do with a laugh. I'll send you my new address.'

But Danny had never sent me his old one. He was caught up in an exciting new world, and had little in common with someone who was staying behind in the town that time – and he – was determined to forget.

CHAPTER THIRTY-THREE

Life's Little Surprises

In a small town there are a lot of familiar faces. But even though I watched the girl passing by from my gnome stool in the arcade, I didn't realise that it was Julia until she turned back and walked towards me.

'Kay?' she asked in disbelief.

I hardly recognised her at all. For a start, she had a figure. She had lost her puppy fat and seemed taller, but there was something else about her, a rawness, a new energy that dispelled her former air of lethargic disinterest. She had grown her hair. Her face was thinner, so that her blue eyes now seemed large and searching.

'Kay?' She slowed in mid-stride, shocked by my appearance. 'My God, is that you?'

I knew that I had also changed, and not for the better. The stress I had been through, worrying over my brother, and the fears about my health and sanity, had taken their toll. My face was gaunt and liverish; I was as skinny as a hat-rack.

She, on the other hand, was as radiant as a summer morning. She should have taken one look at me and run a mile, but instead she took another faltering step forward, then reached out for my hand without thinking. 'You poor sausage, I've been meaning to come and see you but things have been so crazy . . .'

'I didn't think you'd ever want to see me again,' I began.

'Believe me, for a while I really didn't, but I have missed you. Are you okay? You're working here at the arcade? We've got some catching up to do, you and I.'

I might have known she would never hold a grudge. She had no temperament for bitterness or anger. 'I would like that.'

'So what do you think of the new me?' She stepped back and looked down at herself. 'Good, huh? A waist like Sabrina, my mum says.'

'Listen, Julia, that day on the pier, I never meant to harm you, I was sorting out some problems—'

'You can sit and tell me all your problems, isn't that what we used to do? How long have I known you?'

I tried to remember when we had first met. She couldn't have been more than six years old. Her family lived two streets over from Balaclava Terrace. As far as I knew, they were still there. 'I don't know,' I replied. 'You were very small.'

She laughed. 'I was never very small. It's the only thing that's changed about me. I still tell my troubles to the sea. Still stand on the pier, like I used to do when I was young. Do you have time to grab a cup of coffee?'

'I can't today.' I could, but something made me turn down the offer. I felt at a disadvantage. I'd been caught off guard, and her bright confidence had unnerved me.

'What's the matter? Is something wrong?'

'There are things I have to do.' I watched as disappointment dampened her spirits. 'We can always get together another time.'

'I guess so. I'd like to keep in touch.'

'Sure.' I nodded, falsely cheerful. 'I won't let you down.'

'The ball's in your court, Kay. It always has been.'

'You're a real sight for sore eyes,' I told her as she drew close once more. And she was. Her cheeks were no longer smothered in spot-hiding makeup. She was wearing a light summer dress that showed off her tanned legs, and she moved about me with a loose-limbed grace she had never shown before. Now that she had a reason to feel good, there was a sense of bravery about her. I wished I wasn't wearing my old brown elephant cords and my ratty fisherman's jumper.

'Anyway, it's good to see that you're – well.' I realised that the shock of seeing me again was settling in, and she clearly didn't think I looked so good. My defences suddenly return-ed. She had not spoken to me since the day I had frightened her on the pier. Why would she bother now, if not to gloat over the fact that she had managed to effect a change in her-self, while I remained the same old loser she had known at school?

'I didn't know you were working here,' she explained, searching for something else to say. 'I don't come down this end of town much anymore.' I decided that this had to be a lie, because the school was nearby and the bus came along the promenade before turning inland by the roundabout past my arcade.

'Oh, I'm here rain or shine. Almost a local monument, pointed out by tour guides. People arrange to meet each other in front of me. Well, I imagine you have lots of better things to do with your time than hang around in this area.' I didn't even try to keep the bitterness from creeping into my voice.

'I left school, Kay.' She squinted up at the sky, checking the weather. 'Dad moved to Spain and divorced my mother.'

'I'm sorry to hear that.'

'Don't be. It was for the best.' Her smile became a little less sunny. 'Nobody seemed very surprised except me. He doesn't even bother to keep in touch. There wasn't any money coming in at home, so I had to find a job.'

'But you wanted to be a biologist.'

'Yeah, well. It's like that Stones song. You can't always get what you want.'

'It looks like you got some of what you wanted.'

'I decided that if I couldn't get to be a biologist, I could make a few other changes.' She looked down at her figure. 'It bloody nearly killed me.'

'Well, it's paid off. I barely recognised you.'

'I've been catalogue modelling, making a bit of money. I'm in Littlewoods under Brassieres and Sun Loungers. To be honest, I was struggling with my biology grades. It would have been a long and lonely battle. So don't laugh – I've got a beauty salon. Just a small place, but it's a start. Not just hair – therapeutic massage as well. Taking the stress out of house-wives. It's doing rather well, considering how many people around here are out of work.'

'Well done, you.' Any moment now I felt sure she would tell me she was engaged to someone I hated. At least I knew Malcolm Slattery was already spoken for.

'You're making fun of me.'

'No – forgive me – I didn't mean it to sound that way. I'm not.'

'It's just applying the things you read about in psychology books. If you can understand the reason why people feel bad about themselves, it's easier to find a way to make them feel good. Sometimes I see them come into the shop, and I know exactly what they're feeling.'

'Maybe I should tell my mum to visit you.'

'How are your parents?'

'I moved out. I live above here.'

'Oh.' She searched for something to say, and I didn't help her out. 'How are things? Are you happy?'

'Am I happy?' I asked. 'What kind of a question is that to chuck at someone? Fucking hell, does it look like I'm happy?' I tried to stay calm, but something inside me gave way. 'Why would I stay around here if I wanted to be happy? My dad's about to be made redundant, my brother's in jail, and I'm stuck here because I've got the lungs of a sixty-five-year-old chain smoker. How much worse can it get?'

'I heard about them planning to close down the Scheherazade. Didn't they find mice in the restaurant or something? And I read about your brother. They're trying to get him released early, aren't they?'

'It was rats. They found rats. They would have had to have been the size of Shetland ponies and stampeding around Bob in herds before he noticed them, but he is the catering manager there, so you can see the problem.' I took a deep breath and tried to calm myself. 'The legal people at the British Consulate say they might be able to get Sean released early on a technical point about the sentencing procedure, but the same lawyers also said he'd get a reduced sentence in the first place because he'd been the innocent victim of a smuggling plot.'

'But the papers said—'

'The papers repeat whatever they're told, and they even get that wrong. Sean had no idea what he was carrying.'

'I thought the authorities caught him because he was suffering from an overdose?'

'Oh, *that*. It was a con. O'Donnelly's pals. They jacked him up with the overdose themselves. Put something in a bowl of soup and fed it to him, would you believe. They wanted him to get caught.'

'But I don't understand,' said Julia. 'Why would they do that?'

'My brother has a big mouth,' I explained. 'He upsets people. The consul got hold of the wrong end of the stick and the paper printed some rubbish about an overdose before anyone had checked the facts.'

'That's terrible.'

'Yeah, life's full of little surprises, isn't it? Sean went off to see the world and lost his arm. The only good thing is that the plan backfired on O'Donnelly and the police got him.'

'I'm sorry to hear about your troubles. I think I'd better go,' she said sadly. 'It was good to see you again.' She started off, then came back. 'I've often thought of you, Kay. It's a shame to see you so—'

'So what?' I asked nastily. 'I'm in great spirits, the rudest of health. Things couldn't possibly be any better.'

Typically, she took my remark at face value. 'Well, it doesn't look that way. Look, if you ever want to talk—' She dug into her handbag and found a business card: *The Oasis – Stress Therapy Centre*. '—you can reach me on this number.'

I stared dumbly at the proferred card. I really wanted to refuse it.

'Please, Kay, take it. I always wanted us to be friends.' She hesitated, then decided to speak. 'Well, perhaps more than friends. But you wouldn't do anything about it. Everything just stayed the same between us. You never seemed to want – well, to see inside of me. It was like I didn't matter to you.'

'Are you trying to tell me you fancied me?'

'Well, yes, of course.' She looked embarrassed, and cleared her throat. 'Of course. I was in love with you. I thought you knew that.'

I was amazed. 'But why?'

'I don't know. You always had so many ideas in your head,

240   C a l a b a s h

you were so full of possibilities. I felt sure that you would do something special.'

I had no answer for her. Dumbfounded, I watched her walk off along the sunstruck pavement, a little less confident than when I had seen her arrive.

CHAPTER THIRTY-FOUR

Sea Change

And I suppose that's how things might have stayed forever.

In the days that followed, I sat on my stool in the doorway of the arcade and imagined myself in middle age, living on the outskirts of town in a semi-detached redbrick villa, weather-watching at the window, staring at the narrow grey band of sea that showed between the more expensive houses opposite. Perhaps I had married the shy girl who drank alone in the pub near the arcade. Perhaps I had bought myself a little business and failed to 'make a go' of it, so that now I worked in slot machine rentals, travelling along the coast in my Vauxhall Viva, lazily fantasising about pretty, young hitch-hikers, getting drunk in dingy third-rate hotels, fat and wheezy and free of desire. My dreams of Calabash were as distant as childhood memories.

After a tentative summer, autumn drew in early. In a half-hearted attempt to make amends for my wasted life, I stepped up my hours as a hospital visitor at Cole Bay General. I took an evening course and began sitting with seriously ill children, reading to them, just being there to calm their fears and play with them. Perhaps my reasons were selfish; seeing those poor little buggers certainly stopped me feeling so bad about myself. Every time I visited them I thought of Miss Ruth, translucent and frail in her neat white hospital bed, lost without her beloved books.

In a seaside town, the first sign of autumn is the reappearance of condensation on car roofs. There's a bite in the air when you move into the shadows. The summer stalls begin closing up. After replacing the town's vandalised floral clock half a dozen times, the council threw in the towel and paved it over. Calabash became a distant warm reverie, like a half-remembered holiday. As if to place the kingdom even further out of reach, the end of the pier was declared unsafe, and when the public money required to effect repairs proved unforthcoming, it was blocked off with scaffolding, bags of concrete and barbed wire.

The helter skelter, the ghost train and the dodgems were boarded up and left to the ravages of the elements. The candy-floss kiosk was moved into the main arcade, but Katherine no longer worked there. Cottesloe informed me that she was pregnant and preparing to become a mum. He didn't say who the father was, but I had a good idea. The pier, once Royal Victorian Cole Bay's centrepiece of civic pride, became a blunted stump occupied by a handful of tacky amusements that amused no-one. Day-trippers left feeling short-changed, vandalism increased, and the town lost out. The resort was passed over by the companies who used to book the Churchill Suite of the Scheherazade for their annual general meetings, and most of Bob's staff were laid off. In order to keep his own position he was put on short hours, and had to take a second job as a park-keeper.

I began drinking in the bar on the pier chiefly because nobody I knew would have dreamt of drinking there. The toilets were labelled 'Buoys' and 'Gulls'. Some nights I would nod to Mr Cottesloe and send him over a beer. His theatre was failing; the summer attendances for his ancient Agatha Christie plays had hit an all-time low. Even the town's old age pensioners could spot the identity of the murderer before the final curtain. Cottesloe swore he could hear them all muttering to each other, 'It's the one in the cream jumper,' before the end of the first act.

From my seat in the bar I could see the red metal warning sign on the pier's scaffolding, taunting me. One rainy Tuesday night, ten minutes before the final bell, I drained my sixth pint of bitter and rose unsteadily to my feet, determined to do something about the sign. The barmaid, a woman who looked as if any remaining pleasurable responses had been removed from her by aversion therapy, didn't even bother to glance up as I left.

Outside, the cold rain hit my face and I fell back against the wall, gasping for breath. Following the side of the building I reached the sheets of corrugated iron that had been bolted over the scaffolding, and squinted angrily at the offending notice. This was the closest I had been to the sealed-off section, and now I could see how easy it would be to climb through. Hoping that the council were too mean to pay for a security patrol, I clambered awkwardly between the poles, snagging my coat and tripping, but emerging unhurt on the other side. The way ahead was unlit, but I could make out the black hulk of the ghost train. The top of the helter skelter had blown down, leaving its ribs exposed like the remains of a half-devoured animal. The boards beneath my feet were slippery, but felt solid enough to support me. Although the rain was falling hard, the sea was flat and no storms were forecast, so I made my way to the very end of the pier, where I knew the lower fishing platform to be. But here it was too dark to see the steps at all, and, drunk as I was, I figured my chances of surviving a fall into the sea from this height were lousy.

I knew that I needed to see the platform, just to be sure that it was still in place. There was only one other site from which I could do such a thing. The pier had its own speed-boat, a great heavy motor-launch built in the 1930s, with SKYLARK stencilled across the bow. It was permanently moored beneath the pier a few hundred yards along from the platform, no longer used for pleasure trips, but kept in good order for use in emergencies; not that any had arisen since the escapologist who used to be thrown from the pier in a chained sack got pissed on stout one Sunday morning and didn't come back up.

Leading down to the Skylark's embarkation point was a broad set of steel steps. I searched for the entrance and found it, ducking beneath the wooden admittance bar and hanging on to the railing. Several times I nearly slipped over on the seaweed-slick staircase. I stayed just above the water level, but here beneath the struts I could not make out the platform. The whole thing seemed to have disappeared. Perhaps it had been washed away.

It was the clinking sound that attracted my attention. I looked down at the step below my shoes, and saw the object washing against it, caught in the green fronds that eddied around the stanchion. Reaching down to pull it from the water, I lost my balance and almost fell in. I knew at once what it was; I could tell from its strange stopper that this was the bottle I had thrown into the harbour in Calabash, in an earlier, happier life.

Clutching the bottle, I ran back up the steps, my heart punching against my ribs. I slipped and stumbled across the boards to the barricade, then climbed through, scraping the skin from the palms of my hands. I did not allow myself to examine the object inside my jacket until I reached the lights of the esplanade. I stopped beneath a lamp-post and held the scuffed glass high in the drizzle-misted light. The inside still appeared to be dry. After a great deal of difficulty I managed to unscrew the stopper. I tipped the bottle over my out-stretched hand, thumping the end with my right fist. And there they were, the pieces of card that had puzzled me so much.

Lee Hill Grammar School For Boys South Do

This homework book is the property of Simon Jonathan Saun

And on the other side, in my own handwriting:

Kay James Goodwin,

Residing at 14, Balaclava Terrace, Cole Bay, Southern England

And Also A Resident Of The Kingdom Of Calabash.

CHAPTER THIRTY-FIVE

The Electrified Citadel

But what did it really prove? Couldn't I have deluded myself into filling the damned thing out at the end of the pier? The bottle might simply have been lodged there in the seaweed all this time. Still, finding it filled me with resolve. Looking back, it was odd that this should have been the catalyst to my rediscovered sense of purpose, but I suddenly realised how long it had been since I had last taken any kind of positive action about anything in Cole Bay. At least in Calabash I had been able to effect changes, even though my actions had wrought potentially disastrous results. Here, my attitude towards Julia had been typical; moody, selfish and pathetic. But now I was determined to end my life adrift. I felt sure that the bottle was in some way a call to arms, even though I had thrown it into the sea myself. It had been washed to the steps of the pier for a reason.

The following morning I began my investigation. If I had found the bottle on the pier and invented a story around it, I wanted to know why. If it turned out that my mental fortitude was as weak as my physical health, I needed to be able to understand myself before I could do anything about it.

I examined the piece of paper again. The boy's last name had to be Saunders, or perhaps Saunderson. They were the most popular choices listed in the telephone book. 'South Do' presented more of a problem. I began by searching places that came to mind: South Dorking, South Dorchester, South Doncaster, and so on. I tried nearly a dozen of these, but drew blanks. No sign of a Lee Hill Grammar School in any of them. Then it struck me that the name might be more of a description; South Downs. Along this stretch of coastline, most of the hilly plains above the sea were described as downs.

This time I was in luck. Lee Hill turned out to be a small private grammar school for boys just outside of Worthing. The school secretary was understandably reluctant to give out details of individual pupils over the telephone, but I persuaded her to check the register for boys with the surname of Saunders or Saunderson. She had nothing beginning with the first four letters at all. She sounded busy and anxious to end the call, so I appealed to her vanity. I told her I was a local journalist preparing an article on education, and I had heard that the school's academic record was excellent. I explained that I was tracing students from the area who had gone on to great things. The secretary couldn't help me but thought that Mr Gregory, a senior teacher who had retired but still fulfilled the role of school archivist, might be able to draw up a list if I asked him nicely. She gave me his home telephone number.

The boy's name, it transpired, was Simon Jonathan Saunders. Well-remembered by Mr Gregory, and well-liked. A pupil with distinction. A successful career in the foreign office, all the more impressive because Simon had been crippled by polio at an early age, and had attended the school in a wheelchair. He had left Lee Hill in 1946. A few years later he had made a bit of a name for himself as a writer of fantasy and science fiction. But illness reclaimed him, and he died before achieving lasting fame.

This raised more questions than it answered. What was a handicapped schoolboy doing in Calabash a quarter of a century before my arrival? I knew that there was only one way to find out. Whatever the effect it might have on my sanity, it was time to try and return.

My first barrier was a physical one. The scaffolded wall that sectioned off the end of the pier looked even more daunting in the sober light of day. It was a dry, cold morning, but the sea was churning foam along its wave crests and looked unforgiving. A vicious current pulled around the pylons. I waited until the area nearest the barrier was deserted, then clambered through once more, walking past the shuttered ghost train, the heads of its skeleton passengers rain-streaked and halted in mid-nod, to the upper fishing platform.

I peered over the side, but could see nothing. Slipping under the chain, I carefully began my descent, then realised why the lower platform could not be seen. The chains that anchored it to the nearside pillars had been severed, and the grille had tipped so that most of it was now underwater. The whole thing was lifting and dropping with the sway of the tide, shifting back and forth. The last three steps leading to it had rusted off, and lay twisted in the murky water. Most of the chain railings had come loose and fallen away. If I got down there, it might not be possible to climb back up.

The thought stopped me cold. I had been raised in a coastal town, and yet was unable to swim more than a couple of yards. I had never felt comfortable in water, always aware of the pressure on my damaged lungs. I looked back at the coastline of Cole Bay, at the rows of little grey houses that were banked up behind the tatty esplanade, huddled together as if frightened of being pushed into the sea. The bitter green ocean churned beneath my feet. *Shit*, I thought, *I've got nothing left to lose now except my mind*, and I jumped down.

The shock of cold water over my shoes nearly unbalanced me. The platform shifted violently with my weight. I looked about for something to hold on to and lurched over to one of the main pillars, throwing my arms around it. The grille had become more slippery now that it was immersed. I had to stand further towards the edge, at a point where I would be able to align the reflected lights from the harbour statues. Releasing my grip on the pillar, I took one step, then another. The grille began to sink beneath my feet. The water was up to my kneecaps, then over them. Trying not to panic, I looked at the horizon and forced myself to remember that first day, the need I had felt, the same need I had now.

Above me, the sun broke through the clouds. But instead of a single broad light shining on the water, there were two. The twin beams snaked across the distant waves, lines of emerald luminescence heading slowly towards me, their inter-section arriving exactly at the point where I was standing. Suddenly the glare was stinging my eyes like seasalt, and I was tipping backwards – falling into the icy sea.

No, not the sea, on to the deck of the little fishing boat that was rubbing against the limestone harbour walls of Calabash. A familiar heat washed over me like a warm bath, reviving my chilled bones as I looked up into the now cloudless sky. As I clambered from the rocking boat I was already starting to sweat. Elated, I pulled off my overcoat and threw it on to the dock, then shielded my eyes and looked towards the city.

At first I thought the light was playing tricks. Nothing was where it was supposed to be. The walls of the kingdom seemed to have been rearranged, demolished in some places, rebuilt in others. The maze of sunbleached domes and min-arets that surrounded the palace had vanished altogether. A pall of brown smoke hung over the hilltops. The dock was deserted, the nets and lobster pots laying broken and empty in great rope piles. There were no fishing boats in the harbour other than my own. Mooring the boat beside the nearest capstan, I set off along the main road towards the city. The first thing I noticed was that there was no-one in the fields to greet me as I passed. Where was everybody?

As I approached the village, what I saw shocked and disoriented me. The ochre villas were derelict. Several of them had been put to the torch. The roads were unkempt and partially grown-over. Vines had crawled up the sides of buildings, digging their roots into mud and plaster, cracking walls into rubble. In the village square, weeds had burst through a mosaic of the Sultan, shattering it in a dozen places. I arrived at my own villa to find the front door hanging from its hinges. I called Parizade's name, but there was no answer. Inside, the few items of furniture we had possessed had been tipped over and broken apart. A single rush sandal lay on its side, the strap broken. I ran out into the garden. It had become completely overgrown. I pushed a path through the brambles and saw scavenging cats, so bony that their ribs poked out, creeping under the weeds at my approach. A goat lay bloated and dead on its tether, its rotted carcass covered in flies. In the shadows I caught the glittering eyes of a darting rat.

The entire village was deserted, as if the residents had been spirited away; no, not spirited, dragged, for in every home there were signs that the owners had not gone quietly. Water jugs lay smashed, jars and pots lay in pieces in the grass. Two of the largest houses were completely gutted, burned out some time ago, judging by the way the vines had managed to grow across the blackened debris. The well had been filled with the carcasses of dogs in order to foul its water.

The sun was searing the back of my neck. I pulled off my

sweater and discarded it, running on to the home of Dr Trebunculus. Here, the destruction was even more complete. Everything had been torn from the doctor's laboratory and destroyed. The grand astrolabe appeared to have been singled out for special attention. All that remained of it were a few pieces of twisted metal. The planetary globes had been ground into diamond shards. I picked my way across a crystalline rainbow, past the shelves of rare herbs, pickled creatures in jars and preserved specimens that had been torn down and shattered, to lie stinking and rotting in the corners of the room. It was as if a military coup had taken place, swooping one night while the townspeople slept. Now I began to fear for their lives, for it was clear that nothing lived here anymore. Back in the dead, stale heat I turned and ran towards the city walls. The few animals I passed on the way were untethered and starving. Others lay dehydrated beneath the bleaching sun, their opalescent eyes turned up into the light.

The greatest shock was yet to come. I mounted the steps to the inner city with a sense of growing dread, but nothing prepared me for the sight within. The narrow streets had been filled with trash. There was nothing of value or beauty left. A pair of brawling drunks spilled out across the highway, bellowing obscenities at each other. Another, so far gone that he could hardly stand, was urinating into the dried-up basin of a broken fountain. They wore the disarrayed uniforms of soldiers on leave.

Someone was being copiously sick in the entrance of a make-shift brothel. Garishly painted whores leaned from the windows, angrily calling down to him. Strangest of all, Calabash had somehow discovered electricity. Every shadowed building blinked with fluorescent tubes of bare white light. The buzz of unregulated voltage filled the air. The distant samba beat had been replaced with what sounded like a thousand badly tuned radio stations; distorted tracks that assaulted my ears in a blurry wall of white noise. Where peace and harmony had once settled across the days, a philistine lunacy now swarmed and massed.

I searched for the entrance to the palace, but it was hard to spot between the outcrops of makeshift shacks. The streets stank of alcohol, vomit and faeces. Marauders stumbled past the graffiti-smeared walls, drugged and dazed, begging and brawling from one food-stand to the next. I saw no friendly, familiar faces, only the isolating anger of strangers.

I finally located the forecourt of the former palace beneath a ruptured wooden banner advertising live sex shows. The placid Nubian guards had gone, and the mosaics of the dry fountains that stood within were cracked and faded, their basins filled with detritus. Huge pornographic drawings had been scrawled across the delicately painted walls of the formal gardens. The trees had been torn down and used for firewood. There were no children anywhere. With a deepening sense of horror and desolation, I saw that what had happened here was some kind of decline so steep, swift and total that it had irreversibly destroyed the city from within.

I pushed aside two more drunks who reached out and grabbed at my shirt, running on towards the inner courtyard. Here, instead of the perpetually open entrance to the Sultan's quarters, had been erected a great rusty door, locked and bolted with bars that cut deep into the walls. Iron shafts had been hammered into place across all the windows, turning the building into a prison.

My mind reeling, I slumped against the wall of a drained pond and tried to think. What could have happened here? A suspicion was growing inside me that somehow this was all my fault. As I watched, a heavy-set man in a ludicrously Western pin-striped suit of grey worsted walked briskly past with a briefcase in each hand. The shoulders of his jacket sported steel military epaulettes and raised brass buttons. The legs of his trousers had thin red lines running down their outer sides, and he was shod in highly polished riding boots, a footsoldier in an army of commerce. He reached the great door and stamped to attention, waiting impatiently. Someone must have witnessed his approach from an upper window, for a narrow section in the lower part of the door opened just enough to allow him entrance, and he was gone. A few moments later, the door opened again and another similarly suited businessman hurried out.

'Hey!' I called, 'Wait!'

The little man looked up, startled, then renewed his pace, slipping away into the back alleys. My shout also attracted the attention of the pair of drunken soldiers. I quickly slipped back into the shadows.

The key to whatever had happened here clearly lay inside this fortified compound. My instincts warned me that any attempt to trick my way in would place me in danger, so I decided to complete my circuit of the grounds and determine what action to take once I could comprehend the situation. Fear and guilt spurred me on through the maze of now-derelict courtyards, to the farthest end of the palace. Rounding the corner, I found myself facing a phalanx of military bureaucrats. They were marching smartly towards me with their briefcases held across their chests like the butts of rifles. I dropped back into the alleyway and pressed close against the wall, holding my breath, waiting for them to pass.

I recognised the next courtyard as the one where I had first been received by the Sultan and his retinue, but now the silken banners were gone, and the sheltering fig trees had been hacked down to sap-baked stumps. In the distance, martial brass-band music played through tinny speakers. More blank-faced business-militia marched past in pairs, to vanish within the fortified labyrinth of the inner palace.

I followed the shaded wall at my back, but my sense of direction had deserted me. Soon I could go no further forward. The way was blocked by a monstrous curving wall of stone. The building was of circular construction, a disproportionate stump with a vast sinister portico and a single tiny entrance. The only windows I could see were right at the top, near what I presumed was a flat roof. I cautiously approached the rough iron doors set beneath the portico.

To my surprise, they sprang apart with an electrical snap just as I reached them. Out rode a soldier dressed in a tunic of the *sipahi*, followed by a small band of sickly prisoners chained together at the wrists and ankles. As they passed through the entrance I ran in, and the doors immediately slammed shut behind me with an echoing bang.

The first thing I saw lying on the littered floor of the foyer was a top hat of purple velvet. Only one man in Calabash wore such an item.

'Trebunculus!' I shouted. 'It's me, Kay! Can you hear me?'

The building appeared to be some kind of giant amusement arcade, an illuminated pleasure dome of gaming tables and funfair rides, but nothing looked as if it worked properly. Bare wires had been knotted together above slot machines, where they fizzed and crackled, twisting back and forth with errant electrical force. The place looked as if it might catch fire and burn down at any minute. An acrid stench of burnt rubber and stale bodies hung in the air. I stepped across a pool of oil and peered into the juddering maelstrom of machinery. Ahead, a faultily illuminated funhouse creaked and banged, shorting out as the corpse of an elderly man was repeatedly slammed against the rollers of its tilting walkway. There was broken glass everywhere, much of it stained with blood. A number of dead bodies lay wedged into corners like shattered mannequins. Some drunk soldiers hung from the frame of a wooden roller coaster, bellowing at a carriage as it thundered past. I felt as though I had walked into a physical manifestation of madness.

'Trebunculus!' I called above the cacophony of the electric fairground. 'Where are you?'

There was no sign of the doctor other than his hat. My head throbbing, I ran back to the entrance and pushed at the great iron doors, but they remained shut. There had to be a mechanism for opening them from the inside, but I could not find it. Whatever force had brought me to this deranged place had taken care to seal me within.

Around the edge of the auditorium ran a ricketty wooden staircase that I now set out to climb, vaulting several steps at a time. I knew that if I could see from above, I would have a better chance of spotting someone alive. The staircase ended in a great platform of thrown-together planks that crossed beneath the dome of the building. Now that I was level with the windows below the roof, I ran to one and looked down at the world outside.

From here I could see the full extent of the destruction. The city I had loved and left lay gutted like a corpse before me, and in its place scavengers roamed through the shattered remains, abandoned to an unknown fate. I pressed forward against the sandalwood lattice of the window, trying to see more, when the entire panel against which I lay tipped suddenly forward, launching me into the foetid air outside.

CHAPTER THIRTY-SIX

Migrating Kingdoms

I looked down at the world spinning tipsily at my feet, then back across the fretworked wooden panel, which was creaking away from the wall on its damaged hinges. A gloved hand reached from the gloom behind me. In order to grab it I would have to release my grip on the sides of the frame, and the moment I did so, I began sliding away. I kicked my feet down hard and pushed to stop myself from falling any further, but the great hinged window swung sharply down, separating me from my rescuer.

I stamped at the wood, but it would not give. Dragged by gravity, I felt myself sliding further along the marquetry, and knew that the only chance I had of saving my life was to wait until I had reached the bottom of the panel before kicking inwards and praying that whoever was on the inside was quick-thinking enough to pull me in. For a stomach-lurching moment I was in freefall, suspended in the air below the window, then strong hands were grabbing at my legs. With a crack, I hit the lower part of the frame and swung over so that I was hanging upside down against the wall. Moments later a second, bonier pair of hands grabbed at my clothes, and I was hauled back inside.

'If you were attempting to effect some kind of rescue, it wasn't very elegantly planned,' panted Dr Trebunculus, as he and his assistant released me on to the floor of the plank platform.

'Doctor, Menavino, you're both alive!' I tried to pull myself upright, but could barely feel my legs.

'No thanks to you, I must say.'

'Your laboratory – I felt sure—'

Trebunculus yanked me to my feet and bashed at my arms and shoulders. If he was checking for broken bones, he had an odd way of going about it. 'Oh, a few splinters but you'll live. We very nearly didn't. We've only managed to escape execution this long by using trickery.'

'What's going on? Where is Rosamunde? Is she all right?'

'The Princess is still alive, if that's what you mean. After defying her husband she was taken to one of the city's brothels, but the last we heard, she had managed to bribe one of the guards and escape. Wherever she is now, I don't suppose that she'll want to see you.'

'And Parizade?'

'Ah, well. Fate was not so kind with her.'

'What do you mean?'

'She died badly, with your name upon her lips.' The doctor fixed me with a beady green eye. 'She felt sure you would return in time to save us all.'

'What happened?'

'The soldiers took her away. We found her later, and buried her.'

'This is awful!'

'You realise, I suppose, that all this is your fault.'

'I don't understand what could have occurred to change everything so much.'

'Come. The Semanticor has found us temporary quarters. This is the home of all the so-called "subversives" who have not yet been executed, but there are no subversives here, merely drunks and madmen. They've been leaving us alone because they know we have no power to harm them, but once word gets out that you are here our days of safety will be over. Let me show you what has become of your great dream city.'

Above us, a smashed fretwork panel allowed a cool evening breeze to enter from outside and relieve the stale atmosphere. Menavino and the doctor manoeuvred a flimsy wooden ladder beneath it and we climbed up, to emerge on the flat rooftop of the building. There were a handful of them, tattered, skinny rebels, who looked so bewildered and exhausted that they barely seemed to notice the new arrival in their midst. The Semanticor was curled in a corner like a bundle of rags, fast asleep. Menavino dragged a sack across the floor and upturned it. Out fell chunks of stale bread and half-rotten pieces of fruit. The rebels dropped upon the haul and devoured it as though they had been presented with sweetmeats from one of the Sultan's feasts.

'What has happened here?' I asked.

'What do you think happened?' replied Trebunculus angrily. 'You must have suspected. The kingdom has followed its line of least resistance.'

'What do you mean?'

'The Sultan was deposed. The city was taken over by General Bassa's men, and they brought in a consortium of merchants. There is an old saying: "Take a Turk from the saddle and he becomes a bureaucrat". They had such grand plans, new inventions—'

'Wait a minute, why was the Sultan deposed? You told me he had ruled here for countless generations.'

Trebunculus looked sadly at the others. His anger seemed to dissipate in a single breath. 'You set it all in motion, didn't you? Laying with the Princess. Once you had served your purpose and delivered your scientific advancement to General Bassa, the Lord Chancellor could reveal the truth about your secret trysts. Major Maximus no longer wanted his bride. He beat her soundly, and exposed her as a whore and a deceiver. She had brought shame to the royal family and was expelled at once, to be sold into harlotry. Leaving the General, with his troops under the command of his son, to cleanse the land and place it under military rule.'

'But how could everything suddenly change overnight? Surely there had been uprisings before.'

'Do you still not understand the purpose of our kingdom? Correct me if I am wrong, but your biggest problem with the existence of Calabash stems from your inability to tell if we are real or if this is all a part of your – forgive me – adolescent imagination?'

'It's why I left,' I replied, seating myself beside him. 'I knew it couldn't be real, and yet here I felt more alive than in my own world. I feared I was going mad.'

'Then,' he said wearily, 'perhaps we are partly to blame. How can I best explain this? We are men of science, yes? The man from Vienna. You have read Freud? You understand a little of the id and the ego?'

'A little. The first is instinct and the second is individuality. The *ego* has to control the *id* and stop it from being destructive.'

'In a nutshell. Do you believe in the so-called collective subconscious?'

'I suppose so. There are certain shared ideals, hopes—'

'And dreams?'

'Yes. Are you telling me that this is all a dream?'

'No, Kay, it is not a dream. Oh, it is something far greater.' He looked down at the dusty fires dotting the landscape. 'It is – if you like – the subconscious life of mankind. A separate reality from yours.' He picked up a broken stick and drew a circle in the dust on the floor. 'Here is your world. A great diverse civilisation, heated in calamity, tempered in suffering, scalded in pain and sorrow. But it survives natural disasters and the man-made horrors of religions and wars. A great kingdom that somehow abides. How can it do so? Why should it? Because there is something more to a man than bone and muscle. Man aspires. He seeks to know the un-knowable, to grasp the impossible, to measure the infinite. Man dreams. His lifespan is nothing, and yet he fights, and dies trying to know more. What is he trying to reach?'

The doctor drew a second circle overlapping the first. 'Many people never come into contact with us at all. They pass their entire lives asleep. And there are those who only awake for a brief period, often in early adolescence, before they are told that such things are impossible. Once in a while, though, someone has a deeper need. Then we cease to appear as a passing phase, and our reality grows. Our worlds touch.' He marked the points where the circles overlapped. 'But this combining of spheres brings its own dangers. It can make those who reach us forget their own lives completely, locking them out of their own world.'

'You mean it can drive people mad.'

'Yes. Think of the Indian legends, the Greek myths, the Arabian Nights, Grimm's fairy tales, the lands of Oz, Middle Earth, Wonderland, Xanadu, Lilliput, Narnia, and how they share the same attributes. Your people choose to see us in different ways, but since time began, they have delved deep into our lands for inspiration. Calabash is a dream city, passed on among its dreamers, from one to the next. And everybody dreams of Calabash, in one form or another, even if they fail to realise it. It has survived under a million different names; it is the restlessness you feel in youth, the longing of missed opportunities in middle life, and the wistful memories of old age. Calabash is inside you all.'

The doctor looked away at the red sky, saddened. He drew breath, then continued.

'But as is so often in the natural way of things, there is a terrible paradox at its heart. The kingdom needs new minds to renew it, but it eventually destroys minds. Every hour spent in Calabash damages the dreamer's real life. In your world, aren't you told not to daydream? Aren't you constantly warned about the dangers of failing to face reality?'

'Yes, but—'

'When you are away, Calabash grows weak and susceptible to harm. Once there were hundreds of great visionaries in your world, dreamers who enriched and strengthened us into mighty lands. Until your twentieth century. Ah, what a dreadful time that has been! The visionaries died out, or had no need of us, and slowly the language of dreaming was lost. By the time the middle of the century was reached, only a handful of visitors managed to make the journey across. Before you arrived, we were in the most desperate straits. Our final visitor had died suddenly—'

'Simon Jonathan Saunders.'

'You know of him?' Trebunculus's eyes widened in surprise. 'A prodigious mind, he filled the city with wonders. We had great hopes for him. He drew all of his inspiration from us. His death threw us into disarray. And we liked the boy. Some of the people who have been here— well, you can imagine. We were more the Greek ideal then; Gods and temples. Of course, the best people are very hard to come by. We needed to make contact with a strong new mind, and luckily we managed to locate you before it was too late.'

'You made contact with me?'

'Most certainly. Our world is not accessible from many places. When you first arrived here, you doubtless wondered why there were no muezzins. So long as one person believes in Calabash, it needs no other faith. It is a kingdom kept alive by fantasies, and each dreamer remakes it in his own style. We provide all the raw material people like you need to survive. That is how it has always worked. But you changed us, and then abandoned us.'

'You were killing me, Trebunculus. Using me.'

'And you would not abide by our rules. Those who dream of Calabash must be strong. The process is one of – how you say – symbiosis.'

I thought of my real father. Had he, too, been crushed beneath the weight of his dreams? 'But I thought I was free to do whatever I liked here, all the things I couldn't do at home.'

'Within the limits of our society. Only you didn't do them,' said Trebunculus sadly. 'You could have had daring adventures, you could have improved our kingdom and become a great leader, but instead you did nothing except sow the seeds of our destruction.'

'There's enough uncertainty and anxiety at home – I just wanted to be somewhere where I could feel happiness. Where I could be at peace with myself. Without having to prove anything to anyone.'

'Then I suppose you achieved your aim. But you chose to leave just when the city was laid bare to predatory evil. You knew the Sultan had grown weak and lazy. The kingdom was sinking into a reverie which could only endanger our way of life. After you left, Calabash was like a rudderless ship. We drifted on a collective tide of half-thoughts, tuning into the selfish desires of whoever passed nearest. As the dream began to break up it became spoiled. In the absence of an effective ruler, it fell prey to its own weaknesses, and the Lord Chancellor assumed control.'

'You told me you trusted him.'

'I told you he always kept the welfare of the state at heart. What I failed to foresee was his determination to preserve it at any cost. Once you solved the mystery of Eliya's death, the Chancellor's ambitions were revealed to me. How many years had he waited for this moment! It was his responsibility to keep the kingdom strong. He saw the deepening lassitude in the royal family and sided with the militia. He saw it as his duty. He hastened the process, removing the Sultan's wife to prevent further heirs, waiting for your arrival, bargaining with you to supply a scientific discovery for General Bassa, and then taking action once you had removed yourself – as he knew you would. He saw your weaknesses long ago, Kay.'

I suddenly felt very ashamed.

'Our Lord Chancellor merged the Sultan's army with the nation's businessmen, and installed his bureaucrats as the new heads of government. The land was quickly carved into lots and sold off. The Sultan was too weak to fight back, even when he saw that everything was so badly run that the economy was collapsing. Most of the former courtiers are in prison. The royal family is rumoured to be alive deep inside the palace, but the Lord Chancellor has built a *yilditz* filled with windows coated in chainmail, and standing upon a floor of lethal booby traps.' He sighed deeply. 'But who knows what is true anymore? The Sultan does not need to cut the heads from the songbirds now. They have all been killed and eaten.' He looked around at the hopeless faces of the others. 'And just when all resolve has gone, and the last hope has utterly faded, you reappear! Well, it's too late to undo the harm you caused, so don't even think about it.'

'*I* caused!' I shouted indignantly. 'It might have helped if you'd explained all of this at the beginning.'

'Well, I'm sorry your subconscious doesn't come with an instruction manual, but it can't be helped. Now that you're here, I must warn you – there is no way back.'

'What do you mean?'

'How are you going to get home? Tell yourself it's all still in your imagination? That won't work. Now that you know the truth, you're stuck here with us.'

'I don't see why—'

Trebunculus raised his hands to the sky. 'How can the boy be so slow-witted?' he asked the passing clouds.

Suddenly my predicament began to clarify itself. 'I'm no longer in charge of my own dream,' I said quietly.

'Well done. It has passed far beyond your control. It is following its own chaotic decline, a mirror image to your own world.' He studied my puzzled face. 'You must have known that. The two, you see, are one. They always have been.'

'You say the Lord Chancellor used me to pass science on to the General, but I didn't. The device I gave him was made of a substance called plastic. It was correct in principle only, he couldn't have created electricity from it. He would have needed a practical working model of something electrical to copy its principles.'

'You must have given him something. Bassa has constructed a great electric war machine called the Belligeratron, in which he plans to lead his invasion. It is said to be a great advancement on our meagre weapons. He boasts that you helped him to invent it.'

'But I gave him nothing!' I insisted.

'Then perhaps you did so without knowing.'

'You say he plans to lead an invasion? Who is he invading?'

The doctor grimaced in pain as he shifted his knees. 'Why, I would have thought it was obvious. He has subjugated Calabash, and has decided the time has come to wage war with a more worthy opponent. His mighty army is going to invade your world.'

CHAPTER THIRTY-SEVEN

For Two Worlds

The land was aglow with distant fires. A smoke-haze drifted across the dying sun, bloodying the clouded horizon. Trebunculus sat back on his haunches; his pale kneecaps showed through the holes in his velvet trousers. He snapped his stick in half and threw the pieces aside. 'The Lord Chancellor wanted to know everything about you. Incredible as it might seem, he once feared you. Poor Parizade refused to tell him anything and was put to death. It is told that she professed her love for you even as her final breath left her body.'

'All right, Doctor. I feel bad enough as it is.'

'The Princess Rosamunde was allowed to escape with her life out of respect for the honour of her father. Maximus Peason hunts her, but so far he has failed to discover her hiding place.'

'How do you know all this?'

'I'll show you. Scammer!' A small sooty boy appeared at the end of the roof. His blackened hair stuck up from his head as though he had recently received an electric shock. He seemed unable to stand upright, but ran hunched over to the doctor's side. His eyes were large and bright blue. 'Scammer switched loyalties after the Chancellor beat him once too often. Now he operates as our eyes and ears.'

'Do you trust him?' I asked.

'Oh, you can trust me, sir,' said the imp. 'Beaten black and blue I was. No more, I said, no more. The doctor's kind. He feeds poor Scammer, he does.'

'If we can spy on the enemy, perhaps there is still a chance to put things right.'

'Absolutely not. Calabash is adrift now. You had your chance.'

'This is more horrible than Cole Bay.'

'How would we know? None of us have been to your blighted world yet, although we will if the Lord Chancellor and General Bassa have their way.'

'Do you really think they can?'

'I don't see why not. You managed to get here. Anyway, this kingdom as you knew it is dead. We have run out of time. Once Calabash is gone, no-one in your world will ever find it again. Your people will be without their dreams forever. Do you know what happens to a civilisation that cannot imagine anything better for itself?'

'Perhaps I can change the way things are.'

'Perhaps I'll pass stools in the shape of starfish.' Trebunculus shook his head. 'Remember, the longer you are here, the weaker your corporeal form grows. And the General's army grows stronger with each passing hour.'

'Tell me something, Doctor. How long am I away from my physical self when I cross over?'

'Well, that's the question, isn't it? Remember I once told you about the relativity of time? How a second on one plane might last hours on another?'

'Yes, but—'

'Every hour you spend here in Calabash is but a brief moment in your world.'

'But this time it's different. In the past, the worst that's happened is I've caught a cold. This time – I'm not safe.'

'What do you mean? Where is your physical self?'

'It's balancing on an iron platform that's sinking into the English Channel.'

'God's teeth, how on earth— What's the temperature?'

'I don't know – I guess around zero.'

'You guess! How long do you think you'll be able to survive?'

'I hadn't planned it out. I mean, I'm not wearing a wet suit.'

'What is a wet suit?'

'It doesn't matter. I can't swim. It means there's not much time. What can we do to restore this world?'

The doctor snorted derisively. 'The Lord Chancellor would have to be deposed. General Bassa's army would have to be halted before it attempts to cross over in the Belligeratron.'

'Couldn't we try to storm the palace?'

'What with? An army of flying monkeys? This is not your world to make anymore, remember?'

'But what would I have to do?' I pleaded.

'Let's see. First it sounds as though you would have to go back and save yourself. Then you would somehow have to find a way to return here. Challenge the Lord Chancellor and his men. Vanquish the General and his army before they set off for your world. And safely reach home after restoring the Sultan to power.'

'So, nothing too complicated then.'

'No, it really is extremely complicated, you see—'

'I was being sarcastic, Doctor. It's a popular English conversational form. What should I do first?'

'Go back and save yourself, Kay. Then you must find a way to return here before it is too late. It is said that in the final moments of our lives, as the city faces its apocalypse, it will become visible to your world. That is when General Bassa and his army will make their crossing. If that time comes, you will see us. You must be vigilant for the signs.'

'Then I must go now. We can't wait until nightfall to escape.'

'I don't see how we can escape at all. They locked us up in here weeks ago. We draw straws to see who slips out when the doors open to admit soldiers, and scavenge the ruins for food, but only a few of us have successfully returned. You hear that distant hammering?' Trebunculus cupped his hand around his ear. 'The General has ordered all the roads from the city to be taken up. He's sealing us off.'

'There must be another way out.'

'Only the entry door. It can only be triggered by Bassa's men, who are free to come and go as they please. You are one of the few outsiders to effect admittance since we arrived.'

'Can't we lure someone in and – I don't know, hold them hostage or something?' I was not, by nature, an adventurer. I couldn't begin to see how I might help Trebunculus and his band of hopelessly ill-prepared rebels.

'There is no way of making contact with anyone below, not without giving ourselves away. There are no windows on the lower levels.'

'Then perhaps we could go down the outside from the top of the roof where the window is broken. Do you have any rope or fishing nets we could unravel?'

'In here? Of course not.'

I looked down at the electrical cables traversing the auditorium. 'Then we'll have to make our own,' I said.

The citadel's electrical wiring was primitive, and came apart easily. We tore lengths of wire from the machines, braiding their ends together, but it was difficult to tell how much we would need for the drop. When every available exposed section of cable had been hacked free and used, we climbed back to the platform beneath the opening in the roof, and I was lifted out on to the parapet. I tied one end of the cable behind my thighs while Menavino knotted the other end around a wooden post.

'Remember,' warned Trebunculus, 'your imagination constructed Calabash subject to the laws of physics. That means you can fall to your death here.'

'We'll play out the cable as quickly as we can,' said the Semanticor, who had woken up and was starting to take an interest. 'They'll be able to spot you from below, and some of them are armed with crossbows. They're very good shots. I taught many of them when they were children.'

'Oh, great.' I braced my legs against the curved wall. 'Well, wish me luck.' I pushed off from the side, but there was a cry from above and I dropped much faster than anyone had allowed for, slipping and catching against the stone as I fell.

'You've put on weight,' yelled Trebunculus, hauling back on the cable.

At about thirty feet above the ground, my descent was painfully halted. I looked up and saw Trebunculus indicating that we had run out of wiring. I twisted helplessly on the side of the citadel as a drunken crowd slowly gathered beneath me. I looked down through my legs and calculated my chances. Pushing off from the side of the wall, I began to swing back and forth.

'Don't do that, we won't be able to hold you!' someone shouted from the roof.

Two members of the General's militia fired their crossbows, but now I was a moving target. Their arrows zinged and bounced against my shifting feet. At the peak of my swing to the left, I slipped from my wire noose and fell down on to – and through – the stretched linen awning of the stall I had spotted, demolishing it. People screamed and fell back from my path as I clambered to my feet.

More militiamen were moving in my direction. Without daring to look back, I broke free through the crowd and began running for the gates of the city. I knew that if I failed now it would spell the end of not one, but two worlds.

CHAPTER THIRTY-EIGHT

Custodian of the Empire

As I began running, I doubted my ability to do anything that would save Calabash. I was not brave, or strong. My heroes were figures from history, artists, thinkers, not fictional swordsmen or jet pilots. As if to prove the point, my legs gave way as I ran forward and I fell flat on my face in the middle of the old market square. When I tried to rise, my jellified thighs refused to support my weight. The tension of the last few hours had caught up with me. At the corner of the square I could see a troop of pin-striped militia shoving their way through drugged-up beggars and drunks. There was a high ululating cry as one of them raised the alarm, and their slender crossbows rose up to shoulder height.

It was only the burst of adrenalin that came from seeing so many weapons pointed in my direction that brought me scrambling to my feet. One thing I've always been able to do is outdistance my enemies. I felt sure that my only chance was to stay in the chaotic backstreets; I knew that as soon as I reached the open country surrounding the harbour, I would present a clear target.

The appearance of the city had changed so drastically that I barely recognised its topography. I ran through the reeking, bellowing mob, recalling only that the palace was built on raised ground, so that it made sense to keep moving to lower levels. Aware that my brown leather jacket stood out against the robes and djellabahs, I thought of yanking a linen sheet from a merchant's display and dragging it around my chest, but knew that doing so would impede my escape.

A crossbow arrow cleaved the air above my head and smacked against the wall of a fried-nut stall, and I had an idea. With a wild shout I charged at the stall, causing the merchants to jump back, and I upset the table on which stood their copper bowls of boiling palm-oil. People screamed and fell over themselves, scalded as the round-bottomed vats rolled over. The oil washed across the narrow street, creating a smoking slick that separated me from my pursuers.

I arrived back at the unguarded city entrance and galloped through it, out on to the surrounding road, then into the grasslands, staying near the edge of the great wood, running over the dead untilled earth until I thought my heart would burst. By the time I reached my old village, I saw that my pursuers had fallen back, and that I was beyond the range of their crossbows.

There was only a short stretch left before the harbour, but it was exposed. Keeping low to the ground and moving quickly, I ran behind the hanging nets that had hardened in the heat from lack of use, and arrived at the water's edge, dropping into the little ketch from the harbour wall, still wondering how I would manage to make the crossing now that I knew some of the truth about Calabash.

The afternoon sun was shining between the bronze shields of the statues, blinding me. The searing sunlight stabbed my eyes. I lost my balance and slipped, cracking my head on the side of the boat. The world retreated in a flash of pain.

I felt the temperature tumbling, and when I lowered my hands I found myself on the fishing platform once more, sinking in the freezing green water. My limbs were so cold that at first they refused to move. I wondered how long I had been unconscious. I had been able to travel back because my mind – and my imagination – had ceased to function.

If I slipped and fell in now, I was sure to drown. I leaned forward as far as I dared, but still could not reach the nearest post. I threw myself forward, knowing that all was lost if I missed. My hands connected with the top of the post. My palms were slashed on the sharp barnacles that had grown in clusters over it, but I managed to haul myself across, then began wading back over the weed-covered grille.

I sat hunched beside the electric fire in my bedroom and pulled the eiderdown tightly around my sore chest. I had been coughing for hours. Prolonged immersion into cold water was not, I recognised bitterly, to be recommended for someone prone to pneumonia.

I tried to analyse my new knowledge and apply it, but something was still missing. I had let everyone down by allowing Calabash to collapse. Was this what our own land would do, without the inspiration of a phantom world to guide it, facing invasion from an invisible, impossible army? Even if I could come up with a plan, how could the future of both worlds ever be assured? I had the pieces of the puzzle before me, but I couldn't fit them into a recognisable picture.

Perhaps people no longer felt they needed the freedom of an unfettered imagination. Even if she had bothered to read my notebooks before consigning them to the flames, my mother would not have believed a word I'd written in them.

Her refusal to count dreams as anything but wasted time bothered me. It seemed that there was no room left in our practical new world for speculation, and yet without it, surely we would stumble and fall?

No matter how I looked at the problem, I couldn't see how to proceed. All I knew was that I had to act at once. So I did what I always do when I'm trying to think things through; I took a walk around the secondhand bookshops that cluttered the backstreets of Cole Bay. The town was the colour of a stagnant pond. It was raining again, and most of the shops were deserted. I was wandering among damp stacks of encyclopedias, listening to the rain falling on the roof, when a thought occurred to me.

'Have you ever heard of a science fiction writer called Simon Jonathan Saunders?' I asked the shop-owner.

'The name rings a bell,' he replied, 'let's see.' He pulled down a paperback encyclopedia of science fiction and began to check through it unhurriedly. 'Here we are. S. J. Saunders. A collection of short stories, *Past Futures*, that's his first published work, 1953. Two volumes published in the mid-Fifties, *Beyond The Solar Seas* and *Mind In Flight*, both out of print now.'

'Did he write anything else?'

'Oh yes. According to this, he's still in print. Here, take a look.'

I checked the entry.

Best remembered for the Arcadia *novels, a linked set of books published from 1959 until his death, featuring the adventures of a young space cadet in a far-off mystical land. Although initially based on his studies of archaeological sites in ancient Greece, Saunders increasingly drew on his own imagination until undergoing a severe mental breakdown. A sufferer from recurrent childhood illness, he committed suicide in 1970. He is regarded by many fans as the last of the great science fiction fabulists, before the next era of 'hard' SF. His final novel,* Arcadia Endures, *was published post-humously by Crabtree Press.*

I must have been staring at him, because the bookseller gave me a really strange look.

'Have you ever seen any of his stuff come through here?' I asked.

'I don't think so. All of these books were put out by small publishing houses. I don't suppose the print-runs would have been very high.'

I visited every secondhand bookshop in the area that afternoon, but nobody had ever seen copies of Saunders' work. I decided to call the custodian of Lee Hill Grammar School again. This time, I explained that I was writing a piece about the novels of their former star pupil. Sometimes, I knew, authors sent copies of their published works back to their old school libraries as gifts. Had this been the case with Saunders?

'It's hard to say,' the custodian told me, 'he might have done. It's probably best if you speak to the chief librarian.'

So I rang the school.

'There's nothing by him on any of the shelves,' the librarian told me, after placing me on hold while she checked. 'I've been here for many years, and I don't remember seeing anything.' I was about to thank her and replace the receiver when she added, 'It might have been a private gift to his teacher. Old boys sometimes prefer to do that, in which case we wouldn't have a record of it.'

I asked if she remembered who his English teacher had

been. 'Oh, yes. That would've been Miss Hill, she took all the A-stream English pupils.'

'Ruth Hill?' I asked, holding my breath.

'That's right. She taught here for many years. Lee Hill School was named after her grandfather.'

'*I have some special books for you,*' Miss Ruth had told me in the hospital. '*By an old pupil of mine.*' But Miss Ruth had died. So what had happened to her library?

Calabash. Arcadia. Xanadu. Middle Earth. Wonderland. Call it whatever you like, the mythical subconscious, the wellspring of all imagination, existing through all time and space, wherever there were human beings. Surviving from one generation to the next, and in turn feeding the need for freedom of thought. A collective mental ecosystem growing ever more fragile with each decade, already at the point of collapse by the time I tapped into it. And now almost gone forever.

I followed the idea in my head.

Calabash, the common link between all peoples and nations, the shared need for invention, for inspiration, for harmony and peace, for respect, for resolve, for spiritual succour. A part of our brains as basic as numeracy or the ability to recognise one another. It was the most logical thing in the world to translate this concept into an image of a place, a special land that would bear similar markings wherever it appeared. Why should we not carry the hopes and dreams of our ancestors within us? Organisms were drawn together. Animals grew in families and ran in packs. It would have been more unnatural to believe the opposite, that we were born separate from one another and stayed that way until death.

We were not meant to stay separate from one another. I was sure of that now.

Suddenly, whether Calabash existed in the physical sense became irrelevant. The fact was, it existed within me, within all of us, and was about to die unless something was done. I should have asked Miss Ruth about the books. She had intended them for me. Now it was too late, and she was gone.

CHAPTER THIRTY-NINE

Containing the Imagination

I ran along the esplanade, watching the lowering sky. The stormy weather that had been threatened for the weekend broke overhead, heavy thunderclouds rolling towards the shoreline. The sea had turned to an opaque, glaucous shade that darkened at the horizon. I asked myself for the strength to believe what I had learned. My head was aching, my brain filled with figures from history; Socrates, Plato and Aristotle developing ethical systems of philosophy, Archimedes inventing mathematical solutions, Ptolemy and Copernicus mapping the heavens, Chaucer and Shakespeare developing the language of the emotions, Donne, Shelley and Yeats giving form to feelings, Michelangelo shaping Western art. And the little kingdom of Calabash acting as a source of solace and inspiration through time, providing centuries of use as a haven for those who sought to advance the sum total of their lives, until visitors became fewer, until the land was barely remembered and hardly seen anymore, to die from sheer neglect when the world that had used it no longer needed to feed its dreams.

And of course I failed to realise, even now, that I had got the whole thing slightly wrong. Growing up is, I suppose, a series of mis-steps and corrections.

I knew that Calabash had survived through the darkest times, through the loss of all hope, through wars, plagues, death and starvation. But suppose it had now passed beyond a sustainable point? Whether I was mad or sane, I was sure I had to return and try to save the scraps that were left. I would never be able to forgive myself if I let it die forever. But what could I do? How could I stop its tumbledown destruction from spilling over into this world, my reality? The odds against me were inconceivable. In the eyes of Calabash I was part of the problem; I had gained access to the kingdom, only to become the cause of its final decline.

I kept coming back to Miss Ruth's books, and her link with the boy who had last renewed Calabash. I decided to go back to her apartment.

At first I couldn't find the right front door because it had been freshly painted. The young Scottish woman who answered my knock explained that she had just bought the place. She had been redirecting Miss Hill's mail to a relative in Surrey. No, she had no idea what had happened to the fixtures and fittings. Wait though, the books had been left to a school, she remembered that because they had promised to send a van to collect them, but it had failed to turn up, and she had lost a day's pay waiting in the flat for it to arrive. She had finally arranged for the collection herself.

Miss Ruth had wanted me to go back to my studies. I knew then what she had done with the books given to her by her favourite pupil. She had left them to my school library, her last happy home of employment.

I felt sure that if I failed to act at this very moment, something extraordinary would be lost forever. To an outsider

I know I must have seemed like some kind of paranoiac, fantasising that the fate of mankind's humanity hung on my ability to rescue it from oblivion. A single human being with the power to change the fate of the entire world, wasn't that the ultimate psychotic delusion?

I headed back to my old school. Keeping out of sight as much as I could, I crossed the quadrangle. Luckily it was still raining, classes were in session and there were few teachers about. The library was tucked away at the rear of the building, and was usually empty at this hour. I checked through the window; the place looked dead. A woman I had never seen before was seated in the back room, absorbed in a ledger, and did not look up when I entered. I headed for the small science fiction section – they were the kind of books the school did not approve of – and found Simon Saunders' *Arcadia* novels there, an orderly set of six hardbacks that had not been stamped out to anyone since their arrival. Keeping an eye on the woman, I slipped them into my shoulder bag and made for the door, just as old Beardwood the headmaster entered. His eyes widened theatrically when he saw me.

'Mr Goodwin? What the devil are you doing here? You're not a pupil of this school anymore.'

'I came to see a friend, sir,' I answered.

'Which friend? I see no friend. You appear to be quite friendless. And you're not supposed to be in here.' Hearing his booming voice, the woman in the back room looked up. The book bag weighed heavily on my shoulder. 'What have you got in there?'

'Where?' I looked wildly about.

'There, boy, the bulging great loot sack on your shoulder.'

'Nothing, sir.' I knew I didn't have to call him 'sir' anymore, it just came out through force of habit.

'Let's have a look at "nothing", shall we? Let's see what

"nothing" looks like.' He tapped the bag with a bony fore-finger. In his black cloak he reminded me of the Lord Chancellor. I was sunk. I started to slide the bag from my shoulder.

'Come on, boy, I don't have all day. Let's see if "nothing" takes some kind of corporeal form.' He smirked from the shadows, reaching towards me, and began to pull open the top of the bag. Behind him I could see that a crowd was gathering. Several of the kids who used to be in my class were there. Schoolkids can sense a fight brewing from a quarter of a mile away, and be there to goad the weaker opponent in seconds.

I had no idea how the books would help me, but I knew that if he took them away now, I would never get a chance to see them again. I pulled the bag up and swung it away from him, catching him off guard and off balance. He was forced to seize the edge of the table to stop himself from falling on top of me. He threw out a bony hand, grabbed at my collar and missed. Something snapped inside me; I saw my clenched fist travelling towards him before I was aware of making the decision to hit him. I caught him very hard, right on the nose. A great excited yell went up, and I realised they were cheering me, all the kids who I thought hated me. They screamed and yelled and punched the air and stamped their feet. The noise they made would stay with me forever.

And with Beardwood clutching his bloodied nose behind me, I ran for the library exit.

Out into the corridor, through one set of double doors, then another, and out into the rain. I dashed across the quad-rangle with the headmaster now in pursuit. A group of teachers were spread out across the concrete path ahead. I heard Beardwood call out to them to stop me, but they just looked back at him in puzzlement. I cut on to the wet grass, fighting to keep my balance, threw myself over the low railings and ran off into the trees.

I ran on along the deserted promenade, past the rock shop and the ice-cream parlour, past the Guinness clock, the aquarium and the penny arcade. As I ran, I kept watching the distant rain-blurred sea. I had just reached the green wooden shelter beside the pier when I saw it. The light from the bronze shields of the harbour statues was glimmering across the water in a faint X. Calabash was in danger of disappearing forever. The moment of invasion had arrived.

The rain began falling even harder, and moments later the end of the pier vanished in a heavy grey mist. The shelter was full of drunken Chavs who looked as though they were spoiling for a fight. I needed to be somewhere dry and quiet, where I could examine the books in my bag. I thought for a moment, then remembered Apsley's Field, a waterlogged green patch behind the high street shops that housed a dozen dilapidated caravans.

Why anyone would want to spend a fortnight in a caravan, fetching water across the mud in a plastic churn, changing cylinders of Calor Gas, and washing in a breezeblock outhouse reeking of disinfectant and filled with spiders was a mystery to me, but I knew that at this time of the day the visitors' room would be empty. I made my way down an alley between the shops, and up into the entrance of the field. There was always somebody on the site who stood against the wire fence staring into the next field at the sheep. Even now, in the teeming rain, an elderly man stood beneath a golf umbrella watching the sodden, miserable animals. Perhaps he was trying to decide who was worst off. I reached the visitors' room, an inhospitable cinder-brick box with condensation running down the windows, and entered.

Throwing myself into a corner, I tore open the bag and

spilled the contents out on to the bench. I began to examine the books. I placed them in order, then started skimming through them one at a time. The characters of Arcadia bore little resemblance to anyone I had met in Calabash, yet they seemed somehow familiar, as though the writer had drawn his ideas from a similar source. There were adventures, political intrigues, battles and romances, all the twists of fate that one expected to occur to the residents of an exotic, far-off land. As my eye travelled through the chapters, the adventures blurred together. It seemed rather tame stuff, enjoyable if you were sick in bed, nothing more. Disappointed, I ploughed on, only to find more of the same. I turned to the final book.

It was towards the end of this posthumously published volume, *Arcadia Endures*, that I found myself reading the following exchange:

The old man shielded his eyes from the blazing sun. 'It is too hot to go further today,' he announced. He pulled his camel to its knees and dismounted, making for the oasis where Pip sat. Opening his cloak, he produced a large orange gourd, dried and hollowed into a water container. He dipped the gourd into the shaded clear water of the oasis and raised it, but did not drink. Instead, he held it at the boy's chest, and asked him, 'Tell me, Pip, what do you see?'

Pip looked down and saw his reflection smiling back. 'I see myself,' he replied.

'You see a mirror-image of yourself,' said the old man, 'for what use is a dry gourd but as a receptacle to contain something precious? Just as water brings forth life, so this is a container for your life-giving imagination. You need imagination just as much as you need water. Think, Pip, a

mirror to your life. One half of your reflection.' He smiled and allowed the boy to drink. 'When a gourd like this is hollowed out for such a purpose, it is called a—'

'Calabash,' I said aloud. 'It's a calabash.'

Something that contained the other half of you. Somewhere to put all of the frustrated ideas, all the things you couldn't use, all the dreams you couldn't achieve. That's what I'd been using Calabash for. The stupid thing was that I'd been keeping it separate, closed off from my so-called real life. The more I thought about it, the more everything suddenly made sense.

My eyes rose to the lightning flickering beyond the rooftops. I pushed the books back into the bag and stood. Now, for the first time in my life, I knew exactly what I had to do.

CHAPTER FORTY

Breaking Through

My chest had started to hurt. My ribcage felt as though someone was standing on it. When I breathed deep, a sharp pain stabbed at my lungs in a way that reminded me of the feeling I got just before a bout of pneumonia. *Not now*, I prayed, *not when I'm so close*. As I returned to the esplanade, the rain mist momentarily lifted, and I halted at the railing to catch my breath.

The clearing air revealed a great cross of yellow light shining over the water, growing brighter with every passing second. The time had come. Calabash was falling, and the General was preparing to bring his war machine across. Perhaps I was already too late. I pushed away from the railing and limped on. As I passed the Las Vegas arcade I saw Julia standing outside, dressed in a bright yellow rain mac. I crossed the road and called out to her.

'I've been looking for you,' she said. 'I ran into your mum. She's been trying to call you. She says you've got to go home.'

'I can't,' I answered, taking quick, shallow breaths. 'Not now. There's something I've got to do.'

'Come on, Kay, she misses you. They both do. Couldn't you just go and see them for a few minutes? I'm walking back that way.'

'I can't right now. But I will, as soon as I've done this, I promise.'

She gave me an imploring look. 'What have you got to do that's so important?'

'I'm not sure you'd understand if I told you.'

'You could try to explain for once.'

'I'm sorting everything out. You'll be the first to know if I manage it, I promise.'

I walked forward, half-expecting her to flinch, but she didn't so I kissed her gently on the lips. She tasted fantastic. Her eyes widened in surprise, but she didn't move away. 'Go ahead,' I told her, 'I won't be long. I'll catch you up.' *If I come back in one piece.*

My lungs had stopped hurting. I ran off again, crossing the road and swinging through the turnstile of the pier as the rain began to intensify. I ran into the arcade and threw my bag into a dark corner, hoping that I could still go through to the end of the pier and reach the access point from the gap in the scaffolding.

Someone was blocking my way. Hearing familiar laughter, I turned and looked across the gloomy game-room. Malcolm Slattery was standing near the upper exit, punching the glass side of a mechanical claw machine as it failed to raise a furry gonk in its arms. Laurence, doomed to spend his life watching from the sidelines, was indeed watching him.

Slattery looked up in surprise as I approached, and the gonk slithered from the clutch of the steel grab. Slapping the machine with the flat of his hand he moved over to a model of a lighthouse in a glass case. Two helicopters, one red, the other blue, stuck out on wires from either side. Laurence dropped money into the slots, and the pair of them began furiously turning the circular steel handles at the front of the case, causing the helicopters to race skywards.

'Oi, Goodwin, what are you doing here?' Slattery called as I passed him. He was hunched over the machine, noisily spinning the wheel, all of his concentration centred on beating Laurence to the top of the lighthouse. I figured he usually won.

'It's nothing to do with you, Slattery,' I replied, but I knew I had to get around him to reach the arcade door and the end of the pier.

He released his hand from the wheel, allowing it to spin on. We squared off against each other while Laurence, puzzled, took his helicopter on to the top, ringing the bell. I don't think he liked winning.

'Why didn't you just piss off out of this town while you could still stand up?' Slattery took a step towards me, flexing his fists. 'You were a loony at school, and you're still a loony.'

And suddenly he was grabbing at me, trying to swing a punch, just like the days when I was still in his class, and Laurence was bouncing around beside him, urging him to hit me. Too bad he hadn't seen me deck the headmaster. I was still riding high. I ducked and dropped back as he ran forward, then stuck out my leg so that he fell sprawling on to the floor.

'I've seen you creeping around,' he gasped, standing up. 'Kate's not there anymore. What is it down the end of the pier that's so bloody important?' He threw a punch at my face, but it fell short. I ran around behind him, only to have Laurence grab my shirt and hold me in place. Slattery came charging forward, punching me hard in the stomach, knocking the air from my lungs. I twisted hard as I fell, throwing Laurence into his path, crashing them together into the angled perspex of the Penny Falls game. A copper cascade poured over the ledge of the machine and bounced into the winnings tray. It was the first time I'd ever seen the machine pay out. Mesmerised, Laurence dropped to his knees and began scooping out coins like an otter pawing minnows from a brook.

Rising, I turned and slammed out through the arcade doors with Slattery in pursuit, just as I had when all this had begun. The rain was smashing down now, bouncing up from the planks beneath my feet as I ran to the builders' barrier, climbed up and scrambled through with my old enemy closing in on me. I dropped to the other side and pounded past the bare ribs of the helter skelter, the empty rusting dodgem rink and the shuttered ghost train, on towards the back of the pier . . .

Only to slide to a stop just before plunging down into the angry waves.

It had gone. All of it. The whole of the back of the pier had fallen into the sea. Not just the upper and lower fishing platforms but the boardwalk, the candyfloss kiosk and the sundeck, just splintered away into a churning wreckage of wood and iron. There was no way of getting back. Calabash was sealed off for good.

I knew that the only way this business could be brought to an end was with one final journey. Now that journey could not take place. I stared hopelessly down at the desolate storm-damage.

I needed to get to the point where the beams crossed. Not stopping to see where Slattery was, I wheeled back on myself, catching the corner edge of the building housing the saloon with my outstretched arm, and swung in through the bar door. I knew where Cottesloe kept the keys to the *Skylark*, on the hook behind the counter, and grabbed them before the barmaid could even register that I had entered the room.

The boat was still moored on its hoist near the bottom of the steps beside the arcade, covered in a green tarpaulin. With the keys in my hand and Slattery only yards behind, I raced towards it. I stumbled over the top step leading to the boarding platform and nearly fell headlong down the staircase. Ahead of me was the winch that lowered the boat into the water. I ducked under the chain, grabbed its handle and began to turn. Nothing happened at first, then the greased cable unwound with a groan, and the winch started turning so fast that the handle was pulled out of my grasp.

'You bloody nutcase,' Slattery was calling, 'what do you think you're doing? You'll kill yourself!' But by that time the *Skylark* had thumped into the rocking sea with a bang, and I was off down the stairs. I jumped the last two and landed on the broad deck of the boat. Pulling free the mooring harnesses – something I'd had plenty of practice doing in Calabash harbour – and tearing open a section of tarp on the driver's side, I was tipped into the seat by the force of the waves rising and plunging around the bow.

The *Skylark* had been specifically designed for heavy weather. It could plough through virtually anything. The engine turned over first time, and the whole boat shook with a great throaty roar. Clouds of thick blue petrol smoke billowed from the stern. I opened the throttle and roared away from the stanchions of the pier, then swung the wheel hard and turned her around, heading back towards the site where the fishing platform had stood, praying that the hull would miss the jagged remains of the iron posts that now lay beneath the water.

I had never tried to cross into Calabash with any solid object, but I was going too fast to stop now. If I didn't hit the spot where the harbour lights intersected, I saw that I would plough into the struts of the pier and most likely be killed.

The gap closed fast. The pier came soaring up towards me as the boat leapt from the top of one wave into the trough of the next with a bone-shaking crash, soaking me. Up rose the launch again, water cascading from the bow, as I crested the great green wave before the black wall of iron struts. The *Skylark*'s engine screamed as the propellor left the water.

I had reached the cross of light. The boat was nearly vertical. The water rolling beneath the hull made it sound as though we were punching across a series of concrete blocks. The pier stanchions filled my vision. My hands were torn from the wheel. I threw my arms across my face and fell back.

The *Skylark* came down in the calm blue sea off the coast of Calabash.

CHAPTER FORTY-ONE

To Rescue a Princess

Clouds drifted sluggishly across the water. Calabash was ablaze. General Bassa and his men had put the city to the torch. The afternoon sun was lost in a vermilion haze as I moored the *Skylark* against the harbour jetty. Climbing the steps, I ran into a wall of billowing, choking smoke. From all around came the sound of hammering. Soldiers were building a wooden structure along the top of the harbour wall. The city was a distant flickering beacon, the damned dark land of a Breughel painting.

There were people running in every direction. Some had their belongings bundled into baskets, while others whipped laden donkeys, but nobody seemed to know where to go. Many of the fields were ablaze, and the few boats remaining in the bay did not appear seaworthy enough for trips of any duration. Even so, families were attempting to board them. One was already sinking. A father struggled towards his children as they floundered in the rising water. All was confusion. In the crackle of fire, the howling of infants, the braying of asses, there were no commanding voices to be heard. Several platoons of soldiers stood silently ranked on the grounds of the gutted fish sheds. They seemed to be waiting for some kind of signal before springing into action. I had only taken a few steps forward when I stumbled into Menavino, who indicated that he had been sent to keep watch for me.

'What's happening?' I cried, momentarily forgetting that the boy had no power of speech. I studied his frantic motions, hands flying in front of his face, fists knotting threateningly, fingers opening to form a box around him.

'They've sealed off the city. The others are still inside. Has anyone seen the Princess?'

Menavino nodded violently, gesturing with his fingers once more. He grabbed my hand and began to pull me away. We ran through the panicking crowds. There were soldiers everywhere, herding villagers into groups. I knew that when troops did this, deaths soon followed. Following Menavino's lead, I veered from the road and headed across the ploughed fields towards the woodland.

It took us an hour to cut a path through the dense undergrowth where I had found the ruins of the Grecian temples, the remains of Saunders' youthful dreams. I wondered how many other dream cities lay buried beneath our feet.

The main gate to the city had been closed off with a lattice-work of crude iron bars. We followed the wall as closely as we could, and eventually reached a place where the stones had been smashed to a level that we could clamber over. The new regime was having trouble implementing its plans for security and fortification. Scrambling across the blackened rubble, we dropped to the other side and ran on.

The inner courtyard of the old palace had been sealed with fresh clay walls, but they had been so hastily finished that it was easy to gain a foothold on the outcroppings of the stones they had used. We soon arrived at the citadel where Trebunculus and his rebels had been hiding. The walls were black with smoke, but the building seemed undamaged.

If General Bassa was hoping for discipline from his men, he was to be sorely disappointed. Several lounged beside the burning house of a sherbet seller, drinking from goatskin pouches. I hoped they were so drunk that their senses would be dulled. The nearest soldier was alone and set back from the others, shielded from his friends by the side of the building. I realised that he was attempting to pee, and indicated to Menavino that we should take him. I had seen this performed many times in films, but wasn't sure how well it would actually work.

Menavino slipped his hand across the soldier's mouth and nose as I placed a knee against his spine and tipped him back, dropping both my knees across his throat. He fought violently, so I dropped down harder. He still fought, so Menavino strangled him. After a few moments he lost consciousness, so we dragged him back into the shadows and stripped him of his uniform. The grey and silver folds of his tunic were loose-fitting enough to conceal the fact that it didn't fit me. I unhooked the *kukhri* knife at his belt and raised Menavino before me, as though I had taken him prisoner. Then we walked forward to the citadel.

We waited in the oily smoke haze beside the building's doors, ready to dart in as soon as they opened. But they didn't open. We waited, and waited.

'What on earth do you think you're doing?' asked the doctor, who had appeared at my back with several of his rebels. 'You look utterly ridiculous in that outfit.'

'I've come back to rescue you and the Princess,' I explained, pushing the soldier's cap back from my eyes.

'And Menavino, you should know better,' Trebunculus chided. 'Honestly, the pair of you are as much use as a cow's eardrums. We effected our escape from the rear while you were making such a commotion, tumbling down the side of the building.'

'So I did help you,' I argued.

'I just hope you have a plan now. We had to leave the Semanticor behind, he couldn't manage the stairs. It's no way to run a rebellion. And the news we have received from our lookouts is far from encouraging.'

'What's happened?' I fell into step beside the doctor as we set off through alleyways efflorescent with smoke.

'Why, the army has betrayed the Lord Chancellor. Septimus Peason wanted control of the kingdom, but General Bassa has set alight to the entire land. He is behaving like a madman, destroying everything. Such is his hatred for the ruling body of Calabash that he desires to see it utterly razed to the ground before he and his men set off in the Belligeratron to claim your country. Peason has ordered the ministers who are still loyal to him to attack the generals.'

'Where is the Sultan and his family?' I shouted above the crash of falling masonry. 'Do they survive?'

'They are still imprisoned within the *yildiz* once known as the Keep of Destitution, at the centre of the armoury in the old palace, and the Princess is now being kept with them. She refused to go back with her husband, and has been abandoned with her father. The Sultan remains a prize for both sides. He is of pure blood, the living representative of the gods on earth, and no harm can come to him or his family without his tormentor suffering a fate of eternal damnation.'

'So he's safe, then?'

'Unless the building drops on his head,' said Trebunculus uncertainly, 'or General Bassa decides to risk the damnation of the gods.'

'I think we had better get them all out, don't you?'

'You make it sound easy. It won't be. The *yildiz* is now

known as the *tekke* of General Bassa, the Dervish Lodge. It has been refortified, and its construction contains the hidden essence of the General's *tughra*.'

'What is that?'

'His signature. It bears his mark, the stamp of his personality.'

'And what is that?' I asked.

'Treachery and deceit. It is safe to expect that the *tekke* will be filled with traps.'

'Oh, great.' I turned to look at Trebunculus. He was walking ahead, and seemed assured that I would follow him. 'I came back for you. I thought I might at least get a welcome.'

'Oh, I knew you would come back.'

'How?'

'The Princess. No-one can become a hero without rescuing a princess. I am right, no?'

'You are right, yes,' I agreed.

'Your business here wasn't finished, was it?'

'Well, no.'

'You couldn't live in one world, and you can't live in the other. You came back because you know now what you have to do.'

The doctor always seemed to know how I felt. He irritated me when he was like this.

'Doesn't it annoy you, being right all the time?' I asked.

'Oh, I'm not, I assure you. I just remember what it's like to grow up. It's all right, you know, it happens to a lot of young people.' He looked back over his shoulder and gave a crooked smile. 'And for what it's worth, I'm glad you came back for us.'

Climbing on through the smouldering rubble, our hopeless band of ragamuffins turned off in the direction of General Bassa's fortified Dervish Lodge.

CHAPTER FORTY-TWO

The Dervish Lodge

'What kind of traps?' I asked. 'Mousetraps, knives on springs, pits full of spikes, what sort of thing are you talking about?'

'I'm not entirely sure,' said the Semanticor, who, much to our surprise, was waiting for us outside the entrance to the Dervish Lodge. He informed us that he had been helped down from his rooftop prison in a makeshift wooden cradle, but it had dropped him into the ashes of a bonfire and he was blackened from head to foot. 'I burned my arse,' he complained, 'but at my age one's arse is always in pain.'

'The traps,' I reminded him.

'Ah, yes. The Sultan originally had them installed to protect the armoury from pillage, but as no-one has ever attacked us they gradually fell into disuse. General Bassa is supposed to have restored some of them, but most were beyond the point where they could be returned to order, so they are a danger to everyone. The Sultan's grandfather built wonderful traps. He had the right mind for such cruelties, on account of having to breakfast with his wife each morning. A woman of commanding stature but a face like a camel's ringpiece. The old man passed his flair for invention on to his son. I remember when the Sultan was in my mathematics class, how he used to remove the spines from mice with just a piece of string, some heated wax, a bent needle and a tiny piece of cheese.'

'He is resourceful,' agreed Trebunculus, 'but so are you, Kay. You found a way to return to us.'

'And, of course, his teeth,' added the Semanticor. 'But he was never deliberately cruel. General Bassa has a nasty streak. In the old days, the atmosphere in the royal court was very tense because all business affairs were performed in total silence. The General once shattered a pane of glass with a catapult, causing the Keeper of Concubines to die of shock. In those days, nobody wore the same clothes twice for fear of—'

'This is no time for your faulty reminiscences,' snapped the doctor. 'Come, let us enter the lion's den.' We looked up at the forbidding walls of the former armoury. Here, away from the arson and looting of the town, an eerie silence had fallen across the courtyard. There were no songbirds, only circling buzzards. The sun was obscured by drifting smoke. We walked slowly forward through the shadowed archway into the lodge. Menavino and I studied the walls as we moved along, listening for the springing of traps. We had reached the middle of the first covered passage when there came the twanging sound of wires stretching, the unwinding of a rusty clockwork spring.

'Everybody back!' I shouted, but we were not fast enough. An iron wall rose swiftly behind us, slamming shut at the ceiling, sealing us inside.

'Clever,' said Trebunculus, 'closing at the top, not the bottom. Harder to pull open, you see.'

My ears pricked back; the clockwork ratcheting behind the bricks had not ceased. 'Down!' I shouted, as a dozen iron spears corkscrewed rather too slowly out of the walls, rattling in their firing cases and embedding themselves in the far side of the passage. Although the spears were slow the Semanticor was slower, and stood pinned by his robes against the wall. He appeared more confused than frightened.

'You were right,' he said shakily, 'knives on springs. Obvious, but effective. The mechanism needs greasing with tallow, though.' Menavino and the others set about tearing him free.

'It's not safe to advance like this. Isn't there some other way?' I peered into the darkness ahead, but could see nothing more than indistinct outlines. The passage ahead separated into three identical corridors. 'We'll be killed before we reach the interior.'

'Then what do you suggest?' asked Trebunculus.

'Send Scammer to the Sultan's prison. He can get into places we can't reach.'

'I only hope we can trust him not to betray us. We haven't been able to feed him for days. Scammer!' called Trebunculus. The feral child appeared beside him, bobbing and crouching like a sooty meerkat. 'Scammer, you know how to reach the inner sanctum?'

The boy nodded. 'Easy, master, I climb through the holes in the roof like a bird. I crawl in the spaces under the tiles like a spider.'

'You also lie through your teeth like a politician.'

'No, Doctor, no! I'll be quick. I'll be quiet. Nobody ever sees the Scammer.' This was not strictly true, for I had seen him a number of times, darting across the roofs of the city.

'Then you must find out exactly what lies ahead. Listen carefully and make a note of all you hear. Tell the Sultan that we can only rescue him if we are armed with this knowledge.'

'Watch how I fly!' cried Scammer, springing across to an

abutment, jumping and looping his arms about a rafter. He pushed his way through the dry rushes in the roof, drew up his thin legs and scuttled off. We heard the ceiling crunching and cracking as he made his way across.

'All we can do for the moment is wait,' I said, gingerly seating myself below the thicket of spears.

'Time is our enemy,' warned the doctor. 'By burning the kingdom, General Bassa absolves himself, for fire is a natural force, and if the Sultan dies in the conflagration, he cannot be held responsible. The pyres have been set all around the city walls. It is said that even the hungry wolves shun bodies that have been blackened by the fires of—'

'You're a real miseryguts sometimes,' I complained. 'Try to be a little more positive, will you?' Our group fell into silent reverie. All that could be heard was the distant crash and roar of burning timber. Several minutes passed. When Scammer suddenly dropped back into our midst he made everyone jump. A crooked grin shone on his filthy face. He threw his arms in the air, gripping his left elbow with his right fist like an orang-utan.

'Scammer knows which way to go.'

'You've seen the Sultan?' asked the Semanticor, dusting himself down.

'Aye, and his Royal Mother, and the beautiful Princess Rosamunde, escaped from the seragalio, escaped from Maximus, recaptured by his father.' Scammer hissed. 'I told her you were here. Excited, like so,' he waggled his filthy arms. 'Brave and strong. She hugs her father, she gives him strength. She thanks the Scammer for his news. Come, I show you.'

He was about to run off when I grabbed his scrawny neck and hauled him back. 'Wait. You don't go anywhere without us now, you understand? Doctor, give me your belt.'

I took the leather strap that usually held the doctor's medical bag to his side, and buckled it around Scammer's neck in a slip-knot. 'All right, lead on. Scammer, what did the Sultan say to you?'

'Hello there Scammer, he says.' The boy strained at his lead the way Gyp used to when I took him to the park. 'Bring no torches. Always curve to the right, always stay on the left.'

'What does that mean?'

'It makes sense,' said Trebunculus. 'We keep turning into the building, but we stay in the side of shadow, beneath the embrasures. Without torches, most people would try to walk in the path of the available light. Weapons would be targetted on that side, so we must do the opposite.'

We maintained a single file behind the urchin and crept forward. Beside us, the ground suddenly dropped away in a spray of sand, so that we were moving along a narrow tiled ledge. 'Someone hold on to the Semanticor,' warned Trebunculus. 'He's not very sure-footed.'

Ahead stood what appeared to be a large sculpted rock. As we came closer, I saw that it was carved in the face of a seated djinn. There was very little light here. The only windows were the high arrow-slits, and smoke was wafting through them, reducing visibility still further. The malevolent djinn grinned out at us as we approached, daring us to come closer.

'Stay left, stay left!' warned Scammer, pulling at the lead. Just as he spoke, the djinn's mouth dropped open with a grind of stone, and hundreds of small black objects were ejected from its throat.

'Scorpions,' warned Trebunculus, 'oldest trick in the book.' Even so, several of them had already found their target. Screams erupted in our band. Men were dancing around themselves, batting at their tunics. One lost his balance and fell down into the pit that had opened beside us. Panicked, the column broke apart as everyone ran forward, but fresh screams brought us to a halt. Before us was a deep trough. My feet stopped at the very edge. Others were not so lucky.

'Now what are we supposed to do?' asked the doctor, clearly exasperated.

'Scammer, you said to stay on the left. Can we get around the pit?'

'Is easy,' called the boy. 'Up at your head. Soldiers had to get in here as well as prisoners.'

'He's right,' agreed Trebunculus. 'Bassa's troops aren't very bright. One must presume that when he restored the traps he couldn't make it too difficult for them.'

I reached up and found a rust-flaked iron bar within my grasp. There were several, set within an arm's reach of each other. Still, I doubted that the Semanticor would be able to manage. 'We'll have to carry him between us,' I told the doctor. 'We can make a sling from robes.'

'No thank you,' the old teacher waved his hands at us. 'You look far too puny to lift me. I'll stay here.'

'Then let me go ahead with Scammer.' Annoyingly, everyone readily agreed to my suggestion.

There seemed to be something moving in the pit below. It sounded like a very large snake. I looked down and saw a series of drifting coils, and a pair of glittering lidless yellow eyes watching me. I thought of the murky green ocean surrounding Cole Bay. Suddenly, being cast adrift in the rough sea beyond the pier seemed an attractive alternative to being here.

'How much further?' I asked Scammer.

'Easy now,' said the boy, jigging about. 'Just across the *derbendci*.'

'The guardian of the pass,' called Trebunculus.

I looked down the tunnel. The pit was about thirty feet

long. The overhead rungs offered the only passage across. 'Is there no other way?'

'No other. You swing from the bars, see.' Scammer had hopped up and was hanging from the first bar with one hand. He reminded me of Malcolm Slattery in the school cloakroom. 'Keep moving forward so *derbendci* cannot strike.'

'That's easy for you to say,' I muttered, reluctantly reaching for the bar above my head. 'I'm not used to physical exercise.' As I pulled myself from the ground, I heard the great snake shifting in its pit. I looked down in time to see its coils tensing, ready to strike. I swung myself back to the ground just as it shot forward, glancing its great head against the roof of the passage, then dropping back into the pit. Scammer was tiny and agile, but I could not believe that even he had passed this way.

'You're lying,' I said softly, closing the fingers of my right hand around his throat. 'Show us the right passage or I will end your life here in this tunnel.'

'You will not ascend to heaven if you die in here,' promised the doctor, watching from the edge of the pit.

'Fair enough,' shrugged Scammer, 'I was just testing.' And swinging back, he jumped up into the entrance of a small square tunnel that stood in the shadows beside us.

CHAPTER FORTY-THREE

A Special Occasion

Pauline rebuttoned the neck of the blouse, but the fit was still too tight. 'I don't understand,' she complained. 'It used to hang perfectly. It's not as if I've put on weight. Chance would be a fine thing with you lot worrying the life out of me. I'm sure rayon's supposed to give.'

'You haven't worn it since Kay was a boy,' said Bob. 'I don't understand what you want to dress up for, you'll only get it ruined. I don't see why we can't just wait here. I've got things I could be getting on with. It's pissing down outside.'

'I wish you'd mind your language, Robert, this isn't a barracks. I should have had a perm.' She attacked the blouse again, then abandoned it for a grey jumper with small fake pearls sewn down the front.

Bob had been resoldering the toaster when he had received the summons to get dressed. Pauline had given him the soldering iron for his birthday. Consequently, almost everything in the house that contained metal had been resoldered whether it needed it or not. The house reeked of burnt flux.

Now he was being forced to put on a clean white shirt and the spivvy hand-painted tie Janine had bought him last Christmas.

'You're not staying here by yourself, the mess you make,' threatened Pauline. 'I wish you'd finish one job at a time. I thought you were boxing in the bannisters. There's half a dozen sheets of hardboard by the cellar door. And you were going to cover the breakfast hatch with perspex. Just as well I wasn't holding my breath. Stuff everywhere. Janine nearly broke her ankle on a tin of undercoat.'

'Nearly doesn't count. Anyway, I thought the idea was not to make a fuss,' Bob muttered, pulling on the knot until it was as small and hard as an acorn. 'I wish you'd warned the boy.'

'Didn't I try?' asked Pauline, squirming about in her skirt. 'There's no answer from that dreadful penny arcade, and he's not on the phone in the flat. What am I supposed to do, stand on the roof and yell at the top of my lungs? I saw that Greek girl in the high street. She said she'll have a word if she sees him. She's turned out nice, that one. Lost her puppy fat. Janine could take a tip there.'

'You and bloody Janine,' grunted Bob.

'Before you say anything rude, remember she was very nearly family. I've sent her round to look for him. She should have been back by now.'

'Janine! Bloody hell. Couldn't you have kept her out of our affairs just once?' Bob looked at his sleeves and gave a low moan. 'These are bloody double cuffs.'

'Well, you have some cufflinks.'

'The enamel ones the hotel gave me as a farewell gift? They're in the shape of golf balls. And they're bright red. They look like little pairs of bollocks. That's what all my years with that hotel amounted to: bollocks.'

'There's no need to be crude. I don't know what's got into you today. Anyway, no-one will see them.'

'Then what's the bloody point of wearing them?' He held out his arms. 'You'll have to do them up. I'll let you in on a secret, Pauline. There's not a man alive with half his wits who can stand to wear cufflinks. They make you look like you're in a cigarette advert. They're just something that soft women buy for blokes when they've run out of ideas.'

'Like you and the perfume you always get me. I never wear any of it, you know. I've got a wardrobe full of atomisers. Honestly, I used to dread Christmas presents from the men in this family. You and your 4-7-11 . . .'

'I thought you liked 4-7-11.'

'It's for old ladies! I wouldn't have minded Atar of Roses, but no. Then lavender bath-salt cubes from Kay, and oven gloves from Sean. One Christmas you gave me a grate. Said it was self-griddling and would save my back. I ask you, what woman would want to be given a grate?'

'I never think of you as—'

'Don't say it,' she warned, glaring. The doorbell sounded. 'That'll be Janine. I asked her to pick up some cakes.' She dropped Bob's sleeve, and he sank miserably into the nearest armchair. *That's all I need today,* he thought, *Ten-Ton Tessie armed with her Battenbergs and Iced Rounds. I wanted this to be a private do.*

But it wasn't Janine. It was a woman, all right, but some-one with a completely different voice. Pauline pushed open the door, and standing there next to her was Julia, in her yellow plastic mackintosh and rainhood.

'I think we'd better go with her,' Pauline was saying. 'Kay's got himself in some kind of trouble. Today of all days.'

Julia took a tentative step into the hall, nearly banging her head on a set of hanging wrought-iron soldered ducks. 'I saw him on the esplanade, Mr Goodwin,' she explained. 'I tried to get him to come back with me but he said he couldn't stop.'

'Where was he off to?'

'The pier.'

'What's he want on the pier in this weather, for God's sake?'

'He's gone off in the *Skylark*, the boat Mr Cottesloe keeps there.'

'What do you mean, he's gone off? Who's with him?'

'Nobody. I think he's sort of stolen it.'

'Bloody hell! He doesn't know the first thing about boats.'

'Well,' said Julia defensively, 'he seemed to be driving it all right.'

'You don't drive boats, you pilot them,' explained Bob.

'Well, what are we going to do?' Pauline asked.

'I suppose we'd better go down there before somebody calls the police.' He searched around for his raincoat.

'If Janine turns up she'll find herself locked out. She'll be stuck on the doorstep. She won't be pleased.' Pauline pointed at his feet. 'Are you planning to wear those out?'

'Bloody hell,' said Bob again, hopping about on one foot while he tried to pull off his carpet slippers and hunt for his shoes as Julia looked on, trying to hide her embarrassment.

CHAPTER FORTY-FOUR

The Inner Sanctum

We stood in a curving corridor that passed around an oval stone chamber lined with lurid decorative figures and iron pikestaffs. Smoke was starting to fill the passage. 'They're inside,' whispered Scammer. 'Can't get in, not big people like you. Scammer goes in through there.' He waved a reed-thin arm at a gap in the rafters.

'Where is the entry door?' I asked. Menavino pointed to a tall iron panel, recessed into the corridor wall.

'Can't we force it open?'

'Not without destroying the chamber,' Trebunculus replied. 'Such inner rooms used to house the secret weapons of the royal armoury. Rather than allow them to fall into enemy hands, the Sultan provided the means with which to destroy them, should the building's defences be breached.'

'Push the iron from this side, sparks fly, gunpowder ignites. Can't open the door, not without blowing up,' Scammer repeated. 'I told you, through the roof.'

'But that doesn't help us, does it?' The little homunculus was beginning to annoy me until I realised what he was saying. 'You can open it? From the inside? It won't trigger the chamber's destruction?'

'I can open it, save everyone. What's it worth to the Scammer?'

Trebunculus made to slap him.

'Doctor, no!' I warned. We needed his help. 'We'll decide a reward for you, think of something you'll like, but you must go through the rafters now, hurry!' The smoke in the passage was becoming thicker. I knew I would have to remove Scammer's collar. I released the imp from his lead and he shot up the wall, clambering over the walnut bas-reliefs of dying warriors that covered the corridor. Once more he wriggled up through the hole in the ceiling until only his feet showed, then they, too, were gone.

We waited and listened, but heard nothing from within. After several minutes had passed, during which time the smoke in the narrow corridor grew so dense and dark that we could barely breathe, a terrible bone-grinding sound rent the air, and the iron door before us began to part. The walls of the oval armoury were inset with extraordinary weapons, their purposes as forgotten as their dates of manufacture. Here were rotating maces with metal pincers, shields that blossomed with razor-sharp porcupine quills at the touch of a switch, and gunpowder-operated shoulder-mounted cannons that no man would be able to discharge. It was no wonder the kingdom had few enemies abroad. They had probably all been decimated centuries earlier.

I knew now that the only enemies of Calabash came from within. And within the armoury stood a lone figure; not the Grand Sultan, but Septimus Peason, the Lord Chancellor, resplendent in a black and green peacock-feather turban and a cloak that fell to his knuckly ankles.

'I was beginning to wonder how long it would take you to

get here,' he said, looking down at the tenebrous child that clung to his side and ruffling his hair, the action of which raised a small cloud of soot and blackened Peason's bony hand. 'Well done, boy.' He raised his eyes to me. 'Why on earth did you come the long way around? You nearly got yourselves killed. Surely it was obvious even to you that the Sultan would have his own passageway into the armoury.'

'I thought you said Scammer was on your side,' I whispered to the doctor in dismay.

'I knew I should have held back some treats with which to feed him,' shrugged Trebunculus. 'He likes bitter chocolate.'

'It's rather late to think of that now.'

'And oil-fried chicken.'

'What have you done with the royal retinue?' I demanded to know of Septimus Peason.

'General Bassa has conducted them to the new meeting square at the harbour.' A number of guards crowded into the rear of the room, bristling with arrow-points. 'I think we should all adjourn there. You want to witness the execution of the entire royal family before his warriors depart for your shores, don't you?'

Trebunculus gasped. 'You wouldn't dare. They are the mortal representatives of the celestial heavens. Why, if you harm so much as one hair—'

'Oh, come on,' snapped the Lord Chancellor, 'you don't really believe all that, do you? The kingdom as you know it has gone forever. There's nothing left. The last of the old order must be removed.' He stepped aside to reveal Rosamunde, chained on the floor behind him. 'This one is the most unrepentant of them all.'

The Princess twisted on her chain and spat at him. She was dressed in the saffron veils of a harem girl, as beautiful as my memories of her. 'Don't listen to him, Kay. He has betrayed us all. He murdered my mother.'

'And you, young lady, are not fit to be called Princess. Your royal hymen pierced before your sham of a marriage—'

'Your son is an arrogant bully who hates women, just like his father.'

'We only hate harlots,' sneered the Lord Chancellor. 'I had hoped you might change your attitude towards me in order to save your father, but now I can see that you deserve to die alongside him.' He snapped open Rosamunde's chain and hauled her to her feet.

'Don't touch me, you pig. You care nothing for our kingdom, only for yourself.' She threw out her hand, raking his cheek with her nails. The Lord Chancellor's men tensed themselves, ready to strike at his command. Rosamunde pulled free of Peason's grip and ran to my side.

'You came back for me, Kay, just as I knew you would.'

'There's a longstanding historical precedent set in rescuing princesses,' I admitted. 'I couldn't leave you here.'

'I never loved Maximus. I only thought of you.'

'And I you.'

She smiled. 'How does it feel to be a hero?'

I smiled back. 'I'll let you know if I make it through this alive.'

'This reunion is most touching, but we must set off.' The Lord Chancellor signalled his men from the chamber. 'I'm sure you don't want to be late for your own execution.'

'Well, I have to say that I'm very disappointed in this turn of events,' said Trebunculus as he was goaded towards the Sultan's passage with the tip of a pike.

'Not half as much as I am,' I said. 'What are we going to do now?'

'At a rough guess I imagine we'll be forced to watch the

massacre of the Sultan's family before we face our own grisly, lingering deaths, then the General will lay waste to your land, enslave your people and destroy your civilisation.' The doctor pouted gloomily. 'I suppose I should be sorry I got you into this.'

'You *suppose*?' I shouted as we were shoved into another tunnel. 'I had it all worked out. I knew what I needed to do when I came back here. Now you've gone and mucked it all up.'

'It's not my fault that nobody does what you want them to. We never had this trouble with the other boy. He used to pop over, build a couple of temples, have a swordfight or two, a couple of court intrigues, a bit of adventure, then go home. Finally he came to stay for months at a time.'

'And look what happened to him,' I hissed. 'He took his own life.'

'Ah,' said the doctor awkwardly, 'now that I didn't know.'

Pushed forward by our common enemy, we emerged blinking into the light.

CHAPTER FORTY-FIVE

Heads

'**Excuse me,**' called Danny. He had been trying to check the side profile of the attractive girl walking in front of him by watching her in the shop windows they passed, but had fallen over a revolving Walls' ice-cream sign. Hearing the clatter behind her, the girl turned and squinted at him, tipping the brim of her rain-hat up to keep the water from her eyes.

'Are you all right?' she asked. 'They're lethal those things. Last week one of them blew over and killed a Yorkshire Terrier.'

Danny wiped the mud-splashes from his trousers and made a tentative pointing gesture. 'Are you who I think you are?'

'That depends.' Julia stood back. 'Who do you think I am?'

'You're Kay Goodwin's friend. You run that hairdressers up by the station.'

'It's a therapy centre,' corrected Julia. 'What's brought you back to Cole Bay? I thought you lived in London now.'

'I do. I still come down to visit my mum, though. She's hanging on, poor love. There's no other reason for me coming back here, I'll tell you that. How's our boy doing?'

'Our boy.' She considered the phrase. 'Not so well. I think he's been having a tough time of it lately. And then today.' She explained about Kay stealing the pier's motor launch. 'I've just come back from seeing his parents. Mr Cottesloe thinks he's off his head on drugs. He's threatening to call in the police unless they do something about him.'

'Are you sure it was Kay?' asked Danny. 'It's not the sort of thing he would do.'

'How do you know what he would do?' asked Julia defensively.

'I know because he never does anything. He never gets around to doing anything at all. He waits for things to happen, but they never do. He just sits there in his arcade, rotting away in this dismal, awful town.'

Julia bristled. 'Some of us still live here. This town is all right if you know how to make the most of it. It's a state of mind, all that moping about, put into his head by other people who should know better.'

'Do you mean people like me?' Danny bridled. 'Is that what you're saying? Are you getting at me because I had the nerve to get out of here?'

'Oh, is that what they're calling it nowadays? I just thought there weren't enough boys around here for you. I know what you were like, up in the dunes, looking for sex. I used to see you. You had to move on because you'd been rumbled around here. London's a bigger playground for you, that's all.'

'I was lonely,' said Danny, stung. 'Don't tell me you were never lonely.' He thought for a moment, then remembered something. 'You used to be as fat as a pig. Really greasy. All the kids in school used to make fun of you. Don't tell me you never wanted to get out because I don't believe you.'

'All right, I suppose I did.' Her good humour returned. Like Continental sunshine, it never stayed away for long. 'And I suppose you were in love with him as well.'

'A little bit, perhaps,' Danny admitted. 'But not in the way you think.'

'You don't know how I think.' She smiled. 'We've all got our fantasies, haven't we? Tell you what, I'm going back to the pier. It might not be too late to stop Kay from doing something he might regret. Do you want to come with me?'

'Yes,' Danny admitted, as he fell into step beside her. 'So, about this "therapy centre" of yours. What do you do if you don't do hair?'

'There's other ways of straightening out people's heads,' she replied, linking her arm in his.

Calabash

CHAPTER FORTY-SIX

The Attack of the Belligeratron

As we reached the hill above the harbour, the smoke from the burning villages became thinner and I saw the crowd, a ragged spiritless band, herded up to witness something they clearly had no desire to see. A dense semi-circle had formed around the wooden platform that had been hastily constructed and hung with scarlet cloth near the former fish-weighing station. Upon it stood six chopping blocks and six tall-handled axes. Before the platform, their backs turned to the dull green water, stood the massed ranks of General Bassa's army, their polished finery absurd and vulgar in a land whose people now fought over scraps of stale bread.

The Lord Chancellor strode forward, his guards prodding us each time we started to lag behind. As we stumbled on over the hard ridges of earth, following the line of the forest, I wondered if we were being invited to witness the royal executions, or to participate in them. In a military exercise of this kind, it usually became hard to tell where the killing would stop.

I possessed the essence of a plan; indeed, I had arrived with one forming in my head, but now that I had seen the site of our battleground, and remembered the ricketty wooden stands that had been built for the royal production of *The Pirates of Penzance*, its implementation became clearer. As we marched across the furrows, I fell back to 'speak' with Menavino, who, ever alert for opportunities of escape, watched my gestures carefully. Side by side, we moved up until we were level with Scammer. The horrible child fell and bounced at the doctor's heels like a rag doll on a string, and Trebunculus in turn walked just behind Septimus Peason, who was seeking admiration for his own ingenuity.

'It was no accident, sir, none at all, that brought my son into the eligible sphere of the Princess. As she grew to be of marriageable age, it was I, who had done so much to estrange the Sultan from his army, who suggested a way to heal the rift, by betrothal to Maximus, General Bassa's most trusted aide. Naturally, the Sultan saw the wisdom in my words and arranged the nuptials with such undue haste that I thought for a while Rosamunde must be with child. You see, sir, the manipulative ability of an active mind in a dormant kingdom. Why, it takes but a single action in a place as gone-to-sleep as ours to effect a permanent change.'

'But I simply don't understand why you should want to change it,' said Trebunculus, struggling to keep up.

'Power, sir, power, an underrated commodity here but a necessity if we are to go forth after centuries of lethargy, I assure you. You think this tiny island all there is of the world, when we know the boy comes from another?'

'But they are different planes, different spheres entirely,' argued Trebunculus. 'One has as little to do with the other as the sea has to do with the sky.'

'And yet they cannot exist apart. I thought this was the gist of the argument that you first presented to the Sultan and myself when we sought to discover a new benefactor.'

'Yes, indeed it was, but now I know so much more, and surely you can see for yourself how we can no longer survive in the old ways.'

'Exactly, sir, exactly, and that is why the General has taken steps to ensure that the dawn of a bright red future is upon us. Once the might of his great war machine is felt, worlds will fall.'

Meanwhile, Menavino and I had bullied Scammer into dropping back with us. The filthy little creature hopped about in his rags, rolling his great blue eyes in a pathetic bid for sympathy. 'I shall follow you, for I've not my wits, and so I rely on kindnesses,' he hissed and sighed. 'The Scammer is blown by the winds, this way and that. Whoever is the stronger, why, that's who I go with.'

'Well, if you want to get through this with your head still attached to your shoulders,' I suggested, 'you'd better stay with us this time.'

I carefully instructed Menavino, who waited until our party was closest to the woods before grabbing our grubby little spy and dropping aside with him in such a simple single motion that their disappearance was as if a breeze had lightly murmured in the branches of the trees. Menavino was invisible at the best of times, and now his camouflage skills came to the fore.

'And so with the passing of the old order comes a brave new reign, where lassitude no longer passes for government of the people,' said Septimus Peason, strutting on across the peaks of the ruts. 'These are new times, ripe for grand change, and harsh measures are called for.' Still no-one had noticed the absence of Menavino and Scammer. I felt sure that they would be able to reach the harbour unseen, but wondered whether they would be able to accomplish the remainder of the task I had just outlined.

Trebunculus was engaging the Lord Chancellor in an increasingly academic-sounding argument about the future of the kingdom. There came a point with the doctor when he usually started to lose his audience. I hoped it would not be before we reached the dock.

The crowd before us had swelled now, herded in by the General's men, the whole area steaming and smoking with a crimson-tinged mist that imbued the harbour with the air of a medieval witch-hunt. Even if the doctor could not see it, I knew that our necks would surely follow the Sultan's on to the row of blocks arranged on the platform. As we reached the back of the crowd, we saw the Sultan, his long-suffering mother, the Royal Concubine, and several officials, being pushed above the heads of the gathering by the pikes of Bassa's militia.

Six enormous Nubians, the six former guards of the royal palace, now mounted the steps in black leather hoods and ludicrous codpieces, and each stood beside the handle of his axe. The army's bandsmen introduced a sinister low roll on their drums. The sustained note trundled through the assembly like a plague rumour. The crowd began to shift uneasily. Something – or someone – was expected.

The guards positioned each prisoner in front of a block. Now General Bassa himself appeared before the less-than-enthusiastic crowd. The dictator was low and heavy beside his executioners, with tiny legs and a barrel chest built to carry racks of medals, and stamped about with his silver cap pulled down to the bridge of his nose, bellowing commands that no-one out of service would be able to fathom. His ceremonial marching drill finally came to an end. He stamped both boots and turned to face the line of prisoners, drawing his sword and lifting it in a prepared signal.

The Lord Chancellor had brought us to the front of the congregation. As he gathered our little group into a knot he looked about angrily. 'Who are we missing?' he called out. 'Where is the chimney-child? Where is the dumb-boy?'

Trebunculus shrugged, genuinely puzzled. I pantomimed the same.

Septimus Peason's wrath settled on his guards. 'Better a sheepdog to round up our strays than you,' he snorted. 'Half of you go to find them, quickly. This is no time for truants. Now, Princess, it is time for you to join your ill-fated family.'

Cries of anguish were suddenly heard as the Princess Rosamunde shook herself free of the Lord Chancellor's hand and rose upon the wooden steps. She looked even more beautiful than the day I had first met her, clad in scarlet and gold wire, and she accepted her fate with pride and high bearing. I wished I had been able to warn her of my strategy.

Our chance of escape increased as several of our guards made their way into the confused mob. As it was, all attention was focused on the preparations on the platform. The band's prolonged drum-roll increased in intensity. The members of the Sultan's retinue were forced gently to their knees, and when the Sultan himself refused to obey, he was struck across the backs of his legs so that he fell forward. Rosamunde defied all demands to bend herself. Her honeyed eyes glared out above the heads of the crowd, defiant and dry. I wanted to cry out to her, to show her that I knew what I was doing, but did not dare for fear of calling attention to myself. If Menavino and Scammer did their work, all would be well. It was essential to hold my ground and remain calm to the last moment.

A giant, primitively constructed microphone was dragged before General Bassa as a pair of soldiers attempted to untangle a rats-nest of sparking cable. He was forced to tip on to the toes of his boots to speak into it. An electric squeal resonated through our bones.

'UPON THIS DAY,' the amplified words bounced out across the harbour square, 'THE HISTORY OF CALABASH REACHES AN END.' The crowd twitched beneath the deafening, echoing onslaught of his words. 'IN A LAND WHERE THE HANDS OF TIME HAVE BEEN STILLED FOR SO LONG, IN A KINGDOM WHERE THE RULERS HAVE DENIED US THE RIGHT TO SHOW THE WORLD OUR STRENGTH, WHERE INERTIA AND SLOTH HAVE ERODED OUR MANHOOD, WE MUST RESTORE OUR BIRTHRIGHT, STRENGTHEN OUR RESOLVE, GRASP THE SPINES OF POWER, TAKE UP OUR WEAPONS AND TEACH OUR ENEMIES TO TREMBLE BEFORE THE MIGHT OF A BRAVE NEW NATION.'

His words did not appear to have the galvanising effect he was hoping for. Farmers and fishermen shuffled awkwardly amongst each other. Women fearfully clutched their children to their breasts. The bare-chested girls from the fields appeared angry and dismayed. General Bassa had failed to give the populace a reason to follow him. They had been denied nothing until his militia seized power. They were not disgruntled citizens, but a happily settled people who had known nothing but peace and prosperity. They were unsure how to react to this onslaught.

'MY POOR CITIZENS, YOU HAVE BEEN SO RE-PRESSED,' bellowed the General. 'THE SCALES HAVE NOT YET FALLEN FROM YOUR EYES, BUT THIS MOMENT WILL LONG BE REMEMBERED. FROM THIS MOMENT ON OUR NATION BECOMES A MIGHTY FORCE. A TIME OF REVOLUTION BEGINS NOW. DEATH TO THE OPPRESSING TYRANTS OF CALABASH. OUR MASTERY OF WORLDS BEGINS TODAY.'

The Nubians grasped their axe handles and stood beside the exposed necks of their victims. A terrible stillness fell across the faces of the crowd. Executions were clearly not what they wanted. The General's own sword quivered with tension. The drum-roll ceased. Nothing moved. This was the second when everything hung in the balance. I had been a fool to trust our fate to a mute boy and a dishonest child. I buried my face in my hands, too frightened to look. And in that frozen moment, all that could be heard was a strange muffled hammering.

Suddenly, with a great tearing groan, the back of the execution platform angled sharply and dropped away, falling to the ground with a splintering crash, tipping everyone, the Sultan, his mother, his concubine, the Princess, his retinue and the Nubian executioners backwards on to the nets at the harbour wall, and bouncing some, including, inevitably, a handful of tiresome performing dwarves, right over them and into the sea.

Menavino, I knew, was a brilliant carpenter. The men who had erected the wooden platforms and benches for the Sultan and General Bassa were not. The mute apprentice appeared from the profusion of splintered wooden bones with one of the great execution axes balanced across his shoulder. I had seen them stacked at the side of the platform as we approached the harbour. Even Scammer was dragging a chopper almost as tall as himself. A few strategically accurate blows had been enough to loosen the entire structure.

With a great roar the crowd went wild, surging forward to surround the tipped platform, overrunning the startled militia, snatching their muskets and discharging them into the sky. In the ensuing chaos I grabbed the doctor's hand and pulled him to the harbour edge. General Bassa had fallen to the ground a few yards short of the dock, and was already back on his feet, yelling at his disarrayed troops.

At that moment a strange new sound was heard. It echoed over the hillside, booming out across the harbour, startling clouds of starlings from the trees, and all the while growing louder and louder, an ominous clanking, grinding noise, as that of a hundred camshafts hammering, peppered with the bang and crackle of electrical connections. Everyone stopped what they were doing and looked up in confusion as the smoke-belching monstrosity hove into view, tearing and shredding its way out of the woodlands. I knew that here was the General's great war machine, the Belligeratron, designed to wage war on the people of Cole Bay.

The great wooden carcass was designed to hold hundreds of soldiers in its belly. It moved across the fields on immense iron stilts, lifted and dropped by pistons. Within its oaken cage I could see searing flares and bolts of electricity, rubbing plates, flailing cables, iron cogs, and flywheels lethally spinning. Everyone on board looked terrified. Along the sides, cannon bays had been constructed from panels of riveted iron and shafts of wood, but the cannons had not been properly secured, so that every time the war machine moved forward they shifted back and forth, crushing the men who had been assigned to operate them. At the rear, pulsing exhaust pipes belched oily black trails. Oil was also pouring from a dozen different valves and tubes. The air stung our nostrils with the cuprous tang of unshielded voltage. It was a wonder the whole thing hadn't exploded into a ferocious fireball.

I could see Major Maximus balancing at the helm, trying to calm his men as the contraption twisted and shifted over the land. Every few moments a metal boom swooped over his head, completing a powerful electric circuit. He had to keep ducking to avoid it.

The General was elated. He pointed and yelled to the cowering populace. 'Behold, our new weapon of conquest! Let our enemies witness this sight and tremble!'

A small explosion rocked the rear of the machine and several soldiers screamed and fell off, dropping sixty feet to the ground. The crowd scattered as the eight stamping legs of the Belligeratron approached, looking like an angry animated version of the Pavilion Pier. It managed to make the roller coaster at the Cole Bay Kursaal look like a safe ride.

'Are you sure he got this idea from me?' I asked Trebunculus.

The General turned and saw me. 'You brought us the science, boy,' he confirmed. 'We followed your design.'

'No, I gave you a jet engine that didn't work.'

'Not that piece of rubbish, this, this!' He held up the sleeve of his tunic and yanked it back, revealing my wristwatch. I checked my own arm and found nothing.

I remembered how I was always losing things in Calabash. I remembered being stripped and bathed by handmaidens in a rockpool. I remembered placing my watch on a rock. I didn't remember putting it back on. It was one of the new ones with a button on the side that made it light up, the type that came out just before digital quartz watches arrived in the shops. It was mechanical, but electric.

All timepieces had been banned in Calabash; the closest method of temporal calibration they possessed was the shadow of the Tower of Trezibaba, acting as a sundial across the city. The General had taken my wristwatch apart and copied it on an immense scale. But the result, manufactured with the wrong materials and without the remotest under-standing of the principles at work, was out of balance, off-kilter and lethal to everyone inside, outside, above and below it.

The piston legs crashed down singly, in rotation, the way a spider tentatively walks. Occasionally, because some of the larger cogs were shearing teeth, two or even three legs lifted at once, and the entire war machine lurched to one side, causing shouts of alarm to rise from within its troop-cage.

'The Belligeratron will stride through our shallow waters to the crossing point that will take us to your world,' explained the General. 'So you see, boy, we no longer have need of you.' Bassa bared his teeth as he unsheathed his dress sword and waved it menacingly at me, aiming the tip at my throat.

'Kay, I'm behind you!'

The doctor threw me a sword he had yanked from one of the dropped soldiers, and I managed to catch it by the handle. It looked as though this was where my school fencing lessons would finally pay off. I parried the General's thrust, deflecting the point of his blade from beneath my chin, and advanced on him, driving him back to the dock steps. Behind us I could hear the crackling, smoking war machine advancing to the edge of the harbour.

Our blades clashed again. The General was strong, but I had the advantage of height, and pushed forward. Unfortunately, I stepped on to a roll of netting and my foot slipped. I came down heavily on to one knee as the General pressed his advantage, bringing the glinting tip of his sword over my heart. With my foot tangled hopelessly in the coils of the net, I flinched, preparing to feel the steel shaft pierce my flesh.

I'll say this for General Bassa; he was always confident in his contemplation of victory. He was certainly not expecting to be hit on the back of the head with a ten-foot oar. Rosamunde brought the blade down with a powerful crack across his skull and he dropped the sword, falling backwards into the harbour.

'Kay, get out of the way!' called the doctor. The

Belligeratron was almost upon us. I grabbed Rosamunde's hand and we ran clear as the clanking war machine took its first apprehensive steps over the side of the dock.

On reflection, this probably wasn't the best move for such a patently unstable mechanical device. The front two legs drove down into the water but failed to secure a stable footing on the shifting sandy bottom of the bay. As the great cage lurched forward at a forty-five-degree angle, men tumbled from its many platforms, but there was worse to come.

It was now obvious that the General had not entirely grasped the fundamental problems of dealing with high-voltage electrical devices. My watch had possessed a water-proof case. The Belligeratron did not. The first of the un-sheathed cables hit the ocean with a spectacular bang. Others followed, trailing sparks across the water just as the General came screaming out of the sea like a smoking rocket, only to arc across the bow of the Belligeratron and fall back into the water again. Fish shot six feet into the air, instantly fried, and fell back. The other legs of the war machine flailed vainly in an attempt to find a foothold, but it was too late. The centre of gravity had shifted too far, and in a cascade of deafening electrical explosions the entire device slid away from the dock as it went over into the boiling sea.

CHAPTER FORTY-SEVEN

Waking Up

'If there's damage, I'm holding you financially responsible,' warned Cottesloe.

'I don't see how,' said Pauline. 'My son is an independent agent. He might not yet have the key of the door but he's old enough to sort out his own debts. Besides, my husband's out of work, so just where you think the money would come from's a mystery.'

Bob shifted uncomfortably on the pebbled slope. 'How much petrol did you say was in that thing?'

'Enough to get him a fair way out, it's a big tank. They don't make them like that anymore; 1933, the *Skylark*, and built to last, it can get through the heaviest seas.'

The sinking rain-mist was the colour of tracing paper. It made the ocean opaque and flat, and reduced visibility across the water to little more than fifty yards. 'I don't hear it.' Pauline spoke softly, almost to herself. 'If it was anywhere near you'd think you'd hear it.'

'He's not a strong boy,' said Bob worriedly, 'he could be thrown out. He can't swim because of his chest. You should have kept the keys locked away. It's plain irresponsibility allowing them to—'

'To what?' Cottesloe rounded on Bob. 'To be stolen by some young thief who I've trusted and employed out of the goodness of my heart when God knows he could have been getting himself into all sorts of mischief, hanging out with the little sods on the front who jam up my machines with aluminium discs and chewing gum and Belgian coins? You're lucky I decided not to call the police. And this is the thanks I get?'

That was enough for Pauline. She twisted her head to blow the hair from her eyes and came a threatening step closer to Cottesloe. 'You think we should give you thanks? When it's you who's persuading the hotel management to shut down the Scheherazade? Don't think we don't know what goes on around here. It's because of you my husband's out of a job. If you weren't so short-sighted and money-mad you might see what could be done to the place instead of wanting to board it up. The council is just waiting for an opportunity to tear it down and chuck up a couple of concrete office blocks so they can get a quick return on the land. They'll cut you out of whatever sordid deal you think you've got going with them, and you'll wonder why even fewer people come down here to spend money in your poxy arcade. They won't come down here, Mr Cottesloe, because people like you will have turned Cole Bay into a shit-hole, excuse my language. Just take a look around you and see what's happened to the front, it's falling to bits, and the only way it will get any better is if the people with influence like you use it to do a bit of good instead of lining their own bloody pockets.'

Bob was used to hearing his wife speak her mind, but even he was startled by her outburst. Under normal circumstances he would have told her to calm down, but these were not normal circumstances, nearly a dozen of them huddled together on the beach in the drizzle, staring out into the rain-blurred sea, and the crowd slowly growing because people sensed that something was happening, and nothing ever happened in Cole Bay, events only occurred by the absence of things happening, which made today strange and somehow special.

'So you go on and worry about your precious motor launch. My son's not healthy—'

'Aye, not healthy in the head either—'

'What do you mean?'

'I knew his old man, remember? I was there the day he ran down the street without his trousers on, shouting at the top of his voice. I saw where you had to put him, to stop him from being a harm to himself. Like father, like son, I should have known right from the outset.'

Pauline's eyes narrowed in fury. 'If I wasn't a lady I'd tell you exactly what I think of men who behave like pigs in troughs. My son has a mind of his own, and if he decides to waste his life working in that smelly, filthy, dishonest, germ-infested drug den you call a penny arcade that's his business, and you should be thankful that *he* hasn't called in the police because they'd close you down if they knew half the things that went on.'

'That's slander, Mrs Goodwin, you want to be careful what you say to me. I run respectable establishments—'

'Like The Crow's Nest, I suppose, and perhaps if you hadn't replaced Dudley Salterton with strippers and smutty comedians and fired him from a job he lived for, he might not have gone home and killed himself.'

'Pauline!' said Bob, shocked. 'You don't know that. Nobody said that.'

He placed a restraining hand on her arm but she pushed it off. 'You're just as bad. Why you can't stick up for yourself is

Calabash

beyond me. Just once you could have put your foot down, but no, you spent your time creeping around behind my back seeing that blowsy cleaner Doreen what's-her-name, a woman with no qualifications in anything except bathroom maintenance, rinsing yourself with her cheap soap and thinking I wouldn't notice. I heard you apologising to her down the phone, thinking I was out.'

'It didn't mean anything, Pauline. It's all over. I meant to say something to her ages ago but she kept on.'

'Nobody ever says what they mean until it's too late to make a difference.' Pauline was nearly in tears. 'Nobody wants to take the blame, for anything, for anyone, and it all gets left to other people—' she faltered, then rallied so sharply on Mr Cottesloe that he nearly fell backward over the pebbles. 'And don't think I don't know what's going on with the pier. You're on the committee for that as well, aren't you, deliberately letting it run down and fall into the sea rather than fix it up—' She marched on him, backing him up against the groynes.

'You know as well as I do that the pier has been advertising for a buyer for years now, that the council would sell it for one penny if they really thought that someone wanted it—'

'Then what is wrong with you and the residents of this town?' She turned to the crowd, hysterical now. Years of unheeded complaints and angry letter-writing, years of polishing the silverware in the front room cabinet and longing for a better life, years of sitting alone in cinemas watching lands she would never visit, years of witnessing the restrained acquiescence of her husband and sons; it all poured out in one great emotional fireball. She threw her arms up in a despairing gesture. 'What is it that keeps you from taking back what belongs to you? Why can't you feel some pride? You let your children waste their lives, you sit back and do nothing when all it would take is one little push, one step, that's all.' Again she snapped back to Cottesloe, who had foolishly thought he was safe for a moment. 'And before you say it, yes, I know my sons haven't done so well either, but I'm still proud of them, and I'd give anything to see their lives work out—'

The crowd, as crowds still do nowadays, remained silent and stupefied. Even Bob could see that his wife's anger was as much directed at the men she had loved and lost as it was at the townspeople who stood by and watched. He reached out his arms to catch her as sadness overcame her and she fell against his shoulder with a strangled sob.

Ernest Cottesloe was a man who rarely passed a day without initiating an argument. He was also a believer in the old saying, 'Let not the sun set upon your wrath', but as he could see no easy way of placating this extremely angry woman, he attempted an alternative gambit and changed the subject entirely.

'If your husband's out of work, why are you both so dressed up?' He stared at Bob's testicular cufflinks in puzzlement.

'Because it's a special day, only you've gone and ruined it,' replied Pauline without managing to provide an adequate explanation. 'Our clothes are soaked and we wanted to look nice, and Kay's missing—' She accepted a Kleenex from Bob and wiped her dripping nose.

They made a miserable little group on the beach, windswept, rained-on, like a funeral party who had been accidentally set down at the wrong venue. Danny and Julia arrived, along with some local children, and the man who did the Punch and Judy shows, and a youngster from the *Cole Bay Mercury* started asking people questions and making notes in a book he kept tucked in his windcheater. And they all stared out at the sea and wondered if Kay had suffered an asthma attack, overturned the boat and – God forbid – drowned himself in the icy green waters of the Channel while they stood bickering.

CHAPTER FORTY-EIGHT

Through the Crash Barrier

Floundering among the fried fish in the harbour water, the smouldering General Bassa was having trouble remaining afloat. His glistening steel epaulets were twisted around his blackened neck from the force of the electric shocks, and his gold chains weighed him down heavily. The fur on his helmet was still alight. With a final anguished scream, he went under.

'Kay, what in heaven is going on?' asked Trebunculus.

'Menavino and Scammer brought down the platform,' I shouted. 'We must get into the water too. It's safe now. The Belligeratron has shorted out.'

But the way ahead was barred by the dark form of the Lord Chancellor. Buffeted on all sides, he stood his ground, separating us from the sea, his grimace mirthless, his anger infinite. He searched my face for a sign.

'So, the donkey finally bucks its master,' he said. 'You fail in one world and try to spread your failure to another.'

'No,' I replied. 'It's taken me a long while to understand, but what I need to do is unite them both.'

'Treason, then. You wish me harm.'

'I have no desire to harm you, Septimus. You have simply acted according to your nature. Calabash, such as you have made it, now falls to you. Look upon your new kingdom. It is all but destroyed.'

Looking behind us, we could see the population in pitched battle with the guards, and it was already obvious that the leaderless army was being routed. Stepping around the disheartened Lord Chancellor, I dragged Trebunculus along with me and pushed him on to the stone steps leading to the *Skylark*.

The motor launch was built to carry twelve passengers and could probably take more. Together, the doctor and I began pulling Bassa's surviving prisoners from the water. Menavino lifted the Sultan's wife and the Royal Concubine, for whom he had a private fondness, from the tangle of netting into which they had been thrown, and the doctor hauled apologetically at the Sultan, who swatted irritably at his fluttering hands. Rosamunde came running, to loop her arms around my neck as I deposited her on to the seat of the launch, at my side.

'I was always sure that you would find a way to reunite us,' she said. 'I knew you would come to understand our deeper intention.'

'I'm just sorry it took me so long.'

'Rosamunde, you brazen strumpet, soiled jade, painted harlot, return here at once! You can't go there, it will be the end of everything!' On the dock, her estranged husband Maximus ranted and bellowed at her, held back by a rippling wall of fishermen and farmers.

'Ignore him, Kay. It won't be the end, it'll be the beginning. Complete your task.'

Before I had time to consider her remark, an explosion in the water returned my urgency of purpose. Some of the

General's men had found a working cannon on the dock. With the boat filled to capacity and the sea thrashed white with the floundering of soldiers, I turned the ignition of the *Skylark* and opened the engine to full throttle.

As I did so, it seemed that I was granted a sign from the gods, for the clouds parted to release sunlight on to the great shields of the harbour warriors. Powering the launch to its greatest acceleration, our hull lifted us in the placid sea as we raced forward towards the illuminating cross. With just a hundred yards to go, I looked back to the kingdom of my dreams for one last sight of Calabash. The city seemed like any other now, grey and smoke-stained, rather drab and ordinary, lost beneath the swarming weight of its people, torn down from within, to be further razed in preparation for rebirth.

Above us, a flock of bluebirds swooped and folded, following the motor launch. I turned back to face the streaming wind, and raced the *Skylark* into the sun. The speedboat hit the dazzling intersection of light and found itself at the peak of an immense wave. We left the water and leapt the rift, to crash down on a sliding green wall of ocean that broke across our bow and almost swamped us. But the launch uprighted itself in time for me to spin the wheel and bring her around from the dark thicket of struts at the end of the ruined pier.

'You did it!' shouted Rosamunde excitedly, throwing her arms around my neck as I steered the boat towards the shoreline. The Sultan attempted to rise and make a pronouncement, but was tipped back into his seat by another wave. I realised now that we had emerged from the centre of a sea-storm. The turbulent currents beneath our rudder snatched the wheel from my hands, and the throttle stayed jammed down even though my foot was no longer on it. Blue petrol fumes blasted into our wake as the engine howled and laboured under the swell.

'This is going to be a very bumpy landing,' I called back as we were caught in the next wave rising to shore and thrown forward. I saw the brown pebble slope of the beach and the knot of people gathered on it before I realised just how fast we were travelling. The waiting assembly scattered as the *Skylark*, gripped by a great incoming wave, shot forward, cresting the shallow water to plough waves of stones up either side of the hull.

The effect was that of hitting a brick wall at high speed. I was thrown from behind the wheel, into the air and on to the wet stones, while the motor launch, its engine screaming, ran out of beach and shot driverless through the gap in the railings and across the esplanade. With their brakes screeching, cars skittered and skewed in both lanes of the main road. Barely impeded, the *Skylark* mounted the kerb on the other side. The doorman of the Scheherazade Hotel watched in horror as the great boat headed straight for him. He leapt aside, and the bow of the cruiser ploughed into the giant picture-window next to the revolving doors with an awesome crash, imploding it in a million glistening shards. It finally came to rest against a bank of tables in the empty restaurant, the propellor still turning.

I found myself being lifted from the crater I had made in the pebbles and set upright by an erupting red-faced man who bore some passing resemblance to my employer Mr Cottesloe.

'You bloody moron!' he bellowed into my startled face, flicking spit over me. 'Look what you've done!'

Someone said, 'Stop shaking him, you idiot! His bones may be broken!'

Someone else said, 'Hang on, son, there'll be an ambulance here in a minute.'

But Cottesloe seemed unable to stop himself, and continued to yell, 'Look what you've done! Just take a look at what you've done!' The crowd drew itself in around us, as if for warmth, and so I looked.

Here is what I saw:

The rain had stopped and the sky was clearing. The afternoon had turned to evening, and stars had begun to glimmer through the deep blue void above my head. The mist on the sea had lightened to a slight softness of lines, and the end of the pier could now be seen. The dying sun shone upon the glistening beach so that the stones appeared as bright as boiled sweets. The *Skylark* had gouged a path to the esplanade, then left a black trail across the road to the demolished window of the hotel. The crowd that had gathered around me began to take on individual personalities. I could see Julia and Danny, and my mother and father, bizarrely dressed as though they had been detoured on the way to church, and other people I knew and loved, like Dudley Salterton and Miss Ruth, even though I knew they were dead so it couldn't possibly be them, and I realised then that I was suffering from concussion, because behind them all, walking along the esplanade, turning this way and that to take in everything they saw, I recognised the delighted Grand Sultan and his mother, and the Royal Concubine, followed by Menavino, Scammer and Dr Trebunculus, and led by my beloved Rosamunde.

But as they reached the group assembled on the beach, they walked into the crowd and began to merge with them, blurring in my sight so that I could not tell any of them apart, and soon everything had grown as soft as the distant mist. Rosamunde was the last to leave my vision. And in the very final moment, like the green ray that appears just as the sun dips below the line of the sea, she looked up, caught my eye, and smiled.

Far above Rosamunde, the flock of bluebirds that had followed the motor launch on its voyage between two worlds dispersed across the storm-clouded sky like scattering slivers of silk.

'I'm all right,' I said shakily, turning to the figures who remained.

'He's all right,' said Bob. 'He's woken up, haven't you, lad?' I later thought that he might have said, 'He's shaken up, aren't you, lad?' but it's not the way I remember it.

Suddenly Pauline shoved forward from the others and was holding me in her arms, and I knew things were different somehow, that I had indeed woken myself to the world. I think I saw the Semanticor talking with Miss Ruth as though they were old friends enjoying a school reunion. I think I saw Scammer and Dudley Salterton shaking hands. The Royal Concubine kissed Danny on the forehead. For a moment even Parizade was there in the crowd, her face slowly tilting to the evening sky.

As my mother cried, I looked over her shoulder to Julia, who gave a shocked smile, and I noticed for the first time how much her eyes were like Rosamunde's. The strangest sight I saw that night was the Grand Sultan pushing Mr Cottesloe aside to stand before me, his eyes bulging with pleasure as he spoke. 'You did it, Kay. You freed us. You've freed yourself.' And he stepped back inside someone who could only have been my father, and was gone.

But the real thing I remember, the real moment I hold inside my head, was looking away from the crowd to see the broad figure walking down towards us across the canyon of pebbles as the promenade lights flickered on. I thought the ambulance had arrived because he was carrying a leather holdall, but it was my brother, Sean, who walked up and stood before me.

'We were getting ready to go to the station,' said Bob, 'when the Greek girl came and called for us, and told us you were in trouble. Pauline made me wear this shirt. I wanted to stop and change.'

Sean stepped closer. He had lost some weight in his face and looked older than his years. His eyes were dark and tired, and he needed a shave. The lower half of his left sleeve hung empty. 'It's good to see you, little brother,' he said, awkwardly placing my hands in his palm. He used to do that when I had trouble breathing, hold me until the panic passed.

'I'm sorry, Sean,' I said.

'So am I,' said Sean. 'You don't know how much.'

'I didn't know you were coming back today.'

'I didn't get much notice myself. Nothing was settled. Then it all happened very quickly.'

'You're really here, aren't you?'

'Yes,' he laughed. 'I'm here.'

An outraged voice cut through the gathering. 'Here, what about my boat?'

'Bugger your boat,' said Pauline. And everyone began talking at once.

CHAPTER FORTY-NINE

Reborn in Dreams

'He's waiting for you,' said the nurse. 'You're twenty minutes late.'

'The buses are all delayed,' I explained. 'It's started snowing. It's cold enough to freeze the—'

'Don't you dare,' she warned, 'there's children here. Go on in, then. I'll bring you a mug of tea in a while.'

I sat on the edge of the hospital bed where I always sat, not in the chair, because he liked me closer. He moved less and less these days, but I knew because he always strained to move nearer beneath the bedclothes. His name was Alan Wickes, his condition degenerative to the point where his mother could no longer care for him at home. I had first seen him on my way to visit Miss Ruth in her ward. When I became a hospital visitor, his nurse asked me if I would sit with him and read. The library was a jumble of broken-backed romance novels, so I asked his mother what he liked, and brought in books from my own collection.

When the Simon Saunders *Arcadia* novels came into my possession, I read those to him. He enjoyed them so much that I read them all again. Then, one bitter winter night, after Sean was home and life had settled into something very different from how it was before, I told him about Calabash. I told him how it gained its name, of the legend of the gourd, the receptacle of the imagination that could bring life to the driest desert, and how I had finally managed to make the kingdom pour itself out into the real world, bringing new life, new colour, new hope.

After that I saw him change. Although he was losing the use of his limbs, he seemed less restless. I knew why. I knew where he was going. I could no longer go there, but I had no need to now.

Sometimes I imagine Alan's flight into the city, and what he finds there when he arrives. I see the buildings and people rise up before him, twisting and changing to fit their new owner's dreams. I suppose the name of Calabash has joined all the others in a list that stretches back to the beginning of time. I like to think that in a forgotten part of the woods there lie a few remnants of the Sultan's magnificent palace, the iridescent turquoise tiles of its spires and golden fountains catching the sunlight through the ferns, polished pieces of walnut and sandalwood from its intricately carved windows half buried in the warm soil. I wonder if he favours an adventurous life, galloping across the skyline to the outposts of the kingdom, or if he prefers to lie in the arms of a girl like Rosamunde, watching the sunlit sea beyond the city walls. And I know that, unlike me, he has no need to leave it all behind, because with each passing day there is less to keep him here.

His mother has no illusions. She understands what is happening to Alan, and I think she has some inkling of where he goes. I know she wishes she could go with him just once, to see what it is that provides her son with such comfort. Although he deteriorates, his continued well-being has come as a surprise to the nurses, who now talk of a time when he might stabilise. His mother knows I am part of the solution to the mystery of her son's survival, but cannot bring herself to talk with me. Instead she sits beside me sometimes, touching the books and watching the boy's eyes, as though one day she might catch a glimpse of the extraordinary world that lies beyond, a land denied to some, destructive to others, and always slightly out of reach.

My Life

'Now I know why you like standing here,' she said, looking
out from the shelter to the sea. 'You can see the end of the
pier.' Her hand felt small in mine, but there was a strength in
her that I had not sensed before. She released my hand and
walked forward into the cold sunlight. 'You can feel the sea
on your skin this morning.' She pulled the hood of her coat
back and ran her fingers through her ragged fair hair, closing
her eyes. 'Smell the salt.'

For a minute we just stood there, breathing the air. My
chest was clear today.

'Do you want to go on the pier?'

I thought for a moment. 'No, it's fine. We'll be late for
lunch. You know how they get.' Pauline and Bob were still
basking in the attention the family had received. My mari-
time collision with a stationary hotel had made national
news. More alarmingly for the Cole Bay council, it had
placed the resort under an unwelcome spotlight. Sensing a
broader human-interest story, a couple of ambitious young
journalists from one of the Sunday papers had discovered

some sloppily hidden but fairly spectacular funding irregularities. Their investigation resulted in several front-page exclusives, a spate of arrests, some firings, an independent inquiry and the reopening of the Scheherazade under private management. Although I had been the unwitting catalyst for this, I nearly went to jail, and had been required to pay a share of the damages.

Julia looked up at the pier. The Crow's Nest had a new artistic director, and had just been prevented by the council from showing *Hair* with its nudity intact. Not such a far cry from the days of Barnacle Bill and his saucy sea shanties. 'Come on, just to the end and back. There's time yet.'

'No, another day.' We were due to have lunch with Sean, and I didn't want to be late.

'You still see them, don't you?' Her manner was matter-of-fact. It was a question she knew the answer to.

'Yes, sometimes.'

'Do you see her in me?'

'I guess I see bits of them in all of you,' I replied evasively. She knew I could see Rosamunde in her eyes. 'It's not just them. The buildings, too. I never thought about the buildings, how oriental-looking they are.'

'Most English seaside towns look a bit oriental.'

'I can see that now. So much of Calabash is here.'

'It was always here.' She brushed a strand of hair from her placid, kind eyes.

'So were you, Julia. I was wrapped up in myself— '

She dismissed the thought. 'We were different people then. Being a teenager is a time for being different. I feel sorry for people who never know that feeling. It's a barrier you have to pass through. Let's walk to the shoreline, Kay.'

I watched her jump down on to the stones and start marching. I had to run to reach her side.

'Don't you miss your maps?' she asked.

'Atlantis. Babylon. Mesopotamia. All dead civilisations.'

'Except Calabash. It could have killed you, you know.'

'I know,' I replied. 'But it brought me life.'

For a moment I thought I saw the shields of the great bronze warriors reflecting on the water, but it was only the sunlight on the waves.

'God, the sea looks cold,' she said, walking to the edge of the tide.

'It must be nearly freezing,' I agreed. 'It doesn't look very clean.'

'I dread to think what's in it.'

'I guess we'll never know.'

But by the time we had finished talking, we had waded right in.